Hopscotch

DENYSE DEVLIN

PENGUIN
IRELAND

PENGUIN IRELAND

Published by the Penguin Group
Penguin Ireland, 25 St Stephen's Green, Dublin 2, Ireland
(a division of Penguin Books Ltd)
Penguin Books Ltd, 80 Strand, London WC2R ORL, England
Penguin Group (USA) Inc., 375 Hudson Street, New York, New York 10014, USA
Penguin Group (Australia), 250 Camberwell Road,
Camberwell, Victoria 3124, Australia (a division of Pearson Australia Group Pty Ltd)
Penguin Group (Canada), 90 Eglinton Avenue East, Suite 700, Toronto, Ontario, Canada M4P 2Y3
(a division of Pearson Penguin Canada Inc.)
Penguin Books India Pvt Ltd, 11 Community Centre,
Panchsheel Park, New Delhi – 110 017, India
Penguin Group (NZ), cnr Airborne and Rosedale Roads, Albany,
Auckland 1310, New Zealand (a division of Pearson New Zealand Ltd)
Penguin Books (South Africa) (Pty) Ltd, 24 Sturdee Avenue,
Rosebank, Johannesburg 2196, South Africa

Penguin Books Ltd, Registered Offices: 80 Strand, London WC2R ORL, England

www.penguin.com

First published 2006
1

Set in 12/14.75 pt Monotype Dante
Typeset by Rowland Phototypesetting Ltd, Bury St Edmunds, Suffolk
Printed in Great Britain by Clays Ltd, St Ives plc

A CIP catalogue record for this book is available from the British Library

HARDBACK
ISBN-13: 978-1-844-88063-8
ISBN-10: 1-844-88063-X

TRADE PAPERBACK
ISBN-13: 978-1-844-88118-5
ISBN-10: 1-844-88118-0

Hopscotch

Denyse Devlin is the daughter of an Irish diplomat. As a result of that, and an ongoing interest in the Middle East, she has travelled extensively and had many homes around the world. In 1987 she settled in Co. Cork with her husband. They have two teenage daughters. *Hopscotch* is her fourth novel.

By the same author

The Catalpa Tree

As Denyse Woods

Overnight to Innsbruck
Like Nowhere Else

For
Finola and Tamzin,
with love

I have two daughters.
They are all I ever wanted from the earth.
Or almost all.

from 'The Lost Land',
Eavan Boland

The room was dim. Quiet. I opened one eye. A blue room. Curtains closed. Bedcovers askew. I put my hand on my forehead, and allowed a broader chink of light into my head, as I emerged not from sleep but from some kind of oblivion. My throat was dry, my bladder full. I moved my head, slowly, and scanned the room – great wooden wardrobe on the left, wide timber bed beneath me, a window and . . . *feet*.

I scrambled into an upright position and pressed myself against the bedstead.

A man's feet were protruding from a raised alcove in the right-hand corner of the room. His legs were stretched out, his boots hovering on the edge of the step. My head thumped in fright, my heart banged in an attempt to break out of my chest and run. 'Who's that?' I said.

One of the feet lifted slowly, and dropped to the ground. Then it lifted, and dropped again.

'Who's there?' I was pinned to the bedstead, my knees against my chest, the blanket pulled close. I glanced down. I was dressed. My whole body was shaking.

The boot moved again.

It was tapping.

I shuffled to the side of the bed, casting an eye round and taking in my holdall, a haversack I didn't recognize, and a mattress on the floor. It had been slept on. *Jesus*. What had I done? What had been done to me? Had someone spiked my drink? Drugged me and brought me here? The headache . . .

My legs barely holding my weight, I moved tentatively towards the alcove. 'Hello?'

He cleared his throat quietly, which made me recoil.

Then, with one swift, forward movement, I stepped out to where I could be seen. The man jumped to his feet. A stranger. His book tumbled to the floor, but he caught his Discman before that, too, fell. Pulling the plugs from his ears, he spoke at me hastily.

'Get out!' I said. 'Get out of here!' I backed away until my calves hit the bed.

'No, look –'

'Leave my room!' *Is it my room?*

'But –'

'I'll call the police!' *But where am I?*

He stepped off the low platform.

'Don't come near me!'

He raised one hand. 'Okay, okay,' he said, picking up the haversack. 'Calm down. I –'

'Out!'

He stepped past me, shaking his head, and opened the door. 'But don't you remember –'

'Please go!'

'I'm going, I'm going.'

I slammed the door behind him, then opened it quickly and said, 'Where am I?'

He was a few steps down a staircase on the left and called out, as he rounded the corner and disappeared, 'Transylvania.'

I slammed the door again, shaking so violently that I fell on to the bed, clutching my temples. *What?* The headache thrashed about in my veins, on a rampage of pain. Transyl-fucking-*vania*? And what did he mean, 'remember'?

I calmed myself, breathing deeply, which eased the throbbing, but not the trembling. Who was that person? He didn't look evil. He looked like a student, well-built, tanned, and . . . relaxed. So ridiculously relaxed, sitting there, reading and listening to music in *my* room. *'But don't you remember?'* I scraped my fingers through my hair. What was it I should have remembered?

. . . The train. Jesus, the train. And the pain: nauseating, incapacitating. The rest came back in a rush of mortifying recognition. The country: Romania. The town: no idea. The story: oh, God, the story . . .

The ache swept back with coherent thought, gleeful to return to its favoured place, and lay against me, spooned against my body like an invisible lover.

I remembered Cork airport, that's what I remembered. Cork airport, a week earlier and the fierce rain and the dull, exhausting misery.

I

For some reason the pilot had parked his jet half a mile from the terminal. In a winter downpour, passengers had to run, whipped by cold November rain, all the way to the building. When we got to the doors, the security guard didn't seem to be expecting our flight. 'Where have you come from?' he asked three hundred shivering people, who were crowding round his entrance.

'Where do you think we've come from?' someone screamed. 'Mars?'

Although my clothes were cold against me, I barely felt the wet. I was more aware of the lump in my belly – a hardness, like a large stone, making me feel full to the throat.

We were ungraciously granted access. I placed myself near the fountain, away from the fuss round the carousel, and took my mobile phone from my bag. Its blank screen stared up at me, ready to go into action. I knew what was out there, waiting to get into my phone: messages, dozens of messages, all with the same request. *Phone me. I don't understand. Call me.* It would certainly buzz and maybe even ring as soon as I switched it on. Around me, people were jigging about, trying to get warm. They were laughing now, about the plane parking two fields away from the terminal and the man who wouldn't let them in. Many were switching on their mobile phones. Voices rang out. 'Can you pick me up in ten?' 'Where are you?' I wished I was them. Any one of them. Anyone other than myself.

I looked at the phone resting in my palm. It stood ready to deliver the voice I longed to hear, to put my life back on track.

By switching it on, I could override the last forty-eight hours and make everyone happy again: my fiancé, his parents, my family, friends, the caterers and photographer and dressmaker. All I had to do was push the button and enter my PIN. The carousel began to move. Wet suitcases filed past the waiting trolleys; I stood away from the mêlée. I had time. I could wait.

My holdall retrieved, I headed towards the exit. When I came past a rubbish bin, I tossed my phone into it.

Dad was waiting, not so much for me as for an explanation. He hugged me without a word and took my bag. We stopped at the machine to pay for parking.

'Milenko has called. Several times,' he said. 'He wouldn't tell me any more than you have.'

I nodded.

We hurried to the car. When Dad sat in beside me and shook himself off, he said, 'So?'

What an itsy-bitsy little word, I thought, by which to instigate such a narrative. 'You don't really expect me to blurt it all out, do you? I mean, I will tell you, but don't press me because . . . it's . . . I can't.'

'Fair enough. But is it absolutely final? Surely there's some chance . . .'

'None.'

'But –'

'It's off, Dad. End of story.'

'What about the wedding? Your job?'

'I'll have to sort all that out.'

He turned to me as we pulled out of the car-park. 'So you want to go home? Not to the flat?'

'Please.'

We drove mostly in silence and got home just under an hour later. The house was as I needed it to be – warm, cosy, with a great open fire burning in the sitting room. Dad made

6

me cocoa, just as I had hoped he would. For days, I had longed for this moment in this sanctuary. I couldn't face my apartment, where The Dress was hanging on the wardrobe door and my flatmate would gape at my unexpected return. I had to formulate reasons, excuses, before I took on the world.

Dad had his own special way with cocoa, whipping up a foamy head on the milk then sprinkling Bournvita on top, but I wasn't convinced I'd be able to get it past my gullet. I had not eaten for two days and could not foresee a time when I would ever eat again, but the cocoa went down with only the slightest quibble. It even melted that brick in my belly a little.

Dad stoked the fire. 'We'll get you right, love, whatever's happened.'

'I know.'

'But I'm concerned about Milenko. Maybe I shouldn't be – he's obviously done something foul. It's just . . . he didn't sound good.'

I couldn't speak.

'Maybe you could talk to him?'

'Dad, stop.'

He went to the kitchen to make his own cocoa. When he came back, I said, 'Seems you won't be getting rid of me after all.'

'Kadie . . .'

The tears came at last. Not in great heaving sobs, but one by one, as if they had been queuing up in an orderly manner, awaiting their turn, each, to slip down my face, full and watery.

Dad gave me his hanky. He could not bear my distress, nor I his, so we sat there, upsetting each other. 'What has he done to you?' he asked, bewildered.

'Don't blame Milenko. I won't have it. It's me, all right?'

'But –'

'When I go to bed, will you deal with all these photos?' I glanced at the mantelpiece and the framed photo of our

7

engagement party – the happy couple surrounded by friends and families, Milenko in that lovely dark suit, arms tight round me. His coy smile was imprinted on my mind like a scar. 'And will you tell people?'

'Tell them *what*, exactly?'

'Say I chickened out. Changed my mind about Croatia and the whole move. The cultural thing.'

'As if they'll believe that.'

'*Make* them believe it.'

'You don't have to be so loyal to him, you know.'

'Above all, tell them I don't want to discuss it.'

'You're setting out a lot of rules for someone who's turned everything upside-down for a lot of people. You call it off, with three weeks' notice, without explanation, and I have to tell everyone, but say nothing?'

'Dad, it's private. It's . . . *deeply* personal, not just to me but to Milenko, and I don't see why I should have to share it with everyone.'

'Because you're cancelling a wedding, that's why. The invitations are out, the replies are in.'

'But it's just a wedding to them. It's a whole life for me.' Tears dropped into my cocoa and made it salty. It was good to have licence to cry, now that the fleeing was done. Against the odds, I had managed to get myself home.

Dad patted my knee, and wondered.

When I went to bed, nausea crept in, churning the cocoa. Sometimes I didn't know if I was asleep or awake. I was in a car, a jeep, on a really wet day in Connemara, and Milenko was there, wet too, saying that someone had made us tea to keep us warm. It wasn't quite a dream, but it wasn't a memory either. We had never been to Connemara, but I could smell the damp of his coat, could hear us talking to whoever was driving . . .

I sat up. I was sweating, but at least I was sweating at home. I thanked God I'd got home.

There was some sleep in the early hours, when exhaustion claimed me. The phone rang at half nine, waking me from that mindless, blanked-out state. The word was out; Dad would be making calls. Mum first – and that would take hours – then the aunts, the priest, the caterers. I could hear the murmur of his voice. I curled into a ball. What a lot of work I'd given him. *Just do it.* And now he was downstairs, dutifully doing my bidding, and the calls were already bouncing back. My bed was warm and comfortable, belying what lay in it. My heart was beating on, speedier than usual, but otherwise continuing. Neither shattered nor torn apart, it went on with its work, pumping life through me, in spite of myself. And yet this load in my chest, this rock of horror, there now for the third awful day, gnawed at me.

The calls were coming fast and furious – ringing only once before Dad picked up. Typical, I thought, how they'd been asked to leave me alone but could not. They had to maul at the news. They wanted to be the first, perhaps, with the coup, the first to know the why of it. Throwing away my mobile had been a stroke of genius. Whatever about Milenko, no one else could reach me either – a tiny reprieve in a ghastly mess.

It came back to me, pounced on me like a tiger. *Revulsion, revulsion.* I leapt from the bed and tried to shake it off. Then I fled the room. I wasn't hungry, but I would eat. I would eat down the memory and keep it in the pit of my stomach, like the ulcer it was. It would probably burst eventually, but I might be stronger then.

Dad was in the hall, pulling on his wellington boots. He turned to greet me as I came down, and smiled. He looked good. He always did, in spite of his silver hair being rock-star long, and sometimes even pulled back in a ponytail. I loathed the ponytail, but feared that if he ever cut his hair, he would

9

instantly appear old, so I let him be. Besides, with hollowed cheeks and green eyes, he carried the long locks well for a man of fifty-six. 'Morning, sweetness,' he said. 'I'm off for a walk. Did you sleep?'

'Hardly.'

'Try to eat something. Don't pick up if anyone calls. The word is out.'

'I heard.'

'Clara wanted to leave work and come rushing down here, but she can't leave the new girl unsupervised.'

I nodded. Clara and I had worked together for five years. She was one of my closest friends, but even she would have to wait.

'She said she'd let your other friends know, if that's what you want?'

'Yeah, whatever.'

He headed out into the November morning. I stood by the front door and watched him walk down the long, winding drive towards the lake beyond the gate. It glittered, ever reliable, winking at me like a chum.

The kitchen was warm. I put the kettle on the Aga and stood by the sink, gazing out at our back garden. Only two weeks earlier, I had stood there in a very different mood, gazing out at the garden where I had grown up. It had been a moment laced with regret, because I was soon to leave, and with delight, because of what lay ahead. My imminent departure had made this house a poignant place recently, but even that sweet poignancy had been ripped away. I would not be leaving so the garden didn't seem quite so special. I was stuck with it. I sat down at the table and cried, convulsively, the tears no longer polite.

By the time my overworked tear ducts had been emptied, half an hour had passed. I tried again with breakfast. The morning had been long already; the prospect of slouching around all day was dreadful, but there was nowhere to go and nobody I wanted to see. The travel agency where I had worked with Clara was no longer expecting me. I had left the job two weeks earlier.

Sheep's Head, a peninsula further west, called out. A T-shaped headland there, near Kilcrohane, was my place of retreat, the place where I kept my soul. 'But that would be mad,' I said out loud. The toast was soggy. The phone started up again. 'Really, really stupid.'

But where was I to go, to get away from the calls – from family and businesses and people further down the chain? My friends were at work or at home with babies – and all, probably, were on the phone, talking about me. But they wouldn't phone me: they would know I'd speak to them when I felt able. They'd be ready to catch me, to drag me through the cesspit towards recovery – if such a thing could happen. It seemed unlikely, but people get over extraordinary things. Dad did. He suffered horribly when Mum walked out. We'd lived through it, the two of us, but I had never asked Dad how he had managed to get from the beginning to the end of days like this.

I had sent only two texts from Croatia, to Steph and Killian: 'I've called it off. Don't ask.' There had been an immediate response from Killian. 'Bloody eejit. What have you done now?' If he hadn't been away, he would probably have parked himself on my doorstep first thing that morning to admonish me, because that's the kind of irritating full-on ex-boyfriend he could be. He liked Milenko – they had become excellent friends, but then Milenko had been integrated into every part of my life and would be missed in every quarter. Killian liked nothing better than an opportunity to lecture me about the shambles I made of my love life. As my first love, and lover, he flattered himself – before Milenko came along – that no one knew me as he did. Mind you, he'd pretty much made a shambles of things himself when, after we'd spent twenty-six high-flying months together, he had cheated on me. It had been a once-off, a bad moment. He paid for it. To his considerable despair, which was matched only by mine, I never had him back. I felt then the way I felt now: nauseous and shattered, but this was much, much worse. This time I had lost not only my lover, but my future. This time my hands shook. Shock, probably. Yes, I thought, glancing at them, I am probably in shock.

I brought Killian with me when I got into the car and pointed it towards Sheep's Head. He came along, in my head, for no reason I could think of, but it was typical of him to be away, in Stockholm, just when I needed him. He was one of only two people to whom I felt able to speak about this, and with his support, it would have been easier to face everyone else. The other person to whom I could reveal all was his wife, Steph, who also happened to be my best friend, but she was fragile at the moment.

The road was empty. Monday morning. Everyone going about their business except me, because I no longer had any business. I would not be able to get my job back and couldn't even begin to think about where to find work. The move to Croatia had indeed been, as it often seemed, too good to be true. Not just personally, but professionally. Tourism was taking off there and I was marrying into a family of hoteliers. For years Milenko's father had run an old hotel on the island of Korčula. It was state-owned, as most hotels were in the former Yugoslavia, but they also had a couple of houses that they rented out on holiday lets, and with my experience and contacts, I was well placed to make my own significant contribution. We had made many plans about how we would run our business, and our lives . . . Hurt pulled at my inner chest, on the left of my ribcage.

I drove through Durrus. It was stupid to come back here. Self-flagellation, no less. If I'd had my phone, I would have called Steph and said, 'Make me turn back.' In response to which Steph would have thrown up. That was all she did these days. Only on television soaps is morning sickness restricted to mornings. In real life, it seems to go on all day and for longer than three months. Nonetheless Steph was an acute case. She felt ill all day every day, and was now almost five months gone. It was miserable, and she looked miserable. I would have to be careful: I could not tax her with my mangled insides, which was why I wished Killian was home. I longed to try the story out on him, from beginning to end, and see what he made of it. Unlike my girlfriends, he would not examine, discuss or dismantle: he would be a man about it and simply react. If I had been foolish, he would tell me so; but I knew in my gut that he would not and I longed, but longed, for that vindication.

A few miles beyond Kilcrohane, I took the left turn that led down to a pier, but before reaching it, I pulled on to the verge. Killian would not go away. I felt him sitting there in the passenger seat, felt him looking at me.

'What?' I said.

He dropped the corners of his mouth. 'Nothing.'

'What are you doing here?'

'I don't know.'

Wishful thinking.

I got out, climbed over a gate, and made my way along the dirt track, which dwindled away in a spread of long grass, which in turn led to the sea. Every step exposed me to searing memories. It was not Killian who clambered around that headland with me: it was Milenko. My future become my past.

2

Steph was pale, but on her feet. She opened the door, shaking her head. 'Short of leaving him standing at the altar . . .'

'Down, you rotten mongrels!' Three puppies – Irish wolf-hounds, all of four months old but the size of small donkeys – jumped up and nearly knocked me over.

Steph made them sit in the hall and led me into the kitchen, where their mother was having a well-earned break in a sunny patch on the carpet.

'How are you feeling?' I asked.

'Better, actually. The first week you were away I stopped getting sick and the nausea eased off, and sometimes I even eat breakfast.'

'Good. It was hard to enjoy my food with you puking all the time.'

'But it helped you lose weight for the wedding! . . . Oh, God. I've said it already. I've mentioned the W word.'

'I might as well get used to it.'

'Tea?'

'I'll make it,' I said. 'Do you want some?'

'I want it and crave it, but it just won't go down.'

The puppies pushed on the door and let themselves in. Steph put her hand down so they could lick her fingers.

'You shouldn't let them do that. Cats and dogs can be very bad for pregnant women. You can get–'

'Toxoplasmosis . . . Yeah. If I eat their shit.' She made baby-talk with the adoring hounds. 'Look at those eyes. How can you be unmoved?'

With the smell of dog in this house – very easily. The cottage kitchen was a mess. Dogsville. There were dog dishes on the counter, puppy toys strewn about the surfaces, and torn towels that had been fought over on the floor. As for the rest of the place . . . Some kind of half-turned sculpture on a pottery wheel, an open laptop on the table, and flour on the counter. She was baking. As usual, Steph was doing three things at once. She was scatty, hippie-dippy, infuriating – and indispensable to me. At least now I would not have to do without her. She had spent much of our friendship skittering off here and there to do stints in foreign countries as the urge took her – her attention span was limited – and as soon as she settled back in Cork, I decided to leave. It was a prospect neither of us had relished, so I watched her now with affection, as she pottered around her disorder looking for clean mugs, her long skirt floating round her ankles, the tails of her shirt drifting down to her thighs. Even before she became pregnant, Steph wore loose, layered clothes and always seemed to float about. Her feet were never on the ground; my feet, in contrast, had always been firmly planted in reality, although Steph loved to make me levitate sometimes, by dissecting my dreams or reading my tarot and unveiling me to myself.

'Your dad called,' she said, finding one clean mug. 'Said I wasn't to ask you anything about anything.'

'Sorry. You weren't on that list.'

'Good. Does that mean I get to hear what's going on?'

'Are you up to it?'

'Of course.'

'It's . . . tough stuff.'

She frowned and sat down. 'I'm made of tough stuff.'

'Well, I'll tell you so.'

'Thank God. Then I can tell Killian and he can tell Milenko.'

'Steph!'

'He hasn't the faintest clue what's happening, Killian says.'

I was gutted. 'He's spoken to Milenko?'

'Called him from Stockholm.'

'Why didn't he call *me*?'

'Your phone has been off for days!'

'But Killian's not supposed to do that. He's *my* friend!'

'Milenko is our friend too. And he's devastated, by the way. He hung up on Killian.'

'Why?'

'He couldn't continue.'

Oh, God.

'Look, until you tell me why you left him not a month before his wedding, I have some sympathy for the guy. He can't have cheated on you. I don't believe he's capable of it, so you'd better have a very good reason.'

I put my mug on the table, poured milk into it, stirred the tea, and finally said, 'I do, but it's pretty horrible.'

'Go on.'

I rubbed my forehead with my fingers and searched for the beginning. But where, exactly, was the beginning? And how had I not seen it? 'It . . . It seems I missed something.'

'What?'

From all corners of my head, I gathered words into some sort of coherence. 'Last week, Milenko had to go to a conference in Zagreb and –'

The doorbell rang. 'Oh, bloody hell,' said Steph. 'Let's leave it.'

'No, get it. I'm not going anywhere.'

'But imagine if it's Mum,' she whispered. 'She'll be here for hours. What do you mean you missed something?'

My eyes filled.

The doorbell went again.

'Get rid of them,' I said. 'Pretend to be sick.'

Steph got up and glanced into the hallway. 'It looks like the Mother, all right.' She tiptoed away from the door. 'She'll go away. I'll call later and say I was asleep.'

'My car's out there.'

The doorbell rang again, three times in succession. 'Jesus, but that woman is persistent! She's just come to nag me about eating.'

Her mother called out Steph's name.

'You'll have to go.'

'Coming! Jesus, Mum!'

I stayed at the table. The last thing I wanted was to be seen like this, even by Angela, Steph's dotty but adorable mother. I waited to hear the whispers in the hallway, 'Please, Mum, give her some space,' but there were no whispers. There was no sound at all. There was instead a stillness, like a shockwave filling the house. I got up and looked into the hall. Steph was standing at the front door, staring past her mother at the two gardaí behind her. A woman and a man.

'Steph,' her mother said.

'What? What's happened? Is it Dad?'

'May we step in?' asked the policewoman.

I pulled Steph backwards as they came into the hall.

'Maybe we could . . .' The policewoman gestured towards the living room. Dutifully, silently, we all shuffled in.

'What is it?' said Steph. 'Mum?'

'Steph, dear . . . This is . . .' She hesitated, turned to the policewoman.

'Mrs Enright, I'm very sorry to –'

'It's Killian,' her mother said quickly, not wanting to fail in what she had come to do.

Killian, in short, was dead. That's what they came to tell us, though I don't remember anyone saying it. There was a screech. I thought it was Steph, but it was me. Steph was sitting on the couch. Her mother bent over her, hugging and weeping. The police people said things, muttered stuff. I couldn't breathe.

Killian had died.

Steph's eyes stood out. Her mother rubbed her back, gripping her hand, crying, crying. The gardaí sat down, so as not to tower over them, leaving only me on my feet. Words came at us. Car accident. Stockholm. Killed instantly. Didn't suffer. I heard the 'No' word a lot. Might have been me.

Steph ran from the room and vomited into the kitchen sink. I followed and stood by her, wetting a teacloth in warm water, but the activity brought no relief. Steph's face spun into mine, her eyes wild, as if expecting me to save her, to tell her that if she turned round there would be no one there, that there had been no ring on the doorbell, but I was as bewildered as she was and could not make this go away.

The policewoman came into the kitchen. We sat Steph at the table. 'It's a mistake,' she kept saying. 'We're having a baby.'

'When?' I asked. 'When did it happen?'

'This morning, during rush-hour. He was on his way to the airport. Conditions were treacherous.'

'But are you sure? Maybe it was someone else?'

'I'm afraid not. The taxi driver was also killed.'

But he wasn't in Stockholm this morning, I thought. He was with me, in Kilcrohane. I had not imagined him. He *had* been there.

'Mrs Enright, would you like assistance in notifying other members of his family?'

'Oh, God!' I said. 'His mother. Deirdre.'

'They should be told immediately. These things have a way of getting out.'

But there was no sense to be had from Steph. Angela came to her and keened with her.

The cop turned to me. 'Is there anyone else? A son or a brother, perhaps?'

'He *is* the son. He is the brother.'

The policewoman looked at Steph. 'I'm so sorry.'

'What'll we do?' I said to Angela. 'What about Deirdre and Marjorie?'

'You go, dear. You tell them.'

'*Me?* No. Ferdia.' I turned to the guard. 'Deirdre's husband should do it.'

'He's in Dublin,' Steph said, suddenly clear and matter-of-fact.

'We can send someone, if you like?' the guard suggested.

'God, no,' I said. 'Not like this. Gardaí arriving . . . no.'

'Well, perhaps you and I could go?' the woman asked. 'Do you know his sister?'

'I've known her most of my life, but I can't leave Steph.'

'She'll be fine with her mother.'

No, I thought, she'll never be fine again.

Angela reached out to me. 'There's no one else. Hurry, dear.'

The guard advised that we go first to Killian's sister and allow her to break the news to his mother. 'Where would she be at the minute?'

I glanced at the clock. Three. 'Still at work. At the bank on Patrick's Bridge.'

Before I knew it, I was in a squad car. We dropped the guard at the station, and the policewoman, introducing herself as Bernie, drove me into town. The radio buzzed and beeped and voices filtered in and out of the car and in and out of my head. I didn't think backwards, I thought only forwards: telling Deirdre. How to do it. What to say. What could be said?

'You're a close friend of Mrs Enright's?'

'Of both of them. Killian . . . We go back . . . We . . . Years.'

We pulled up right outside the redbrick building. No parking problem in a squad car. 'I'll come in with you,' said Bernie. 'It's better not to beat around. Get straight to the point.'

I got out. I wanted to run – down the street, along the river and on until I left all this behind in someone else's life.

The bank was busy. I headed straight for Foreign Exchange at the far end. Deirdre was dealing with a customer. She glanced up and saw me, but not the uniform behind me, and nodded vaguely, turning back to the customer. I wasn't sure what to do – push the customer aside, place myself in front of the glass partition and say, 'Your brother's dead'? There was something I had not told Bernie. I had known Deirdre most of my life, yes, but I could not abide her and the feeling was entirely mutual. Steph did not come off much better. Deirdre and her mother had not approved of Killian's choice of women, and were particularly horrified when he had married someone who wrote poetry, taught English and made pottery. A 'floater', they called her, using the word with distaste, and showed no interest at all in Steph's work, scorning her 'little book of poems' as if they were teenage doodles. But it was impossible, even as Deirdre threw me a glance of bored disinterest, to feel anything but devastating compassion.

The customer moved on. 'What can I do for you?' Deirdre asked. 'Want to trade in your Croatian cash?'

'Can you come out?'

'What on earth for? Can't you see I'm –'

'Please, Deirdre. Come out.'

She looked uneasy, glanced at her colleague, then stood up and went to the door. She came out with eyebrows raised, and it was then she saw Bernie. 'What is it?'

'In here.' I pushed open the door that led to the rest of the building.

Deirdre looked at us with increasing terror. 'What's going on?'

The news threw her against the wall. She kept saying, 'No. No,' then slid to the floor with a howl. One of her colleagues came down the stairs and hurried to her side, turning to us for an explanation.

'Her brother's been killed,' said Bernie.

'Oh, God, Deirdre!'

I moved to a free space of wall and leant into it, trying to keep hold. Like fish caught in a net, I thought, that's how we are. Flapping, flapping, gasping for air and freedom from this trap into which we had so innocently wandered.

Bernie crouched beside the women on the floor. 'Is there somewhere we can take her?'

'Upstairs.' They manhandled Deirdre up the stairs and into a boardroom.

'I'll get some tea,' the colleague said.

'I'm afraid we don't have time. Water, perhaps,' said Bernie. 'Deirdre, I'm sorry, but it's important we tell your mother as soon as possible.' This prompted another heart-rending wail. I'd never realized death was so noisy but, then, I'd never seen it up close like this.

And so on to the next awful stop. There was no escape. I did not belong in that car; it should not have been me comforting Deirdre through my own tears. I should have been with Steph. When we pulled up outside Mrs Enright's house, Deirdre stared at the front door. 'What will I say? How am I supposed to . . .'

'If you like, I'll do it,' said Bernie. 'You just need to be there.'

Deirdre was still staring at the house. 'Daddy just died.'

'Oh, I'm so sorry.'

'Two years ago,' I said, because it needed clarifying.

They got out. I didn't move. There was no point all of us lumping in, dancing attendance round the Grim Reaper. The sun shone into the car. Voices still emerged from the radio. Sitting in the back, I must have looked like a suspect to passers-by.

I regretted that bin – the tempting bin into which I had hurled my phone. I desperately needed to call Dad and Clara and Ger and . . . Milenko.

This was it. This was the chance to fold, to capitulate, to

wrap myself in his love, happily defeated. I could not be expected to get through this without him. Killian was my childhood friend, my mentor, my conscience. Losing him put everything else into the shade. I would call Milenko and tell him our best friend was lost. But I had no phone. How long would I have to wait while they did their dreadful business inside?

A schoolboy came along the street, his tie loose, his shirt undone, with a backpack hanging off his shoulder. He would have a mobile. All kids did. I got out of the car so quickly that he leapt back in fright.

'You have a phone,' I said. 'I'll bet you have a phone, right? Can I use it? It's an emergency, but I'll pay for it. I'll give you a tenner if you could just let me make one call.'

His eyes went left and right. A crazed-looking woman with a puffy face jumps out of the back of a squad car, demanding his phone . . . He leant towards the car to see if there was anyone else in it, and he glanced at my wrists. No handcuffs. I could see him add it up: a tenner's worth of credit for the price of one call. He handed me his phone.

But it wasn't Milenko I dialled. Dad's number came instinctively and when I heard his voice I floundered. The boy shifted awkwardly on his feet as I sobbed over the squad car.

'Kadie, where are you?' Dad said. 'I'll come and get you.'

'No, no, it's something else, you won't believe it. You won't believe what's happened.'

By the time Dad and I got back to Steph's, the cottage had filled with neighbours and friends: the tide of support was coming in, wave after wave. There were whispers of disbelief, of hows and whys and what-the-hells. Grief-stricken friends hugged every wall like a layer of condensation. Steph was still sitting at the kitchen table, which was covered with cups, milk cartons and biscuit crumbs. I muscled through the crowds with Dad and slipped behind Steph's chair, squeezing her shoulder. Dad hugged her, wordless and bereft, and I thought of Milenko and how I hadn't told him yet.

'Thanks, Rollo,' said Steph. 'You're very good.' How amazing, I thought, that she manages to speak.

Killian's mother was in the living room, surrounded by her own entourage. Dad and I embraced her. She could not be blamed for not acknowledging us: she scarcely seemed to know where she was.

The night had no beginning and no end. Tea was made, and made again, and again.

'Where do all the coffee-drinkers go,' Clara asked, 'whenever there's a death?'

I wandered about. Children – nephews and nieces and friends' kids – were playing cards in one of the bedrooms, creating their own safe haven, away from the frightening upset of the adults. The local hurling team had turned up, Killian's team; burly men reduced to stunned monoliths taking up space in the hall.

In Steph's room I lay in the dark on top of all the coats. My first love, gone, without as much as a wave. So swift, so simple. He had crawled from his sheets that morning, in his hotel room, swallowed some breakfast and hailed a cab, and that was the end of his life. Whipped away, like a house in a tornado, leaving the occupants of his life homeless.

No tears would come. Crying would be some sort of release, yet there was no release from this. My desolate friend, the fatherless baby, the widow called upon to bury her son . . . Expelling a few saltwater droplets would do nothing about any of it. We had come upon a very dark passage, and I knew only one thing. My heart was shattered, scattered, and I would never again get all the pieces back.

There was a gentle tap on the door; Clara put her head in. 'Kadie?'

'Yeah.'

She came in – a dark shape moving towards me – and sat on the bed. A hand rested on my hip. 'Are you okay?'

'Yeah. You?'

Clara sighed heavily. 'With all these people here, I keep expecting him to arrive, late as usual, and burst in laughing at us all.'

'Mmm.'

'I hope Steph doesn't go into labour.'

'God.'

'I had a bad feeling when I woke up this morning,' she said.

'Me too, but that was something else entirely.'

'What on earth happened?'

I sighed. 'Not now.'

'Is it really off?'

'Yeah.'

'But your job. Everything. What will you do?'

'Getting through the next few hours would be a start.'

Much later, after hours of comings and goings and weeping and whispering, I found myself seated with Steph.

She said, 'I have to go.'

'Where?'

'Stockholm. I have to go and get him.'

'Oh, Steph, no. Not you. Someone else.'

'How can it be someone else? He has to be . . . identified.'

'Anyone can do that.'

'And brought home.' Her eyes were glazed. 'They keep talking about bringing him home.'

'But it doesn't have to be you. It would be too much.'

'You hardly expect me to let Deirdre do it? Or any of that lot?'

'You have to put the baby first.'

'I have to put Killian first,' she said. 'I have to go to him.'

24

'But in view of –'

'I have to go to him.'

I bit my lip.

'So, you'll come with me?' she said.

'To Sweden? Yeah, of course. Clara can organize flights first thing in the morning.'

'Dad offered to come, but he's not up to it, and Mum would fuss too much.'

'What about the Enrights?'

'I don't know, do I? They've closed themselves into the other room as if they're at a whole different wake. She's hardly spoken to me. Can you believe it?'

I could believe it. Killian's mother could be a hard, self-centred old cow. 'She's too upset,' I said. 'She looks like she doesn't know what's happening.'

'I won't have Deirdre coming to Stockholm, do you hear? She'll try to take over, but I'm not going to start playing happy families now.'

'You might have to.'

'We'll have to get in touch with Henrik. We'll need him.'

'I'll do it,' I said. 'Where's his number?'

'It's with all Killian's numbers – in his mobile. It's his address book. There's loads of people we haven't been able to call yet.'

'We'll do it when we get there, then.'

Someone interrupted us to say goodnight to Steph. A wordless hug, a nod of acknowledgement.

'Steph?' I said, when we were alone again. 'I saw him today.'

'What?'

'Killian. At Kilcrohane. He was sitting in the car with me, staring at the sea.'

Her eyes filled.

'He looked good.'

'What time was that?' she whispered.

'It must have been about three hours after . . .'

'So he *did* come home.'

'Seems like it.'

An elderly neighbour, sitting on the couch behind us with a cup of tea on her lap, tugged at my sleeve. 'They say the departed make a grand tour of all the people and places they loved before they go on their way.'

Steph turned. 'Why did he not come to me, then, Nell?'

'Because he hasn't left you, dear, and never will.'

'I thought I was playing mind games,' I said, 'thinking about Killian to stop me thinking about everything else.'

'But it was him thinking about you,' said Steph.

'Maybe.'

'Steph!' Killian's robust cousin Paul pulled up a chair and sat down. He was a nice man, amiable and reliable, and a fairly good friend of Killian's. 'The family have asked me to make arrangements for, you know . . .'

'For what?' I asked.

'Killian's return, God rest him.'

Trouble already. The bypass was under way. The Enrights were taking over.

'I'm sorry?' said Steph.

'Someone has to go to Sweden, pet. I've offered to go along with Deirdre.'

The coarse presumption sickened me. And there would be more of it.

Steph said, '*I* will be the one to go to Sweden.'

'But, sure, you won't want to travel in your condition.'

'My condition has nothing to do with it. I need to be with my husband.'

'Ach, I understand that but, really, in view of –'

'Paul,' I interceded, 'it's all organized. Steph and I are going to Sweden and we will bring Killian home.'

He was shaking his head. 'But the family feels –'

'His family has already made a decision,' I said.

'Thanks for the offer, Paul,' said Steph, 'but there'll be plenty to do back here.'

'Are you absolutely sure you wouldn't like me to go in your place?' he said warmly. 'It's a difficult business, and I'd hate to see you put yourself through it.'

'I want to see him.'

'All right. I'll speak to Marjorie so.'

'We have to get her permission,' Steph muttered to me.

The house phone rang, as it had been doing all night. A neighbour called out, 'It's for Kadie. It's Milenko.'

My eyes sought out my father. He came across the room. 'Why is he phoning me here? How does he know?'

'He doesn't know. He's phoning here for the same reason he's phoning everywhere else – he'll go on until he finds you.'

'Oh, God.'

'Take the call,' Dad said.

'I can't. I don't want to be the one to tell him.'

'You can and you will.'

'No, I've told enough people.'

'Don't you want to speak to him even now? Surely you can put aside whatever . . .'

I shook my head, slowly but repeatedly, until Dad went out to the hall to take the call.

Even from the kitchen, above the mumblings of the bereaved, I could hear his low, grave voice delivering the news, and then, after a pause, the dreadful details.

I locked myself into the bathroom to stop myself grabbing the phone just to hear his voice, because if I spoke to him I would go back to him, and I could not do that. He would have to handle this in whatever way he could, all alone, in Korčula.

When I emerged, Dad was waiting for me. 'It must be very bad,' he said, 'what he's done.'

3

In the small hours of the morning after Killian's death, a meeting was held in the cottage during which both branches of his family managed to reach agreement. Paul undertook to organize the funeral with Deirdre's husband, while Steph, Deirdre and I went to Sweden. Clara got us on to the Stockholm flight out of Dublin that afternoon.

We were told that it would take a couple of days to release the body, so the funeral was tentatively arranged on the basis that we would be home within three days. Killian had friends and family in America and Europe, many of whom were already making plans to travel to the service.

My sole interest and occupation was to get Steph to where she wanted to be, but that meant managing the Deirdre Factor. As much as his wife and his friend, she wanted to go to her brother, and her determination was matched only by Steph's, so they cancelled one another out and both travelled.

The flight from Dublin was dreadful. It undid every coping mechanism I had learnt to control my fear of flying – a phobia so incapacitating that I had been forced to address it when I acquired a Croatian boyfriend. A course of hypnosis had worked, in part. I could now step on to a plane unaided and, with all sorts of mind games, could survive most European flights without hyperventilating. I didn't enjoy it, but I could do it, especially when Milenko was at the other end. But as we flew to Stockholm, my nerves were not as robust as usual, I had already stretched them on the flight from Cork to Dublin in a small propeller-type job, and Steph was holding my hand in comfort, when it should have been the other way round. I squeezed her fingertips until they were white.

We were otherwise composed. A calm had settled on Steph. The business of death is the salvation of the bereaved: so many people to see, hands to shake, plans to make. If nothing else, the very tedium of it numbs the senses. The same platitudes repeated over and over had rocked us into a daze.

But Steph was not as dazed as one might have expected. She would not be led around like an invalid of bereavement. She was clear-sighted, and knew what she needed to do. In contrast, as the steady friend who was meant to hold every-thing together, I should have been doing better. I was doubly, trebly, shocked now, and my own turmoil had not retreated one inch. In spite of everything, I missed Milenko, and the missing was like a burning stake inside me. To have to get through all this without his support was brutal. My stomach went over and over like a tumble-dryer. It would not be still. Steph was not eating, and it was hard to encourage her to do so when my own appetite had shut down.

The aircraft shuddered. 'Jesus! What's that?'

'Calm down,' said Steph. 'You should be used to all the bumps by now.'

'Bumps? Into what?'

'Air pockets, clouds, I don't know!'

Deirdre leant forward to look past Steph. 'And you a travel agent. Really.'

Oh, fuck off. 'As if I haven't heard that one before,' I muttered.

'I thought the hypnosis helped?'

'It did. You should have seen me before.'

'How *did* you end up like this?' Deirdre asked. 'Were you in an accident or something?'

'Don't use that word.'

'Yes,' said Steph, 'do tell how you ended up such a basket case.'

There had been no mid-air trauma, no accident. My fear of flying had come upon me stealthily during one of the smoothest flights of my life in my late teens. Dad and I travelled a fair bit when I was small, often to a friend's villa in the Caribbean, and flying had never perturbed me then. I liked to look out and gape at the beautiful globe, the uniform clouds, the vibrant blue of the ocean. But on that particular flight home, I had looked out at the same clouds and the same sea and suddenly noticed how very, very far down they were, and how very, very far up I was. What was stopping this multi-tonne cylinder of aluminium from hurtling down like a paper plane through those clouds and into that deep ocean? Nothing. Air was the only thing between me and disaster, and I suffered a horrifying vision of falling all the way to the ground. It was the first of many dreams that subsequently tormented me – like the one in which I was hanging off the end of a plane watching a man in a green suit behind me let go and fall, knowing it was me who had to fall next.

I had never returned to the Caribbean and subsequently flew only under duress. For holidays, Dad and I went to the Continent on the car ferry. It didn't bother me that I might never again go beyond the ever-widening boundaries of Europe. Europe would do fine: vast and varied, and the whole lot could be seen, top to bottom, east to west, *on the ground*. I flew occasionally for work, until I met Milenko, who presented a serious challenge. It was then I took the airline Fear of Flying course and had hypnotherapy. My therapist searched my past for some anxiety-riddled event that had rendered me so nervous and decided that my mother's departure when I was four was at the root of my inner sense of insecurity. Codswallop, of course, but I was rehabilitated enough to get to and from Croatia as necessary, which was all that mattered.

All that progress, however, was about to be undone by my mercy flight with Steph.

'Who's meeting us?' Deirdre asked.

'Meeting us?'

'Surely somebody from the embassy should be there?'

She'd like that, I thought. Lots of fuss and officials flapping around her. She was a deeply silly woman. The oddest things impressed her and her mother, like how people enunciated their vowels and whether they shopped in Brown Thomas.

'The embassy offered consular assistance,' said Steph. 'I told them we'd ask if we needed anything.'

'Oh,' said Deirdre. 'Is that wise?'

'We'll have Henrik. I'd rather be with friends.'

'Are we going straight to the morgue?'

'*Deirdre*,' I hissed.

'Well.'

'We have to phone the police when we get there,' I said.

It was then the fun began. Our descent into Stockholm was an aerophobe's nightmare. After announcing that we would be on the ground in five minutes – music to my ears – we found ourselves still in the air half an hour later, bouncing around the sky like a shuttlecock. The conditions had become foul: we were flying through a gale-force wind. The pilot tried to land and came within feet of the runway, but instead of enjoying that wonderful moment of contact with the ground, there was a terrifying acceleration. The aircraft was heaving and straining and doing everything but landing. Sweat poured off me. We tumbled upwards in disarray. Even Deirdre had turned grey, and as the tumult went on, a passenger across the way reached for a sick bag. I closed my eyes. There was no explanation, no steady, calm announcement from a sexy-voiced pilot explaining why he had aborted the landing.

'Why aren't they saying anything?'

'He's a bit busy,' said Steph, who sat with her head back, utterly calm. She had nothing to fear. Half of her was already dead.

'Jesus!' Another tussle with the storm flung us sideways. We didn't seem to be turning round.

'We must be going on to Helsinki,' said Steph.

'I don't care where we go as long as we *land*.'

'Use your mind-game thingies,' she said. 'Rollo on the lake, isn't it? Rowing his little boat?'

'This is no time for that shit!'

A flight attendant struggled down the passageway, looking alarmed.

'We'll be fine,' said Deirdre. 'Killian wouldn't let anything happen to us.'

I liked her enormously at that moment, until she added pleadingly, 'Would he?'

'Maybe he wants us along,' Steph said. 'Maybe he's come to get us.'

'We're done for,' I said.

'Don't start hyperventilating,' she said. 'Breathe normally. There's nothing you can do, so relax.'

I hyperventilated.

The plane was speeding up. The engines whined. I braced myself for impact. We were about to hit something.

With a heavy *bumph*, we hit the ground. There were gasps of relief, then everyone clapped. We waited to hear where we were. Oslo? Helsinki? There was no sexy apology. The pilot simply said, 'Welcome to Stockholm.'

'What is it with me and planes? It was so wet in Cork the other day that we skidded on the runway and slid sideways.'

'All your bad vibes do it,' said Steph. 'All that negative energy plays havoc with the electro-magnetic field.'

'Cork to Dublin was fine,' said Deirdre.

'I don't care. I'm going back overland.'

Steph said drily, 'You live on an island.'

'For heaven's sake,' said Deirdre, 'what a fuss.'

I was a snivelling, miserable wreck of a being when we disembarked. Bereavement? What bereavement? All that mattered was the ground. The glorious, wonderful, solid earth. I wanted to lie on it, and very nearly had to, because there were no seats in the baggage-reclaim area. The terminal was so quiet, it might have been the middle of the night, but it was only four o'clock. The concourses were empty. Steph and Deirdre stood by the carousel waiting for our bags, while I sat on the floor against the wall, planning: ferry to Denmark, train to Belgium, ferry, train, ferry all the way home. It would mean missing the funeral. I didn't care.

There was no one to meet us; no one about. Strings of white Christmas lights hung like curtains over the vast windows of the airport. The travel agent who was meant to lead the way – me – was more disoriented than the widow, but we managed to find the train that went into the city centre, and from there took a taxi to our hotel.

The manager appeared almost as soon as we stepped into the lobby to offer his condolences. Because I was not a relative, I was singled out as the person to speak to. He took me slightly to the side and said the hotel would do everything they could to help; we simply had to ask. Mr Enright had been a valued customer.

A long way down one corridor and at the far end of another, we found our rooms on the third floor: two were singles; one had a double bed and was larger than the others.

'I'll have this one,' Deirdre said.

'It's always nice to have a choice, isn't it?' Steph said to me.

Our rooms were tiny, smaller even than the cabins on a car ferry. I threw my bag on to the bed, pulled out my pyjamas and toilet-bag. I had packed in a daze, hurling in enough clothes to get me through two cold days in the north: a few shirts, another pair of jeans, a second sweater, socks and underwear. The room was stifling. When I was putting my toilet-bag in the bathroom, a packet of contraceptive pills protruded. I took it out, and consulted myself in the mirror. What a wreck: my reddish fair hair was turned up in a twist; it usually looked funky that way, all spiky at the back, but after travelling it was more like a self-made knot. My eyes – supposedly inherited from Dad, but never as twinkly or mischievous as his – were slightly crazed with exhaustion, and because I hadn't been eating, my high cheekbones stood out, as in an exaggerated drawing of a skeleton. All in all, I looked like I'd been trampled on by something unpleasant. Not quite the beautiful bride I had hoped I might make a few weeks later. On the matter of the pills, my haggard reflection agreed with me. I chucked them into the bin. What a lot of dumping I was doing.

When I went in to Steph, she told me she had made arrangements with the police for us to go to the mortuary first thing the next morning.

'Good. We all need an early night.'

She was sitting on her narrow bed. 'We must call Henrik.'

'We can't without Killian's phone. It must be with his belongings.'

'He must be told. He was the last person to see Killian.'

'Let's get something to eat,' I said. 'Then we'll figure it out.'

We collected Deirdre from her room and made our way out to the broad street below. It was cold with fresh, thin air, invigorating after the overheated hotel. Every time a car drove past there was a satisfying scrunch on the ground. I thought the roads must be gritted, but it was the snow-tyres on certain cars that scrunched. In an Italian restaurant a few blocks away, we took a table by the window. A Christmas party was in full swing – about twenty women and two men at one end of the room, laughing and celebrating.

Exhaustion pulled on me. I'd lost count of the sleepless nights. That morning, Dad had taken me home some time after three. I'd had to pack and try for sleep before we travelled. But try for sleep was as much as I had been able to do when I lay in the old bed that had recently reclaimed me, with images from the day screaming out of nowhere like holograms – the doorbell ringing, the screech of horror that never left Steph's mouth, the weeping, the squad car and Deirdre on the ground.

We picked at our pasta. Steph's face glowed in the candle-light. 'We could go and tell Henrik, face to face.'

'Now? Tonight?'

'As far as he knows, Kill went home yesterday. He can't go on thinking –'

'I'll do it,' I said. 'Where does he live?'

'No, I want to.' She glanced out. 'He's at work. Killian told me he's on the evening shift this week.' She turned back to us. 'We'll go there. He mustn't hear it from someone else.'

Outside, a taxi stopped to pick us up and drove us to the television station where Henrik worked. I was in dread again. I knew Henrik from the early days, when he had lived in Cork for a year. He was a cheerful guy, and one of Killian's oldest friends; coming with this news to him was like coming at a tree with an axe.

We made our way into the building. There was a canteen on one side, a reception desk on the other. Steph asked for Henrik. I admired her resolve. She could have stayed at home, the whimpering widow, and left all this to others.

'I'm sorry,' said the receptionist, glancing at the many screens on the wall, 'but Henrik is working.' On a screen behind him, Henrik was reading the news.

'How long will he be?' I asked.

'About ten minutes.' He motioned towards a bench. 'If you would like to wait, I will call him when he's ready.'

Steph and Deirdre sat down. I paced.

Bad news has a look, an international uniform, and the receptionist recognized it. 'Is everything all right?' he asked me, when I passed his desk.

'A good friend of Henrik's has died. We need to tell him.'

He immediately picked up the phone and spoke in a low, sombre voice. 'One of his colleagues will come.'

'Thank you.'

Henrik went about his day's work, staring out at us, churning out bad news. Incomprehensible.

Some minutes later a woman in jeans and a sweater came through the doors. 'Hey,' she said to the receptionist. He pointed towards us. She extended her hand. 'I'm Freja. Please, this way.' We followed her upstairs, pulling off our coats. The building was hot. Outside the newsroom, she stopped and said, 'Who is it who has died?'

'Killian,' said Deirdre. 'My brother.'

'His Irish friend? Oh, my God, he was here the other day.'

The newsroom was crackling. Staff moved from desk to desk or leant back in swinging chairs, talking to one another with one eye on their screens. Freja led us into a room full of monitors and computers. It was dim and humming with tension. A woman spoke into a microphone, another handed her a sheet of paper. We could see into the studio, through a large pane of glass, but Henrik could not see us. When the news rolled to an end, he stacked his papers, chatting to his fellow newsreader as he stood up, fixing his jacket. The tension in the newsroom relaxed. I wished something would stop it, stop the moment, but Henrik came through into the hub and saw us there.

He realized very quickly that something unspeakable had happened. It was Freja who actually said it to him. Steph hugged him. He was robust at first, deflecting the blows, until he sank defeated into a chair and sat staring hard at the floor. 'But I saw him . . . But we were together the other day . . .'

Killian had left us with a heavy burden of buts.

We had coffee in the cafeteria. Henrik kept shaking his head. What pathetic gestures we make, I thought. How useless we all are. Steph's growing child had become like a black eye that people felt inclined to look beyond, so as not to remind the mother, or themselves, of the fatherless child, and Henrik did it too.

I didn't expect anyone to take into account the four sleepless nights I'd had before this calamity struck, but the tiredness was beginning to catch up with me – overrun me, in fact – and if I did not sleep soon, I would probably walk under a tram, so I suggested we get Steph back to the hotel. 'Of course,' Henrik said. 'I will get my car.'

Deirdre did most of the talking on the way back. She seemed able to talk her way through this, to get comfort from the patter of her own voice, while the rest of us were stranded in a linguistic wasteland where only easy words came and even they repeated themselves over and over. Perhaps having Deirdre along was not such a bad idea. In the back seat, I took Steph's hand and was startled by how thin she had become. Her wrist was like a reed. There had been concern about her weight through all those months of sickness, and if she did not start eating now, how would she withstand the next few days?

The city was cheerfully lit for Christmas and, in almost every window, a little triangle of lights, like a row of candles, glowed against the long Swedish night. I had always wanted to see Stockholm, but this was not at all like being in Stockholm. It was there, a setting, a backdrop. We stood in front of it, not in it. Not for us the canals and shops, the cosy cafés that were hiding among the downtown streets. For us it would be mortuaries, hotels, sullen faces. We weren't really in Sweden. We were in Killian's death.

The pedestrians made me envious. Normal people doing normal things. But what did I know? What could I tell from a passing glance? That woman there, heading into the underground, might be dragging through her own ordeal. That day, in Stockholm, people broke up, marriages ended, affairs began. That day, in Stockholm as in Cork, people were bereaved. Other people, other families, felt as we did. They were somewhere in my backdrop, but knowing as much brought me no closer to Stockholm, though it lived and breathed and was trampled on by the well-insulated soles of its inhabitants.

'A single bed,' said Steph, as she lay back and pulled the duvet over her.

'I hope you'll sleep.'

She looked at the window. 'I suppose . . . I suppose we'll be okay for money?'

'Of course you will. Your mortgage will be paid off and Killian's dad left you a neat little sum, didn't he?'

She nodded, but tears slipped down the side of her face. I wiped one away. 'He did so well on the Estonian deal, you know . . . A big chunk of commission . . . As if . . .'

'You'll be fine. Killian has seen to it. Don't worry about that stuff now.'

I turned out the light and quietly left the room. Steph had never in her life worried about money. She used to joke she didn't have any to worry about. She made little from her work, and had always lived sparsely. Indeed, Killian's high earnings had initially been bewildering to her. He enjoyed money, and was quite materialistic; she was comfortable with very little. As a result, their home was a curious mixture of hi-tech and Bohemian. No doubt Killian had life assurance and there would probably be an insurance pay-out because of the accident, and with their recent inheritance, wise investments would offer Steph a reasonable income in the long-term, or at least until she could go back to work.

I went to my box-room and slept better than I had for days, which wasn't saying much. The room was hot and the window resisted being opened more than an inch. I tossed a lot, but blanked out for an hour or so every hour or so.

Henrik collected us the next morning to take us to the mortuary. The police had offered to do so, but Steph had declined and arranged to meet them there instead. It was so good to have him with us. From my bedroom window it had looked like a bright sunny day, but the sun had barely risen above the buildings, so at ground level, when we emerged on to the street, it was dull.

Stockholm was indeed a beautiful city. We gazed at it with heavy curiosity, this strange place that had taken Killian. The Venice of the North. Water everywhere. Steph had been there before. There was nowhere she and Killian had not been together. They had met on the move, had courted on the move, and only the pregnancy had drawn them to stillness. Steph had been too ill to mind being grounded, but Killian had never really stopped since becoming a sales manager for his company. He travelled to Sweden once a month and to other European capitals regularly.

Henrik wasn't sure where to go and made phone calls while he drove, and pointed at the City Hall as we crossed a bridge. 'Where the Nobel Prize is awarded,' he said, his phone in one hand. It was a beautiful building on the waterfront, a deep, rusty red with a golden cupola on the tower.

The morgue was part of the university hospital, a vast suburb of a place. Deirdre wasn't so talkative now, Steph was shaking and I felt sick. Eventually we pulled into a car-park surrounded by redbrick buildings. I asked Steph if she wanted me to wait outside, but she gripped my hand. I reached for Deirdre and, in a tense huddle, we made our way inside. A policeman met us at the door. Sombre introductions were made, and we were shuffled into a whispering waiting room. A few chairs, a plant, a low table. I fantasized that it would not be him. As in the movies, we would draw back and exclaim, 'But that isn't Killian!' and there would be consternation and joy all round, and no concern for the victim.

We were shown into a large, bright, unadorned room. A trolley stood in the middle. There was little furniture – nowhere for Steph to sit, just a few skylights throwing a grey light on to the draped body. A nurse stood by. With a nod from Steph, she pulled back the sheet. It was indeed Killian who was uncovered.

Steph made only the slightest sound. It was Deirdre and I who ripped the respectful quiet. The nurse stood back. Henrik put his fist over his mouth. Deirdre leant over her brother's still chest, sobbing. 'No!'

A tear grew on Steph's lower lid and stayed there.

Those minutes ate into my bones. They would never go away. The morgue, the white-clad nurse, dug a trench in my head and buried themselves there, because Killian's new face – grey, bruised, *hurt* – was not the face he had worn at Kilcrohane. It was not peaceful. He was not at rest, but dead and battered. He had no expression; no heavenly expression of peace. We put our fingers through his cold dark hair, whispering endearments, reproaches, and touched his hands as if to squeeze into them some belated comfort, even some life. Odd little gestures of affection that were quite wasted on him, but helpful to us.

Deirdre kept whispering, 'He's gone. He's gone.'

And so he was. He would not open those bright eyes and

grin. He would not do anything. I kissed his hand. They had already removed his wedding ring.

We were led, at some point, from the room. 'I don't want to,' I said, looking over my shoulder at the shrouded figure. We were reassured that we could see him again when the undertakers had done their work. For now we were given seats in the smaller room. No one spoke. We sat, staring at the floor, until the nurse stepped in; in one hand, she carried Killian's briefcase, in the other, his suitcase.

We stared at his belongings, affronted. Henrik jumped to his feet, took the cases and left the room. When he returned, we felt ready to leave. I hesitated in the entrance, wanting to wait for Killian to come.

We returned to the car, limp with weeping. Huge mounds of snow and grit, left over from a recent heavy fall, lay about on street corners, waiting to melt. Steph was increasingly blank, removed, and we had yet to face the undertaker.

Henrik was a gentle guide, efficient and tactful. He recommended a hot drink and drove us to a dim coffee shop with a worn carpet and a big white cat painted on the wall. We took seats on an old couch and armchairs while he ordered drinks.

'Traditional,' he said, bringing over a plate of saffron buns, 'at this time of year.'

'Try,' I said to Steph. 'You barely touched breakfast.'

'I'm not hungry.'

'I'll bet the baby is. And it helps the nausea.'

'I'm not nauseous any more. Not much, anyway.'

Our drinks came – tall glasses of hot milk, with chocolate lollipops on a plate. 'You put the stick in like this,' said Henrik, whirling his chocolate ball in the milk until it melted.

Deirdre's phone rang. She went outside to take the call.

'Would you call Mum for me?' asked Steph. 'Tell her I'm fine, et cetera. Here, use my phone.'

I went outside. I reassured Angela that Steph was fine and promised she would ring when she could. I put the phone in my pocket, staring at the park across the road. Steph was not fine: she was slipping further and further inside herself.

When I got back to the table, Deirdre was all earnestness, while Steph watched her with still eyes. I wanted to throw her a lifeline, but there was nothing to hand.

'Mam has chosen Killian's favourite readings for the service,' Deirdre was saying.

'He didn't have any favourite readings,' said Steph. 'He was agnostic.'

'Oh, I think Mam would know best in that regard.' She listed the selected readings.

'But they're completely hackneyed,' said Steph.

Deirdre sighed. 'Since you never set foot in a church, how could you possibly know?'

I had seen this brewing – from a *long* way off – but had formed no strategy for dealing with it.

'Killian wouldn't want any holy jazz,' Steph insisted. 'We won't be doing the whole Catholic bit.'

Deirdre's jaw dropped. 'What do you mean? Of course he must have a Catholic service. He was born and brought up a Catholic.'

'Surely we can make these decisions when we get home,' I ventured, already out of my depth.

'There isn't time,' said Deirdre. 'It has to be organized. People are coming from all over for the funeral.'

Those chocolate lollipop sticks came in very handy. Henrik and I swirled them around in our glasses, frowning at the milk, as if there were answers to be found in the whirling chocolate tails.

Steph said nothing, so Deirdre boldly went on. 'For the hymns, Mam wants "Abide with me"–'

'Oh, for God's sake,' said Steph, throwing down the bun she'd been nibbling.

'What?' said Deirdre.

'He was thirty-two years old,' I said. 'Can't we lighten it up a bit?'

'It's a funeral service, not a party.'

'It *should* be a party,' I retorted. 'That's what Killian would have wanted.'

'Oh, and you'd know,' said Deirdre.

'Absolutely.' God, we hated each other. She had been thrilled when Killian and I had split up, but I had had my revenge when he took up with Steph – arty-farty type, humanist, Amnesty International activist and Greenie, God help them. They had never learnt to handle it.

Deirdre ploughed on. I should have been sympathetic. She had, after all, lost the younger brother she adored, but a brother, too, whom she had bullied as a child and tried to control as an adult, and all to no avail, because he had steadfastly resisted his family's wishes in every instance. To their continuing frustration, he had somehow escaped the grasp of these two powerful women. Perhaps that was why Deirdre was determined to take possession of him now. 'Father Patrick will celebrate the Mass in our local church,' she said.

Steph sighed. 'Father who?'

'He's a family friend, from the parish in Carrigaline. He married me and Ferdia, remember?'

'You can't have it in Carrigaline,' I said. 'Steph and Killian live near Passage West. That's where–'

'But they never go to that church. He was christened and made his Holy Communion in Carrigaline.'

'You can't make all these decisions,' Steph said mildly.

'But Dad is buried there. The grave will be reopened.'

'Wait,' I said. 'Wait, wait, *wait*! Steph, did you and Killian ever discuss . . . this stuff?'

'We were planning a nursery, not a grave.'

'So wouldn't you prefer Killian to be near you, in your local cemetery?'

'But Steph might marry again,' said Deirdre pertly, 'and move away.'

I almost spluttered hot chocolate all over the table.

'You can't steal this from me,' Steph said quietly. 'I am his next-of-kin and I will make the decisions.'

'And *you* can't steal it from Mam. You already took his wedding away from her. She has the right to give her son a proper funeral!'

Ah, the wedding. It had been only a matter of time.

'And *my* rights?' asked Steph.

Deirdre was flustered. 'Look, my mother buried her husband two years ago and now she has to bury her only son . . .' Her voice broke. 'Surely she has some right to say what kind of funeral he gets?'

'No one's disputing that,' I said, 'but you can't bulldoze Steph either.'

'But Steph is an atheist. Killian wasn't.'

'He was seriously lapsed,' I said.

'There has to be *a Mass*.' There was desperation in her voice.

'Your mother's afraid we'll dance around thistles, I suppose,' said Steph. 'She always thought I was a witch. So, I'm to have nothing to do with this, am I?'

'Don't be silly,' I said quickly, but Deirdre was uneasy. 'Deirdre?'

'We can't have a repeat of the wedding,' she said. 'That upset everyone.'

'This is no time to rehash all that,' I said firmly.

Henrik looked decidedly uncomfortable, as if he felt he

should contribute something, but couldn't work out what.

'Mam feels that, in view of your beliefs, this is her call. That's reasonable, isn't it?'

'But you're even deciding where to bury him,' I argued, 'near your mother's house!'

'Yes, because Mam would want to visit the grave every week. Steph probably . . . won't.'

Steph pushed herself forward on the low leather armchair. 'I'm not going to bargain over this. Killian may have been brought up a Catholic, but he didn't die one, and the worst thing I could do to him now would be to send him back into a church.'

'You can't do that! Steph, you can't. It would kill Mam.'

'It would kill me to do it any other way.' She stood up and went through an alcove to the back of the café.

I caught up with her in a vestibule in front of the ladies' room. 'Are you sure about this?' I asked her. 'About Killian, I mean.'

'I'm sure he's dead.'

'*Steph!* Did he ever say he didn't want a Catholic do? Because we have to get it right, we have to put his stamp on it, but if there isn't some kind of religious service, his mother . . . It would be very hard on her.'

'They've been very hard on me. And on Killian. Why should they have their way now? When he can't stand up to them? I have to do that for him.'

'I know, but –'

'Whose side are you on?'

'Killian's. Look, I'll do the negotiating – we can compromise, some of your stuff, some of theirs. You tell me what you want and –'

'I want him back. Can you do that for me?'

'We should have some of your poetry,' I rushed on. 'He'd want that, and music – Dad could get some guys together.'

'Can I pee now?'

'The point is, whatever we may think about her, Killian loved his mother, and we do have some responsibility towards her.'

'My primary responsibility is to Killian. And you're right – he will not be buried in Carrigaline.'

I went straight through the café again and on to the street, pulling out Steph's phone. 'Dad?'

'Hullo. How's it going?'

'We've done the morgue.'

'Oh, love. How was it?'

It was sunny on this broad street, but there was no warmth in it.

'Well,' he said gently, 'the worst is behind you now.'

'But the arguing has started. The Enrights are taking over.'

'Tell me about it. I'm getting instructions every day.'

'They're so full-on, it's getting Steph's back up. She's refusing to have a Mass. I don't know how much I should . . . you know, try to influence her.'

'Don't intercede, just support her. Whatever you do, don't bring in your own issues. How is Steph bearing up?'

'She's in a fog some of the time, and then suddenly she's as sharp as a blade. She's hardly eaten a thing. How are things there?'

'Well, guess who got stuck with feeding those rotten puppies?'

'Not Clara?'

'*Me.*'

'You fed the puppies?'

'I had no choice. On the way out of the airport, Ferdia asked if I'd mind checking them on the way home. And they'd probably need a walk, he said. I said, "Man, I'm no dog-walker." So I went to the house and fed them and went home. Then Ferdia rang this morning and asked if I could feed them again. When I got there, they were wired. So I tried to walk it off them – along the streets of Passage. I mean, Christ, I only have two hands. They wrapped themselves round me and knocked me over! A passer-by had to untangle me. I felt a right wally.'

The image of Rollo walking Steph's highly strung pedigree chums took some beating. He loathed dogs. They were thick, in his view. Not bright at all. It was a big thing for him to walk them. 'That's great, Dad.'

'Yeah, and that's not all.'

'What?'

'I brought them home.'

'You *what*?'

'Well! I'm not going to hike over there twice a day to feed the wretches, and if they're left unwatched, Steph will come home to devastation. They'll get plenty of exercise here around the hills.'

'But you can't let them loose – they'll kill the sheep!'

'You think?'

'Dad, you're clueless. Can't someone else do it?'

'Killian's mother isn't able. Ferdia says he couldn't fit four large dogs into a semi-d with three kids in a cul-de-sac, and he might have a point. It's easier here. At least if they drag me across the hills on my arse I won't be humiliated like I was earlier.'

'Well, good on you. Steph will be so . . .' *horrified*

'. . . relieved. I'd better go.'

'One more thing. Your mother is coming over for the funeral – and Milenko.'

'No! Dad, no! Stop him.'

'I can't stop him. He's as entitled to pay his respects as the next person. He feels indebted to Killian. It's only right he should want to come.'

'Fine, but I won't go if he's there. I couldn't face him.'

'You'll have to. And you *will* be there.'

'Dad –'

'He said something that was fairly shocking.'

I waited, biting my lip. Cars scrunched along the street.

'He asked me if I had any idea why you'd left him. How can he not know, Kadie?'

Steph had still not returned to the table. *Don't bring in your own issues.* Right. Be sympathetic to Deirdre. Be understanding towards this woman who, some years before, had let it slip, oh-so-accidentally, that her brother had slept with someone else on my shift.

Deirdre also was conciliatory. 'It's just Mam,' she said, when I sat down. 'I'm afraid . . . She needs a proper Requiem Mass. I'm afraid of how she'll cope if Steph goes all hippie about it.'

'With all due respect, this isn't about your mother; it's about Killian. Maybe he wasn't an active humanist, but he wasn't a practising Catholic either. This service, if there is one, should have some sense of Killian – not of your mother.' *Oops. Sorry, Dad.*

Steph came out through the alcove and, for a moment, seemed not to know where she was, as if she had just woken from a confusing dream. I pushed her phone into her hand.

Henrik checked his watch. 'We must go. The traffic might be bad, and the undertaker is expecting us at one.'

The undertaker's office, on a small square on the other side of the lake, had, from the outside, all the appearance of a smart boutique. She met us as we came in and brought us to a narrow room, largely taken up by a boardroom table. She was a slight, dark-haired woman, in a black suit and white blouse.

Her first question was whether or not Steph wished for Killian to be cremated.

'Goodness, no,' said Deirdre. 'We want to take him home.'

'You will take him home,' the undertaker hunched her shoulders, 'either way.'

'Yes, but . . . I mean a coffin.'

The undertaker turned to Steph. 'Mrs Enright?'

'I would like him to be cremated, yes.'

Deirdre's shock was so overt that it camouflaged my own. The undertaker nodded.

'No, no,' said Deirdre. 'He is to be buried in Cork!'

Everyone looked at Steph.

She said again, 'I want him cremated.'

'Perhaps you would like time to discuss it?' said the undertaker. 'It doesn't have to be decided now.'

'What usually happens,' I asked, 'in cases like this?'

'Oh, cremation. Nearly everyone. It is easier with the airlines. An urn is easier to transport, and much cheaper. But it can be a hard decision and, even with cremation, you will need to select a coffin.' She explained that if there was to be a traditional burial, she would liaise with an undertaker in Cork. The coffin would have to be lined with zinc, as was required when the deceased are repatriated, but if Steph wished, they could leave a window in it, so that his family back home could see Killian before he was buried. But first there were official procedures – the body could not be released until the all-clear had been given on certain transmissible diseases, and papers had to be signed at the Irish embassy. The undertaker suggested we could deal directly with the embassy and she would handle all other aspects of the repatriation.

'Will we be able to get the same flight,' Deirdre asked, 'as the . . . you know . . . ?'

'I hope so. Usually there is no problem.'

'How long will all this take?' she then asked.

'If we move along very quickly, only a few days, once you have decided . . .' She was looking at Steph. 'But you have been through a great . . .' she asked Henrik for the word –

trauma. 'Do not rush. In Sweden it is often weeks between a death and a funeral. Mr Enright can be held in the mortuary for some time. Now, for the casket . . .'

She spread out a brochure. Coffins: big ones, narrow ones, pine, simple, elaborate – even those big American ones that open in two parts, with silk lining. Steph recoiled, as if someone was showing her dismembered bodies.

I couldn't concentrate, and didn't care to. It was out of my hands. Deirdre was right. I wasn't there to decide anything. I had not come to protect Killian's memory, but I would have liked to see things done his way. There was talk of available flights, but until the cremation issue had been resolved, there wasn't much point going into details. Steph nodded a lot, her complexion grey. I longed to take all this away from her and put it somewhere else.

Deirdre asked the cost of a great heavy elaborate thing.

'That's horrible,' said Steph.

And, as it turned out, expensive.

'We'll all help out,' said Deirdre, 'with the expenses.'

'Thank you,' said Steph. 'That won't be necessary.'

Deirdre pulled the brochure back towards her, licked her finger as if she were at the hairdresser's skimming through a magazine, turned a page and pointed at another coffin.

'Too fussy,' said Steph. 'I want simple. And it isn't a question of cost. It should be as plain as possible.'

The undertaker said, 'Ah,' and suggested a solid but plain alternative.

Deirdre sighed. 'But that will look . . .'

'What?' I said.

'A bit mean. Basic. When it comes into the church.'

'It'll be covered with flowers.'

'We don't want people to think we didn't get the best for him. That we were . . . cutting corners.'

This was becoming increasingly difficult for Deirdre, agitating for Steph, and impossible for me. Henrik was nervously twiddling his thumbs.

'Very often families disagree about such things,' the undertaker said.

For several moments, no one spoke, all staring at the brochures with reproach.

'Look,' I said, 'if you two can't decide, I'll pick one. And I'll pick the readings too. A bit of agreement here would be good.'

Steph eyeballed me, across the table. 'He will have a simple coffin. That one.'

The undertaker put the brochure away, saying, 'Finally – in what would you like him to . . . his clothes, you know. Here in Sweden, the deceased, they wear a type of gown, but people from other countries often prefer their loved one to wear their own clothes. What would you like for your husband?'

Steph looked at her, bewildered. 'I'm sorry?'

'Your husband – we will dress him in whatever it is you wish for him to be . . .'

'Laid out,' I said.

'Oh, not the gown,' said Deirdre. 'In Ireland, we select a favourite suit or –'

The undertaker interrupted: 'I regret that his suit, in the accident, was . . .'

Henrik caught my eye. Once again, I was the soft target. Not family: someone who was not hurting as much as the others. 'Perhaps you and I should go through his suitcase?' he suggested.

'We'll all do it,' said Deirdre. 'Back at the hotel.'

'This is too hard,' Steph said vaguely.

'This is exactly why you shouldn't have come,' Deirdre suddenly snapped. 'You're not up to it. You don't know what you want.'

Steph stood up, very slowly, and left.

'Steph, wait!' I called.

'Oh, very helpful,' said Deirdre.

'My thoughts exactly!' I followed Steph on to the street. 'Steph!' The sound of my voice put an extra kick into her step. I caught up with her as she turned into a main road.

'This is horrible!' she said.

'I know, it's a nightmare, but you'll get through it. It doesn't seem like it now, but you will.'

'I can't deal with those people.'

'What people? The undertakers?'

'Everyone. Why . . . What do they want from me?'

'It's just how it's done, and we have to go with it. It's the only way.'

'Not for me, and not for Killian.'

'Steph!' I tried to grab her, but she forged on along the pavement. It was bitterly cold. Steph's central heating – the baby – wouldn't hold it off for long.

'I don't have to do it their way.'

'Okay. Fine.'

'Killian's gone. There's nothing left, so why all this other stuff?'

'It's the way people cope. The organizing. It's a crutch, but it works.'

'How would you know?'

'Please let's go back. The undertaker needs decisions.'

'She didn't seem to be in any hurry.'

There was nothing for it but to follow her as she walked on, past one art gallery after another. 'God, this air is good,' she said.

We came to the water, and a bridge, beyond which the city presented itself at its most poster-esque. A façade of tall, thin houses, cream and orange, ochre and yellow, faced out across the water. The sun was dipping, although it was barely two o'clock, and the shadow of Stockholm's latitude was creeping up the front of its buildings. The lower storeys were in deep shade, while the upper ones glowed in late, winter sunshine. We crossed the bridge. I looked over my shoulder, hoping Henrik and Deirdre might be following in the car. We would not be going back, clearly. The undertaker would have to wait.

'I need to pee,' said Steph.

'Good. For once your bladder is working to our advantage. Let's find us a cup of tea and get out of this cold.'

We turned into a side-street, away from the quays, and chanced upon a small square with a Christmas tree in the middle. 'Just the job – look,' I said. 'Tea rooms.'

While Steph went to the ladies', I selected saffron buns and helped myself to tea. It was the kind of place I loved: cakes and pastries, china cups, and a great copper urn in the middle of the room, where people replenished their coffee. Perhaps I could open something like it in Korčula, I thought, forgetting momentarily that there would be no more Korčula for me.

To our left, two women were holding up their young babies, their feet dangling on the table. One baby stared at the other, unsure as to what it was. Its more gregarious companion was charmed by their introduction and gurgled in delight. Steph stared at them. This little place didn't seem quite so charming any more. I mentally urged the mothers to leave.

'I like the idea of a gown,' said Steph. 'Classic.'

'We could go for that. Or we can get out some jeans and a nice shirt. Something he hung out in.'

'He ironed them. His clothes. Before he left.'

I sipped my tea.

'He didn't iron them so he could be buried in them.'

'Once all this is decided,' I said, 'the worst will be over.'

She sighed heavily. 'The worst hasn't even begun yet.'

'Steph, about cremation . . . You haven't forgotten, have you?'

'What?'

'That conversation we had with Killian. When his father died. About how he'd hate it.'

'He was joking,' she said.

'He wasn't.'

'He was.'

'Look, I know he joked about how the ashes get all mixed up in the furnace and that he didn't want some old lady's legs in *his* urn,' I said. 'He was being funny about that, but it gave him the creeps, you know it did, and he was deadly earnest about not wanting it for himself.'

'Well,' she said, 'he wasn't to know he'd die abroad.'

'Stop moving that bun around your plate and *eat it*, will you? You're fading away.'

'*He*'ll fade,' she said, in that distracted way. 'He'll fade from me, and then one day he'll be completely gone.'

'Never.'

'They said we wouldn't last, the Enrights did. They were right.'

She had not taken her eyes from the mothers and their babies, but when I turned, it was a different set: different mothers, different babies – this time newborns asleep in their prams. 'When did *that* happen?'

'They left. Others came. You've brought me to a crèche.' Steph broke open the bun. 'My baby's an embarrassment, have you noticed? This bump is like a great unmentionable pox on my face. Did you see Henrik? Any other time, he'd have made a fuss of me being pregnant, but he acts as if it isn't happening, and I can't bear the pity.' She looked up at me. 'I can't bear it for me and I can't bear it for the baby. I dread going home, Kadie. You're all so busy with your flights and your coffins, but I dread those pitying faces and hearses and flowers and churches and crowds, and no one wanting to look at me. At *us*! I can't face it. Why can't I deal with this in my own way? Why should I abide by form – by this hackneyed ritual?'

'Because it works. It's been tried and tested for centuries. It helps us grieve.'

'I don't need any help grieving. I'm doing perfectly well without it. I'm not going to play the widow the way they want me to, and my bump is not going to play the part of the tragic, fatherless child. Our baby is not tragic.'

'Don't mistake sadness for pity.' I put my hand on her belly. 'They feel for you, that's all.'

'Killian wouldn't like fuss. He'd want to slip away, unnoticed.'

'No, he wouldn't. He'd want a big bash. Lots of friends and noise.'

She shot me a look of panic. 'I couldn't face that! You know what Cork funerals are like – hundreds upon hundreds of people, stretching all the way to the next village. Killian shook hands for two hours after his dad died. But it's supposed to be *private*.'

'It isn't. That the whole point. It's a community thing, whether you like it or not. Death has to be shared, Steph. It's how people get through it.'

'I just want to get away. That's how I'd get through it. Not sharing it with anyone.'

'After.' I squeezed her hand. 'We'll go away afterwards. You and me. Wherever you want. Except Croatia.'

We walked, not knowing where we were going, and arrived back on the quays. The Grand Hotel, across the way, was bedecked in white Christmas lights. Another building had icicle-shaped lights dripping off its roof. A Viking longboat, closed for the winter, was tied up at the quayside, and the remnants of the day shone through a black latticed steeple.

We went on, through a tree-lined square and past a fountain that had been turned into an ice-rink, where children were skating about in safety helmets. It was almost dark, which struck me as odd, not only because it was not yet four o'clock but because this felt like a day that would never end. No night would ever claim it and give us peace. My feet were aching in boots not meant for walking, and I wondered would Steph get into a taxi if I hailed one. Her eyes were set, her pace steady. I needed to hang on to her. She was like a hot-air balloon trying to lift, and I worried that I wouldn't be able to stop her drifting off.

. . . No. What really worried me was that she was wrong about Killian. How could I claim to know better than his wife? I did, that was all.

We ended up in a busy shopping street. Steph needed to pee again – the baby fighting for space with all those cups of tea – so we stepped into a huge department store and I waited on the ground floor beneath a Christmas tree four storeys high. The Swedes knew how to do Christmas, I'd give them that, but for us, Christmas had become an affront in all its manifestations. There would be no happy gatherings this year. Instead of the Irish-Croatian celebration in Dad's place we'd been planning, it would be a day to be endured, got through, in the long shadow of Killian's death.

I frowned. Thought back a week. Milenko and I arguing in our almost-finished house. An insubstantial matter, a minor domestic, which rose exponentially nonetheless until it took the roof off. My screeching insistence, his voice coarse with anger. Pre-wedding, pre-marriage stress, perhaps, but it felt so bad, to be trapped inside it, and neither of us with the slightest inkling of the devastation heading our way.

Steph didn't want a taxi, so we walked on, past buildings pouring out their seasonal cheer at our feet and street stalls selling Christmas wreaths. Eventually we found an underground station.

★

56

At the hotel, Deirdre was sitting at one end of the broad lobby. 'There you are!' She sprang to her feet. 'What were you thinking, for God's sake? I've been out of my mind!'

'We were just walking.'

'But there's so much to be done!'

Steph raised her chin, her hands deep in the pockets of her overcoat.

'I didn't know what to say to the undertaker. I mean –'

I peeled off my coat, roasting already, and stepped towards Deirdre. 'Don't.'

She sat down. To my relief, Steph did too. On the wall near us, a fake fire glowed on a video screen. I could swear there was heat coming off it. 'Where's Henrik?' I asked after ordering drinks.

'Gone to work. He's making arrangements to travel over for the funeral. I told him he could stay with Rollo. Is that all right?'

I nodded. 'You didn't . . . You haven't selected the clothes, have you?'

She shook her head.

Thank God, I thought. One row diverted. 'Good. Because Steph wants to go with the gown.'

Deirdre didn't look up. 'He should be in a suit. His best suit.'

'Why?' I said. 'He isn't going to work.'

'He looks so smart in a –'

'Leave it, Deirdre. Anyway, no one's going to see him.'

The thing about Deirdre was, she wasn't very bright. And stupidity can be dangerous. When our drinks came, she pulled out a notebook and got stuck in. It was getting harder, keeping the balance, holding the calm, although Steph didn't seem to be quite there any more.

'Mam really wants to get on with booking a venue for the post-funeral gathering and they thought . . .'

The more Deirdre waffled on, the more Steph retreated. She was being blotted out, made irrelevant. Normally she would have fought them, like she had on the wedding, and held her course. Now it was too easy to overpower her. She had not even flinched when Deirdre said Henrik was going to the funeral – as if there *would* indeed be a traditional funeral – so perhaps she had given up the battle. I wished she would. Still, it was hard to see her undermined, with no Killian to take her part. I could not make up for him.

Deirdre bulldozed on: 'According to Mam, people are coming from all over. There'll be quite a gathering at the airport when we arrive.'

'Oh, God,' Steph murmured. Here, exactly, was the scenario she dreaded – crowds of strangers pressing towards the poor pregnant widow; people who hadn't seen Killian for years and were nothing to her, trying to get a piece of her grief.

'And then what?' I asked.

'Then we'll proceed to the church.' Deirdre's eyes were bright, excited almost at the prospect of being at the centre of this dramatic repatriation.

'You mean, have the removal straight from the airport?'

'Yes. Everyone will be there.'

Milenko among them, I thought. And my London-based mother, according to Dad. Three weeks before the wedding that wasn't to be, we would all gather nonetheless, to celebrate Killian's life, and everyone from the bottom up would be watching me and Milenko, trying to see if this tragedy would cancel my silliness and give them something to look forward to after all. I stared at the video fake fire and, for a moment, it felt as if we were there, at the airport, and he was standing close behind me; his warmth, his height, his strength standing by just for me, when all the focus was on others. He would know that losing Killian was like having a chunk taken out of my side, that I would for ever more be slightly off-balance, and he would mind my special loneliness when no one else could see it.

Even before Killian died, it had seemed to me that things could not get worse, but they had done so progressively and dramatically with every day that passed, and there was a long way down still to go.

Steph startled me by saying, 'I have agreed to none of this.'

And round again . . .

I'd had enough. I'd had too much. 'I need some air,' I said, getting up. Killian had been lost somewhere. He didn't come into it any more. Steph wanted only to steer her own course, while his family were hurrying to send him off with lamentable dirges and dreary, predictable biblical passages. They had no imagination.

I went through the huge circular door on to the street. Two teenage girls were huddled in the corner, giggling over a mobile phone. Both plans were wrong: Steph's and the Enrights'. Killian would want . . . But I couldn't remember what Killian would want because tears had overcome me. I leant against the cold marble wall, needing Milenko so badly that I could barely stay on my feet. He would know: he would tell me how to cope. Milenko knew about the sudden death of young men.

In my box-room, I watched Henrik read the news. He seemed slightly out of it, fiddling in a way he hadn't done the night before, and at one point he wasn't ready to read the next item.

Steph came knocking, saying she was suddenly very hungry and had to eat. We gathered Deirdre and headed to a sports-themed restaurant on the corner. It was packed with young people watching ice-hockey on large screens, and was thick with cigarette smoke. As we stood waiting to be seated, Steph turned to me and said, 'I'm going.'

'Where?'

And she slithered to the ground in a faint.

'Steph!'

A waiter hurried over; people stood up to get a better look.

'Steph, Steph!' Deirdre was saying. The waiter held people back. 'Water.'

'Bugger it! I've been trying to make her eat all day!'

'She's coming round.'

Steph rejoined us, slowly. They cleared a table. We sat her at it and fed her soup, and walked her back to the hotel when she was stronger. The faint had made her feel much better, and even more cheerful. She thought it was funny – the way it had come over her, knowing that she had gone past the point of no return, and the only thing left for her was to concertina to the floor.

'It wasn't amusing from our end,' I said.

'I've never fainted before. It's quite an interesting experience.'

'Henrik!' I called, delighted to find him waiting in the lobby. We had a quick meal with him in the hotel restaurant. Steph had colour in her face, and even picked at my dinner. It was such a relief to see her eat. One battle less to fight.

But I had lost another battle – with exhaustion. I could no longer sit up. 'You should turn in,' I said to Steph. 'Long day. I'm going to.'

'You go.' She glanced at Deirdre. 'I want to talk to Henrik.'

In the lift Deirdre said, 'You can imagine what she wants to talk to him about.' The purple rings round her eyes now extended to her jaw. 'When he last saw him, what he said, how he was . . . Poor Henrik.'

In my room, I put my arms round a pillow and tried to shut out the memory of Killian's pallid, wounded face.

Someone was knocking quietly on my door. I stumbled from the bed, disoriented, and turned on the light. It was two o'clock. The stifling wakeful hours had been passing with agonizing torpidity. I pushed open the door. Steph was standing in the corridor. She looked girlish in her pyjamas, vulnerable, not the sassy person I knew. 'Can't sleep?'

'Sorry for waking you,' she said.

'I wish you had. I wish I'd been asleep.'

She came in, agitated, breathing too fast. The benefit of the food had worn off; she was unwell again. I sat her down and rubbed her back. She was tired, probably dangerously so. All that emotion, all that walking, and now no sleep.

'Come away with me,' she said.

'What?'

'I can't be part of this. It isn't what I want, and the Enrights don't want me either.'

I opened my mouth. Nothing came out.

'We could leave first thing, slip away and go to Hungary.'

'Hungary?'

'We could stay with Ágnes, until all this is over.'

'Steph, calm down. Everything's going to be fine. You just need sleep. Why don't you lie down and I'll turn out the light and sit here?'

'I've done what we came to do. We've seen Killian, identified him. They don't need me for anything else. I can't go back into . . . all that.'

'Putting it off isn't going to make it go away.'

'I'm not putting it off. How could I possibly put it off? It's right here, *in* me. So if the family must have their Mass, let them have it, but I don't have to be part of it.'

'You can't miss the . . . the *service*, no matter how we do it.'

'Why not?'

I looked at her grey eyes and wavy hair dangling over her face and I wasn't very sure why anyone should do anything at a time like this, except get through it, whatever way they could. 'Listen, going through the motions, even if you don't believe in it, helps. That's why every culture in the world has some kind of ritual.'

'But why must it be *their* ritual? Why must they be allowed to mourn in their way, but I can't do it in mine?'

I could formulate no good answer. Ritual is one thing; social constraints quite another. 'And how would you mourn him in Hungary?'

'I need to *be* with Killian, to have a sense of him, a grasp on him, before he goes any further away. I can still feel him near me and I could still hear his voice until Deirdre's screeching got inside my head. I won't let them take what's left of him. When we touch down in Cork, it'll be over for me. I'll be a cog, a performer. When Killian's dad died, it was a circus. Killian would hate that. It's very private, being dead. I mean, lots of people don't have big jamborees for funerals.'

'Which can be hard on the extended family. People need an outlet. *I* need an outlet. I need to stand with a crowd and claim him. I want to be part of his army. Doesn't that make any sense to you?'

'Not really.' She rubbed the end of her nose.

'You're thinking too much. Just go with the flow, Steph, and it'll be over before you know it. We'll go home and –'

'Stop talking about home! I don't want to go anywhere near the cottage, with the baby's room he was decorating, and his mugs and his videos of All Ireland finals. Please, Kadie, come away with me. Let's clear out. They're obviously able to organize the whole thing over the top of my head, so let them at it.'

'But if you take off, there won't be a funeral of any kind. They won't go ahead without you.'

'All the better. No service at all.'

I sat back. 'And what about Killian?'

'If I could have my way, we'd have him cremated – straight away – no fuss, no bother, like the Swedes do it.'

'But he didn't *want* to be cremated.' I went to the window. *Christ.* Should I ring Deirdre? No, she was part of the problem. Should I give in? Be the loyal friend and go wherever Steph wanted to take me? This was probably a standard reaction – the urge to run, flee – and it was up to me to keep her on track, to pull her through the tough bits. That was surely why I was there. Or was it? Steph was unlike anyone else – she was an individualist to the core of her being – but there were others to consider. To be an individual, you have to live in a crowd.

'Look, I'm all for going away with you,' I said. 'Let's face it, I don't have any other commitments. We can go to Budapest to see Ágnes, and even go on from there if you like. We could do it all – Bucharest, where you got engaged, and Verona, where you had that fight, and Goa . . . We'll go back the way you came, to all the places that meant something to you, but we *have* to get through the next three days first. That's all it takes – a lousy three days and then it's done.'

She stood up. 'They've got you right where they want you – on their side. And I thought you came for me.'

'Steph, don't be so pig-headed! I'm only trying to –'

But the fire door banged behind her.

4

The very act of waking was a considerable achievement. I marvelled at it. I was waking up; therefore, I had been to sleep. I had actually passed into the oblivion for which I had yearned for nearly a week, wresting a few hours away from Milenko, and Killian. In the space of three days, two of the most important people in my life had been taken from me. Milenko was alive and well, or well enough, but he had been removed as comprehensively as Killian had been. There was no comparison, and yet I compared them, the living with the dead.

I made tea, bolstering myself for the day's work: guiding Steph, manoeuvring her in the right direction while also respecting her wishes. As I drank it, Deirdre knocked frantically. 'Kadie?'

'Coming, coming.'

When I let her in, she barked, 'Where is she?'

'Who?'

'Steph. She's checked out.'

'*What?*'

'The undertaker rang. Said she couldn't get through to Steph so she rang me. I went to her room and knocked and knocked, and then went downstairs to see if she'd gone for breakfast. They told me she checked out two hours ago.'

I sat on the bed.

'What on earth does she think she's doing?' Deirdre asked.

My voice wouldn't work.

'I know she was finding this difficult, but who isn't?'

'Fuck. Have you tried her mobile?'

'No reply.'

I picked up the phone and dialled Reception. 'We've got to get into her room.'

The manager sent a chambermaid to give us access, but there was nothing of Steph's left in the room. Deirdre stepped back and forth, her arms crossed, muttering and wondering *what* she was going to tell her mother! 'Where *could* she be?' she asked.

'She's just gone, all right?'

'Yes, but *where?*'

'Try her mobile again.'

'She's not picking up.'

If only I had mine, I thought. She might pick up for me. 'Give it to me.' I grabbed Deirdre's phone and punched in a text. 'Steph. It's Kadie. I'm really sorry. I should have gone with you. I'll come now. Where are you?'

Deirdre read it over my shoulder. 'Did you know about this?'

'I thought I'd talked her out of it.'

'Out of what?'

'Just . . . getting away.'

'But – who'd want to get away at a time like this?'

'Someone who is really, really struggling. Believe me, I know the feeling!'

I had no expectation of a reply to my text. Steph had spelt it out for me, not only the night before but also the day before on the freezing pavement, and I had been too numb to hear her; too caught up in form, following the norm. How could I have forgotten that Steph's entire life had been spent escaping the norm?

'It'll be okay,' I said to Deirdre. 'It'll be fine.'

'You don't sound very convinced.'

The phone beeped. We jumped at it, knocking into each other. 'It's her!' My fingers were trembling, but I managed to open the text, which read: 'Go ahead without me.'

'But that's nonsense!' said Deirdre.

I dialled Steph's number. It rang out. She wasn't picking up.

'We'll have to hang on to her by text,' said Deirdre. 'At least she's answering. Ask her again where she is. If she's still in Stockholm, we might be able to change her mind.'

I tapped in, 'Are you still in Stockholm?' Then I held the phone in my hand like an injured chick, waiting for it to take another breath. No reply came, though we tried to pace it into being, bumping into each other in the tiny space between bed and dresser.

I tried another tack. 'Steph, don't do this to me. Killian must be brought home. We can't leave without you.'

We breathed at the phone and jumped again when the incoming text beeped.

'I've already left,' she wrote. 'I'm going back the way we came. Over and out.'

Going back the way we came. My very words.

We heard a phone ringing and stepped into the corridor. 'Your room,' said Deirdre, running. She got there first, then held it out to me. 'For you. Some Swede.'

'Hello?'

Nothing.

'Hello?'

'Kadie.'

Milenko.

'Don't hang up!' he said. 'Please don't!'

How could I put the phone down when I could not move? Hearing him breathe immobilized me, and he was breathing heavily with the effort of keeping me on the line. 'Are you okay?' he asked quietly.

'Of course not.'

'I'll be in Cork. When you get back. I'll be there with you.'

'Don't.'

'Kadie,' he said, in quiet exasperation. I loved the way he pronounced my name, Kay-dee, almost in reproach. 'We should be together at this time.'

'That's not possible.'

'I must pay respect.'

'Please don't, Milenko. Please. It's too much.'

He sighed heavily. 'It's good to hear you.'

I blubbered and snivelled into his ear.

'Kadie, what . . . Why . . . *Why* have you done this?'

'I have to go. Steph's gone missing.'

'I'm sorry?'

'She's gone off somewhere. We have to find her. Don't come, Milenko. Please, please, don't.' I hung up and fell back on the bed.

'Henrik's on his way,' said Deirdre, holding her own phone.

I managed to sit up. This was a losing battle. No one knew their own mind as Steph knew hers. No matter what she said or how outlandish the claim, she never deviated. We had handled this so badly. *I* had handled it deplorably.

'What an unbelievably selfish indulgence!' Deirdre sniffed, but I could not begrudge her. She wanted only to take her brother home and bring her mother some comfort.

'If you can't be selfish when your husband's dead and your baby's coming, when can you?'

'I have to tell Mam. How do you think this is going to go down?'

Her mother, surprisingly, did not throw one of her fits or declare that she expected no better of Steph. Rather, she was bewildered, and asked would her son still be coming home.

'I didn't know what to say,' Deirdre said. 'I mean, what are we to do about the funeral arrangements, the priest . . . everything?'

'Frankly, I'm more concerned about Steph. She might go

passing out in strange places. I've been such an idiot!' I picked up my handbag and hurled it across the room, smashing it into the mirror.

Deirdre looked at the contents strewn across the shelf. 'And that helps?'

'Enormously.' I began pulling on some clothes. 'I'm getting out of here.'

'Oh, you too? My, but you two are helpful!'

'I mean out of this stifling hotel. Let's get some air.'

'But what about Henrik?'

'He'll find us.'

The Stockholm pavement again. Sunny up top; grey on the ground. Cars scrunching past – as if they were tiptoeing across gravel. I needed to walk. I needed streets, people, faces rushing past, preoccupied and frazzled by the normal run of things. In failing to harness Steph, I had failed Killian, and everyone else too. But it was Steph I had let down most. I should have gone with her, unquestioning, and would have done so had I known she seriously meant to leave.

We walked and walked. Henrik phoned and asked us where we were. We didn't know. There was a bridge and some trains. We were near the main station, he told us.

'I need a coffee,' said Deirdre. I wanted more of that fresh light air, but Deirdre was done in. Henrik directed us to a café in a street in Gamla Stan. I was glad, when we got there, for the warmth and the friendly guy behind the counter. There was a platform by the window with cushions and a low table. We took off our shoes and sat against the cushions. Fir branches were bunched round the window, candles flickered on every table, and customers were chatting over coffee. How normal Deirdre and I must also have looked, in jeans and sweaters, curled up with our drinks in the window – apart from our red noses, of course, and puffy eyes.

Time to own up. 'I think she's gone to Budapest,' I said.

'Budapest!'

'She said something about going there to keep her head down until everything is over and done with.'

Deirdre frowned. 'But why Budapest?'

'They got together there, remember?' It was Deirdre herself who had told me about it, with relish. 'And she wanted to see Ágnes.'

'Who's she?'

'They worked together. They were close.'

'And what are we supposed to do while she's off gallivanting?'

'Hardly gallivanting.'

'Text her again. Ask her what she wants us to do.'

'She's already told us to go ahead.'

'But we must keep up contact.'

I struggled over the phone before writing 'Should we wait for you here?'

'This is a joke,' said Deirdre. 'A bloody bad joke.'

'I hope she's not having some kind of breakdown. Or fainting all over the place.'

Henrik came in. We gestured to him.

'I thought it was bad losing two friends in three days,' I said to Deirdre. 'Now I've lost three friends in five days.'

'And a baby.'

'Hey,' said Henrik, joining us. 'Hey' seemed to be the standard greeting in Sweden.

'Here,' I said, 'sit.'

'What's going on?' he asked. 'Why has she gone away? And where?'

'Kadie thinks she's gone to Budapest. That's where it all started, with Killian.'

'They met in Budapest?'

'They'd already met, through me, at home. But she lived

there for a year, working in an orphanage, and when Killian was over on business something sparked.'

'Wouldn't she need a visa?' Deirdre asked. 'And it can't be that easy to get flights, can it?'

'She wouldn't need a visa for Hungary, and flights are easy to come by if you're not fussy about how you get there,' I said. 'God, I wish I'd gone with her.'

'This is my fault,' said Henrik. 'I was the last person to speak with her.'

'How was she when you left her?' Deirdre asked. 'Was there anything that might have upset her?'

He thought about it. 'I told her he talked a lot about the baby . . . how he hoped not to travel so much . . . I must have upset her.'

'You weren't the last person to see her,' I said. 'I was.'

'You?' said Deirdre. 'When?'

'In the middle of the night. So if this is anyone's fault, it's mine. I may even have put the idea into her head. When she says, "I'm going back the way we came," she means retracing their steps, going to places that were significant, just like I . . . said we could, last night, but I meant for us to do it *after* the funeral. For all I know, she could be on her way to Goa by now.'

'Oh, for God's sake!'

'I was trying to stop her bolting!'

'Why didn't you call me?' Deirdre threw up her hands. 'I'd have talked sense into her.'

'Deirdre, you are a large part of the problem. You and your mother. Keeping Steph on the sidelines. You made her feel redundant. You as good as told her this wasn't her call. So what was there for her to stay *for*?'

Deirdre blushed. 'That's all very well, but what are we going to do?'

'Let's just get Killian home,' I said. 'That's our priority.'

'But there's a problem,' said Henrik. 'She hasn't signed the paperwork at the embassy and, well, will they release . . . him . . . if she doesn't consent to it?'

'Can't Deirdre give consent?'

He pulled out his phone. 'I'll find out.'

Deirdre's phone rang. Ferdia, her husband. She took it outside and walked up and down the cobblestone street, shivering and waving her hand about. Henrik ended his call. 'The undertaker is very reluctant to proceed without Steph. She says that in cases like this, where there is a disagreement within the family, they can offer the services of a counsellor, but ultimately they will go with the wife's wishes. They need to know from Steph what they are to do. Cremate him here? Repatriate him? They need to know.'

'Great. And what happens in the meantime?'

'They will keep him at the morgue.'

Deirdre came back in. 'Mam isn't good. This has really thrown her. Relatives are flying in from all over to be there when we get home, but how can we go back without Steph?'

'And maybe even without Killian,' I said.

'How do you mean?'

Henrik inclined his head. 'They need to know there is agreement within the family before they make any arrangements. They won't overrule his wife's wishes and . . . yesterday Steph was very clear about cremation.'

'Oh, *God*,' said Deirdre.

'I can't believe I let her go,' I said. 'I never dreamt she'd take off without me.'

'What I can't believe is that you put that stupid idea into her head!'

'*Your* family – '

'Please,' said Henrik. 'We can't blame.'

'Someone must prevail upon her.' Deirdre gripped my arm. 'Kadie, listen. We can't leave her wandering around Europe. Especially with the baby.'

'Oh? Some concern at last?'

'Of course I'm concerned. You should go after her.'

'No. Let her be. She just wants to grieve in her own way. Why don't we leave her in peace?'

'Because the undertaker wants to know what's happening and because my mother deserves some peace too.'

'But I don't have an address for Ágnes, *if* that's where she's gone.'

'Ferdia can get her email address from Steph's laptop and we can email her and tell her that if Steph turns up, she's not to let her out of her sight until you get there.'

'Get there? You seriously expect me to go to Budapest?' I looked at them both.

'It's a good plan,' said Henrik.

It was a good plan, but no one knew how battered I was. I was on the brink, had been for a week, and had no clue where to find the necessary resolve to stretch myself further.

'Kadie?'

'I'm not well,' I said, to no one in particular.

'This isn't the plane thing, is it?' said Deirdre. 'It's not like you'd be going to Antarctica.'

I felt as if I was being peeled, layer after layer. Milenko first, Killian, now Steph. They were my triangle, my sanity and trinity. It was too much. I could not be without Steph as well.

The toilet across the room had seen a steady stream of people going in and out. Maybe it was all the coffee they were drinking. It was just then unoccupied, so I took my chance. It was in a little cubby-hole, lit by a candle. In the dim, flickering light, I tried but failed to remember the last time Steph had asked something of me. She was a giver, a nurturer, and consequently very bad at looking after herself. And yet the night before, when she was frightened and confused, I had sent her from my room with an admonishment worthy of

Deirdre. *Don't be so pig-headed.* I had sent her back to bed like a child who had been unable to escape its nightmare.

There was nothing at all that Deirdre and Henrik could say that would persuade me to go to Hungary. Had hordes of thousands been descending on County Cork for the funeral of the century, it would not have swayed me. I would go to Budapest only because Killian was lying in a freezing chamber and because Steph had asked me to go, and it wasn't much to ask.

There was a flight to Budapest at eight the following morning. Armed with Deirdre's phone and three days' worth of clothes, I left Stockholm. Deirdre saw me off at the railway station. So contemptuous on the inward flight, she now displayed some sympathy that I had to fly alone. 'Pretend you're going to Croatia,' she said, then pulled back her lower lip in apology for mentioning the C-word. Sitting on the airport train, my nerves all of a jumble, I thought she might be right. Perhaps meditating on better times would get me through the flight.

An email address for Ágnes had been found in Steph's laptop. Clara had emailed her. By the time I got to Budapest, there might be some response. As for Steph, we had not told her that I was in pursuit, for fear of provoking another dash, and there had been no further word from her. I was furious with myself, with her and with her in-laws. She was living up to all their expectations. Just like her, they'd be saying back home, to abandon her dead husband. For Killian, it had been another night in cold storage; like a murder victim in the morgue, waiting for his nearest and dearest to claim him. If it took a hundred flights in damaged aircraft, I would do it. If it meant dragging Steph back by her long, wavy hair, I would do it, if that's what it would take to get Killian into the warm Cork earth.

★

The airport was quiet when I made my way along its broad parquet corridors. At the gate I did my pre-flight exercises. Businessmen and -women sat with coffee and newspapers. I went to the lavatory three times. The flight was called. It was silly to fret in the middle of a crisis, but I couldn't help myself. We queued. Our plane had only recently pulled in to the gate. Had they checked every little bolt? Every nut? Had they had time to refuel? Were the European skies not terribly crowded at this time of day? Were we not likely to hit another commuter plane?

I handed over my boarding card and made my way down to the aircraft, saying out loud, 'Deep breathing. Deep breathing,' the very process of which was causing me to take quick, shallow breaths. Installed in my seat, I continued to work on my breathing, but I was too jittery. I wanted to rush to the door, fight my way from the cabin. My mouth was so dry it felt crackly, and the palms of my hands were like taps. Time for creative visualization: Dad on his boat on the lake on a warm summer's day . . . But Dad is looking over his shoulder, forlorn, because he knows I'm about to go down in a horrible plane crash and that he'll never see me again. No good. Taking advice from Deirdre of all people, I turned my thoughts to Milenko: sweet thoughts, not sad ones. The first time I had seen him, not the last.

I closed my eyes, adrenaline pumping through my veins, my death imminent in the Baltic Sea, and sent myself back to that first night: to the pounding rain, a rocking boat, a hand on a suitcase and a faceless being in yellow raingear.

5

Croatia, that land of sunny isles basking in the azure Adriatic, had been revealed to us in flashes of sheet lightning. From the window of the mini-bus, our first view was not of lush islands dozing in late-summer heat, but of the outlines of black mountains drawn by white lightning. Another flash revealed a harbour, as we neared Dubrovnik, and the dark shapes of cypress trees. A country revealing itself through electricity.

Our transfer to Korčula was much longer than I'd expected, and took us along winding coastal roads. The bus was alternately stuffy and chilly, cooled by fluctuating air-conditioning. The moon seemed to be short-circuiting as the storm grumbled on, and I grumbled to Clara about the quoted ninety-minute transfer now heading into its third hour.

'Sorry,' she said. 'My mistake.'

'Tsk. And you a travel agent.'

By the time we neared the island, the lightning was almost incessant and the ghostly negatives of olive groves and vineyards hinted at the landscape we expected. The bus finally pulled on to a quayside. The driver looked out into the blackness.

'Great,' I said. 'No ferry.'

The driver made a phone call. The dozen passengers stepped out to stretch. Twenty minutes, the driver said, before the boat would come. It was one a.m. I was cranky and hungry, but couldn't hope to eat before morning.

'This is why I don't travel,' I said to Clara and Geraldine, when it started raining again, and we trooped back on to the bus.

'But it'll be gorgeous tomorrow,' said Ger. 'Hot and sunny.'

'Optimist.'

'Grouch,' said Clara.

We were perfect travelling companions. They both knew me well, which made it all the more amazing that they had invited me along. I'd known Ger longer than Clara – we'd done a tourism course together after we'd left college. She now worked in the tourist office selling Ireland, while we sold everywhere else.

A boat puttered out of a mist of heavy rain. A voice behind me said, 'That's not the ferry, is it?'

'No wonder this holiday was so cheap,' a teenager muttered to her mother.

'Excellent.' I groaned.

'You were right, you know,' Ger said to me.

'I know I was.'

'We *should* have left you at home.'

The boat was rising and falling so dramatically that boarding was treacherous. Inside, we sat on benches, soaked through. Clara and Ger looked like children who had fallen into a pond – the long dark hair of one like an oil-spill on her head; the short blonde curls of the other flattened. Outside, the driver was passing our luggage to the boatman. The crossing was alarming. We rolled so severely that it seemed we would tip right over. For the umpteenth time that day, I gripped my seat. First it had been the plane – such a weird thing, with the wings at the back, that the girls had had to force me up the steps. Then three hours on the bus, speeding round hairpin bends, with regular spurts of daylight revealing perilous drops at the edge of the road. Now this – but at least we were almost there.

The boat stopped rolling and the lights of Korčula island came closer. A voice called out, 'Hotel Soline!'

'That's us,' said Clara.

The downpour had not eased. A figure standing on the quayside in yellow raingear also shouted, 'Hotel Soline!' and everyone disembarked in a miserable rush, assuming the luggage would be taken off by the boatmen, as it had been loaded. There was no hotel to be seen – only a long promenade and a beach, so a few of us ran to take cover under an arch at the bottom of some steps. The man in oilskins was losing his rag. Not only had we hopped off without taking our luggage, but *everyone* had hopped off, including passengers due to continue to another hotel. He yelled at us to come back for our bags, then roared at a couple huddled under the archway who were bound for the other hotel. They couldn't hear him in the drone of rain, and remained where they were. As I took my case, he shouted, 'Jesus Christ! Almoro Hotel!' I ducked past him, making a mental note: 'Welcome: could be improved on.'

Pulling my suitcase on its wheels, I rushed over to the couple and sent them back. We sheltered under the arch, peering up the steps into a darkness of trees.

'Is the hotel up there?' someone called out.

'Can't be anywhere else.'

The faceless being in oilskins was untying the ferry. 'Yes, yes. Up, up, up!' he called. There seemed to be no one inside the yellow hood, like the Black Riders in *Lord of the Rings* – all hood and no face.

We began dragging our bags up the broad steps, which were flooded and pouring water like a set of rapids. Breathless, I was busy formulating letters of complaint to the travel agent.

'*We*'re the travel agent!' Clara roared.

'We're not the operator. I'll get on to the –'

'Remind me,' Ger said to Clara, 'why *did* we bring her along?'

'I heard that,' I called, several steps behind them.

They went ahead, with their lighter bags, giggling, and even

77

stopped to splash in the puddles, while I went on cursing my cumbersome suitcase. Suddenly a hand touched mine and took the handle from me. The suitcase flew on up the steps, as the oilskins disappeared with it beneath the trees.

We followed him until we found an entrance to the hotel. Seven people stood at Reception, gasping and dripping on to the marble floor. A tall aristocratic man checked us in. Slightly bald, with a dark moustache, he was very charming. He made no reference to the weather, but gave us keys to our rooms, which more or less equated him with God.

Five hours later, the sound of a deep baritone voice singing along to an accordion pushed into my drowsy brain. It was seven o'clock. My letter of complaint was getting longer. There were cheerful voices, and that grating accordion. I wondered if it was a wedding, or a dream, and imagined the Pied Piper of Hamelin leading a party of cleaners through the gardens.

Later that morning, when we were sitting on a pebbly beach, piling on sunscreen and looking out across the inlet of crystal Adriatic, I might have said it had been worth it. But that was before another interrupted night, this time courtesy of a crowd of youngsters partying into the night. Other guests called down from balconies, presumably telling the youngsters to be quiet, so now the noise below was provoking loud voices above. A Frenchwoman called out, 'Go away. I have baby. Go to beach.'

And they did go to the beach, shouting, 'Fuck the French. Fuck the English. Fuck everything.'

Charming. Silence. Sleep.

Drums woke me. I thought I was imagining it but, no, someone somewhere was playing the drums. All that was missing now was a great brass band marching up and down on the terrace below.

★

The promenade offered several nice spots to lie on. The grounds of the hotel – a faded villa, possibly a holiday retreat for the Communist bigwigs of Tito's era – were vast, and the neglected gardens had huge potential for development, with the tourist boom that Croatia was beginning to enjoy. The broad steps, shaded by cypresses, led down to the promenade, which began on the right, where there was a small beach in the curve of the bay, then ran for several hundred yards along the waterfront until the sea became a creek. Beside the beach, there was a broad quay for the mainland launch to come in, a smaller pier for the water-taxis to Korčula town, and another shorter pier further on. Beyond that there was a narrow pebbly beach and a semi-circular concrete platform. This roughly hewn platform became our spot.

I lay on my stomach on the hard cement, gazing out from under the rim of my black hat at an entrancing view. Just beside me, over the edge of the pier, the sea was limpid, and the stones on the seabed appeared to lurch around under the waves. Further out, yachts glided, a catamaran was motoring in, and the rocky, wooded peninsula that embraced the bay stretched into the water like a pointing finger. On the other side of the creek, red roofs peeked out from behind cypress and eucalyptus trees. It was all lovely, and very possibly worth the early-morning disruptions.

Beside me, the girls were snoozing. I lowered myself into the water and swam towards the main beach – a horseshoe of sand in the corner – passing the short piers and paddling about like an old woman. Before reaching the beach, I headed back, but as I came round the end of the first pier, I heard a guttural roar overhead, followed by some kind of screech, and looked up to see a body dropping out of the sky right above me. It landed on top of me and pushed me under. A dead weight pressed me down. Bubbles gurgling; water up my nose; no air in my lungs. I struggled against the downward momentum.

Another body was flailing around in the turbulence. Legs, arms, gushing sea.

I got out of its way, pushed for the surface and reached it, coughing and choking.

'My God! I am sorry! Very sorry,' I heard.

I inhaled sharply.

'Are you okay?' I turned. A spluttering Croatian, all black hair and smooth chest, was flapping around behind me. 'Let me help you,' he said.

Too stunned to respond, and still catching my breath, I allowed him to guide me towards the beach, blabbering apologies. 'I didn't see you. I just . . . I jumped. No one saw you.'

Some lads were watching from the pier, abashed. But he was no lad, no boy; he looked to be late twenties, I thought, or even thirty.

'It's all right.' I was shaking, but the door that had landed on me – that was what it felt like – appeared even more traumatized. Knee-high in water, I sat on the gravel, because my legs weren't ready to hobble on to the stony beach.

'Can I get you something?' he asked. 'Some water?'

Wet hair fell over his face and the dimple in his chin was so deep it looked like a closed-up piercing.

'I've had enough water, thanks.'

'Did I hurt you?'

I put my hand to the side of my neck, which was throbbing.

'Let me get you some tea,' he said, motioning towards the bar on the promenade.

'No, I'm fine, really.' I wouldn't, however, have said no to a couple of concerned friends, but they were busy sunbathing, with their Discmans plugged into their ears, so they had not heard the anguished yelp that went out when this man realized, mid-air, that there was an obstacle in his way. Me. 'Please don't worry. I'm okay.'

He stood up. I got up too, to reassure him, but he hurried off, picked up his towel and disappeared up the steps. I went over to the girls, lay down and began to recover.

It wasn't until we were having dinner that night, in the old town of Korčula around the headland, that Clara noticed I was pulling at my neck.

'What's wrong?'

'I hurt my neck today when I was swimming.'

'How?'

'Some Croatian bloke fell out of the sky and landed on top of me.'

'Was he good-looking?'

The drumming started up again the following morning. It wasn't early, but it wasn't late either, and although it wasn't very close, it drilled into my head. I had enough of this at home – live music all hours of the night – without putting up with it on holidays. I tossed about, taking care to hold my sore neck. Enough was enough. We could not endure another such night. As soon as we had had breakfast, I marched over to Reception.

The lady receptionist was dealing with a young couple, but while I stood waiting, another receptionist wandered out of the back office. My mouth fell open. So did his. The Dive-bomber.

His expression was at first alarmed, then sheepish, then resigned. He lifted his chin in a slightly arrogant way and said, with a sideways glance, 'How is your neck?'

'A little bruised.'

'You have come to make a complaint?'

'Yes.'

He nodded. Now I understood why he had been so nervous, and why he had vanished up the steps. He worked at the hotel. I could make this difficult for him – an employee jumping on a guest and nearly breaking her neck. For a moment, I considered it. What *was* an employee doing leaping about and putting other people in danger?

'I'm sorry,' I said, 'but why the hell was an employee of this hotel jumping on guests?'

He didn't flinch. 'Cooling down after a long day's work. So, you wish to complain?'

'Yes, I do. We have not had one good night's sleep since arriving. When it isn't singers, it's young kids shouting the place down, and if that wasn't bad enough – someone plays the drums early every morning.'

He frowned. 'You want to complain about *noise*?'

'Yes.'

'Not about . . . me?'

He was so adorably contrite. 'No, I'm not going to complain about you – although I now know what a crab feels like when a foot presses it into the sand.'

He was too relieved even to smile.

'We were lucky,' I said. 'It could have been more serious.'

He nodded again and dismissed it. 'The noise?'

I smiled. After years in the business, I know that complaints should come sweetened. I will always do more for a disgruntled customer if they're nice to me. So I said ever-so-nicely that I was *terribly* sorry, but wondered if *anything* could be done about the nocturnal disruption? After all, we *were* on holiday, the general purpose of which is to have a *good rest*. I didn't wish to be difficult, but we'd had a *frantic* season back home at the travel agency, and we were done in.

He caught my eye. He'd picked up on it, the dig about being in the business, but he wasn't going to bite. Instead, it annoyed him and made him determined to be as unhelpful as possible. To do otherwise would be to suggest he needed our custom and this man wasn't going to admit to needing anyone. Or that was my reading, when his mouth straightened.

'I am very sorry your sleep has been disturbed,' he said, 'but other guests are trying to enjoy their holidays also.'

'Yes, but they can surely enjoy themselves away from the bedrooms. As for the drumming . . .'

'That is in a neighbouring house, but we will do what we can about the singing,' he said, which meant: precisely nothing.

'Thank you. After all, I don't want to have to tell my clients that Croatia is great as long as you don't need any sleep.' I turned and walked across the lobby.

'They're going to do what they can,' I told the girls, when I got back to the stony beach.

Clara shaded her face. 'Kadie, will you please chill? What have you to do all day except sleep off the night before?'

I sat down. 'I hate holidays. Why do I earn my living sending people to places where they won't get any sleep?'

'Most people don't want to sleep on holidays.'

'Whoa,' said Clara, a few minutes later. 'Six o'clock, girls.'

We lifted our heads. 'Where the bejayzus is six o'clock?'

'Over your shoulder.'

I strained around. 'Ow, this bloody neck.'

'Where?' said Ger.

'On the pier.'

A sultry handsome type was helping a woman and child on to the water-taxi that ferried guests in and out of Korčula.

'I saw him earlier in the bar,' said Clara. 'The Handsome Waiter: a must for any holiday.'

'Him?' I said. 'He's the Dive-bomber.'

'*He* is? Why didn't you say so?'

'I am saying so.'

'I mean, why didn't you say he was drop-dead gorgeous?'

'Well, people tend to look a bit hazy under water, and after we'd struggled to the surface, well, what with the stars spinning round, it was a bit hard to see anything clearly.'

Clara was shaking her head. 'This is just like you.'

'What is?'

'Having someone like *that* fall out of the sky on top of you!'

'He is also the person I complained to earlier. He works at Reception.'

'So you've met him twice and you still haven't introduced us?'

'The Latin Lover,' said Ger. 'In person.'

Clara said, 'He's a bit beautiful.'

'If you like that kind of thing,' I said, putting my head down.

'And you don't?' said Clara.

'You know very well I like 'em rough and scraggy. Worn round the edges.'

'Translation: *older*,' said Ger.

'Gone, already.' Clara sighed, as the Dive-bomber went back up to the hotel. 'Maybe we should go and have tea by the pool? I want to see what he looks like up close.'

We humoured her: we placed bookmarks in our novels, put on our hats, pushed up our sunglasses, pulled our sarongs round us, tied a knot over our boobs, folded our towels, slipped our feet into flip-flops, picked up the sunscreen, and finally made our way up the steps to the pool, where we took seats under a brolly, and waited.

Ger and I read, while Clara gazed around with intent. Her long dark hair was up in a bun, her shoulders were already tanned, and she looked gorgeous. She also managed to appear all dreamy and faraway, but every time something moved near the entrance, her eyes shot left. She was eventually rewarded. Handsome Waiter came out, a tray with three coffees balanced on his hand.

'Let's order something,' said Clara.

'Like what?' said Ger. 'A good shag?' We snorted.

Clara raised her hand and waved.

He came over. He was wearing a white shirt and jeans, and raised his chin to ask what we wanted.

I said, 'Yes, we'd like . . . erm . . . Ger? What did you say you wanted?'

'I said I wanted a good –'

'Coffee!' said Clara. 'Some good coffee, please.'

We cracked up again. He bit his lip, as though embarrassed, but this was probably a regular, if not daily, occurrence – foreign women behaving like schoolgirls.

'For all three?' he asked, looking at me.

'I'll have tea, actually.'

'Indian or . . .'

'Yes, Indian, with milk. That would be lovely.'

He left us.

'Wow,' said Clara. 'He's dead dishy up close.'

'Cool down,' said Ger. 'We're here for time out, remember? You're not allowed to pick up waiters.'

'And if you really *must* pick someone up,' I said, 'let it be a guy with a yacht in the harbour, so we can all benefit. Preferably that nice catamaran.'

'But if a girls' week away doesn't involve flirting, what hope is there?'

'Flirting is one thing,' said Ger, 'but if he'd stood there a moment longer, you'd have thrown yourself on top of him.'

'I would have.' Clara sighed. 'I would.'

The plan backfired. A different waiter brought the tea and coffee.

'You frightened him off,' Ger muttered.

A few minutes later, another man came out – the manager, who had checked us in on arrival – and stopped by our table to ask if everything was to our satisfaction. He was gracious and handsome, and had a very quiet voice.

'Now,' I said, after he'd moved on. 'That's my kind of man. Mature. Wrinkled. Attractive. And so well dressed. Did you see the creases in his shirtsleeves? You'd cut yourself on them.'

The object of Clara's interest eventually reappeared, but he sat down next to a woman in a very slim bikini on the other side of the pool. 'Flirting on the job,' I said. 'Typical.'

'Sod him,' said Clara.

'You came on too strong,' said Ger.

'And what's *she* doing?'

'There's only one of her.'

'Yeah, must have been the deeply alluring adolescent behaviour we exhibited,' I said.

The woman made him laugh.

'He probably thinks he's a real babe magnet,' I added.

'The rat,' said Clara.

'He's a waiter in a hotel full of near-naked women,' said Ger. 'You can't blame the guy for chatting them up.'

'It's no good,' said Clara, staring across the pool. 'I'm in love. For the moment, anyway.'

'Well, that's bad news,' I said, 'because the only person *that* man is going to fall in love with is himself. Same as all other beautiful men.'

In spite of Clara's best efforts (she spent much of the day wandering around hoping to run into him) we didn't see the dishy waiter again until the next morning, when he appeared on the terrace at breakfast. 'Now he's chatting up the waitress,' she grumbled.

He moved away from the waitress to the same woman he had been speaking to the day before, then came to our table. 'Good morning.'

'Morning.'

'Everything okay?'

'Lovely, thanks,' said Ger. 'Really lovely. This is such a beautiful place.'

'Thank you.'

He nodded. We nodded.

He said, 'You have some plans for today?'

'Not really,' said Clara. 'What would you recommend?'

'Oh, there are many things. You could hire a boat and take it round the coast.'

Ger looked at us, wide-eyed. 'That'd be cool!'

'Yes, but we wouldn't know how to . . . you know, make it go,' I said.

'What kind of boat?' Clara asked.

'A small motorboat. It's easy.'

'You'd be able for that, Clara, wouldn't you?' said Ger.

'I sail,' Clara said to the waiter, 'but, yeah, I'm sure I could handle it.'

'Excellent,' said Ger.

'But we might hit something,' I said, 'or sink, or crash on to the rocks.'

He smiled. 'Of course not.'

'Come on, Kadie, it'd be fun.'

'Enjoy it, so,' I said.

Ger looked up at him. 'Our friend is the adventurous type. Bungee-jumping, hang-gliding, that kind of thing.'

'I'm not going out on anything that floats with you two in charge.'

'She's used to chauffeurs,' Clara explained. 'Comes from a very wealthy family. A bit spoilt, you know?'

'Sod off.'

'Come with us, then,' Ger said to me. 'It'll be great *craic*.'

'Would you be able to organize it?' Clara asked the waiter.

'Of course. I'll get some details.' He went off.

'Good work,' Ger said to Clara. 'You have him running after you already.'

He soon returned, brandishing leaflets that he spread out on the table beside Clara. He was looking at photos of boats; she was looking at his wrists, his belt, his shirt buttons, and he knew very well that she was. 'These are available for four hundred and fifty kuna per day – about fifty euro.'

I leant over. 'But that's a speedboat!'

'Cool,' said Ger.

'We'd kill ourselves.'

'It's easier than driving a car,' said the Croatian, 'and there are no bends on the road.'

'Let's take it,' said Clara.

'Yeah,' said Ger. 'I'm game.'

'I can show you where to go,' he said, 'islands near here.'

'Can you book it for us?' Clara asked.

'Of course. For when?'

'Is it possible straight away? We've only got a week and we haven't done much yet.'

'No problem.'

He folded up his leaflets, but Clara wasn't ready to let him go. 'Are you from around here?' she asked.

'I was born in Zagreb, but have lived most of my life in Korčula.' He pronounced it Korchula.

'And you've never gone away?'

'To study, yes, and to war.'

'Oh, right,' she said.

'Where did you study?' Ger asked.

'Dubrovnik.'

'Your English is excellent.'

'It has to be.'

'We're in the travel business too,' said Ger.

He glanced at me. 'Your friend mentioned this.'

'But I'm afraid our Croatian isn't up to much.'

'Yes, but how many Croatian visitors do you have in Ireland?'

'Not enough,' said Ger. 'You must send some over.'

'You should come yourself,' said Clara.

'That would be very nice. We have more and more Irish visitors now. Before the war, it was mostly Austrians, Germans and Italians, of course, but not many Irish.'

'Well, Croatia is the in place right now,' said Clara, 'which is why we thought we'd better check you out for ourselves.'

'And how are we doing?' he asked me.

'Very well,' I said.

'Not too noisy?'

I smiled. There was a short silence.

Clara leant over to shake his hand. 'I'm Clara, and this is Ger, and Kadie.'

'Milenko Lalić. Pleased to meet you.'

'So have you worked here for long?' Ger asked.

'I, eh . . . along with my father . . . run the hotel.'

'Oh, right. Lovely,' said Clara.

He glanced at me again – to make a point? – then dipped his head and almost clicked his heels. 'Enjoy your breakfast. I will make arrangements about the boat for later this morning.'

'Good one, Clara,' I muttered.

'So much for chatting up a waiter,' said Ger. 'You've been chatting up the manager.'

A yellow speedboat was brought to the quay an hour later by a young guy with blond dreadlocks and reflecting shades. I stood on *terra firma*, while he showed Ger and Clara how it worked. They were giggling too much to take anything in.

'Girls, concentrate!' I said. 'Otherwise, you'll be picked up off the Italian coast in a few days' time.'

'No need to be nervous,' a voice said behind me.

Milenko.

'Nervous? I'm not a bit nervous. I'm not going with them.'

His eyebrows went up. 'But it is very safe.'

'You really think so?' I asked, looking at them. They had collapsed once again into hysterical laughter, making the boat rock so much the dreadlocked one had to grab a seat to stop himself falling into the water – and they weren't even moving yet. Milenko dipped his head sideways as if to suggest that I might have a point.

Clara had taken the controls. The boat went backwards, then forwards, and hit the quayside. Milenko said something to the owner; he nodded and replied.

'What did you say?'

'I said maybe he should go with them. He likes that idea.'

'I hope he's well insured.'

'They'll work it out. But what will you do?'

'I'll enjoy your lovely beach and be here when the corpses are brought back.'

Clara was getting the hang of the controls. She drove the boat round in a circle and managed to bring it alongside. 'I'm impressed,' I called, but when I turned, Milenko had gone.

After the speedboat had disappeared round the headland, I lay on the pebbly beach near the pier for the smaller, private boats, and tried to read, but I was restless, so I had an ice-cream and sat on my towel, watching aqua-aerobics taking place on the main beach. A young woman with a CD-player was standing on the rocks, directing about twenty people, spread out in the sea, through a series of exercises. But my attention was drawn to a solitary woman standing on the promenade, following the routines all by herself in her swimsuit. She was like a solo performer, raising her arms, kicking her feet, bending her knees to the music. Aqua-aerobics on land. It was like being in an East German holiday camp.

I lay down to snooze.

'Hello.'

I shaded my eyes and looked up. Him again. 'Hi.'

Milenko had changed into a T-shirt and shorts. He was standing on the pier, dangling keys in his hand. 'You're not lonely without your friends?'

Not much of a chat-up line. 'I'm grand, thanks.'

He hunkered down. 'They will be okay, I am sure.' He

dangled the keys a bit more. 'I'm finished work for today.'

'Ah. Time for a bit of dive-bombing, I suppose?'

He looked mortified – why did I persist in tormenting him? – and had to scramble around to save the moment. 'Actually, I'm going over to the town.'

'Lovely.' I was having trouble holding my head up.

'Would you like to come?'

Oh, dilemmas. Multifarious dilemmas. One: Clara saw him first. Two: getting into a car alone with a strange man. Three: he didn't look half bad. 'Umm . . .'

'It's okay.' He stood up. 'I thought maybe the day was long for you on your own.'

What a busy man he must be, I thought, if this is what he says to every woman sitting alone. But the truth of it was that the hours *were* dragging, and I was narked that the girls had gone off without me. We were supposed to be spending time together, not going off and leaving one behind, which might be why I said to Milenko, 'Actually, that would be lovely.'

'Good.'

I pulled on my skirt and top. 'But I'll have to get back before the others.'

'Whatever you like.'

'Thanks. Have you things to do in Korčula?'

'Not today.' I stepped up on the pier beside him. 'Just here,' he said.

I looked down. He was pointing at a rubber speedboat. 'Oh.' It was the size of a mattress. A Li-lo with a motor on it.

Sensing my apprehension, he said quickly, 'My boat, then. This belongs to a friend, but we have a bigger one. Over here.' I followed him to the larger pier where there were five or six boats, with awnings and engines, and room for about six people. Much better.

Milenko stepped into one with a yellow awning and put out his hand. 'Welcome to *Zizinica*.'

I'll bet you say that to all the girls.

It was a bit hairy, going to sea with a stranger, but when we came round the headland, my reservations dispersed. There were hills in every direction, mountains across on the mainland, and when we pulled round to the left, the walled town of Korčula, squashed on to a narrow horseshoe-shaped peninsula, rose out of the water, its buildings circling and crowding towards the church at the top of the rise.

'Is it true,' Milenko called over the whine of the engine, 'that you're very rich?'

Nothing like getting to the point. 'They were just teasing.'

'Yes, but . . . is it true?'

I took my eyes from Korčula to look at him. Was he for real? He smiled. His bluntness was disarming. Without exception the men who had dated me because of my perceived wealth had gone to comical lengths to appear disinterested in it. I matched Milenko's effrontery with my own. 'Why do you ask? Are you looking for a rich wife?'

He was still grinning. 'Why would I need a rich wife? Could she buy me this?' He waved at the mountains, the town. 'You can't buy what you already have.'

Because I had never been asked outright before, I decided to give an outright reply. 'My father made a lot of money earlier in his career,' I explained. 'He still makes quite a lot, I suppose.'

'What does he do?'

'He's a musician.'

'Jazz?'

'No. Rock.'

He appeared to lose all interest, which was also a first. Within minutes we were pulling past a busy marina, crowded with yachts, launches and water-taxis. Milenko jumped off, tied up and helped me out. 'You've been to Korčula already?'

'We come over every night for dinner and a wander.'

'You would like to swim here? Off the rocks?'

'God, yes.'

He led me round the ramparts that surrounded the town, down a staircase and across the rocks to roughly hewn steps that dropped into the sea. I spread my towel across a flat concrete platform. 'There can't be many places where you can swim off the city walls.'

The sea was choppy – in fact, pretty rough. Milenko threw off his T-shirt and lowered himself in. I hesitated on the top step. Tossing waves slapped off the rocks. 'Yikes!' It was all something of an inelegant struggle. I turned this way and that, and made a complete arse of myself trying to catch a break between the waves. There was nothing for it but to throw myself in.

Milenko had not mentioned the considerable pull, which dragged me swiftly away from the steps. It was an effort to stay in one spot. Then a couple of motorboats went past, several hundred feet away, and their wake hit us soon after-wards. Large waves flung us about like cans bobbing on the water. It was fun, sort of, but my bikini top was coming off. The sea was too busy to allow me to fix it, and the padded cups were acting like underwater sails, dragging me into the current.

Milenko dived and surfaced like a porpoise. With his wet hair pushed off his face, he didn't look quite so perfect, which was reassuring. There are good looks, and then good looks – improbable and off-putting. No one really wants to shag a descendant of the Archangel Gabriel – the sheen will wear off – so it was good to see that, when wet, Milenko's features were more pronounced. His incisors were slightly crooked, his eyebrows rather prominent, and his skin very sallow. He was a stranger, *un étranger*, in every sense of the word, and here I was, bobbing about in frisky waves, with a bikini top floating an inch away from my chest.

When a large motor-launch passed nearby, the waves became unmanageable. I swam frantically on the spot, getting nowhere. Milenko reached out and pulled me towards him without a trace of flirtation, as if I was a rowboat he needed to tie up.

I screeched as another large wave came down on us, throwing me against him. He had a tight grip on my waist, but I didn't care – I didn't want to be dragged away – although I could have done without the bikini top that had a mind of its own. Milenko swam to the steps, pulling me with him, but even he struggled to get out, with waves breaking against him as he fought to get to a foothold. Eventually, he succeeded and reached back for me. With one hand on my errant top and a great heave of determination, I lifted myself from the water. 'Well, that was interesting.'

'It isn't always like that,' he said.

A handful of elderly locals were sitting around in the sun, the men with their slack tummies sagging over their shorts, the women in large bathing-suits looking healthy and bronzed. A child kept throwing himself into the sea, off the rocks, then calling back to his grandparents.

'That was me,' said Milenko, 'when I was a kid.'

'You came here a lot?'

'All the time. To swim with my cousins.'

'You have no brothers or sisters?'

'I had a brother. He swam here too.'

Oh, God. More deep water. Nothing for it. 'The war?'

'Yes. He died near Dubrovnik. He was twenty-three.'

'I'm so sorry.'

He shrugged.

'Were you in the army too?'

'I was too young, mostly, but I fought for a few months. It was difficult for my mother.'

'I can imagine.'

It seemed a trivial thing to do at such a moment, but my skin was burning and I had to get out the sunscreen. As I was creaming myself, Milenko lay back. No lingering looks, no sleazy offer to help. He was not quite the opportunist I had expected. Though I had thrown myself almost topless at him in the water, he remained unmoved, which was a relief in view of Clara's stake.

Within half an hour, the sea seemed to have calmed down. 'It looks safer now,' I said.

'The wind has dropped.'

'What about the current?'

'Let me see.' He dived straight in. 'Much better,' he called. 'Come on in.'

So, once again I tackled the steps and the sea, and there was less of a pull. We paddled about, relishing the cool, the heave, the clarity. A grandmother, swimming alongside us, urged her granddaughter, in wings, to get in. The little girl reached back for her grandfather's hand. He led her to the edge. No, no, she seemed to say, you go first. So he did, with a great belly-flopping dive.

'Ah!' said his wife. *'Bomba!'*

Suddenly I envied them their lifestyle, as I looked up at the curved wall of the town from my extraordinary viewpoint in the sea.

We had coffee just above where we had been swimming. From our table under the pine trees, I could lean over the wall and watch the sea teasing the rocks below. A man in a wetsuit was pulling an old-fashioned steel helmet over his head. Like something out of Jules Verne, he lowered himself into the water and, but for a few bubbles on the surface, disappeared from sight.

'Thanks,' I said to Milenko. 'That was wonderful.'

He smiled, and stirred his coffee.

Afterwards, we wandered the shaded streets of the medieval town, the paving shiny with use. Milenko told me about his work. 'Most hotels in Croatia are owned by the state, including ours, but we – my father and I – have also built two houses, four apartments, which we let to tourists, and that is our family business. We hope to build more.'

'More houses?'

'Yes. That is the future for me. There is very big potential.'

'I can see that.'

'And this,' he said, 'is the house where Marco Polo was born.'

The speedboat came round the headland and approached the quayside without beheading any swimmers. I watched from the semi-circular platform as the owner of the boat helped Clara to tie up. They stood chatting in the evening sun and eventually came over to me.

'You missed a great day,' said Ger. 'We went out to Badija – the island. There's a gorgeous monastery there, and we passed a nudist colony and swam off the boat. It was blissful.'

Clara was looking over her shoulder. 'I'm in love.'

'We know that,' I said.

'Not with the waiter. With him. Johnnie.'

'He isn't a waiter. And who's Johnnie when he's at home?'

She waved at the dreadlocks. 'Isn't he divine? He's English.'

'You fickle beast,' said Ger. 'What about yer man?'

'He'll be devastated, I know, but I've found someone else.'

'That's good to hear,' I said.

6

A grey winter day. There had to be better times to arrive in Budapest, to arrive anywhere. I negotiated the crush of people outside the airport, and eventually found the taxi rank, as well as the driver from hell. He drove so badly I fully expected to suffer the same fate as Killian. A bank of cloud hung over the low skyline of the city, but it still seemed very bright. The daylight was clear-cut, sharp, not indecisive as it had been in Stockholm.

Steph, I hoped, was in the city somewhere – visiting old haunts, finding comfort in places she had shared with Killian. Perhaps it was a natural instinct to go back to the beginning. Budapest, after all, had been the wet-nurse of their affair, and it was nice to imagine her tiptoeing across memories, until these gentle thoughts were elbowed aside by another scenario: Steph, faint and panicked, with no clear idea of what she was doing. And yet another: Steph, on a long-haul flight to Goa, because I had put that mad idea into her head.

Clara had booked me into the Hilton. The word from home, when I made it to my room, was discouraging. Nobody, but nobody at all, had heard from Steph, and there had been no response from Ágnes. Steph's parents had expressed relief that I was on their daughter's trail, but Dad had his own problems.

'These bloody dogs.'

'Giving you grief, are they?'

'You bet. I can't keep them here, but Steph's in-laws keep saying it makes sense because "You've got so much space."'

'You *do* have space.'

'Which would be great if the mongrels would go outside.'

'They're only little, Dad.'

'*Little*? Irish wolfhounds are never little, not even in the womb! They keep knocking me down and slobbering all over me, and every time I turn, four pairs of eyes gaze up at me. They don't half crave affection.'

'They must be pining,' I said, looking out at a hot-air balloon tethered in the plaza outside the hotel. Curious place to put one.

He sighed. 'They seem a bit confused all right, but they're absolutely wired.'

'You have to tire them out. Take them for long walks.'

'Long walks? Have you any idea how chaotic things are? Your mother's on her way, and three friends of Killian's are arriving over from the UK tonight, all expecting to stay here. Mourners rushing back for a funeral that isn't. But enough of my complaining. How are you bearing up?'

'Okay.' I hesitated. 'Have there been any more calls?'

'What do you think? He hasn't stopped. I've told him there's no point coming to Cork. No funeral, and no you.'

A weight seemed to be dangling off the back of my throat. Hearing about Milenko was like being aware of music playing in another room, but being unable to hear it.

'I wish there was something I could do for the both of you,' Dad said. 'This can be sorted, surely?'

''Bye, Dad. And mind those dogs. They're the ones that will bring Steph back.'

I took out Deirdre's mobile, wishing now that I had not thrown mine away, with all my numbers, because I was cut off from most of my friends. I sent a text to Steph. 'Where are you? Please let me know where you are.'

The message was delivered, and dropped into the great black hole that was cyberspace.

I was washing underwear with hotel soap when the phone rang beside the bed. I lurched out of the bathroom. 'Hello?'

'Ah . . . is that Kadie?'

'Yes.'

'Ah, this is Ágnes.'

'Ágnes! How are you?'

'I am well, thank you. Your friend, Clara, emailed me. We have spoken on the phone just now.'

'Oh, look, thanks for calling. Have you heard anything from Steph?'

'Actually, I am very near your hotel. I will be there in five minutes.'

'Great! I'll meet you in the lobby.'

Ágnes was pointy – sharp chin, narrow nose, bony shoulders. Her black hair was swept up in a scarf. She embraced me warmly. 'Stephanie has spoken of you so often. How horrible to meet like this.'

'I take it she hasn't turned up?'

Ágnes shook her head. We sat down.

'*Damn.* Have you heard from her? Email or text or . . .'

'Text?'

'Yes, text message, by mobile phone.'

'Ah – SMS. Yes, I had an SMS, asking if she could come to see me. I said she would be welcome, but I don't understand . . . when Killian . . . so soon.'

'I know, it's peculiar, but she isn't coping very well with her in-laws and all the arrangements, and she was desperate to get away.'

'But why would she want to come here?'

'To see you, to hide out, to hang on to Killian, I suppose. It makes sense, in a crazy kind of way. After all, this is where they got together so . . .'

Ágnes wrinkled her nose. 'It did not start here.'

'Oh, it did. Killian came over on business, remember? And they hooked up.'

'He came, but they did not,' she waved her hands about, 'begin their romance here.'

'Are you sure?'

'He went on to Bucharest and Stephanie went there to see him. She came back all . . . happy.' Ágnes smiled. 'In love.'

I rubbed my eyes. Had I got it wrong? Mixed things up? 'You mean – I'm in the wrong place?'

She shrugged. 'Perhaps.'

'Excellent.'

'I must go to my work,' she said.

'Yes, of course. Thanks so much for making time for me.'

'What will you do?'

'I'll try to sort this out, and hopefully get some rest. I barely closed my eyes last night.'

Ágnes looked at me as if she was reaching inside my head. 'I can help with that. I come this afternoon. You have swimsuit?'

Um, *no*. Don't usually need a swimsuit in the morgue . . .

The hotel was linked to an 'exclusive' shopping mall, so I went in search not only of a swimsuit – a swim might well help me sleep – but also fresh clothes. It was like a wander through another era. The clothes were garish, loud, and the underwear so coarse and frilly that there was no point buying any, unless I wanted to scratch all the way home. Hand-washing would have to prevail. I did, however, find a swimsuit, a black one-piece that might have been hanging there since the Soviet days.

Then I went to bed, pulling the blankets round me. Going through a close bereavement without my partner, my love, was one thing; going through a broken engagement without my best friend was another. Going through both at the same time without anyone at all was like losing sense.

Guilt throbbed away. So desperate had I been to get home, to curl up under my own duvet of woes, that I had let Steph slip through my grasp. We had rarely been out of touch for more than a few days. There was always a text, a call, an email. We were always in each other's heads, until now, and it was like having a limb amputated.

There was someone in the room. I sat up, heart pounding. It was Killian, sitting on the end of the bed, looking over his shoulder. 'Give me heart failure, why don't you?' I said. Grey light slid into the room but did little to brighten the gloom. 'Where is she?'

But I knew he wouldn't speak, wouldn't tell me. If I didn't know, he could not know, being, as he was, an extension of me. I rolled over and cried, and the crying got worse until I couldn't remember what I was crying about – Killian or Milenko or both. Only one of them, after all, was truly lost. I should reach out, perhaps, to the one who remained. If death can come so viciously – if a husband can die so swiftly on a cold Stockholm morning while his wife force-feeds herself cornflakes back home – should we not keep hold of what happiness we already have?

The phone stared at me. One call. All it took. Images threw themselves at me. I batted them away as I had been doing for a week now. Any discussion, any degree of honesty, would lead to torment for too many people.

I lay in the bath, still sore. It was the first time I had been properly alone since Killian's death, the first time I was able to grasp that I would never again nudge him, or curse him, or stand at the front door watching him and Dad going down to the lake to fish. I would never see him gather his newborn into his arms. Killian was a thread so deeply woven into my life that I would surely unravel without him. He had been there for ever. When Mum left us Marjorie, a near neighbour, had swept in. She was not entirely without compassion in those days and attended to us with genuine care, helping Dad get into the swing of school lifts and ballet classes. Killian and I were often thrown together in various childminding arrangements beneficial to our parents, and we hurried through our childhoods, inventing landscapes and creating adventures in my vast garden. As teenagers, we became even closer when Killian increasingly felt the need to escape his overbearing mother and docile father and found a second home with us. It was the making of him, he said, and the making of Marjorie's antipathy to me. She resented our influence on her son and was cross that we enjoyed so much of his time, but somehow she never held it against Dad, whom she continued to treat as an unfortunate inept; no, she saved all her disdain for me. We never fancied each other, Killian and me – or, at least, not until one sunny day in the music room when we were sitting on the red couch under the window and he looked at me, and I looked at him, and it suddenly seemed like a very good idea. It was.

Now he was sitting on the edge of my Budapest bath, grinning at me in a slightly salacious way, our own intense affair zipping between us. 'I'm glad I didn't marry you,' I said. 'Only to lose you like this.' My eyes welled up again. God, was there no end to this crying? I looked at my body, expecting to see a neat division – a line demarcating which bits of me ached because of Killian and which because of Milenko. It was wrong to connect the two, yet I could not separate them, because each would have been my salvation on the loss of the other. When I thought about Killian, I felt convulsed, *bouleversée*; Milenko created more of a dragging terror, a sickening. How strange that one body could make room for so much hurt, I thought.

In the bedroom, the mobile beeped. I lifted out of the bath. This wasn't any beep. I knew it in my gut. As it opened its inbox, the phone whirred and dallied. Then the name appeared. Steph! It said simply, 'Kadie?' Tentative, of course, because this was Deirdre's phone. I replied, 'Yes. It's me. I have Deirdre's phone. She's in Stockholm.'

'But where are you?'

I laughed. 'You're one to ask!' My fingers would not obey instructions, kept hitting the wrong keys. 'Budapest.'

Message sending ... Message sent ... Beeps. Message received.

I sat down by the desk and rocked. 'Hurry, hurry, hurry.' Minutes. Many, many minutes. My heart beating up my ribcage ... Finally: two beeps.

'Silly dope,' she replied. 'Wrong city.' And then the mobile rang. 'What on earth are you doing in Budapest?' said Steph.

'Looking for you.'

'But I'm not there.'

Oh, joy. The sound of her voice. 'Clearly. Where the hell *are* you?'

'Bucharest.'

'But I thought you wanted to come to Ágnes?'

'I couldn't get a flight, so I came here instead.'

'Yes, but ...' Enough with the inquisition. 'Are you all right?'

'I'm fine.'

'Are you eating?'

'Yes, Mummy.'

Relief and delight quickly evaporated. If I said the wrong thing, she would be gone, as swiftly as she had vanished from Stockholm. She held all the cards. 'Steph, I'm so sorry.'

'Who's got the dogs?'

'I should have gone with you. I was confused. Tired.'

'The puppies get different food from Mirabel.'

'Listen, everyone's frantic. The whole of Cork is –'

'Kadie,' she said sternly, '*who* is looking after the dogs?'

'Dad.'

'What? *Still?* Oh, God. He's useless with anything that doesn't miaow.'

'I couldn't give a toss about the dogs. I'm more concerned about you, and Killian.'

She didn't respond.

'There are certain things that need to be done,' I went on. 'As next-of-kin, you have responsibilities.' I was coming across all Deirdre again.

'I am aware of that, thank you, and I've been trying to meet those responsibilities, but no one will listen to me. What am I supposed to do?'

'Let them take him home at least.'

'Nothing's stopping them doing that.'

'The undertaker won't move without your instructions. Please, Steph, can we just get ourselves back to Cork?'

'No. It's better for me here. I've been eating, like I said, and even sleeping a bit.'

'But where are you?'

'In the hotel.'

'What hotel?' I was looking for a name.

'Where we got together. I'm even in the same room – two three two. It's so strange,' she said, going all wistful. 'It hasn't changed one bit – heavy brown curtains, like hanging carpets, and dull yellow walls, and there's this old radio, like something out of the nineteen fifties, with knobs on – Killian fiddled with it for ages last time. It's nice here, Kadie. It's like he's right behind me, waiting for you and me to stop nattering.'

'*Well, that's all very well,*' I felt like saying. Instead, deflated, I held her voice to my ear. 'Listen, I'll come to Bucharest tomorrow. We'll sort this out together.'

'No way! You go home. It's ridiculous you've even gone to Budapest.'

'But I can't go home without you. They'd never forgive me. Your parents think I'm bringing you back.'

'Mum and Dad know I need space, and this is the perfect place for it. It's an old château, and it's friendly and quiet – and it isn't Cork.'

Where had they stayed in Bucharest? Was it anywhere in my memory bank? Had they mentioned any names? They'd been there twice together, and Killian had proposed to her in a park, where men were sitting at tables playing backgammon surrounded by walls of hedge ... That much I knew, but where had they stayed?

'In fact, it's so quiet,' Steph said, 'I can even hear the wires flapping about in the lift shaft.'

'I thought Bucharest was manic.'

'I'm not in the city, I'm outside town on Lake Pantelimon. It really brings me back, that word. We used to love telling the taxi drivers to take us to Pantelimon.'

I scurried around the room, my towel falling off me, and found a pen in a drawer. Pantelimon. 'But all those memories of Killian, Steph. How can that help?'

'It just does. It's like having a kind of communion with him, you know? It feels right, being away. Besides, I don't have what it takes to deal with all those people coming at me like a great marching crowd.'

'They mean well.'

'They think I'm selfish, but I have to keep calm, Kadie, I have to keep the head. This is my way of dealing with it. Calm, that's what the baby needs, and that's what she'll get.'

'But I'm desperate to get you both home, safe and sound.'

'Just go home yourself, would you? And tell them to leave me alone, to stop ringing and sending texts. They're driving me mad.'

'But what about Killian?' I snapped. 'They won't release his body until you tell them to. You can't leave him in that mortuary!'

'I don't intend to,' she said, and hung up. Just like that.

'Bugger!' I dialled and redialled, but Steph had shut off the phone.

I immediately called Clara on the hotel phone, while simultaneously texting Dad – 'Tell the family she's okay. In Romania. I'm on my way.'

'Clara? She's in Bucharest, at the hotel where they hooked up. I've just spoken to her. We need to find out which hotel that was.'

'Why don't you ask her?'

'Because I don't want to spook her. She made it perfectly clear she doesn't want any interference, but I'm going down there as soon as you can get me a flight. It's a converted château beside Lake Pantelimon. You should be able to find it.'

'Okay.'

'And tell the families to *lay off* her. Can you get me on to a flight tomorrow?'

Clara sighed. 'I'll try.'

She tried every airline every way, but flights were booked solid. 'You could go on stand-by or I could filter you through somewhere else.'

'But that'll take all day.'

'Kadie, you can't expect miracles. I can book you back to London tomorrow and try to get you out from there. It's either that or stand-by. Unless you go overland.'

'Huh?'

'You know – *trains*.'

'Oh, trains!' Beautiful, magical words! No dreaded airport. No gut-churning take-off or wild imaginings. I pulled on some clothes and hurried downstairs.

The young receptionist nodded. 'Yes, there are many trains. Every day.'

'Excellent.'

'Is very long journey.'

'How long?'

'I think . . . twelve hours.'

'Can you get me the times?'

There was a train at eight thirty-five the following morning, ETA Bucharest twenty to twelve that night. Fifteen hours. Perfect. All the time I might have spent fretting in airports could instead be spent sitting in one place, one seat, with no fear or confusion or panic-attacks, and I would probably arrive a day earlier than the airlines could manage.

It was not a swim Ágnes had in mind for me, but a thermal bath – outdoors. The large reserves of mineral waters beneath the Danube spout into a number of spas around the city and, convinced I could benefit from their medicinal properties, she took me to a Turkish bath in City Park. The entrance was like a bus station, with ancient kiosks dispensing tickets, and there was a whole floor of changing booths overlooking the out-door pools. I couldn't believe Ágnes meant for me to wear a swimsuit in that cold, but when she bullied me into the 40°C water, all resistance drained away and I groaned like an elephant rolling in mud on a hot day.

'When I saw you this morning,' she said, 'I thought this is what you needed.'

Men were playing chess on boards floating on the water. Others sat back, like us, leaning against the edge, relaxing.

Ágnes had also heard from Steph – a brief text, apologizing for not turning up – and she approved of my plan to continue to Bucharest. She felt Steph could not be left alone and offered to put me on the train the next morning. I was grateful for the help: unlike Stockholm, there wasn't a lot of English spoken in Budapest. I told her about the disaster that Stockholm had been, but she was bemused by Steph's instincts. 'It would be like torture,' she said. 'Why would she go back to these places?'

'Because going forward is so desperately bleak?'

'Ah, yes.'

*

The spa was soothing, but I did not sleep well that night. I was haunted by Steph's voice. Perhaps the quiet, the lack of fuss, would be better for her and the child, but what they really needed, surely, was for this to be over, and a funeral was the only satisfactory way to end it. Whenever I turned from thoughts of Steph, I saw Killian as he was at that moment, locked into a cold, cold place. A freezing place. I held my head in my hands to shut it out. After hours of tossing, I sought refuge in Milenko – our early days together, not recent events – for there could be no harm reliving the good times, even though they were over. Besides, maybe I would find in there, somewhere, the thing I had missed.

On our last day in Korčula, I went for an early-morning walk. I was in a contented, contemplative mood. I had no blues at that time in my life. I even quite liked myself, at twenty-seven, which had been harder in my early twenties. After Killian had cheated on me, I was further brought down by a series of unsatisfactory relationships and I somehow managed to banjax those that had potential. My mother flitted from lover to lover, always in control, but I was not my mother. I was like my father: loyal, steady, a desperate romantic. I had never been able to take love lightly, so each failed relationship wore me down until I was flattened, dull, my edge blunted to the point where I had no bite. For many years, I was also concerned about Dad. When I was little, he had spared me the discomfort of a new woman moving in on our happy duo, but by the time he hit his mid-forties, it pained me to realize that for my sake he had risked remaining alone for the rest of his life. I thought him old, of course, past it, as fifty loomed, and believed it was all over for him. By then, I had left home, leaving Dad like a basketball floating through a big hall with no basket at either end. The prospect of us ending up together – the spinster daughter minding her old man in the big country house – was not terrifically appealing, but such a fate seemed less likely after I discovered Dad in an affair with his beautiful accountant. He was not in the least embarrassed when he told me the relationship had nothing whatsoever to do with love, leaving me to draw my own conclusions. I was quite shocked.

Another bombshell soon followed: Killian and Steph. It would be unreasonable to pretend it didn't hurt when my ex began seeing my best friend, but the way I found out made it worse. Killian had just come back from a long business trip to Eastern Europe and invited me to lunch. I longed to hear all about Steph's life in Budapest, and when we stepped into Isaacs restaurant together, his sister was on her way out. In the course of doorstep pleasantries, she squeezed my arm and said, 'What *do* you think about Steph and Killian? Aren't they're just *made* for each other?' Then she was gone. Killian, never one to avoid eye-contact, looked at neither the floor nor the ceiling, but straight at me.

'How?' I said. 'How could you tell Deirdre before me?'

'She overheard me on the phone yesterday. Put two and two together.'

We stared at one another. He bit his inner lip, sheepish, yet resolved to face me on this.

'You and Steph. Are you mad?'

'I think so,' he said, nodding. 'And so is Mum, and Deirdre, for all her gushing. Absolutely furious, they are.'

'Your table is ready,' said a waitress.

'Please don't say, "It just happened," ' I said, as we sat down. 'Or "Do we have your blessing?" And above all don't say you're sorry.'

The waitress handed us menus.

'All right,' said Killian, 'but, Kadie,' he spoke over the top of the menu, as if discussing the fare, 'I don't know what it is with Steph or where it might be going, but if you're not happy about this, it isn't going anywhere.'

I glowered over the menu, thinking blackmail, friendship, loyalty. 'You can't make me responsible for this. That's not fair.'

'Nonetheless, it's how I feel, and Steph too. Neither of us can afford to lose you, so if it ends up being no more than a fling, so be it.'

'How dare you have a "fling" with my best friend?'

'But it wasn't, isn't, I mean . . . Oh, Christ.'

'Wasn't just a fling?' I eyeballed him.

'I don't think so.'

'Good. I won't have you getting quick thrills out of my friends.' I glanced at the menu.

'Ready?' asked the waitress, pen and notebook in hand.

'So do we have . . .' Killian looked at me, confused.

'My blessing? I'm not giving it and I'm not withholding it. This has nothing to do with me. Go with it or don't, but don't hang it round my neck.'

The waitress nodded, then asked more optimistically, 'Ready to order?'

Killian wouldn't take his eyes from mine. 'Would it hurt?' he asked simply.

'Not going there.'

'I don't want to hurt you again, so if it'd be too difficult, tell me.'

I looked up at the waitress. She shrugged.

'I'll get over it, Killian, all right? But as for giving Deirdre such good reason to gloat at my expense – fuck you.'

A flicker of a smile passed over his lips. 'The Clonakilty pudding is very good here,' he said.

The hurt passed. I didn't see Steph and Killian together until Steph came back from Budapest months later, and by then I had fallen in love with a fledgling musician. In student venues and grotty bars, I sat entranced by his mediocre lyrics and repetitive tunes, until one night he announced to the crowd that I was his inspiration. I cringed, and the cringing got worse until the relationship was as dried out as a prune, but in the high of it, Steph and Killian were good for a ribbing. 'It can't work!' I teased Steph, when she rang from Budapest. 'You'll never be happy with a business executive!'

'That's what his mother says.'

'Does she? Oh, well, in *that* case, I insist the relationship succeeds.'

It had. Steph, the disordered, untidy poet, had been very happy with her marketing man, and he had been happy with her, so they had married, in far-off Goa, away from us all, and remained as married as pens to their nibs.

By the time I went to Croatia, I was single again and so was Dad, but I didn't worry about him any more. It was clear that he got up to plenty of mischief, with absolute discretion, so he was never as lonely as I had feared. My own single status didn't bother me much either. If I was on the shelf, it was a crowded shelf – not many of my friends had married and the rest of us weren't particularly inclined to – so on my last morning in Korčula, I was pretty happy with my lot. In retrospect, I can see how attractive the happy person is; and how contagious their happiness. The more we know it, the more we find it perhaps.

Breakfast beckoned, but so did Korčula town. I went back to my room to get my bag, then ran for the water-taxi and hopped on. It was a beautiful start to my last day. As Korčula came into view, I felt a longing to return before I'd even left. The mountains across the water were hazy, the sea choppy, but the town was pert in the early-morning light, its red roofs brighter than ever, and the rim of cypress trees leaning over the wall was like a ribbon round a cake.

I walked the shaded ramparts to the place Milenko had taken me, and took a seat. The tarpaulin umbrellas flapped noisily in the breeze. The dark trees drooped overhead, and in an alleyway opposite me, a woman was sweeping the back of a folded carpet. Below the wall, a yellow boat with a white awning sat moored to the rocks. I ordered bread and coffee and took out my last-minute postcards, glancing up occasionally at the early walkers. It was a small town, a village, really, and the same faces appeared again and again in the streets: the boy in the red T-shirt on a skateboard whom we had seen one evening skating down steps; the woman who sat by the main steps selling bottles of holy water from Medjugorje; the flip-flop salesmen from the square. And, as I sipped my coffee, another local came past.

I wasn't aware, at first, that one of the few cars that had access to the ramparts had stopped beside my table. So he beeped, which made me jump. Milenko, in a Fiat Punto.

'Good morning.'

'Oh, hello.'

'Our breakfast is not good at the hotel?'

No, actually, it's crap. 'Of course it is. I just came out for a walk and ended up here.'

He looked down the street, and then back at me.

'What brings you over so early?' I asked. 'Work?'

He looked ahead again, and didn't seem to know what he was doing there.

'Or are you on a day off?'

He turned to me. 'You think I should take a day off?'

'Oh, I . . . I don't know. When was your last day off?'

'Three days ago.'

'Ah, well, possibly not, then.'

Milenko shrugged. A fine set of square shoulders; long fingers on the steering-wheel. 'I work as I please,' he said.

Well, of course you do. Talk about son-of-the-boss syndrome. He was beginning to live up to my preconceptions: an idle Romeo, using his father's hotel to meet babes. Except for the car. The Punto didn't quite live up to the image.

'I was visiting my grandmother,' he said.

Oh. Neither did that. 'She lives in the old town?'

'Yes.'

'I wish I did.'

He ran his fingers round the steering-wheel. The end of the street held considerable fascination for him.

'Well,' I said, holding down my postcards in the wind, 'don't let me keep you.'

'Keep me?'

'I mean . . . don't let me *delay* you.'

'How can you delay me? I'm not going anywhere.'

'What are you doing in a car, then? Having breakfast?' I regretted the quip as soon as it slipped out.

'I haven't had breakfast yet.'

Oh, God, oh, God.

Milenko looked away, sucking in one cheek. He was winding me up.

'They do very good breakfasts at the Hotel Soline,' I said.

He turned suddenly. 'Or I could have it with you?'

What could I do, except smile?

Minus one Fiat Punto, he joined me a few minutes later, gesturing to the waiter. When he spoke in Croatian, it did strange things to my stomach. His language made it rumble with a new kind of hunger. We both looked out at the sea, bright blue, boats plying back and forth.

'Another good day for swimming,' I said.

'You like swimming, I think?'

'I love it. That's why I come to places like this. Warm water. We have wonderful beaches in Ireland, but the Atlantic is pretty chilly.'

Milenko drank his espresso quickly, efficiently. There was something in his body language that suggested he owned everything around him, yet he was not entirely at ease, which was contrary to type and made him more interesting.

'So, what are you doing, you and your friends today?'

'Not much. We leave this afternoon.'

'Ah, yes.'

'So we'll soak up the sun, I suppose.' Below us, a man went past in a small rowing boat. There seemed to be no craft in existence that could not be found around Korčula, from enormous luxury liners to inflatable armchairs.

'It's very beautiful at Pupnatska Luka,' said Milenko. 'Very nice for swimming. I could take you there.' He looked at me full-on again, in that sudden, provocative way. Not quite so intimidated now.

'But is there time? We're leaving at three.'

'So we go straight away.'

'I'd have to ask the girls if they'd like to come.'

'Sure. We can drive by the hotel and pick them up.'

Clara and Ger had no interest in getting into a hot car on a hot day. Their plan was simple: sunbathing to the last minute. The ferry to Orebić on the mainland was coming at three and the flight from Dubrovnik was at nine. They warned me to be back on time, but promised to throw my stuff into my suitcase.

Milenko talked while he drove, more relaxed than he had been during our tense breakfast, sometimes smiling at me in a sexless kind of way. Almost like a taxi driver. He had an interesting mouth. He used it a lot, biting it, turning it down, or one corner up, or straightening it in displeasure, as I would find out.

'You all live together, you and your friends?' he asked.

'Yes.'

'Not like me, still living with my parents.'

'No harm in that. I lived with my father until three years ago and I still go home every chance I get.'

'You have a good relationship with your father?'

'He's all right. We get on pretty well.'

'And your mother? Is she . . .'

'She's alive and well and living in London.'

He didn't say anything, so I went on: 'She left home when I was four.'

Milenko frowned. 'It's unusual, no, for a mother to go?'

As I had learnt, he didn't beat around the bush. 'Yup.'

He waited to hear more. I wondered if it was worth going into the saga. It was usually the stuff of the fourth or fifth date, and in the sweltering sun on my holidays, did I really have the energy to tell my parents' story? I kept it short, but wondered how we had become so personal so quickly.

'We lived in London in the early years, but Mum and Dad decided to move back to Cork, where they both grew up, when I reached school age. It didn't really work out. Dad was away a lot and Mum felt isolated – we were a good bit out from the city – and she missed London, so between one thing and another, she decided to go back. She wanted to take me with her, but Dad wasn't having it. He said she could go if she wanted to, but he wasn't losing me too. So she did. She left.'

He glanced at me again, and shook his head as if to say, 'Just like that?'

'Yeah, I know, but it sort of suited her. She wasn't cut out for the child-rearing thing and wasn't thinking too far ahead either. She planned to come back for me later, when she'd sorted herself out, without realizing that I'd be too settled by then. So Dad got stuck with my full-time care. He had to give up his job to look after me.'

Milenko raised his eyebrows and did something with his mouth. 'It was sad, growing up without your mother?'

'Sometimes. She was in the distance for a few years. I knew she was there, if I needed her, but we didn't see her much – she had another man – and I was really cheesed off when she had two other kids, two girls. She tried to make it up to me when I was a teenager, but I wasn't having any of it. I mean, Dad gave up a job he loved to look after me. Anyway, she persevered, very patiently, and a few years ago I relented, so we're okay now.'

'That's good,' said Milenko. 'It's important to have a good relation with your family.'

The road took us through the centre of the long, rasher-shaped island. Just beyond Pupnat, we turned on to a rough surface that got steadily worse as we went down. It also got windier and steeper, and sometimes Milenko seemed to have only one eye on the road. He stopped half-way down. 'There,' he said, gesturing at the narrow cove way below us. 'Pupnatska Luka.'

The local beauty-spot did what it was meant to do: it twinkled down there in the sunlight. The beach was hugged on both sides by verdant hills, the sea was iridescent, light green in the shallows, thick blue in the depths, and roofs poked out among the trees on one side of the bay. The track got worse when we continued. The cove was famous for the stone terraces that curved along it, and its stone dwellings, and after we had parked on a verge, we followed a path that led through a shaded area where tourists were feasting on olives and sardines. In the corner, there was an open oven with a stoned roof and chimney. Further along the pathway, giant cacti leant over the walls, like gardeners on ladders, and when we came on to the beach, big white and grey pebbles rolled under our feet.

We threw down our towels. The sun was perfect – not too hot, not too cool, a warm coating on my skin. But it wasn't only the sun that was comfortable. I was comfortable, entirely relaxed, in the company of this . . . I glanced at him . . . pleasant man. He was not at all the shallow egotist I had assumed him to be, not quite the Romeo.

'What's the tourist trade like in the winter?' I asked.

'It's quiet after September. Our season is very short.'

'What do you do from September to May?'

'I sleep,' he joked. 'We work eighteen-hour days in the summer, seven days a week sometimes.'

'So you hibernate all winter.'

He shrugged. 'Not really. Before, I travelled or took a job in Zagreb, waiting tables or teaching English. Now, during the winter, we work on our houses. I don't like to go away any more. There is so much to do. Let's swim.'

On the shoreline, the stones shuffled about under the gentle pull of the sea, which, apart from a half-hearted heave every now and then, was calm. Milenko dived in, avoiding the undignified approach of hobbling across the rolling stones the way I did, ouching and slipping. In the end I let myself go and dissolved into the sea. On one side of the bay, sheets of overlapping rock sloped into the water. Underwater, Milenko was slicing above the purple grass that covered parts of the seabed. When he did surface, he didn't speak before diving again, his long legs dropping in a straight line. There was something detached about him. He was chatty, warm, even, but removed. With any other man, this little excursion would have classified as some kind of date, but with Milenko it was more straightforward: I was a visitor, and he had taken me to a local beauty-spot; nothing more about it. He seemed to have no other agenda, which was reassuring when one is stuck in a ravine at the bottom of a winding dirt track with no clear way out. When I stretched out in my best bikini, floating elegantly, Milenko managed to make me feel as if I was shrouded in a nun's habit – devoid of alluring possibilities. This probably had everything to do with my job. He and his father had no doubt agreed he would work extra hard on us, to gain our favour.

But, there was quite another factor at work. He surfaced at some point and swam round me. 'There is a jazz festival in Cork, your friend was saying?'

'Yes. Every October. It's well known internationally. Gets some great names.'

'Like who?'

'God, I don't know. I'm not really into jazz.'

He dived again and resurfaced. 'Maybe I should come some time?'

'You like jazz?'

'Very much.'

'I'll send you some details if you like. Or you could look it up on the Internet.'

'I'll come to Cork.'

'Right. Lovely. You'd be welcome.'

Until that point, the absence of attraction on his part had allowed me to enjoy the day without fear of trespass, but it was beginning to irk. In the shallows, I lay back, enjoying the gentle ruffle of the waves and allowing the sea to pull me out and shove me in, and pull me out again. No massage could have been more effective, no whale music more soothing than the shuffle of the pebbles beneath me. But I was burning, so I battled with the stones that insisted on sliding from under my feet, painfully, while the waves pushed me forward. Whenever I was with Milenko the Adriatic, in which we had been so dramatically introduced, contrived to make me look ridiculous. Milenko scampered out and once again offered me a hand, then hauled me over the slight incline at the water's edge. I found myself about three inches from his chest. I was tempted to touch it, to put my palm over his nipple. When we reached the towels, a glance at Milenko's watch told me it was twelve minutes past eleven. That was the exact time it began for me. He produced a packet of Petit Beurre biscuits. As he offered me one, I came to the bridge between acquaintance and desire, and crossed it.

He was scanning the other women on the beach. The significant moment had not been shared.

The morning passed too quickly. We sat with our feet in the waves, munching Petits Beurres, drinking lime-flavoured water and watching a man push a very large log through the water for no reason that we could understand. The sea shimmered, like a coy seductress, reproaching us for getting out.

Further along the coast, we had lunch in a restaurant on a hill. We heard the singing before we'd even stepped on to the terrace. Inside, some local men were having a party, and they were in full voice. The noise made conversation difficult, even outside.

Milenko smiled. 'At least you have been introduced to Croatian folk songs.'

'Actually, I enjoyed several performances of your folk songs the night I arrived, remember?'

'They were Hungarian,' he said.

'You must have thought me an awful old bag when I complained.'

'A what? An old bag?'

'You know, sour and grumpy.'

'No, but what could I do? During the night I am also asleep.'

I bristled. 'You could approach them during the day. Or put up a notice about noise.'

He shrugged.

'You know, if you're really expecting to improve your business, you need to change your attitude. Where I come from, the customer is always right.'

'You find the customer is always right?'

'Well, no, usually not, but this one is!'

'Mostly,' he said, dipping his head slightly to the side, 'they are – what did you say? – *awful old bags.*'

I looked away, furious. He had me. He just totally had me. His accent was causing havoc. I could have left the island intact, but now I'd be carrying that very expression away with me and it would taunt me for weeks. I'd be sitting at my desk minding my own business and suddenly he'd be there, his hand on the rim of his glass of water, dark eyes fixing me and his voice low, saying conspiratorially in that damn accent, '*awful old bags*'.

As we were contemplating the dessert menu, a young woman and man came in and sat at the table behind me. Milenko's expression altered. He glowered at the woman's back, put down his menu, said, 'Not here. Somewhere else,' and stood up.

As I got up, the woman looked over her shoulder and saw him. Her eyes saddened. They nodded at one another, then Milenko bolted inside to pay.

'What was that about?' I asked, on the street. With anyone else, it wouldn't have been appropriate to pry, but this date was going nowhere so I could feed my curiosity and not go away wondering about the glorious woman with the sultry black hair or the gentle, loaded nod that had passed between them.

He strode towards the car. We got in. He took off, along the coast road, past coves, peninsulas and villas, flowers pouring over their walls. It was touching that he made no attempt to hide whatever it was the woman had sparked.

'We were to marry,' he said eventually.

'Oh.'

He nodded.

'Recently?'

'Two years now.'

'She seemed sad. Did you end it?'

'No.'

'So . . .'

'She said she'd made a mistake.'

'Better to find out before than after, I suppose.'

He looked at me, hurt.

'It's a tough decision, this getting-married business,' I said.

'Not for me.'

'I'm very sorry.'

'We were building a house. It's still there, half built.' His eyes stayed on me for a moment. 'Would you like to see it?'

Oh dear. What territory was this? 'Erm . . . Where is it?'

'Outside Korčula. On the Račiše road.'

'Have we time?'

'You won't miss the ferry.'

He had been nice to me and I wanted to be nice to him. 'Okay.'

By taking me to the house he had been building for someone else, he reconfirmed how things stood between us. We were becoming friends. Lovely. But not what I wanted. What I now wanted was exactly what I had initially believed to be the only thing he was likely to deliver: a harmless, quick, commitment-free and, not to put too fine a point on it – indeed, using Ger's graceful choice of language – *shag*. But friendship was better. Real. He gave the impression that he needed a friend.

He took me to a site surrounded by vineyards, a little way back from the main road with a view of the sea and the limestone mountain on the mainland. I could even see the church half-way up the hillside that always caught my eye from the beach. The foundations of the house had been built, and some walls. It was an ideal spot in an ideal location with a view to die for.

'You should finish building it,' I said. 'This is like a big open wound for you.'

'Maybe, some day.' His eyes were hidden behind sunglasses. I considered stepping over, putting my arms round his neck and kissing him. I had never made a pass at a bloke, so why not this once, with this gorgeous individual, standing among the rubble of the home he had hoped to share with the woman he still, clearly, loved?

He looked at his watch. 'Christ, we're very late now!'

'Oh, Jesus. Ten to three! If I miss the ferry, I'll miss the flight!' We ran back to the car. 'I can't miss the flight. My best friends are going to Goa tomorrow to get married! I have to see them off.'

Milenko took the winding roads at speed. I gripped my seat in full expectation of sailing over the edge, but it was either risk that or risk missing Steph and Killian's send-off, which would be a far slower death. So I let Milenko do his worst, and his worst was pretty hair-raising. His body language was suspiciously relaxed. Obviously, he often drove like this. Crazy Croat.

We reached the hotel five minutes after the ferry was due to leave. I fell from the car and tore down the pathway, hearing Milenko call, 'Run!' Ger and Clara were jumping up and down on the ferry. I skidded across the quay and leapt into the boat, which immediately revved up. Everyone clapped. I turned to see Milenko reaching the quayside. His sunglasses had slid down his nose. I called out thanks. He waved.

'That was a bit close,' said Ger. 'We had to beg them to hang on.'

I was catching my breath, muttering expletives.

'If you'd missed the ferry you'd have missed the flight!' she said.

'But we're fine,' I said, 'because we didn't miss it.' The figure on the quay turned and walked away through the arch and under the trees. I took another gasp of air. 'I just wish I had.'

7

I woke with a start. I had slept for a bit, had stopped my mind churning. It was nearly time to get up: three hours until the train. I had to get upright, pack my few belongings and make my way to the station.

I sent my father a text for when he woke, saying I would probably have no signal on the train. He came straight back to me. 'Morning.'

'Why aren't you asleep?' I asked.

'Dogs baying.'

'Let them out in the fields.'

'They'd kill sheep, you said.'

'So get leads.'

'Did do. Pulled my arms out of sockets. Four of them. One of me.'

'Are they in the house?'

'No. The old pig pen.'

'Good, but Steph will have a miscarriage if she hears. "They're pets," she'll say.'

'They're dogs. If they were meant to sit on sofas, God would have given them fingers to push the buttons on the remote.'

I laughed quietly, but tension was amassing in my forehead. Premenstrual, aggravated by . . . take your pick. A migraine was not an option. Not until the next day at least, and I figured it would hold off until I got to Steph. Stress-related migraines, from which I had suffered since my early twenties, often strike after the accumulated tensions have eased, so I should have a couple of days' grace, since there was more stress to come –

not least the long journey ahead. But the thermal soak made me nervous. Treatments that release tension often release migraines too, and coupled with the fact that I had recently stopped taking the pill, the omens were not good.

Nonetheless, I needed to get this long day under way; I struggled to push back the blanket.

The first four hours passed quickly enough. I was sitting by the door of the compartment, so had no countryside to distract me as we hurtled through Eastern Europe. *Eastern Europe*. I had never thought much about it, and I didn't think much about it then. My mind was like a salt-flat, barren and inhospitable.

Two local women sat opposite each other by the window, headscarves tied under their chins, chatting, chatting, almost without break. One had a whiny voice that pierced right into my head, the other talked through her food. Beside her, a blond, beefy man sat with his legs apart, reading magazines and scratching his crotch. The other seats were mercifully empty.

I had nothing to read. Not a thing. I had only my head to distract me, and there were many compartments inside it that could offer distraction. The last few days; the last few weeks; that moment, about ten days earlier, when Milenko and I had stood in our unpainted, unelectrified kitchen, and smiled at one another, thinking babies and school lunches and Holy Communions. The ache of remembering was somehow sweet; an exquisite pain.

At some point, I took to the corridor. There was no signal on the phone, so I could not call or text home and was more cut off than ever. It was unnerving. I was rattled, and hungry, which was not good. On days like these, I needed high blood-sugar to counteract a migraine, but I had come ill-prepared. Ágnes had given me a picnic, but the cold meat and dry rolls were, several hours later, unappetizing. There were snacks, tea and coffee on the train, but this was not the tourist season, so services were restricted. Locals had brought their own picnics. I began to crave, to *need* a hit of glucose, sucky sweets, and a bottle of sparkling water.

I managed to doze for a couple of hours. When I woke, I calculated the time we had travelled and the time yet to do. To my horror, we were barely beyond the half-way mark. I would have wept with boredom had I not been so wretchedly bored with crying, and short of tissues.

The feeling had already begun, on one side of my forehead: a mere pinprick, a flashing red light of warning when I tilted my head in a particular direction. The headache was at least a day out still; these warnings came in advance. But this was no warning. Within an hour I had reason to suspect that deep trouble lay ahead. I took a strong painkiller, which eased the budding ache, but made me feel sick. The rocking of the carriage, the stuffiness, being unable to eat what and when I should have, all contributed to a growing nausea. This nightmare trip was tilting towards horror.

I hurried to the lavatory and threw up the pills, but the migraine remained at bay for another few hours. In the late afternoon, it began to creep in with more resolve and I had to accept that it probably would not hold back, as I desperately needed it to. My impatience to reach Bucharest was no longer about Steph; it was about a hotel room, dark and quiet, and about stillness and privacy. I kept my eyes shut, my head against the headrest. Lying down, even if I could have, would have made me worse. Occasionally, I opened my eyes and noticed the grey winter light dimming, but the motion made me feel sick again, so I blotted it out, physically and mentally. This would not become full-blown! It couldn't; it simply could not. This would be a headache like any other. A normal person's headache. Not a migraine, when there were still hours to go.

Wishful thinking brought me further along, an hour at most. Beyond that, my determination to hold the headache at bay was losing grip. I took more serious medication – a migraine pill, even though it would knock me out, render me senseless in public – but nothing mattered, except preventing the pain taking over. I cursed Steph and Killian and the whole bloody lot of them for bringing me to this dreadful place. To be home was all I cared about, in my own bed with my father pressing a cold cloth on to the side of my face, and hearing the squeak of the stopper being twisted into the hot-water bottle that was about to come beneath the covers. I wished I was on Korčula, lying on the rocks that curved round the bay. I wished I was anywhere, anywhere at all, but on the train to Bucharest.

My mind became muzzy. I had to increase my efforts to ignore the nausea by blocking any thoughts of another lurching visit to the end of the carriage. Milenko knew my migraines. He saw them coming even before I did – the look in my eyes, he said, and a pallor announced them. But I had not had so many when I was with him. The Croatian climate helped, and the happiness, and the pill. I willed him to me, to come for me, and carry me to a place that didn't move and shake . . .

I fell to daydreaming a lot after the Croatian holiday. I sat at work booking holidays for people who wanted to go to Lanzarote and found myself trying to sell them Korčula and Dubrovnik. It was hard to fathom. Certainly, I had spent a lovely day with Milenko, but nothing had occurred that could by any definition be described as flirtation on his part. I had fancied him for all of three hours, but even that had waned in the cool Cork autumn. What lingered was something else – the easy conversation, the frankness, and his appealing no-bullshit approach. What he thought, he said. What he wanted to know, he asked. So often set upon by sycophants trying to get to my father, I found this refreshing, although it wasn't much good to me in someone who lived so far away.

We had exchanged email addresses, but I had emailed only once, thanking him for lunch.

His first email came a full month later. It was formal, as you'd expect from someone you'd met on holidays, and it delivered a bombshell. He was coming to Cork. I might have been flattered, were it not for the dates he had chosen: the bank holiday weekend at the end of October. His visit coincided with the Cork Jazz Festival.

'The nerve!' I said to Clara.

'Why?'

'The way he just announces he's coming.'

'He's as entitled to come to the jazz festival as anyone else.'

'He could have waited until he'd been invited,' I said.

'We *did* invite him. And it's hardly invitation-only.'

'But what are we going to do with him?'

'Oh, um,' she looked at the ceiling, finger to her chin, 'let me see, we could, er, take him to some jazz maybe?'

'But it's going to be so awkward. We barely know him.'

'*I* won't find it awkward,' she said. 'I look forward to seeing him.'

'He wants me to book him into a guesthouse. Where'll I put him?'

'Rollo's.'

'No way!'

'Come on, Kadie. The guy probably hasn't got much money and your dad's rattling around in that big house . . . He loves visitors, and he loves jazz. It'll be a perfect match.'

'Maybe he's after our money?'

Clara rolled her eyes. 'For once I don't think that's the

problem. It's the jazz festival, and that's exactly what's bugging you. You're narked because he isn't coming to see *you*.'

'I am not. He isn't my type. He's too disgustingly good-looking.' I pulled the wrapping off a packet of ski brochures. 'And well-dressed.'

'And polite.' Clara answered the phone. 'Carter Travel, good morning.'

'Not to mention the accent,' I muttered.

'Mr O'Leary, hello . . . Yes, your ticket is here, so you can collect it any time . . . That would be fine.' She hung up.

I looked at her. 'But apart from being too clean, too particular about his clothes, and a lousy driver –'

'And polite,' said Clara.

'And polite, what do we know about him? Nothing.'

'We know lots,' she said.

'For instance?'

She pulled out a piece of paper. 'Let's make a list.' I rolled over to her on my chair.

'Sexy,' she wrote.

'You're entitled to your view.'

'What else?'

'Owns a little boat called *Zizinica*,' I said.

'How do you spell that?'

'Oh, just write down "boat"!'

'Only remaining child,' she looked at me, 'therefore *tragic*. Charming father. Half owns some houses.'

'Which is better than no houses at all.'

'Roman Catholic – that's *really* important. When you get married, there'll be no hassle.'

I tapped the page. 'One broken engagement.'

She wrote that down, followed by 'Extraordinarily restrained. In fact, maybe,' Clara wrinkled her nose, 'a teensy-weensy bit *frigid*?'

128

'Owns a lot of white shirts . . . which show up his lovely dark skin.'

'Gorgeous hands, good legs.' Clara ran the pen along her chin.

'That's it,' I said. 'That's the sum of it. I won't have a stranger staying in my home.'

'Chill, will you? He's coming over for the jazz, not you.'

'Do you have to be quite so brutal?'

'Anyway, you don't want to get involved with someone who lives in Croatia. It's a non-starter, so show him some Irish hospitality and then find yourself a nice Irishman.'

'Actually, Dad brought home someone lovely last night.'

'*And* get over the older-man thing!'

'I didn't say he was older.'

'What age was he?'

'Late forties,' I mumbled.

'On mature reflection,' Clara said quickly, 'Croatia isn't so far away and Milenko *has* many strong points. He's kind of classy, *and only thirty!*' She slammed a file on to the desk. 'So you should brush up on your jazz.'

Cork airport was busy – bank-holiday busy. The terminal was heaving and a jazz band was playing in the arrivals hall to give enthusiasts a proper welcome. A crowd stood right in front of the doors at Arrivals, so I placed myself off to the side, slightly behind the barrier. I wanted to get a look at Milenko before he saw me.

In contrast to the soul-destroying obstacle course of heart-broken people at Departures, Arrivals was full of happy expectation. A large family had gathered with 'Welcome home, Granddad' balloons tied to the children's prams. Curiosity stung. Where had Granddad been that it warranted being met by the entire family? In prison? Antarctica?

I was suddenly pushed aside by a young girl reaching out for her arrival: an unkempt backpacker. They threw themselves round one another with such deep joy that it spread beyond them, and was almost palpable even in the people who weren't quite looking at them. The reunion was so intense, they couldn't even kiss. He stared ahead, as if blinded by the feel of her in his arms. When, finally, they let go, she touched his T-shirt with shaking fingers, as if afraid to believe he was there, then led him away through the crowd. I was tempted to follow. I wanted to see the kiss. There had to be one, but they disappeared into the swarm and kept it to themselves.

Milenko emerged, chin dipped and eyebrows raised in that slightly bashful way, less urbane than I remembered, almost like a student: young and uncertain. I grabbed his elbow.

'Hello!' Relief all over his face.

'Hi.'

It was awkward, all right. Really, really awkward. He stood, looking down at me. God, he was tall. Should we shake hands? Hug? I launched myself into the crowds. 'This way. It's absolutely manic.'

It was dark and cold outside. 'It's one of the busiest week-ends of the year for Cork airport,' I said, and prattled on in similar vein until we reached the car.

As we drove through the car-park, I saw them. The reunited couple. They were standing in the orange glow of street lighting, between a van and a car, kissing – kissing so hard that the vehicles beside them seemed to be melting. I slowed down.

'What is it?' Milenko asked, following my gaze.

'I saw him arrive.' I leant over the steering-wheel to get a better view. 'It'd make you wonder . . . Who is he? Where'd he come from? How long has it been since he's seen her?' I took my foot off the brake. 'And where did they meet, and how long can he stay?'

★

We spent a pleasant evening at home with my father, who kept things light and easy. He threw a few too many obscure jazz references at Milenko, who was a fan, not an expert, but he mostly kept up.

At the end of the meal, he said to my father, 'But you are more into rock?'

'I am.'

'I suppose everyone says you look just like . . . what's his name . . .'

'Well, that's because I –'

'Michael Bolton.'

'*Who?*'

'Michael Bolton, the American singer.'

'I know who you mean,' said Dad, looking rightly miffed, 'but, no, no one's ever told me that before.'

I sniggered. 'Don't worry, Dad. You're far better-looking than Michael Bolton. It's just a pity you don't have his talent. Cheese, Milenko?'

Over coffee by the fire, I curled up on the couch, tucked my legs under me, and relaxed. It would be all right. Milenko blended in. He was lovely. He was the unexpected. The long weekend would be fine.

It was fine, but it wasn't easy. On the Saturday morning, I woke up steeped to my chin in the turmoil of intense desire. There was no escaping it – I was mad for him, and he was there, in my house, and he probably didn't even fancy me. When he came into the kitchen looking tousled, and tucking in his denim shirt, I greeted him with a seductive smile and asked if he'd slept well. He said yes, as he hurried to the back door to help Dad bring in wood for the stove. That was good, I thought. Mannerly. After breakfast they went for a chummy walk together; I put my head in my hands at the kitchen table.

Clara rang to see how it was going. I had taken that Friday and Saturday off work to mind him. 'Not so much as a lingering look,' I grumbled. 'He's completely enamoured of Dad, of course.'

'You should be used to that.'

'But he doesn't even know who he is. Last night he told him he looked like –'

'Rollo King?'

'Michael Bolton. That poncey American with long blond hair!'

Clara snorted. 'So what's the plan?'

'Kinsale this afternoon, jazz tonight.'

After lunch, I took Milenko to Kinsale, where we walked round Charles Fort on the headland. I could think of nothing to say that did not sound like tourism-speak. I tried to relate the history of the place, something to do with a Spanish invasion, but I couldn't remember any details. Milenko asked lots of questions, which only served to highlight my ignorance. I sell sun holidays to the Irish; I have long since lost the habit of selling Ireland to tourists. My every other line was 'Erm, I'm not sure, really.'

'We come from similar countries,' he said. 'Invasions, Catholicism, civil war.'

Is this a line? A historical flirt?

'And this is such a beautiful country,' he went on, 'just like Croatia.'

'You'll feel at home in Croatia'?

Back at the car, Milenko gazed seaward over the roof. I turned to check out the panorama and make sure the Old Head of Kinsale was doing a reasonable job of competing with Pupnatska Luka. It was. The headlands were deep green, the sea glittering in autumn sunlight. When I turned round, Milenko was looking at me.

Our first jazz session was at the Firkin Crane that night. Babatunde Lea and his band were great, and his sax player was mesmerizing. He wore white robes, had dreadlocks to his knees, and wandered barefoot around the stage as if he were Jesus walking on rice-paper. During the interval, when we were helping ourselves to coffee in a circular theatre downstairs, someone bumped into me causing boiling coffee to splash all over my hand. Milenko swept into action: took the paper cup, grabbed a teacloth, rolled back my steaming hot shirtsleeve.

'Ouch, ouch, *ouch!*'

'Cold water,' he said, to the girl serving the drinks. 'Quick.' She led us to a kitchen, where he put my hand under the cold tap. The relief was tremendous.

'It is very painful?' His hands were all over my fingers. He splashed water along my wrist, rubbed the water gently into it. 'Stupid guy!'

He was busy with my hand, but I couldn't take my eyes from his face, and when he glanced up at me, neither of us looked away.

We returned to the theatre and took fresh coffee. Across the room, just inside the door, the Jesus figure was signing programmes.

'Isn't he beautiful?' I said to Milenko, who was leaning over his knees, his hands round his cup.

But then my father appeared. He was wearing a black suit with a black shirt and he looked the part. People immediately gravitated towards him and the saxophonist hurried over to shake his hand. A photographer took a photo of them together. Milenko looked over his shoulder at me, then back at Dad. Dad beamed over at us; I scowled.

'I asked you to be low-key this weekend!' I hissed at him, when we were pressed together in the mêlée going back into the auditorium. Milenko was out of earshot.

'You can't expect me to stay home all weekend. And he'll find out eventually.'

'Yeah, especially if you insist on doing celebrity turns like this! Honestly, Dad.'

'He probably hasn't even heard of Black Daffodil,' he said.

'He hasn't.'

'Really? Are you sure?'

In Patrick Street the next day, there were drummers at one end, a brass band at the other, and West Indian acrobats in the middle. In the Paul Street plaza, a Dutch band was playing Dixieland on their banjos and washboards. People gathered in a broad semi-circle; some danced. Milenko was enchanted by the way the whole city was turned over to the music. He loved the way the pavements exhaled jazz, how every session fed seamlessly into the next; how we could leave the opera house and walk round the corner to the next venue for sessions that went on into the early hours. I felt myself grow fond of him: the pleasure he derived from it all was as endearing as his appreciation.

When we got home that night, Rollo had two new CDs to share with Milenko. I left them to it and went to bed, but was woken a couple of hours later by a jamming session. Friends of Dad's had shown up, and I was concerned that Milenko was stuck down there, too polite to retire gracefully. I decided to rescue him, or at the very least tell them to wind up – it was four a.m. – and pulled on my dressing-gown. Milenko's bedroom door was open. Coming down the staircase, I heard Dad doing a turn on bass. Jack was on drums – Jack having had a few, from what I could tell, because it wasn't quite flowing as usual. I crossed the hall and went along the corridor to the large music room at the back. Milenko was there all right, and Dad was reaching towards him with a joint. Milenko took it, his foot still beating out that rhythm on the bass drum. He saw me as he inhaled.

I stood akimbo.

'Sorry,' said Dad, stopping. 'Did we wake you?'

I glowered at Milenko. 'And it wouldn't be the first time either.'

He did a drum roll, then raised his hands, smiling.

'He plays the bloody drums,' I told Clara, the following night in the Metropole, when there was a break in the session and we could actually hear one another speak.

'Cool. And very sexy. How's progress?'

'Non-existent. I've flirted till I've turned *myself* off!'

'Try jealousy,' said Clara, nodding at Killian, who was sitting down beside her with a pint. 'See if you get a reaction.'

I leant into Killian and said, 'Look at me as if you wish you'd never let me go.'

'But I do wish I'd never let you go.'

'I'm serious. I'm trying to nail the Croatian.'

Killian glanced at Milenko, who was at the bar. 'You already have nailed him. He can't take his eyes off you.'

I noticed it then, when Milenko returned. He sat fractionally closer to me than he had been. His thigh pressed into mine, and I could feel the warmth of his shoulder right by me. I wanted to be with him. In every possible sense of the word, I wanted to be with him, to be his, be a couple, be in bed, be together. But what was the point? A two-night stand wouldn't do it, not for me, not in this case, and he lived too far away for anything else. All I could do was drag myself through this weekend and, when he was gone, forget all about him and move straight on to someone local . . . One of those hundreds of guys who were beating down my door.

On the long drive home, along the dark, country roads, I could feel Milenko leaning slightly sideways in his seat, watching me while I drove. When I pulled up in front of Dad's, we sat for a moment. That was his chance – I gave it to him, too frisky to let the opportunity pass. Neither of us spoke. His hand hovered over the door handle. We stared ahead. Then, with a heavy sigh, he opened the door and got out.

Inside, Dad got us drinks, then made a strategic retreat. He need not have bothered. We sat on the couch by the fire, talking, but it was strained, and Milenko went to bed, I was sure, as frustrated as I did.

The Monday was long. We went for a walk round the lake, where I showed him my childhood haunts. My hands hung by my sides, in case he wanted to take one, but he kept his buried in his pockets. He kept looking at me with those shifting eyes as if trying to say something I could not interpret.

'This is a very special place to you,' he said, when we were sitting on a rock by the water.

'Very. But I have another rock, on Sheep's Head, further west. That's really my spot, more so than here. I'll take you there some time.' It was out before I could stop it.

His jaw moved about. Again, we made significant eye-contact, the significance of which was lost on me. He dipped his head to the side in an increasingly familiar and almost intimate way, but I had no idea what all these mannerisms meant.

We went to hear Don Baker do his thing with his harmonica in a bar in town that afternoon. Once or twice Milenko smiled, a bashful little smile that seemed to be admitting he knew he had not met my expectations. We sat, huddled round a small table, with little to say. I couldn't wait to get rid of him.

On the way to the airport, he was very excited, giddy almost. And why wouldn't he be? He'd had a good time and was going home, probably to dozens of gorgeous Croatian women. I treated him like a colleague, a tourism hack. 'Well, I think we've shown you the best of Cork. Be sure to tell your friends about us.'

'Agh!' he said, rubbishing my formality. 'Thank you, Kadie. It has been fantastic.'

Glad someone enjoyed it.

'And your father, he is amazing.'

'Yeah. Good old Michael Bolton.'

'He's a very . . . humble man.'

'As indeed Michael Bolton should be.'

'Perhaps,' he said, 'but Rollo has much to be proud of.'

'Like what? Me?' *Oops, flirting again.*

He shrugged. 'To be in such a group and to give it up to look after his child . . . He is a very impressive person.'

'What? You mean . . . What do you mean?'

He made a face. 'We are not in the dark ages in Croatia. We know Black Daffodil, their music.'

'But . . . why didn't you say anything?'

'It's not my business.'

'Well,' I said. 'People don't usually see it that way. They want the autograph, the introduction.'

'He was very kind to me.'

I glanced at him. 'Thanks for not making a big deal of it. It can be difficult.'

'I understand that.'

I smiled. 'It was lovely to see you again.'

He nodded, as if he agreed that, yes, it must indeed have been nice for me to see him again.

The man was exasperating. I could not read him at all. Pulling up in front of the terminal, I told him to check in while I got rid of the car.

'No. I'll come with you.'

We found a space at the far end of the car-park, and were making our way towards the terminal, weaving between cars, when Milenko stopped and looked around.

'What is it?'

He shook his head and walked on, but he kept looking about, at the airport and the exit and even at the ground.

'Have you lost something?'

'Why?'

I strode on, never so eager to despatch someone through Departures, such was the mix of frustration and irritation.

'Here,' he said suddenly.

I stopped between two cars. 'What?'

He took my elbow and, with a gentle yank, pulled me towards him and kissed me. The cars dissolved.

'He met her on holiday. He came a long way. And it's been too long since he saw her,' he said, and kissed me again.

Sick. Feeling sick, so sick, push it away.

The terminal was jam-packed with departing jazz fans.

Push. Hold it back.

At the departure gate, Milenko stood against me, his eyes roving around, then settling on me.

'Why now?' I asked.

No good . . .

'I didn't want you to think I was . . .' he lifted his shoulders '. . . insincere.'

Oh, God, the pain.

Back in Romania, in the carriage, in the pain, the memory of that high moment, of that beginning, ceased to be a distraction and became instead like a shot of despair. There had been some changes in the compartment. Through half-opened eyes, I noticed a tourist, a young man, sitting diagonally across from me. The two women were still gabbing. Oh, for silence. I wanted to be home, in so far as I wanted to be anywhere, because there were only two places – pain and without pain.

It was too late. I'd left it too late. The pill had not taken effect and the nausea was acute. It had vanquished my attempts to stomp it down. It had won the battle and was rising in my gorge. Bucharest had to be another five hours away yet. What were my options? *Christ*, I thought, *what am I going to do?*

I went to the lavatory and threw up. Nothing came, except

bile, because there was nothing in my stomach. The convulsions made my head throb even more violently. At least the lavatory was clean. Pristine, in fact. I sat on the floor by the bowl, holding my head, gasping and panting and wanting to die. For at least half an hour I stayed there, retching at intervals. Then I felt my way back to my seat. As I sat down, I registered the concern of the tourist, a fleeting frown as he caught my eye when I stepped back into the compartment. The two women were too engaged to notice my blotchy face and dreadful demeanour. There was no comfortable way to hold my head; every slight movement made it worse. A sharp, blinding white light pierced my eyeballs and the nausea rose again as the train rattled on, shaking me, rocking, rocking, banging me from side to side to side.

I tried to curl up, sat rigidly upright, leant over my knees, and I know that I groaned out loud. I went to be sick again, and struggled back to my seat, each time to the increasing concern of the foreigner and the groin-scratching blond man. I zoned out for a while, then started squirming around.

'Can I get you something?' said a voice.

I didn't open my eyes. 'Make it stop. Make the train stop moving.'

'Tea, maybe?'

Oh, God. I had to dash. The thought of anything passing my gullet . . . I pushed my way to the toilet and collapsed again on the ground, retching, retching, trying to vomit the ache into the bowl and flush it away. This time my head was going to explode and I was definitely going to die and it couldn't happen soon enough.

I don't know how long I'd been there when there was a hesitant knock on the door, which opened at the touch. I hadn't locked it.

'Migraine,' I said, to his boots.

'Can you take something for it? A painkiller?'

He had done it again. I retched into the bowl.

'There must be something?'

The brakes began to squeal, piercing, stabbing my head. The train slowed. 'Get me off,' I said to the stranger. 'Just get me off this thing.'

I felt him leaning into the cubicle and reaching down for me.

8

I was drifting around the airport car-park, not quite looking
for my car, when my phone beeped. A text from Milenko.
'When are you coming to Korčula?'

I leant against someone's car, smiling, and replied, 'Why
would I want to go to Korčula?'

'Because I am falling in love with you.'

That was the last I heard from him for three months.

9

In the blue room with the raised alcove, I dragged myself into an upright position. I had to find the stranger, thank him. And I had to pee. There was no *en suite*. What kind of hotel didn't have *en-suite* bathrooms? After a few minutes sitting up, the pain shifted to the bearable drone of post-acute. I stood up and opened the door.

There was a bathroom across the hall. After using the loo, I stood at the top of the stairs. I had to catch up with the guy. Such abuse he'd taken after helping me. But what had he been doing in my room? And where exactly were we?

He had maybe five minutes on me, and the benefit of pain-free, normally paced movement. I made my way gingerly round a bend in the stairs, which led into a large sitting room. A couch curved round the wall, facing a television. This was no hotel. It was a home. Where had he brought me?

There was another door diagonally across the room. Every step towards it hurt. Through the soles of my feet, up my leg and past my torso, the carpet assailed my head. Acupressure. I remembered someone going on about acupressure, treating me . . . Had I been treated? The door led into a kitchen – a no-frills, wooden-unit type kitchen. Voices came from another room, but I had to sit down. I perched on the edge of the couch by the kitchen door.

'Oh, God! Dad!' He would be so worried. I tiptoed across the room and went back upstairs, where I grabbed my phone.

'Kadie!'

'Dad.'

'We've been frantic. What's happening? We thought Eastern Europe had swallowed the both of you up.'

'I got a migraine.'

'Oh, my love. Are you okay?'

'Getting there.'

'Inevitable, I suppose.'

'Yeah.'

'What about Steph? Is she all right?'

'Dad – I haven't even got there yet.'

'Where?'

'Bucharest. At least, I don't think that's where I am.' I went to the window. Red roofs huddled together and, beyond, snowy hills covered with black trees. Bright sky. Not a city, anyway.

'So where *are* you?'

'I don't actually know.'

'How do you mean, you don't know?'

'I think I'm in someone's house. I was on the train and the head got out of control, and some guy helped me off and I woke up here.'

'Some man has taken you to his house? Kadie . . .'

'It's okay. He's just a backpacker or something.' I glanced at the mattress on the floor, the sheets askew. Maria. A Maria had met us. 'He was decent to me, I think, but he's gone and . . .' I lay down, weary. I needed food. 'Has anyone heard from Steph?'

'Nothing. You're the only one she's talking to.'

'My mobile's going to go. I'm running out of battery.'

'Have you a charger?'

'Yeah, but no adaptor.'

'Kade, would you please find out where you are and text me the number? Then I can ring you.'

'Yeah, but I'm not exactly Speedy Gonzales at the moment. And I've got to find the guy who brought me here. I treated him like a thug. I can't let him leave without apologizing to him.'

'Be careful.'

''Bye, Dad.' It was coming back to me. There was a woman on the platform. Maria. I had thrown up and she had come over and the two of them had helped me to a seat, where she insisted on pressing between my thumb and forefinger. Acupressure, she kept saying, cures migraine. *No*, I was thinking, *no, leave me alone, don't touch me*, but she pressed and pressed and the nausea lifted enough for me to get out of the station without retching again. She put us in a taxi. I remembered now, falling into this bed – alone at last, just me and the headache, like a saw through my brain. Then I'd slept, badly, until the early hours when I went into a coma-like sleep, from which I had emerged so confused.

My head was spinning. I needed to eat, but it's hard after a migraine and I yearned for stuff I wouldn't be able to get: Marmite, fig-roll biscuits. Time to tackle that kitchen and find a body, anybody, and some food.

I made my way down the shiny wooden steps again. A woman in an apron appeared in the doorway of the kitchen. 'Ah!' she exclaimed.

I aimed for the couch and sat.

'You okay?' This didn't look like Maria. Maria, I felt, would be instantly recognizable.

'Yes, thank you.'

'Very sick.' She made a lot of gestures to indicate what had come in the door the night before.

'Yes.'

'You want tea?'

'Oh, yes, please. And I need to eat.' I also gestured.

She waved towards the stairs. 'I come.'

I could have kissed her slippered feet. 'Em, I came yesterday with someone . . . Do you know where he is?'

'Gone,' she said cheerfully.

'Is he coming back?'

She had gone into an annexe off the kitchen where there was a kettle and a cooker. 'Fruit tea?' she called.

God, no. Eugh. 'Oh, no. Just . . .'

'Black?'

'Please.'

'Go bed. I come.'

'Sorry, but . . . where am I? Where is this place?'

'Brasov!'

'Thank you.' Excellent. I was in Brasov. Wherever the hell that was.

I went back to the room and lay down. I needed a shower. My clothes were filthy. I had managed not to vomit on them, but I'd run out of clean shirts. I wanted to clean up, buy stuff, wear fresh clothes.

There was a rap on the door. I leant over, opened it, and saw boots, not slippers. My roommate. 'Breakfast,' he said, standing tentatively in the doorway.

'Oh, hello.' I sat up too quickly. 'I'm so sorry.'

He was patently relieved. 'That's okay. Can I come in?'

'Yes, please. I didn't mean to be horrible earlier.'

He put down the tray – a mug with teabag, a jug of milk and two pieces of toast with butter and jam. Perfect. 'I couldn't remember anything when I woke up,' I rushed on, 'and, well, I got a fright when I saw you there.'

'Sweet as.'

I waited. Then said, 'Sweet as what?'

'Huh? You know, sweet as. That's fine. No worries.'

'But you missed your train. I didn't mean for you to get off.'

'Was I supposed to chuck you in a heap on the platform?'

I smiled. 'More or less. I would have been perfectly happy to die there, you know.'

'That's cool. I was getting off here anyway. Supposed to be a nice little town, is Brasov.' He glanced out. 'Dracula's castle is near here.'

'But where are we? Is this someone's home?'

'No, it's a hostel. Run by some English guys.'

'I remember someone called Maria at the station. Or did I dream her up?'

'No. This is her place too. She's famous around here. She meets backpackers off the train and drags them to her hostels. I'd read about her in the *Lonely Planet* – she sounded really full-on, so I reckoned I'd give her a wide berth, but when she swooped last night, boy, was I glad to see her.'

'I must thank her.'

He was quite young – younger than my twenty-nine years, anyway – and he had scrappy hair, bleached either by the sun or an expert or both. He was travelling rough, light, alone, and I would love him for ever for getting me off that train.

'I'll leave you to your breakfast.' He opened the door. 'Can I get you anything else?'

'I'm fine, thanks. Once I've eaten I'll pop out and get a few things.'

'Whoa. Wait a minute. You shouldn't be popping anywhere.'

'No, really. I'm okay. So much better, thanks to you.'

'What do you need?'

'I . . . Glucose. Sucky sweets – you know, barley sugar or glucose, or even chocolate. Something to get my blood-sugar up.'

'I thought chocolate *caused* migraine.'

'It can, but it doesn't cause mine, and I'm something of an oddity when it comes to craving it after the event, but it gives me a lift.'

'Any particular type of chocolate?'

I was too weak to argue. 'Preferably something with toffee. Like a Mars bar. But are you sure?'

'Sweet as.'

After he'd left, I lay back, nibbling the toast, insanely grateful, and rang Dad with an update – I had found my knight; he was very kind; getting me chocolate in Transylvania.

'Where's he from?'

'I'm not sure. South African or Australian, or mixed up at any rate. In fact . . . I don't even know his name.'

'Well, he's a good man in my book.'

'I know. I was lucky, but this trip is turning into a nightmare, Dad.'

He said nothing. He was probably pretty desperate, knowing I was wherever I was, and sick.

'But I'll be all right,' I hurried on. 'Don't worry. The worst is over. And I must be near Bucharest. What's happening there?'

'Chaos. A load of people showed up for the removal – but no removal. No casket. No Killian. I tell you, there's some great material for good songs going on here.'

'*Dad.* Are they all still there?'

'The long-distance people have stayed, but people from Dublin and round abouts have gone back. Deirdre's holding tight in Stockholm. She's missing her kids something awful, but she won't leave Killian. Everyone has their hopes pinned on you. You have to get Steph back here, Kadie. These people can't hold on much longer.'

Half an hour later, my backpacker returned, holding several bars of plain milk chocolate like a fan and a bag of garish multi-coloured jellies. It was a beautiful sight. The jellies, I mean.

'This is all I could find.'

I grabbed the bag and took out a jelly. 'Fantastic! That's so good of you. Really, you have no idea. How much do I owe you?'

'Aw, that's all right. You can hook me up later.'

'Thanks. I owe you so much, and I don't even know your name.'

He held out his hand. 'Daniel Blewitt.'

'Kadie Kingston.' *Blew It?*

'Nice to meet you . . . Is that kd as in kd lang?'

'No. Kadie as in Sadie with a *K* and Katie with a *d*. My parents couldn't decide whether to call me Sadie or Katie, so they compromised.' I chewed the jelly – it cleared the rancid taste in my mouth – and moaned. 'This is the second time in twenty-four hours that you've saved my life.'

He reached into his jacket and took out a bottle of mineral water. 'I got this too.'

'Oh, great! You get so dehydrated with a migraine.'

'Not surprising with all that chucking up. Anyway, I've got a cup of tea on the go downstairs, so . . .'

'Bring it up here. Please, Daniel. You've so much to tell me.'

He came back with a mug, took the chair from the raised alcove and sat near the window.

'Tell me what happened,' I said. 'I have a clear recollection of a lavatory bowl and your boots, and the rest is coming back to me in fuzzy bits and pieces. Was it horrible?'

'It was fine. Some people helped me get you and our stuff off the train.'

'I'll bet those two women didn't bat an eyelid.'

'Not a blink. Anyway, you sort of went into a fade and that's when Maria approached. She was a godsend.' *Irish. Was that a hint of an Irish accent?* 'She put us in a friend's taxi and he brought us here. You more or less passed out straight away.'

'But . . .'

'Yeah?'

'Why . . .' I munched on some chocolate. I'd got off to a bad start and didn't know how to finish it. He sat, his knees jigging about, waiting for me to continue. 'Why did you sleep in here?'

He blushed. Then I did. 'That was Maria,' he said. 'She was bossing everyone about and made them bring up a mattress, because . . .'

'Because what?'

'She said I shouldn't sleep on the bed when you were so ill, so I explained we weren't together and she waved that off, saying I'd better stay in here anyway, in case something happened during the night. She said people can get strokes with really bad migraines, and you were pretty sick, so . . . She's not a woman you can really argue with.'

'I got that feeling.'

'Anyway, the only other room up here is taken and the dorms are downstairs – it's a bit of a warren – and if you'd woken up, you wouldn't have known where the hell you were. But I'm sorry for scaring you earlier.'

If he only knew . . . 'I probably scared you more. I'm a bit nervy at the moment.'

He flashed a grin. 'I'm kinda glad you didn't die on me.'

It must have been terrifying for him, in a strange town in the middle of the night, with some woman seriously ill in the bed. 'Where are you from?'

'Auckland.'

'Oh. I was trying to place your accent. You don't sound totally Kiwi.'

'I'm half Irish. My mother sounds like she left Dublin yesterday, and I lived there myself for fourteen months a few years ago. Gotta look after our own, right?'

'But you didn't know I was Irish.'

'Aw, I did. When I heard you say, "Feck this," as you rushed for the bog, I'd a pretty good idea where you were from.'

I smiled. 'So you're one of us.'

'Half, anyway.'

'And your dad?'

'Oh, you know, a Kiwi, yeah. How's the chocolate going?'

'Coursing through my bloodstream. What brings you to Romania in the dead of winter?'

Daniel got up and walked about with his fingers in his hip pockets. 'Just travelling. I did Western Europe last time, so I wanted to come a bit more to the east.'

'But at such a time of year?'

'Cheaper. And not too many bloody tourists.' There was something sad in him, I thought. 'What about you?' he asked.

'I'm meeting a friend in Bucharest. In fact, I absolutely have to get there today. Are there many trains?'

He held out his hand. 'But . . . look at you. You can't travel.'

'I have to. And it can't be far, can it? Another two hours or something?'

'About that.'

'So I'll get some fresh air, have a rest, and with a bit of luck, I'll be fit to move this evening.'

He looked at me doubtfully, then said, 'I'll come with you.'

I tried to say, no, no, don't be ridiculous, there's no need, but in truth, there *was* a need. I was weak, and nervous about getting on a train again. If he was fool enough to offer, I'd be a worse fool for refusing. 'But Dracula's castle,' I said.

'I'll do that this afternoon.'

For a moment, neither of us spoke.

'You didn't half give me a fright,' he said. 'During the night, I thought you'd stopped breathing.'

'Sainthood is the only thing for you, Daniel Blewitt.'

★

Daniel went in search of train times while I had a shower, the effect of which was undermined when I had to get into dirty clothes afterwards. But it was only for a few hours. I could get my clothes laundered in Bucharest.

We agreed on a train at seven thirty, so that I would have time to recuperate and Daniel time to sightsee. On the grounds that a good blast of Carpathian mountain air could only do me good, we went into town for a wander. It was bright and sunny; crisp. Snow-covered hills, their trees bare and black, loomed behind the buildings in the main square. It was a pretty little place, though an industrial city encircled the old town.

'A bear was shot here a few months back,' said Daniel. 'They thought he had rabies. He killed a couple of people.'

I stopped in my tracks. 'There are rabid bears here?'

'He wasn't rabid. Turns out someone offered him a bit of steak they were cooking on a barbie and the fork burnt him. He lost it. Went on a rampage.'

A woman marched past us in a purple suit and a black hat with a feather sticking out of it. 'Straight out of *The Sound of Music*,' I muttered. My legs were wobbly, so I stopped to rest for a moment on a bench and watched children driving around in little motorized cars. When we went on, Daniel took my elbow and supported me the length of a shopping street as if I was his ailing mother. I was desperate for more clothes, but unless they jumped out on to the pavement in front of me, I wasn't going looking for them. 'You're very patient,' I said, 'but you really should be getting on to Dracula's.'

'Let's have a coffee first.'

In a café opposite the Black Church, which was famous, Daniel assured me, looking up from his *Lonely Planet* guide, he had lunch and I had tea and a plain pastry. He told me he was a professional sailor, currently working in Sydney on a private yacht, and that he was coming to the end of a tour that had taken him from Denmark over to Estonia, through Latvia and Hungary. He was now heading to Istanbul, via Bucharest, to pick up his flight home. 'It's been great. You get a totally different look at Europe in the winter.'

A long thin woman smoking a long thin cigarette sat at the window table with an espresso. Everything about her was just so. I envied her the neatness, and the clean clothes.

'So why the rush to get to Bucharest?' Daniel asked.

'You wouldn't believe me if I told you.'

'Yeah? Why not?'

'Because last week I was decorating a house in Croatia,' I began. 'On Sunday I was back home in Cork. On Monday my best friend was killed in Stockholm and on Tuesday I went there to get him with his wife. On Thursday she ran away to Bucharest, and on Friday I followed, except I thought she'd gone to Budapest, so I ended up in the wrong country.'

He had stopped chewing. 'Come again?'

'Now you know what gave me this bloody migraine.'

'Your friend was killed? That's terrible.'

I told him about Killian and Steph, but not about me.

'So you were going to meet her when you got sick?'

'Yeah.'

'Does she know you've been delayed?'

'She doesn't even know I'm coming, so the sooner I get there the better.'

I slept that afternoon; Daniel went to Bran Castle. He tried, but failed, to find an adaptor so that I could recharge Deirdre's phone. Dad got hold of me on the landline before we left for the station. Clara had found a hotel on Lake Pantelimon called the Lebada; it was almost certainly the one Steph had been speaking from – a château-cum-monastery overlooking the lake. He gave me the details and said everyone was relieved that I would be with Steph that night, however late.

I was not recovering as normal. My head was clear, but my body shattered. I was limp and listless. At the station, a big box of a building with no seats in the concourse, I sat on the marble stairs near an old man who was sound asleep, while Daniel negotiated the ticket office. The prospect of getting back on a train filled me with anxiety – the smell, the motion, the crowded seats. Whichever way I turned, I thought I could smell vomit.

Tickets in hand, Daniel found a waiting room upstairs. It was dim, barely lit, with rows of plastic seats. The women all had their heads covered, mostly with scarves, the men wore caps or hats, and the air was thick with smoke.

'How was Dracula's place?' I asked Daniel.

'Like something out of *The Sleeping Beauty*. Not a bit Gothic.'

'Bram Stoker said that place had nothing to do with *his* Dracula.'

'That's not stopping the tourists. It was packed.'

A young couple near us were snogging with healthy enthusiasm.

'I can't stick this smoke,' I said.

So we hung around the concourse until the Bucharest train pulled in, and although Daniel hurried up and down the platform in the cold night air, he couldn't find our carriage. It wasn't there.

'Of course it's there,' I said. 'You must be misreading the tickets!'

'I'm not.'

'Maybe we're on the wrong platform?'

More scurrying. I dreaded to think how I might have managed alone, but that didn't stop me remonstrating with Daniel, who, in a bare twenty-four hours, had become my travelling companion and friend and was therefore open to abuse.

Our carriage, it transpired, had yet to be hooked up to the rest of the train, so I stood in the cold, holding myself together, while the carriage backed towards us. A sleeper for Prague pulled in on the platform opposite; I looked into the compartments and saw young people eating and laughing and standing about in huddles. Not for the first time that week, I tried to propel myself into someone else's journey.

Our own compartment was empty. Daniel turned off the harsh overhead light and sat opposite me. His attentiveness allowed me to rest, listening to Eric Clapton's 'I Shot The Sheriff' on the sound system.

'We're here,' said Daniel.

'Where?'

'Bucharest.'

'What?'

'You slept all the way.'

He insisted on seeing me to Steph's hotel, and it was only when we sat into the taxi that my heart began to rush at the prospect of surprising her, *seeing* her. We made our way along wide boulevards, lined with dark Communist-era apartment blocks that looked as if they would topple over if anyone so much as leaned against them to have a fag. Daniel pointed at a car, low on its axle, filled to the roof with green cabbages, but my eye was drawn to two teenage girls jumping up and down beside a tram, waving a mobile phone at their friends within.

The hotel driveway was lined with cars. We pulled up beside a fountain in front of a very grand building, lit up like a power station. A broad set of white marble steps, with green carpet, led to the entrance.

'Good luck,' said Daniel, peering out at it.

'Aren't you coming in?'

'You kidding? This place is way out of my league.'

'Be my guest, then. Please. It's the very least I can do. It's nearly eleven – way too late to be looking for a hostel. Stay here with us. My treat.'

'No way.'

'Or rather,' I added quickly, 'my father's treat. He's loaded.'

'With all due respect, you don't look any better off than I am.'

'Listen, I have to go to Steph. Please come in. We can argue later. Just let me see Steph and then we can say goodbye properly.'

He shuffled across the seat. 'You can buy me a drink, I suppose.'

'Thanks.'

The lobby was as opulent as the entrance – all white and bright and with a grand marble staircase in the centre. As we stepped in, a little flower-girl in a big white dress ran out of a function room on the left, tripped on a rug, and slid past cus on her belly along the marble floor, watching us as she went by.

The receptionist was cheerful. 'Good evening.'

'Hi, em . . . We'd like to check in, but I'm also looking for a friend of mine who's staying here. Stephanie Enright?'

He went through his books. 'Twin bed or double?'

'Oh, no, not together –'

'Kadie, I'm not staying here.'

'Not now, Daniel. If you could tell me which room my friend is in, I'd like to surprise her.' My hands were shaking.

He frowned. 'Her name?'

'Stephanie Enright.'

'Ah yes,' he said, nodding, 'but Mrs Enright left this morning.'

Daniel had been watching the belly-flopped flower-girl. Now he turned to me. 'What was that?'

'Your friend has left,' the receptionist reiterated.

'No,' I said.

'Yes,' he said, with affronted emphasis. 'Today.'

'But where's she gone?'

'She has left the hotel, madam.'

I thumped the desk. 'Bugger!'

'You should have told her you were coming,' Daniel said tunefully.

'Damn. She must have gone home. She said she only needed a few days.'

'I suppose.'

'Could you please find out where she went?' I said to the receptionist. 'It's very important. Did she leave for the airport and, if so, where was she flying to?'

'This is not –'

'Look,' I said firmly. 'Her husband has just died and she's expecting a baby. Her family in Ireland need to find her!'

He picked up a phone. 'I will ask the concierge.'

'Well, this was totally bloody stupid,' I said to Daniel, 'coming here! I could have saved myself a lot of trouble. And you.'

'Maybe if you'd told her you were coming . . .'

The receptionist put down the telephone. 'Mrs Enright took a taxi to the airport.'

I turned to Daniel, hand on hip. 'She's bloody well gone home!'

'I reckon so.'

'So you wish to check in?' the receptionist asked.

I was too stunned to respond.

'Just one single,' Daniel said to him, and then to me, 'There's a hostel in town –'

'Oh, Daniel, don't be tiresome! It's late. You'll never find it at this time of night, and I have to find Steph. Please don't complicate things.'

'Sorry, but I'm not a charity case.'

'The point is that *you*'ve been incredibly charitable to me, so please let me repay you by putting you up for one night, which will save me having to track you down in the morning. I don't have the head for this now.'

'Your dad's really loaded?'

'Oh, it's disgusting,' I said, 'his money.'

He glanced round again, clearly tempted, but shook his head. 'Sorry.'

'Oh, whatever! At least come up with me while I find out what's going on. I could kill Steph, I really could. I mean, if she was going to take off again, why did she give me all that guff about this being the best place . . .'

The receptionist handed over my key and pointed us towards the lift. We squashed in. 'Steph was telling me about this lift,' I said, 'only the other day.'

In my room on the second floor, I dived for the phone.

'Hello, sweetness,' Dad said, when he picked up. 'You arrived okay?'

'Where's Steph?'

'Huh?'

'She isn't here. She checked out. Please tell me someone knows where she is!'

'Oh, for fuck's sake.'

'Has anyone heard anything?'

'Not so far as I know. Everyone's been waiting to hear from you.'

'Look, my mobile is out. Can you text her on yours – do you have her number?'

'Yeah, but what'll I say?'

'Em . . . "Kadie's phone is down . . ." Wait.' I couldn't make my brain work. 'The thing is, she'd be there by now if she'd gone home, wouldn't she?'

'Depends. Look, I'm sure she's fine. She's obviously on her way. But what about you? How's your head?'

'I'd be fine if I knew where Steph was!'

'I'll call a few people and get back to you.'

I gave him the hotel number, then paced. 'Please, *please*, make her turn up!' *Killian, cold, icy, in that drawer. My beloved.* 'I mean, she *must* be heading home. It stands to reason. Unless . . . she said she'd handle things, for Killian, so maybe she's gone back to Stockholm.'

Daniel was on his hunkers by the fridge, a bottle of juice in his hand. 'You'll get another headache if you're not careful.'

When Dad called, he said the magic words. 'She's heading back.'

'Alleluia!'

'Her mum spoke to her earlier. Apparently Steph said she'd had a rest and was feeling much clearer about things. She must have stopped over somewhere.'

'What about Killian?'

'I'm not sure, but Angela said she'd get straight on to his mum. God, Angela can be vague. She was all flighty, going, "Oh, yes, yes, she's on her way," as if Steph had missed a bus. I felt like saying, "Well, thanks a heap for telling us when *my* daughter's out there looking for her!" These people aren't zoned in at all.'

'Angela's for the birds, you know that.'

'Yeah, well, I don't much care at this point. I'll get Clara to sort out flights for you first thing tomorrow. What did you do with the Kiwi?'

'He's here. He came to the hotel with me.'

'Really? That's very kind of him. Put him on, will you?'

I held the phone out to Daniel. 'My father wants to talk to you.'

He grimaced, but took it. 'Er, hello?'

I went into the bathroom to draw a bath. If my clothes couldn't be clean, I at least could be.

Daniel came to the door.

'What did he want?' I said, looking over my shoulder. 'To tell you not to take advantage of my virtue?'

'He didn't mention your virtue. He asked very nicely if I could hang about until you leave . . . as his guest.'

'Poor Dad. He loses it when I get migraines.'

'At this rate, I might as well go all the way to Ireland with you.'

I held his eye. 'You'd be so welcome.'

'Nah.' He glanced at my bath. 'Gotta get home myself.' And there it was again. The something else. A sadness that pushed out at odd moments.

'So I don't suppose he persuaded you to stay here?' I leant over the bath.

'Actually, he's slightly more persuasive than you are.'

'*Good*. I'd really hate to be stuck out here on my own.'

'If you'd said that in the first place instead of all that "I'm-so-grateful" stuff . . .'

'I didn't want to seem too pathetic.'

'What business is your dad in?'

'Music.'

He dropped the corners of his mouth. 'There's money in that, all right. I'll go check in. See you in the morning.'

'Right,' I said, sliding into the short bath a few minutes later. 'Thus far and no further. I'm going home,' I cooed out loud. 'Thanks be to Jayzuz!'

It had been over twenty-four hours since I had given Milenko more than a fleeting thought. In that time, there had been a smidgen of healing. It didn't feel so raw. I might have to thank Steph for getting me through the painful early days of lost love. Or perhaps I should thank Killian for dying. 'Stupid idiot!' I said out loud. 'What were you thinking?'

He was sitting on the closed loo; there wasn't room on the narrow, stubby bath. 'Like I did it deliberately,' he said.

'I could be at home now, crying on your shoulder and

utterly convinced that absolutely nothing could ever be as bad as losing Milenko.'

'And I could still be alive.'

Lake Pantelimon was frozen. When I got up in the early light and pushed back the heavy yellow curtains, there was a curious silver sheen on the lake. Ice; thin ice.

I met Daniel on the landing. We went down either side of the grand staircase that curved round the outer wall, met in the middle, then hugged the wall again on either side, before meeting again as it descended into the lobby. It was only a matter of time before Daniel tried to slide down the marble banister.

The hotel was quiet, in spite of the wedding the night before, and breakfast was pretty miserable. I kept looking at my watch, waiting for Clara to get to work. It would be at least another hour, so we went down to the water's edge and sat on a stone bench near a willow tree. The tips of its branches lay on the iced water. 'I've got to get my phone charged. Being without it is driving me mad. Don't you have one?'

'Yeah, but I came away to get away, you know? If you bring a phone, everyone's still in your ear. You can't escape.'

Clara, when I got hold of her, was in the process of booking my return, via Prague, the next day. 'It's the easiest way. Prague–Cork. The flight leaves Bucharest at three and you'll be home by nine our time.'

'Wasn't there anything today, through London?'

'London to Cork is booked out. It's just one more night, Kadie.'

'And what am I supposed to do here for another twenty-four hours?'

Daniel, the tourist, had the answer to that. First, we had to see Ceauşescu's People's Palace; then he wanted to check out Piata Universitatii, 'where a thousand students were mown down at the start of the revolution. And I must eat bear,' he added. 'I can't leave Romania without eating bear.'

What else was I to do? Sit around watching Romanian television? We caught a taxi into town, past block after block of blackened Communist housing, some crumbling, some a little sturdier; all ugly. Many of the balconies had been glassed in – a good idea in winter, but surely stifling in summer. Or did the glass keep out mosquitoes? After the clarity and freshness of gracious Stockholm, it was salutary to imagine the millions who lived in this grey place. The trams were crowded, the air thick with pollution, and we saw another car crammed to the roof with cabbages, which was pulling a trailer, also full of cabbages.

Then to Ceauşescu's folly: a great white wedding-cake of a structure at the end of an upmarket boulevard – a monument to ego. Everything was outsize, the doors, the carpets, chandeliers and corridors, everything except for the steps. Ceauşescu was only little, the guide explained, so the great marble staircases had had to be torn down three times and rebuilt with lower steps, so his little legs wouldn't tire going up them.

'This is the second biggest building in the world, after the Pentagon,' she told us, when we stood out on the grand balcony, looking down the boulevard of fountains and trees (several strategic metres longer than the Champs-Élysées). I was fed up. Steph was almost back in Cork and I was stranded in Romania, cut off, out of the loop, and standing on the balcony of the most enormous piece of insanity ever built.

After a long stroll down the boulevard, we ambled into an older part of town and chanced upon a market. Sausages and bread were being grilled on open flames. Gypsy girls pushed sprigs of herbs into our faces. One even put some in Daniel's pocket, then pointed towards the sausages. He declined the offer.

'This place has been hit twice by earthquakes,' he said to

me. 'What chances, do you reckon, of anyone in those blocks surviving another?'

'What do you hope to gain from this?' I asked him. 'Rushing around. You can't learn about a place in a day.'

'Two days.'

'*Please* can we find me an adaptor now?'

After we had done so, with the help of a taxi driver, we went to a café Daniel wanted to check out. 'It's got the best coffee in town.'

'You've been reading your *Lonely Planet* again,' I said.

The place was trendy, all brightly done in yellows and reds, and the coffee *was* exceptional. Daniel's bitter chocolate cappuccino, with a creamy heart poured on to the top, was the best he'd ever had, he told the waiter, who seemed bewildered by such compliments. It was all rather pleasant. We relaxed in leather armchairs by the windows and Daniel chattered on about . . . something. The lilt of his voice, that endearing pronunciation sprinkled with Irishisms, was like whale music to the hyperactivity inside my head. A young couple sat near us. She was plain, he was gorgeous, and she placed the long-stemmed rose he had given her on the table.

'Awesome!' Daniel said, looking past me. 'Look at that.'

I turned. An old woman was sitting on a stool across the road, surrounded by buckets of flowers.

'The Porsche,' he said. 'What a beauty. Most of the cars here are held together with twine, but there's a fair load of shit-hot sports cars too. Far more than you'd ever see in Auckland.'

'And I thought you had a thing for old women.'

The couple were dipping long spoons into tall glasses of lurid-coloured ice-cream, and giggling quietly. Intimately.

'What's wrong?' Daniel asked.

'This place. It reminds me . . .'

'Of Killian?'

I took a moment, then said very quickly, 'I was engaged, until a week ago.' His eyebrows shot up. 'To a Croatian. And while this isn't much like Croatia, it has that same feel of continental Europe. Something . . . I dunno. The smell of coffee and all these tall, attractive men.' I swallowed a mouthful of chocolate and cream.

Poor Daniel was daunted. He fiddled with his earring. Another bloody drama. 'Sorry to hear that. What happened?'

'It doesn't matter what happened. All that matters is that it did happen, and this place reminds me of him.'

'Who left who?'

'Me. I did the leaving.'

Back at the Lebada, I plugged in my phone and waited. Within minutes, a text came through from my father. No sign of Steph. Her mother was now backtracking. Maybe she hadn't meant she was on her way *home*.

I stared at this message for a long time. Then, anguished, I wrote back, 'Would someone please get Killian home?'

We found Daniel's bear that night – he had Bear's Paw for a starter – in a lively restaurant near the university. The bear wasn't only on Daniel's plate. There were bears' heads everywhere, and anything with fur on it had been stapled to the walls, foxes and squirrels and deer; downstairs, a huge stuffed bear looked as if it was about to attack the musicians. We watched the young of Bucharest pile in, the women in tight jeans, displaying their midriffs. Pink was all the rage: pink bags and boots and jackets abounded.

'Where d'you think she's gone?' Daniel asked me tentatively.

'Steph? Don't know. Don't care, right now. The thing about Steph is, she's lived all over. She could go to a dozen different places and get TLC from friends who won't tell her to go home and bury her husband, like I've been doing.'

I chewed on the Arctic Boar in Red Wine that Daniel had made me order so he could taste that too. 'Anyway, it's out of my hands. I've told her the undertaker needs instructions, but she hasn't given any. What more can I do?'

'I don't get what's stopping her. The guy has to be buried or *something*.'

'I know exactly what's stopping her. She knows very well that I'm right – Killian did not want to be cremated – but she doesn't want the family to have their way either, so she's . . . dithering. Escaping the inevitable. Which is all very well, but I feel for his sister too. She can be an awfully silly woman, but to think of her sitting in that boxy hotel room, waiting for someone to tell her she can bring her brother home – it's a bit much.'

Daniel chewed.

'Poor Daniel. And all you were doing was minding your own business on your holidays.'

'It's cool. Weird things happen when you travel – that's what's so great about it, isn't it?'

'I wouldn't know. I only travel if I absolutely have to.'

'But you're a travel agent.'

'So? A vegetarian can be a butcher, you know.'

'Have you ever met a veggie butcher?'

'Well, no, but . . . Anyway, I can't help it. I'm terrified of flying, ferries sink, and trains give me migraines, apparently.'

'And throw you into the path of fascinating individuals like me.'

I smiled. 'Are you fascinating?'

'I like to think so.'

'Go on, then, fascinate me. Tell me about Daniel Blewitt.'

He sighed. 'I'm twenty-six, I live in Sydney, I love sailing, paragliding and whitewater rafting.'

'I said fascinate me, not list your hobbies. Stop holding back.'

'I'm not.'

'You are. Come on, you've picked me off a lavatory floor, saved me from a stroke, seen me at my absolute worst, but I'm not allowed to know anything substantial about you?'

The hidden thing again: no eye-contact.

'You're not on the run too, are you?' I asked.

'Course not. I've a few things to think through, that's all.'

'Career? Love?'

'Both. How's the boar?'

'Fine. How's the bear?' He was chewing too much to answer. 'It's an interesting name, Blewitt – unless it's an accurate reflection of your life experience. Is it?'

'Depends who you ask, I suppose.'

'Where does it come from?'

'Aw, it isn't my name. It's my stepfather's.'

'Oh. You took his name.'

'Didn't have much option. Don't have one of my own.'

'Sorry?'

'I don't know my father's name.'

'But . . . can't your mother tell you?'

He wiped his mouth with the big napkin. 'She doesn't know either.'

'Know what?'

'His name.'

As the first conversation we'd had that wasn't about me, this wasn't going very well.

'She doesn't know . . .' he folded the napkin '. . . who it was.'

'Oh, right . . . But, um . . .'

'You're not going to let this go, are you?'

'You promised me fascination.'

He tossed his head in acknowledgement. He was very cute, and likeable, and I was blessed, in view of whom I *might* have picked up in Transylvania. He was like an adorable baby brother, sweet and coy, but sassy too.

'Mum rebelled, you know? Against the whole Catholic thing and the expectations. She turned hippie. Went to London and did the swinging sixties in the late seventies. Drugs and men. Lots and lots of men. When she got knocked up, she had no idea how she was going to raise a child in grim old London on her own, surrounded by the guys who may or may not have been the father, so she shipped herself off to New Zealand.'

'How many guys?'

'About four, she reckons, were serious contenders. Any one of them could have been my . . . you know, father.'

I exhaled. 'Tough.'

'Sure is. No name, even. The older I get, the more it bugs me – if only because of the amount of flak I take about Blewitt.'

'Can't she give you possibilities? Probabilities, even?'

'She can't remember some of their first names, let alone their surnames. Although one of them was Irish, so I might even be fully Irish.'

'But you're probably half English?'

'More likely, yeah. Believe me, I've been around the tree with her on this. There's nothing there. It was one long party to her, until I showed up.'

'You could've taken *her* name.'

'I could've, if I'd had a choice, but she married him when I was a year old, so it just sort of happened. Anyway, it helped me blend in, sort of shaded the fact that I didn't have my own dad.'

'Does your stepfather compensate?'

He waved his fork sideways. 'My stepfather is a bastard. He's an Episcopalian minister. Sanctimonious, severe. Oh, and did I mention completely bloody humourless? Takes to spouting the scriptures any time life gets interesting.'

'But he married a hippie.'

'No, he *saved* a hippie. She took one look at him and saw Redemption, so she threw away her joints and sandals, and settled down to the quiet life of the minister's wife. I wish she hadn't. I'd rather have been fatherless. Nameless. And you know what his name is?'

'What?'

'Noah. Noah's Ark, that's the way Ma saw it. He took us aboard and saved us from damnation, but you know what? It really *was* like being stuck in an ark. I felt trapped as a kid. That's why, whenever things get a bit . . . well, I take off. Go travelling.'

'So things are a bit . . . that way now, are they?'

'You could say that.'

An urge to rescue him from whatever it was washed over me. There was a hurt in there that I had to get my hands on. It wasn't the father thing – that was an old bruise: there was something else, closer to the surface.

'You should come to New Zealand some day,' he said.

'No way. I hyperventilate at the sight of an aeroplane. I'd be a basket case if I went that far.'

Daniel nodded. 'Yeah, I reckon.'

10

Milenko's declaration of love was followed by a thundering silence, but he didn't hear from me either. I did not reply to that text, or send an email. The 'love' word scared me off. If he was teasing me, it was unkind; if he felt it, it was silly. That was the word my mother used, when she flamboyantly dismissed it: 'How silly. He barely knows you.'

For one dreamy evening, while still in the thrall of that kiss and the words he gave it, I fully intended to return to Croatia at the earliest opportunity. The next morning, I was cooler, and wiser. Rushing to a country I barely knew and a person I knew little about would not only be silly, but scary. Milenko might turn out to be weird. Indeed, he had already proved a little weird. In the shortening winter days, as the effect of that knee-wobbling snog waned, a return to Korčula ceased to hold much attraction.

In idle moments at work, Clara and I concluded that Milenko had been carried away on the moment and that his mad declaration had been a sudden blurt about which now, no doubt, he felt excruciatingly embarrassed. My silence on the matter was possibly the nicest thing I could have done for him. And so, in time, he became the Gorgeous Croatian I almost had, another sigh to be expelled at intervals like all the other sighs of my life. I started seeing an acquaintance of my father's, Carl, who had tantalizing egoless confidence. Weekends in flash hotels were the norm, but the relationship made me wistful, not about Milenko *per se*, but about his relative youth. I found myself longing for tentative uncertainties, occasional gaucheness, freshness and optimism; for someone who didn't have it all worked out, tied up, sorted. The time had come for something challenging, long-term, even, with someone who was game to take chances with me. My friends were right: I needed to get over the older man thing – so I steeled myself for the awkward phone call with my middle-aged lover.

The office was busy that day. It was early February. Customers were lined up three deep in front of the counters, wanting to book their holidays, and Carl was on the phone wanting to book another romantic weekend, when my email inbox blinked: Milenko Lalić.

'The Park Hotel in Kenmare is fantastic,' Carl was saying.

'I know.' *And full of oldies.* I stared at the name on my screen, feeling as if someone had pounced on me from behind. My fingers hovered over the keys.

'We were thinking Lanzarote,' said the woman leaning over the high counter in front of me, 'but isn't that a big volcano?'

I double-clicked. The email opened.

'On the other hand, Portugal is nice, but . . .'

'For a travel agent, you're taking a very long time to book your flight.'

'. . . I've heard all you can get in Portugal is sardines.'

'Kadie?' said Carl.

'I'm with a client, Carl.' I turned a page of the brochure I'd been leafing through in search of this woman's A1 sun holiday.

'I'll pick you up at work, if you like,' he said.

For a travel agent, you're taking a long time to book your flight.

'My friends thought Turkey, but isn't that in the Middle East?'

'Shall we say six on Friday?'

'So, on balance, I think we'd like to go to Majorca again.'

'That sounds lovely, Carl. In fact,' I added in a flash of mischief, 'the timing will be perfect.'

'For what?'

'You know . . . My dates. I've been feeling terribly . . .'

The customer looked at the wall behind my head. I hoped the poster of Tahiti would transport her there for a few moments.

'Terribly what?' Carl asked.

'Broody. And so is Dad, actually. He can't wait to become a grandfather.'

Tahiti couldn't compete. The lady's eyebrows arched as she glared down at me.

I hit the 'Reply' button, typed, *What flight?* and hit 'Send.'

'I mean, let's face it,' I said to Carl, 'you could become a grandfather yourself any day now, so there's no time to lose.'

The client put her hand on the counter to steady herself.

'We need to talk,' said Carl, father of four.

'We do.' I hung up. 'Well, Lanzarote *is* lovely,' I said to the customer.

'I just said we want to go to Majorca.'

My screen flashed. He was on line. *Your flight to Croatia.*

'Croatia,' I said.

'I didn't say anything about Croatia.'

I had booked the woman's holiday in Majorca by the time I got back into my inbox and found that he had sent another: *'Korčula is missing you, Kadie.'*

Milenko drove down to Dubrovnik to meet me at the end of April. I wasn't nervous about seeing him. The flight had burnt out every nerve I owned all by itself. I had taken a tranquillizer to get me on to the plane, and a little old lady on her way to Medjugorje had baptized me with dollops of holy water before take-off, which, curiously, had allowed me some easy breaths. She then spoilt it all by pointing out that far more people died on the roads than in aeroplanes – another platitude frequently churned out for the benefit of sad cases like me.

'Yes,' I retorted, 'but you've a far better chance of surviving a crash on the road than you have in the air.'

The woman said another decade of the rosary and read a pamphlet about Living in Prayer. I gripped the armrests and thought about dying.

Milenko was exactly as I wanted him to be: on firm ground. He suggested we have lunch in Dubrovnik. I didn't comment. I was too busy planning my route home: trains through Italy and France, ferry from Roscoff . . .

In a most unassuming way, Milenko accepted the wreckage of anxiety that was me. He didn't resort to teasing, or tell me that if the plane crashed I wouldn't feel a thing. 'You've never been to Dubrovnik, have you?' he asked, driving in that alluring European way, as if the car was an unpretentious extension of his body. 'Because I was thinking maybe we should stay here tonight. You cannot come to Croatia and not visit Dubrovnik.'

'That's a lovely idea.' Excellent. He was beginning to behave like a red-blooded male. Away from the eyes of his no doubt over-interested parents and my jamming father, we could enjoy some intimacy, if not fully consummate this fledgling affair, in a hotel in the old town of Dubrovnik, Jewel of the Adriatic . . .

But there are few hotels in the old city and Milenko was a gentleman. We took two rooms in a bland hotel nearby, then walked towards the famous city walls. Inside the main gate, Milenko pointed at landmarks. 'St Blaise's Church . . . Onoforio Fountain.' The main thoroughfare was impressive: a pedestrianized broadway, graced by green-shuttered buildings and paved with limestone slabs, worn down to a shine by centuries of feet. Milenko led me up steep steps to the next level, where a whole stretch of restaurants huddled along a narrow, shaded alley. We took a table under an awning; pigeons picked at the crumbs at our feet.

'It's nice to see you again,' he said, after we ordered. Not a man for overstatement, then.

'You too.'

'I didn't know if . . . you would want to come.'

'I didn't, really. I'm not much good at travelling.'

'It was only the flight that worried you?'

'Not just the flight, no.' I held his eye. 'Let's face it – it's not as if you've been pressing me to come. Hounding me with emails since October.'

He looked away, as was his habit, along the alley full of tables, waitresses, awnings and tourists, then turned back abruptly, as also was his habit. 'I had some worries after the jazz weekend.'

'Oh?'

'It took me fifteen hours to get home – a delay in London, and then a long drive from Split in not very good conditions. There was a problem with the ferry . . . It made me think that our countries are very far apart, in many different ways.'

'That's true.'

'I meet a lot of women,' he said candidly, 'from everywhere. I've had girlfriends, you know, from many different places. It isn't good. It . . .' he shrugged '. . . goes nowhere.'

'Is that why I've come here – to go nowhere?'

He shifted about, did things with his mouth, and just when I thought he had no response to make, he said, 'I am the one going nowhere.' The waitress brought water. 'After lunch, we must climb the city walls.'

We climbed on to the ramparts – a stiff trudge up high stone steps – and began to make our way round the massive wall. Milenko pointed at the damage from attacks on Dubrovnik in the early 1990s, and explained how difficult it had been to find replacements for the distinctive red tiles. As a result, fresh orange-tiled roofs lined up against wonky, mismatched greying roofs, and brand new windows stood alongside poky shoe-box windows.

Milenko helped me up a slippy bit of path, worn down to a glossy finish, then leant over the parapet. 'Look.'

'I'm not great with heights.' I peeped over. At the foot of the cliffs, way below, a man wearing very long flippers lay face down in the water. He looked like a dead frog. Further out, the green of a wooded island ran into the all-pervasive blue.

'Beautiful,' I said, turning back to the jumbled roofs, huddled together like conspirators, 'but I prefer Korčula.'

'That's good.'

Swifts squealed overhead, making quite a racket. It had been cool, in the narrow passageways, but the ramparts were taking a direct hit from the sun, and I was sticky with exertion. Pink, and getting pinker. My head was throbbing slightly, especially on the climbs, but it was fascinating to look down into the private gardens inside the great wall, at teacloths hanging and cats sleeping outside kitchen doors. The people who lived there had no privacy, with waves of tourists walking past at roof level, but their garden terraces were covered with vines to give them shelter from the sun and from prying eyes like mine. In some places, the houses were so close to the wall that I could have picked the herbs on their windowsills, and in one case, I was tempted to reach into an attic room and select a book from a shelf crammed with volumes.

'I want to climb in,' I admitted, 'and snoop around.' *And I have a headache*, a voice said inside me. I had been anticipating, longing for, dreading this day since February. Nothing could spoil it.

While I took photos, Milenko stood with one hand on the wall, leaning into it, his sunglasses held between his fingers. To hell with historic Dubrovnik, I thought. Just take me back to that cool, bland hotel room.

'How would you get off this thing if you needed to?' I asked. 'What if you had a heart-attack half-way round?' The drop on either side of the wall was severe, and I began to feel as if I'd quite like to get off the bloody thing myself.

'There is an exit,' said Milenko, 'further along, but then you wouldn't reach the top, where the view is best.' He pointed to a corner tower that was a long way across the town and an even longer way up the hill. I wiped my forehead, promising myself a reviving cup of tea when we were done. Continuing on, we came past a small church with three iron bells hanging in their arches on the roof. Entrancing. Milenko had chosen an unlikely method of seduction, but it was working.

At a bend in the rampart, I stepped into a round look-out tower, the size of a phone booth, and squinted through a hole at the Adriatic.

Milenko squeezed in behind me, put a hand on my waist and kissed the side of my neck. I swooned, but for all the wrong reasons. 'I'm not feeling so great.'

The dullness sitting at the back of my head, a woozy indistinctness, had chosen its moment.

'It's hot,' said Milenko. 'I should not have brought you here.'

'No, it's the tranquillizer. It's catching up with me.'

He sat me on the ground in the shade of the wall and gave me his bottle of water, but the thumping in my head was taking hold. 'I need to get back to the hotel.'

'Okay.' He was quick and clear; not fussed. 'Come, I'll help you,' he said, pulling me to my feet. He lugged me round more and yet more wall, supporting me against his hip, while I held my hand over my eyes, cursing the glaring sun.

Finally we reached an escape valve. A staircase, a gate, shade. I was aware of the smell of cat pee, of cobblestoned alleyways, and tunnels beneath rooms. At the Onoforio Fountain, a mausoleum-like structure, Milenko sprinkled me with the water spewing from lion-heads. It helped, but it was a long hike, through the Pile Gate and up more godforsaken steps, before we reached the hotel, where I hit the pillow and fell asleep.

When I woke, I could not lift my head. The migraine had taken possession in my sleep. Stealthy devils, migraines, and they certainly know how to wreck things. How to Spoil a Date in One Easy Step. Instead of spending a delightful afternoon nurturing a nascent romance in one of Europe's most beautiful cities, I would spend the evening throwing up.

At seven Milenko came tentatively to the door. I managed to get to my feet. He was concerned that I might be hungry and had brought food – strong-smelling cheese, bread and salami. I leapt past him to the bathroom.

Sending him away, I promised I would be all right in the morning.

'Warts and all,' said Ger, in a sympathetic text.

'Yeah. He's certainly getting the warts before the all.'

It was a pleasant night of vomiting, pain and drinking water, but I slept through the early hours and woke after nine, much improved. Milenko sounded immeasurably relieved when I phoned, and with the help of strong sunglasses, painkillers and his arm, we managed to get to a café on a terrace outside the front gate. Our physical closeness had been speeded up by the headache. I couldn't move without holding on to him. 'What did you do last night?' I asked him.

'I had a drink with some college friends.'

Sipping my tea, I groaned with relief. 'There is *nothing* quite like the first cup of tea after an attack.'

'I'm sorry for yesterday,' he said. 'We should not have done the wall.'

'No, really. It was lovely, but migraines often strike after stress and I'd been fretting about that flight for days, and once it was over, I relaxed and – boom.'

'You get them often?'

'Depends.'

'Do you want to leave for Korčula straight away?'

'Not necessarily. I'd hate to miss out on Dubrovnik again. If you can spare the time, I'd love to see a bit more.'

And so we strolled, talking and looking, and holding hands. Sometimes I leant against him and he kissed my forehead, as if we'd been together for years. We took regular breaks – a coffee on a terrace opposite St Blaise's Church and lunch in the square. The town was so easy on the eye, the cream buildings with their green shutters, and easy on the ears, church bells ringing, tenor to the swifts' soprano. Milenko apologized for bringing me food the night before and asked a lot of questions, so that he would know what to do the next time. We had, already, an unspoken understanding: there *would* be a next time. This was not a foreign affair, a flash in the pan. We were starting something more lasting, more difficult, and we both knew it as we meandered the shiny passageways of Dubrovnik.

We left for Korčula in the early evening. It was a spectacular drive along the Dalmatian coast and a significant one. It was not Dubrovnik that lay behind me, but Ireland. As the sun set, it threw a glittering stretch of light across the sea between two islands. A boat was motoring right up the middle of this glowing carpet. On the other side of the road, the mountains were green and rocky. Empty. There were similarities with the Irish wilderness: stone walls running up and over hill-sides, rocks strewn across the ground, barren peaks laden with mystery, but this was not Ireland, as the weather con-firmed, and it asked questions of me that I was not yet ready to answer.

In a car, and with Milenko driving, the journey was much shorter than it had been on the bus – barely two hours. On the peninsula of Orebić, the road wound its way west and north and the sun dipped behind the hills, glowing like a hot coal. The sky turned orange, the hills black, and a gathering of flat purple clouds appeared to be skidding across the sky in pursuit of the sun. The sea, coming in around us, could not have looked more like a Connemara lake, right down to the fish farms, with their plastic markers like grids on the surface. Put a currach on there, I thought, and you'd have the perfect Connemara landscape.

Milenko suddenly swerved.

'That looked like a tortoise!' I said, turning. 'A tortoise crossing the road.'

'There are a lot around here.'

'Stop! I want to see it.'

He reversed a few metres on a long stretch of straight road, and sure enough, half-way across it: a tortoise. We got out.

'He'll get himself squashed.'

'Frequently they are killed.'

'But where's he going?'

Milenko stood, his fist against his hip. 'He's going to the other side of the road.' And he sucked in his cheek to stop himself laughing at me.

Aware that it had unwanted company, the tortoise recoiled bashfully into its shell.

'Well, don't do that,' I said to it. 'You'll get flattened.'

The tortoise considered this, apparently agreed, poked out his head and paws, and resumed his crossing.

'We must go,' said Milenko, bending over to pick him up.

'Don't! He's never been picked up in his life. He'll get vertigo.'

The tortoise made his way laboriously under the car.

'Great,' said Milenko.

'We'll wait until he comes out the other side.'

'Kadie,' he said, and I loved the way he said my name, like

an Italian, with affectionate reproach in each syllable. Kay-*dee*! 'We have a ferry to catch, and our record for catching ferries is, you know . . .'

The tortoise emerged from the other side of the car. He waddled to the edge of the Tarmac and slid down the chippings on his belly – he didn't look in the least surprised, so he had clearly done so before – and landed conveniently at the edge of the field, into which he disappeared.

'Now we can go.'

We got to Orebić with five minutes to spare and drove straight on to the open-deck ferry. I stood up at the front, leaning over the railing. The sun had left a pink glow lying between the dark edges of the mainland and Korčula island, but I hung my eyes on the lights of the town, with the steeple rising out of it like a candle on a cake.

'You see that red light left of the church?' said Milenko. 'It's the same height as the church tower – and it's on a boat. A yacht. You've never seen anything like it. Huge. Gold railings. Probably never sails.'

We sat on the plastic seats. The car ferry slid out from the quay. The sea was so flat, it was hard to tell we were moving, apart from the quiet rumble of the engines.

'This is very different from my last arrival,' I said. 'That miserable storm. The boat rolled around and when we reached the other side, all we got was abuse. This guy was yelling at us to get our baggage and yelling at other people to get back on . . . It was mad. The rain was banging down and we were, like, getting cursed at. Not a great ad for the Croatian tourist board, I have to tell you.'

Milenko put his arm on the back of my seat. 'That was you, in the storm? Late at night?'

'Yeah.'

'I remember. People jumped out and it wasn't even their hotel.'

'That's because we *thought* we were getting on to another transfer bus,' I explained.

'And the suitcases – was I to carry them all?'

'Where were you?' I asked.

'By the boat, helping people get off and . . . yelling, actually.'

'That was you? The faceless one?'

'I had no face?'

'You had a very loud voice and some choice language.'

He laughed.

'You touched my hand,' I said. 'You nearly gave me heart failure. I hadn't heard you coming. You'd been screaming and swearing, and then suddenly you were there, taking my suitcase without a word.'

The water whispered round the bow. Milenko was unshaven, slightly unkempt. He glanced over my shoulder, as if to see who was on the deck, then leant towards me. Our second kiss was everything the first had not been. Slow, lazy. It went down to my roots and came back up for air. There was no flight to catch, no water-taxi waiting. We had a full fifteen minutes to indulge the attraction sparked so many months before.

When the ferry started groaning and braking, Milenko pulled away. 'I hope you're ready for my family.'

'Do I need to be?'

He looked down at the cars, his mouth straight.

Their home was an uninspiring house next to the hotel grounds. Inside, it was dim and cool, cluttered with heavy furniture and decorated with religious icons, virgins and crosses and plates with the Sacred Heart of Jesus. White lace on every surface. The nicest part was the terrace at the back, which, like those in Dubrovnik, was draped in bougainvillaea and backed by geraniums on the wall of the house. There was bamboo furniture, upholstered in green floral cotton, and a long timber table. Milenko's mother, Cecilia, rarely left this spot, pottering about and pulling at the plants, or staring from her chair towards the trees on the boundary and the glimpse of sea between them. She had little else to do. Their meals were sent over from the hotel and their rooms were tidied by hotel cleaners, but her inertia was not a matter of having little to do. She could have made herself busy, but in all my time there, I never saw her step into the hotel, though she occasionally took a walk along the promenade.

Cecilia was like a doll, thin and fragile, and always smiling. It was as if she had some private life going on behind her eyes, an inner paradise from which she looked out, throwing that warm beam upon the rest of the world. But there was no paradise in there. Milenko confirmed that his mother was not quite well. She had always been frail, physically and mentally, and the death of her elder son had aggravated a long-established depression, for which she was medicated. It manifested itself in disengagement. She was distracted most of the time, as if she couldn't quite remember what exactly was going on, yet she remained unfazed when various relatives turned up that first night to check me out. As they crowded round the plastic-covered table and knocked back the local brandy, Cecilia smiled and nodded.

For all her abstraction, she was a warm person – a pretty woman in her early sixties, who wore her greying hair in a loose bun, and dressed in smart items of clothing carelessly thrown on. Her husband loved to buy her nice things, including classy Italian clothes. She could concentrate on conversations for a short time, particularly if it had anything to do with her much adored son, but Milenko believed she was getting worse – that she was filled with anxieties, one being that he was thirty already and had neither wife nor children.

Milenko's father, Marin, was a saint. He was very handsome, even better-looking than his son, and daily set upon by flirtatious women guests, but he was devoted to his wife. He lavished her with attention, hurrying back and forth to their home to check on her and fill her in on developments, in so far as she showed any interest. He ran the hotel with a gentle touch and had all the subtlety, the professionalism and charm required for the job, most of which he had passed on to his son, though not all (as I had discovered when I had complained about the noise).

Milenko's main interest at the time was the website he was designing and marketing, marketing, marketing, but he did little work the week I was there. I stayed in the hotel, as their guest, which saved me having to struggle to make conversation with Cecilia, who had little English. It was hot for April, and in that week Milenko gave me a taste of the lifestyle he had to offer. Every evening we clambered over the rocks that curved round the bay and picked a nice spot where we could enjoy furtive cuddles. There was no question of him coming to my room for any such activities, not with staff and even his father wandering the corridors. His parents wanted him to marry a nice Catholic girl – and be a nice Catholic boy about it.

'But you've been in the army,' I said. 'You've been trained to kill. They can't imagine you've never . . .'

'My mother does. She thinks I'm different from other boys – I am a boy to her still. Pure.' He grinned.

'Which of course you're not.' It was actually a question, because I still wondered, sometimes, about his continuing restraint. Milenko knew it was a question, so he looked away and said nothing, because he had learnt how to taunt me.

We had very little time to be alone, but Milenko seemed unbothered by this lack of opportunity. He just didn't appear to be very *hungry*. A few kisses kept him going, and he was more intent on sharing his day-to-day existence with me, and this, I knew, was not the way he generally carried out courtships: he usually partied with women, and surely slept with them. He was not in the habit of taking them around his daily life, and although this was very touching, it didn't help my escalating physical desperation. Sometimes he toyed with me, as when I was snoozing on the semi-circular platform one afternoon, and he came down from the office and without a word began rubbing sunscreen into the backs of my legs, his fingers moving over my calves, pressing into the backs of my knees, and up and up under my short skirt in slow, deliberate movements, until I was undulating like a caterpillar. Another day I watched him play the drums, and although it was loud and sometimes discordant, he never took his eyes from mine and every beat of the bass drum was like a thrust, into my body and into my soul.

We talked a lot, getting the important stuff out of the way. I told him about those grim early days when my father had struggled to be both mother and father, while seeing his glittering career melt away. And one night when we were sitting in Milenko's boat tied up by the pier, he told me that he was away, fighting, when his parents heard of his brother Dario's death. Since then he had felt he had to be two sons, not one. His parents never treated him with resentment or made him feel he could not make up for his brother's loss. Rather, he felt the weight not only of their grief but of double love. Their love and hopes for Dario were now poured into him, and it was heavy sometimes, he admitted, but inescapable. Children of his own, he hoped, would broaden the isthmus on which his parents currently had to squeeze their expansive love.

We took *Zizinica* out one afternoon and trundled about the coast. I lay on the bow, wondering what I was doing there. We lived in separate countries; he lived an additional three hours' journey from the nearest airport. He would want to meet his family's expectations. As the last remaining son, he had little choice. But the only true obstacle to this relationship was his love of his island, because I loved my own island. He had travelled, but there was nowhere he wanted to be other than this long sliver of land, and I could hardly blame him, as I gazed at the clear sea and at the rocky islands all around us, like prostrate hermits jealously guarding their spot.

Stiff from lying on my belly on a hard surface, I turned to look at Milenko: shirt open, glasses half-way down his nose, shorts. In many ways, he was alien to me – the island boy, former soldier, victim of war and dutiful son; in other ways, less definable, he was utterly familiar. It was as if we had always been in one another's lives, unseen, and now could see no one else.

He was staring out, one hand on the tiller, the snort of the engine harsh and intrusive. We were alone, far from prying eyes, but he was sailing along as if we'd made love that morning and would do so again that night. He seemed, sometimes, to be as disinterested as a doorknob.

He threw down the anchor off a deserted hump of island. 'Let's swim.'

'Isn't it too cold?'

'Not for me.'

He pulled off his shirt and dived, shattering the still of the deep green water, then surfaced and urged me in. 'It's warm, really.'

Why not? I thought. Why not be brave this once? I stood up, held my nose and jumped.

I might as well have jumped into a hole in the ice. The shock took my breath away. I came to the surface squealing.

'What's wrong?' Milenko asked, deadpan.

'You bastard!' I paddled frantically to the back of the boat, but when I got to the ladder Milenko grabbed me and warmed me up with a loaded kiss. Our lips were cold, our tongues hot. He held me with one hand, the steps with the other; I put my legs round him; our chins dipped into the water, as we sucked at one another's faces, shivering. But it was too cold; I clambered on to the boat, grabbed a towel and returned to my spot to lie down. *Zizinica* rocked in the wake of a passing launch, which was pleasant until the same waves bounced off the island and hit us again, almost tipping me into the sea.

When Milenko climbed aboard, I waited. The engine didn't start. If he didn't continue what he'd started, I thought, and touch me where I needed to be touched, I would have to throw myself into the water or risk burning up right there, like a piece of paper under a shard of glass in the sun.

He did come to me, and lay half on me, wet and chilly. His hand pressed into the small of my back, his lips into my shoulder, and he pulled slowly on the string of my bikini until it came undone. I sighed, more with relief than desire, and rolled over. His mouth ran over my goose-bumps.

Milenko gestured over his shoulder. He had laid out towels on the timber floor. Not so disinterested, after all. 'Kadie,' he said, then seemed unsure what to say next.

'Yes?'

He looked at the towels again. 'I have . . . everything.'

I laughed, which affronted him. 'I'm sorry,' I said, 'but a while ago you seemed so unaware of the possibilities.'

'Why do you think I brought you out here on such a bloody cold day?'

'You call this cold?'

'Yes, and the sea is fucking freezing!'

'That's what you get for showing off.' I thumped him affectionately, then said, 'I can't read you at all.'

He slithered away. 'Stop trying to read me and come down here.' He took a condom from his shirt pocket.

'My, you did come prepared.'

'I even have biscuits for afterwards.' He grinned, and love began to creep along my veins.

It was . . . all right. If the earth didn't move, it was because the sea did. *Zizinica* wouldn't stop bobbing about, and having our ankles stuck under a bench didn't help much either. A hard surface can be unforgiving with a weight on top of you; Milenko's elbows suffered on the timber slats; it was too bright. Early intimacy should be undertaken in the dark – the visual can come later . . . although that long, slim body looked very good in daylight, and it tasted salty, all over. A fresh breeze blew around us, making us shiver. Had a boat come round the island, getting myself into a wet bikini would have taken more time than was available, so it was hard to relax. Every time we heard an engine in the distance, I bolted up to see where it was, and Milenko smiled warmly, so warmly that it didn't matter one jot that it wasn't the greatest session of our lives. There would be loads of time for that.

We pulled the towels round us and ate our biscuits.

'How can we manage it,' Milenko said, 'a week here, a week there?'

I put my hand to his face. 'Do you want more than that?'

He kissed the tips of my fingers. 'Very much.'

'Then we'll manage somehow.'

'I can never leave this place. Not the country, after fighting for it, and not my parents after what they've lost.'

'I understand.'

'We have a big problem.'

'Why?'

'Because . . . what I said when I left Cork . . .'

'In the text?'

He nodded. 'It's true, and it's a very big problem.'

11

'Morning.'

'Hi, Daniel.'

'What's happening?'

'No trace of Steph, if that's what you mean. She's really gone this time. What about you?'

'I'm good, but I've been thinking. Let's spare ourselves the hotel breakfast and go back to the café.'

'Hmm. Hot chocolate and croissants. Good idea.'

The trip across town was worth it. Daniel ate and read his *Lonely Planet* guide. He was slightly irritating, if endearing, yet sexy enough to keep at bay too many sisterly inclinations to mind him. He had tattoos, which I loathed, and wore leather strips round his neck with shells hanging off them.

'We should check out the Hilton,' he said. 'It was the German headquarters during the war.'

'If it's all the same to you, I'll just go back to the hotel and pack. I've had enough sightseeing.'

'But you're a travel agent. You should see what the place has to offer so you can tell your clients about it.'

'I'm not a travel agent any more.'

'How come?'

'I've left my job.'

'Why?'

'Oh, keep up, Daniel. The wedding, remember? The big move to Croatia that isn't going to happen?'

'Aw, right. So if you don't mind my asking, what exactly are you going back to Ireland for?'

I turned, irritated now by his jumpy, full-on, in-my-face *tourism.* 'The funeral,' I hissed.

'You mean the funeral that isn't happening?'

'Daniel!'

'You should come to Istanbul instead.'

I gaped.

'Why not? If you go home now, it's going to be pretty damn depressing. All those wedding arrangements to undo, families fighting . . . Wouldn't it be nice to get away from all that?'

'Presumably, yes,' I snapped. 'Presumably that's exactly why Steph has done just that. *Gone away.*'

'My train leaves this afternoon. If you've any sense, you'll come too. You've nothing else to do.'

'Are you joking?'

'No.'

'I didn't think so.'

'And since your old man is loaded, you can afford to take off.'

'Daniel, I don't appreciate this banter. I am in mourning. I've lost my best friend and I don't have the slightest inclination to go skiving around the East.'

'Going home won't bring Killian back.'

'Shut the fuck up!'

We finished breakfast in silence and went on to the street. I hailed a cab. Daniel opened the door for me. 'Get in,' he said, and when I did, he got in beside me.

'What are you doing? I thought you were going sightseeing.'

'I'm sorry for what I said. I was out of line.'

'Look, I appreciate the . . . invitation – it's very sweet, but while this is an adventure for you, I'm in the middle of a disaster.'

'*Allez où?*' asked the taxi driver.

'Pantelimon.'

'I didn't mean to make light of it,' he said, 'but it's been nice travelling with you and I figured . . . well.' His own loneliness was peeking out again.

'I've really enjoyed your company too,' I said, 'but I have to go home. Everyone has to go home eventually. Where'll we drop you?'

A pink tram swung past us.

'I'll come to the hotel and see you off to the airport.'

As soon as we stepped into the Lebada, the receptionist called me. 'Yes?'

He nodded towards the staircase. 'There is someone waiting for you.'

I gripped Daniel's wrist. 'Steph!' We hurried across the lobby and round the central staircase. Behind it, a sitting room led out to the courtyard.

He stood up when we appeared. I let out a cry.

He looked tired. Thin. 'Kadie,' he said, and his voice didn't quite work, got caught somewhere. He cleared his throat and came towards us.

'The ex, right?' Daniel mumbled.

'What the hell are you doing here?'

Milenko dipped his chin and said quietly, 'I've come to take you home.'

'What? I don't need to be taken anywhere!'

'Keep the voice down,' said Daniel.

'You're Daniel?' Milenko asked him.

'Yeah.'

'Milenko Lalić.' They shook hands. 'Kadie's father told me what you did. We're very grateful.'

'Excuse me?' I said. '*Who's* grateful? I don't need anyone to be grateful on my behalf, thank you very much. I can do that all by myself, just like I can get myself to the airport and on to a flight. I don't need help from you or anyone else!'

Milenko blinked. 'You needed help the other day, on the train.'

'I don't need any *now*.'

'I'll leave you guys to it,' said Daniel, backing out.

I glared at Milenko. I had begged him, really begged him, not to come after me, ever. 'How could you do this?'

'How could I not?'

He was standing two feet from me. Hurt, wounded. I went to the couch where he had been sitting; my legs gave out.

'Don't be angry,' he said, sitting on the chair next to me. 'I was going to Cork anyway, so Rollo suggested I come here to accompany you and Steph home, especially after your migraine. You were only one country away ... Clara has booked me on to the same flights.'

There was no point yelling. It must have made sense to Dad, worried as he was about my health, that Milenko should hop across to Bucharest and help me with Steph. I would never have been able to prevent Milenko going to the funeral; or avoided seeing him through all this. 'You do know Steph isn't here?' I asked, as if it was his fault.

He nodded. 'Rollo told me when I landed.'

We sat, inches apart. I wanted to reach out, to grab the beautiful hand and curl against those much-loved shoulders; he also was straining. His restraint was impressive; mine wasn't bad either. If I could get through this one fraught moment, I thought, I might just hang on to my miserable broken engagement, and even succeed in it, but if I touched him at all, I would never again let him go.

'I'm so sorry,' he said, 'about Killian. It's . . .' He shook his head.

I turned my hands over and over in my lap, holding every part of myself in. I didn't know what to think, where to move. Here he was, *with me*, and I was gripping my resolve like a cat with its claws in a far from dead mouse. How could I endure it? The journey home, together; all day, together; Prague, Cork, at home, together. *Impossible*. Dad had engineered this. He was taking advantage of Killian's death to manoeuvre things back to the way everyone wanted them. Killian wouldn't have minded, but I did.

'You and Dad,' I said, 'you shouldn't have done this. I made it clear what I wanted.'

'Yes, but this is a catastrophe, Kadie. Killian gone, Steph missing. How can we stick to your crazy rules?'

'You're manipulating me at the worst possible time, using this catastrophe, as you call it, to get things your way. It's unspeakable.'

'Listen to me.' He leant forward. 'This is not about what you want. Do you think it was easy for Rollo, knowing you were looking for Steph with a bad migraine and no one to help you?'

'I had Daniel.'

'But what if he had not been there? What would have happened?'

'I'm not an invalid. I've dealt with migraine many times in many places. I can look after myself. I don't need you or Dad or Daniel to mind me!'

'We were worried for you.'

'We should all of us be worried about Steph.'

Milenko sat back and sighed, his hand dangling off the armrest. 'Where do you think she has gone?'

'I don't know. "Going back the way we came" – it means nothing and everything. Those two went all over the place.'

'Vietnam?'

I looked up. 'What?'

'Her second home, isn't it?'

'But –'

'And they went on honeymoon there.'

'Oh, God.'

'You don't think?'

'I hadn't thought. I haven't been able to think.'

'It seems obvious,' he said.

'Did you tell anyone? Anyone at home? Has anyone else thought of it?'

'No, I . . . I've only said it to you.'

'But you could be right. I was thinking Goa, maybe, where they got married.'

He wrinkled his nose. 'She didn't like Goa. They both got sick, remember, but Vietnam – her sanctuary, she said, no?'

'Yes, yes. I mean, you're right, it's a possibility, but would she really hike all that way? It wouldn't be good for the baby, so much travelling.' I looked at him. 'Surely?'

'She can't face people,' he said. 'I understand that. When Dario died, I didn't want to go home either. I remember standing in Orebić, looking across at Korčula, and knowing that when I got there, I would not have time even to think about him. It would be my parents, everything for my parents, and the family, and that's how it was. I had to be solid, when all I wanted was to . . .' after a moment the word came '. . . evaporate.'

'That's exactly what Steph's done – evaporated!'

'You have a problem with that? *You?* That's funny.'

I crossed my arms, tight against my chest.

'I'll get us some coffee,' he said.

He knew when I liked my coffee, and how; he knew everything necessary to make my life sweet and companionable. He knew how to seduce me as no one else. And it was almost done. The caring ex-fiancé had gone to fetch coffee while we discussed our next move in the search for the skittish widow. We were together again, almost. It had been seamless. 'I'll get us some coffee.' *Us.* The couple. The almost-marrieds. Nothing had really changed apart from my little brainstorm when I'd tried to wreck our future, but Milenko and Dad were dismantling all that, sending it off into the past, with Killian's help.

Milenko was coming back; still apprehensive. What a tight-rope he walked.

I said, 'Go home, Milenko.'

He stiffened in the seat, his hands between his knees. 'And where would that be – home? Our house? You know the one I mean, Kadie? The house with the big window looking over the sea, and the blue sofa you wanted that we couldn't get into the room. The empty, cold house smelling of paint? Is that the home you mean?'

'*Don't.*'

'I am going to Cork,' he said, 'as we have arranged.'

'But that makes it impossible for me! Why are you being so stubborn?'

'It must be catching, I guess.'

'Milenko.'

'Kadie.'

'If you love me at all, you'll just go – back to your family.'

'I told your father I am bringing you home today and that is what I will do today.'

I looked at him.

'And maybe, somewhere along the way, you'll tell me why you left me,' he said.

'There is nothing to tell, beyond the fact that I was wrong. I didn't love you the right way.'

His eyes held me. 'You love me more than anyone ever will.'

'Jesus, Dad!' I spat into the phone. 'What were you thinking?' I had stepped out into the courtyard and was pacing around on cobblestones. The garden was drab, wintry; the trees were bare and the ground damp. 'What do you think you're doing?'

'Getting you home.'

'That's not it and you bloody well know it. I told you I did not want to see him and there's a very good reason for that! And what about Milenko? Did you think about him?'

'Of course I did. He's been straining at the leash to get involved . . . to help.'

'No, Dad, he just wanted to get *to me*. Don't you see that now I'll have to hurt him all over again? Crush him into little pieces and send him off?' My voice broke. 'How could you do that to him? To *me*?'

'You said yourself he hasn't done anything wrong, so I thought if you saw him –'

'You shouldn't have thought anything!'

'Kadie, please. This is no time for break-ups. With Killian gone, we should all take stock of things. Be grateful for what we have.'

'But that's just the point,' I cried. 'Isn't there enough going on without you complicating things? For God's sake, he's inside now – just waiting for us to leave for the airport. And guess what, Dad – I'm not going!'

'Kadie.'

'No. I can't spend another minute with him. It's too hard and it'll cause misery all over the place.' He tried to interrupt, but I ran on: 'I will *not* be manipulated, and if that means staying in Bucharest or Budapest or wherever the hell I am, then so be it. I won't do this to him. He can go to Cork for all I care, but I'm not going with him!'

'You can't stay away.'

'Watch me.'

I hung up and marched up and down. Rollo was probably doing likewise, in the kitchen. He'd really blown it. It would be coming clear to him how much he'd fucked up, and that he would now have to face the doubly heartbroken Milenko, whose hopes he had himself rebuilt.

Daniel came into the courtyard from the other end – from

the walk round the lake. 'So,' he smiled, 'is everything sweet in paradise again?'

'How can you imagine I could be anywhere other than hell?' I sat down on one of the marble benches, but it was so cold I stood up again.

'Look, ahm, I'd better be heading off,' said Daniel. 'You and Milenko'll be leaving soon, so I'll –'

'I'm not going anywhere with Milenko.'

'Why not?'

'You need to ask? Don't you see – *why can nobody see?* – that that can only make it much worse for *him?* Every minute we spend together gets his hopes up. But he'll still end up without me.'

'Look, he seems like a nice guy. You should go with him, maybe –'

'Stop sounding like my father! You're on my side, right? You have to see it my way. *Somebody* has to see it my way!'

'Right.'

'There is no sorting this out. It cannot be done. I have to persuade him to leave, and if he insists on going to Cork, I'm staying here.'

'I thought you were desperate to get home?'

'I am,' I sat down again, 'but going back with him would be too cruel.'

'It'd only be for a few days.'

'But they'd be hard, *hard* days, Daniel. I wouldn't hold out, I can tell you that right now. I'll barely hold out another hour.'

'So forgive him. Christ, whatever he's done –'

'Maybe it's what *I've* done.'

There were two coffees on the table. Milenko was sitting with his hand over his eyes, his thumb and finger rubbing moist eyelids. 'How can this happen to me again?' he asked, more of himself than of me.

A dull thump landed inside my chest. *Again*. It *had* happened again. It had happened before. Twice, the unexplained broken engagement.

My phone rang. 'Mum.'

'Your father is thick sometimes!'

'Tell me about it.'

'And then sometimes he's right.'

'*Mum.*'

'Come home with Milenko, Kadie, and you and he can sort out your problems when this is over.'

'The problem cannot be sorted. Why does no one understand that?'

Milenko exhaled, as if I had hit him.

'Perhaps because you won't tell us what the problem *is*. And because you and Milenko have every chance of making this work. This is not the time for drastic decisions. You've had a huge shock, losing Killian like this, and you're not thinking clearly, so be sensible. I'm not asking you, Kadie. You're almost thirty years old, but I am *telling* you to come home today with your fiancé.'

'Yes, Mum. Whatever you say, Mum. Goodbye, Mum.'

Milenko chanced it. His fingers reached across the tiny divide between us and touched me. Tentatively, he ran one finger round my knee, the pressure soft and friendly through my jeans. He was so pale.

'I can't go with you, Milenko. Go to Cork, if you must, but if we spend any more time together, we'll both regret it. I swear it.' I got up and ran for the stairs. He came after me. We hurried up the staircase, round the spiral, one floor, two floors, and up to my room. I shut the door in his face. He shouted at me to let him in. I leant against the door, crying. He thumped and shouted some more, then I heard him slide down the door to the ground. I did the same, just behind him on the inside.

'I'm so sorry,' I cried.

'Sorry is no good.'

We sat there for about fifteen minutes. I wished Daniel would come and take Milenko away; send him off to the airport. But there was no need. His anger did that for me. I sensed a change in Milenko's mood, in his voice, which developed its own momentum until he said, 'Okay, Kadie. I am taking these flights to Ireland, and I am going to pay my respect to Killian's family, but don't worry. After that, I will never go to your fucking country again.'

Silence. A dreadful silence in the corridor and in the room and in my head. 'And I'll never go to Croatia again either,' I whispered to the door.

Daniel knocked. 'Can I come in?'

'I'd rather not.'

'He's left for the airport. Are you okay?'

So I would not, after all, sleep in my own bed that night, and instead of me sitting by the fire with Rollo, Milenko would sit with him and they would have a malt whiskey and shake their heads about the errant woman they loved, who would not be there. I could only be where Milenko was not, and that would never change. Twenty years, thirty, would not destroy the draw that sucked me towards him. I could never see him again.

'Kadie, I have to get shifting. Can we at least say goodbye?'

I admired Milenko. He was right not to go back to Korčula at my behest; it was correct that he should express his condolences to Killian's mother. He might even hit on a funeral, but if he did, such a funeral would be very hard on him.

It had not been an entirely wasted day. My broken engagement was intact.

Daniel knocked again. 'All right, all right,' I said, getting up. I let him in.

'You haven't packed yet?'

'No need. I'm not going anywhere.' I went to the window. 'I really wish I knew where Steph is hiding. I'd rather like to be with her right now.'

'But we'll miss the train.'

'What train?'

'The Istanbul sleeper.'

'I'm not going to Istanbul, Daniel.'

'Yeah, you are. I've booked us both on.'

'Since when?'

'Since the Croat left without you.'

I stared at him. 'You really are too much. You shouldn't have made any bookings. I have to ... you know, get to Cork.'

'You're going after him?'

'No, I ... He'll only be there a few days. I'll sit tight here and go back when he's left.'

Daniel looked around. 'Here? Should be fun.'

'I don't need fun.'

'You know what I love about trains, especially sleepers? They give you loads of time to think.'

'Is this just a game to you?'

'No, but ...' he smirked '... your problems have certainly distracted me from mine and –'

'Oh, good. I do so like to be helpful.'

'Thing is, I'd love if you'd come to Istanbul, because you're not bad company when you set your mind to it, and you've nowhere else to be.'

The hotel was so far out, so empty, and the kitchens effectively closed. It didn't even have satellite television. No books. There was nothing but torment for me there.

'Distance, movement,' said Daniel, 'they're good for the soul, you know.'

'You'll dine out on this for years,' I said. 'I can just see it. A great traveller's tale: the loopy Irishwoman and her mad Croat boyfriend.'

'You have to admit . . .'

I felt like hitting him, so I did. I thumped him and cursed and thought I was going to burst into tears. Instead, we started laughing.

'Stop beating me up,' he said. 'The train leaves at two ten. We don't have much time.'

I sank on to the end of the bed. 'And all I really want is . . .'

'Yeah, yeah. Milenko.'

'. . . a washing-machine.'

12

Daniel had a small green rucksack. I followed it into the station in a stupefied daze. I was drained, and on the run now, like Steph, but it was a relief to escape that hotel. To stay there alone, in that grey mist, even for another night, going through the door that he had leant against, crumpled like a child, or walking past that lounge where we had sat, his finger doodling on my leg . . . Following Daniel further south was somehow more rational than sitting in Bucharest torturing myself.

The station was cold. An old woman in black was scavenging in the rubbish bins.

'Food,' I said, veering towards an outlet on the concourse selling croissants. *Fornetti*.

'I've got it covered,' said Daniel.

I bought two bags of pastries anyway. We looked up at the departures board. Prague, Warsaw, Vienna . . . In a blink, my life had become exotic. This was like a nightmare and a dream, running concurrently. Daniel was in the dream, in the unreal; Milenko was in the nightmare, and there was no way of getting him out of it. His distress sucked me into the ground. When I had left him in Croatia, he had been too confused to react, but now his tears were pulling on my conscience, dripping into my heart. I had crippled him. It was as if a bullet had travelled through me and brought him down too, because he was next to me in body and soul. Perhaps it was fair that he should be hurt, but I loved him too much to bear it, which was why when Daniel stopped beside a carriage door and said, 'In you go', in I went.

I had never done anything so bizarre in my entire life. Nor anything, frankly, as interesting. Taking a long-distance train to Turkey when all around me was chaos . . . When, exactly, had reason abandoned me?

There was a collegiate atmosphere in the carriage. Daniel directed me into our compartment. It seemed comfortable enough, but it wasn't what I was used to.

'You didn't book first class?'

He opened his mouth to speak, then closed it.

'Will we have to share with anyone?'

'Probably not at this time of year.'

'How long is this trip?'

'Aw, about eighteen and a half hours.'

My eyes popped out.

'On a good day,' he added.

'You're kidding?'

'It's okay, got lots of chocolate. How's your head?'

'Fine. Just don't stress me!' We laughed. My heart was racing, but it wasn't nerves. It was excitement. I was off on a spree, an adventure – away from parents, responsibilities, funeral and wedding arrangements.

We closed the door, hoping to hold off any invasions, and the only interruption was a guy selling Romanian novels from a plastic bag.

'Do you think I'm abandoning Steph? That I should be following her?'

'Bit difficult when you don't know where she's gone. Anyway, she asked to be left alone and that's fair enough, I reckon.'

The train left right on time. 'God, this is one of the poorest countries in Europe,' I said, 'but they still manage to keep their trains running on schedule.'

'Old Communist habits die hard. What did your dad say about this?'

'I, eh, haven't told him.'

'Come again?'

'How can I when I'm not speaking to him?'

'But he'll phone the hotel and hear you've checked out.'

'I don't think so. He'll give me twenty-four hours to calm down, then start wheedling himself back into favour. As long as my mobile's off, he'll know *I'm* still off.'

Daniel smiled. 'You get on so well with him.'

'That's an odd thing to say when I'm not speaking to him.'

'I can't imagine either of my parents giving a damn if I got my heart broken, let alone trying to mend it for me.'

'But he can't mend it. That's what's going to be so hard on him. He won't be able to fix this.' I looked out. Black Bucharest. I liked it. A city of florists, pharmacies and cabbages, red hairdos and purple trams. It had brawn and guts, and a whiff of the Orient about it. We left it behind and came on to a flat brown plain with black hills further out.

'I've never slept on a train before,' I said.

'What, never?'

'The backpacking-around-Europe thing wasn't really my scene.'

'Not even when you were a student?'

'No.'

Daniel threw his rucksack and my overnight bag on to one of the top berths. 'What exactly did you study?'

'Tourism and languages – French and Italian.'

'Right,' he said, 'so, plenty of opportunity to travel?'

'Yes. Daddy rented villas in Umbria or the Languedoc.'

'I get the picture. Not exactly living, though, is it?'

'I would say a villa in the Umbrian countryside is a very nice kind of living.'

Daniel was untying the top of his rucksack, from which he pulled out a picnic. He certainly had our eating requirements covered – bread, packets of ham and sliced cheese, bottles of water and bars of Milka chocolate.

'Great. I'm starving.'

'You've hardly eaten all day, thanks to the Croat.'

'Stop calling him that.'

'He cheated on you, right?'

That question, again. He had an extraordinary way of moving from the flippant to the serious in the blink of an eyelid. 'A month before your wedding? Total bastard. Doesn't deserve to be called by any name.'

'Remind me – why *am* I going to Istanbul with you?'

'Because,' said Daniel, stuffing one of the cheese croissants I'd bought into his mouth, 'I fancy the company.'

'Pff. You're just using me.'

'Yeah. You're all that's available. What a blow-out – a heartbroken, bereaved and migrainous Irishwoman . . .'

'You are so rude.' The fog was beginning to lift, and so were my treacherous spirits. We sat opposite each other by the window, drinking water. People looked in occasionally but did not intrude. Sharing a compartment with Daniel was one thing; sleeping with strangers would be beyond the pale.

'I wouldn't mind,' he went on cheerfully, 'if I could pass the time hitting on you, but you're a dead loss there too.'

'And why is that?'

'Well, there's the age thing.'

'You're intimidated by older women?'

'How much older?'

'You tell me,' I said.

'Early thirties, I reckon.'

I winced. 'I'm twenty-nine.'

'Way too ancient for me.'

'Yes, well, it takes men so long to mature that you're still in kindergarten as far as I'm concerned, so don't go getting any ideas.'

'Dream on.'

'Oh, God,' I groaned, 'I feel guilty every time I laugh.'

'You can't cry incessantly. Even Killian would get a headache.'

'Where is he, anyway?' I asked, looking around.

'I beg your pardon?'

'Killian,' I said. 'He's never far away, but I haven't seen him since yesterday.'

Daniel had his mouth half-way round the croissant, and he stayed like that, staring at me. Then he put the croissant down.

'What?' I said.

'You *see dead people*?' His eyes were wide and mocking.

'Killian isn't really dead. He's just moved on.'

'That's the spirit,' said Daniel.

We crossed into Bulgaria. Daniel gazed out. Another country to tick off the list, he said.

'This isn't travelling,' I said, 'looking out a window.'

'By the time I get to Turkey, I'll have gone overland from the Gulf of Finland to the Sea of Marmara; Tallinn to Istanbul; eight countries in three weeks. That's travelling in anybody's book.'

The winter landscape was unforgiving in Eastern Europe. Everything appeared drab, dull. The people we rushed past looked cold, the cars and tractors were throwbacks to the era of the Iron Curtain. Over the years I had seen these countries open up, one by one, to my clients, and now I was visiting them, one by one.

It was a very long journey. The compartment remained our own cocoon. During the late afternoon, Daniel fell asleep on the top bunk. I tried to do likewise, but I had never had to sleep on a bench with an overused blanket and an envelope-sized pillow that had had many greasy heads on it. Bed linen should have as little history as possible. And it was impossible to get comfortable in jeans. I enjoyed the motion of the train, but every time it speeded up, I tensed, anticipating a crash, a huge collision, death on the rails. Perhaps I should have told Dad what I was doing. No. But if the train crashed and I was identified among the dead, Rollo would be stunned. Spontaneity was hardly one of my defining characteristics.

The evening dragged. After dark, Daniel produced a pack of cards and taught me a few games. I liked the feel of the train, the odd passenger walking past, the grumble of the undercarriage, and the sound of our voices, ribbing each other. This was no more than the eye of the storm, but what a strange place to find it – on a railway in Bulgaria.

'Are you flying home direct from Istanbul?'

'Changing in Singapore.'

'I'd like to see Asia.'

'You're so blocked,' said Daniel, shaking his head. 'If you got over your fear of flying, just think of the things you could do with your dad's money. The places you could go – especially now you're single.'

'Thanks for reminding me.'

'Sorry.' He sat back. 'Did you ever wonder if you'd got it right with Milenko? Did you ever have doubts?'

'Only once,' I said, but we weren't really talking about me.

Daniel was snoring quietly; Milenko was in my bed, probably, and I hoped he was dead to the world, after his gut-wrenching day. He was beautiful in his sleep and, unlike Daniel, he never snored.

Using Daniel's torch, I found his Discman and the CD pouch and went through his collection. It was good – Dylan, Coldplay, U2, Chili Peppers . . . I had a suspicion that . . . Yes, they were there: Black Daffodil. A recent CD. I slipped it in. Song Five. 'The Ones That Got Away.' One of Dad's best, recently, and although his former colleague, Bruce, did a heart-breaking job, I preferred Dad's own acoustic version. It was about Mum. Almost all his love-songs were. This one was a eulogy to the years and the kids they had never had together. The years they had never had . . .

I liked the hushed rumble of the train. Even in semi-sleep, I was aware of the movement. I kept dropping out of my mind, away from my thoughts, and it was like sliding downhill. Sometimes it felt as if we were going fast, at others very slow, and once I thought we were moving when we weren't. I was no longer tense; in complete contrast to the run to Bucharest, this train was soothing, fun, even. Or maybe that was the Daniel effect.

Vietnam. In the small hours of the morning, the Vietnam word began to repeat. Milenko had a point. If Steph was looking for sanctuary, it was the one place she would find it. She had spent three years there as a teenager, and of all the places her parents had dragged her, it was the one she most loved, so much so that she had gone back in her early twenties to work as a volunteer in an orphanage for street children. Those were happy times for her, but after eighteen months she had been forced to go home when her mother became ill, and she had been unable to finance a return trip, so had ended up in Budapest instead. Since then, she and Killian had been back twice, including their honeymoon, to stay on the island of Phu Quoc, Steph's favourite place in the world.

Images of her sitting on the balcony of the little hotel they had loved came clearly to mind. I'd seen the photos. I knew the view. She would certainly find peace there, but I couldn't countenance it. She was crazy at the moment, granted, but I could not believe she would go to some tropical island when her husband was lying in a morgue.

I stopped the Discman. 'Daniel,' I whispered.

He sighed.

'Daniel, are you deeply asleep or nearly awake?'

He grunted.

'Damn.' I rolled back into the wall.

'Who are you talking to?' he mumbled. 'Killian? Come back, did he?'

'You're awake.'

'I wasn't.'

'Sorry.' I leant over the berth. 'Where's the food? This roughing-it lark really gives me an appetite.'

'This isn't roughing it, Kadie,' he said. 'Hiking through Nepal and sleeping in flea-pits is roughing it.'

'That's *your* roughing it. This is *my* roughing it. Where's the food?'

He threw a bag on to my berth, then hoisted himself up beside me, still grumbling.

'Sorry, but I'm giddy,' I said. 'This is like a school excursion for me. We have to have a midnight feast. Where's the water?'

'Just a minute, madam. I'll get it for you.' He got down again. 'I guess you have a servant to wipe yer bum too.'

'For your information, Dad and I don't have any servants. A woman comes in to tidy his place on a Monday. That's acceptable, isn't it? A bit of help with the housework for a working man?'

'What does he do, exactly?'

'He writes songs.'

'Any I'd have heard?'

'Nah. They're silly little ditties that are big hits in Armenia and Goanna.'

There was a silence in the darkness. 'You really do need to travel more, Kadie, because, as far as I know, a goanna is an animal, not a country. An Aussie animal, at that.'

'I meant Ghana. Or Guinea, or somewhere.'

'Big multicultural appeal, then.'

He was an odd mix, was Daniel Blewitt. He alternated between being mature and serious, coarse and mocking. The sudden shifts made him stimulating, if unpredictable company. His dislike for his stepfather seemed out of proportion to his gentle nature, but he had half-siblings – a sister and two brothers – whom he admitted weren't so bad. 'I hated them when they were born, but they grew up thinking the sun shone out of my ass, so I got quite fond of them.'

I said, 'I *still* don't like my half-sisters. They live the high-life in London, and see me as discarded rubbish, the one their mother left behind who lives a dull life in Ireland, which, of course, I do.'

'Hardly.'

'It's true, and . . . to be absolutely honest, here in the middle of the night, in the middle of wherever we are, I can openly admit that I've often envied them. I would even go so far as to say that I resent them, because they have the mother I never had and a lifestyle I would have enjoyed.'

'Explain.'

'Dad played bass for a band when we were little, and we used to go on tour with him. Then, when I was four, Mum and Dad bought a nice home in County Cork so I could settle into school, which I did, while Dad went off on tour without us.'

'Would I have heard of this band?'

'No. Before your time, sweetie.'

'Try me.'

'Do you want to hear about my tragic childhood or not?'

'Sorry. Go on.'

'Oh, look, it's all a bit rock'n roll. Without Mum there to fight them off, Dad couldn't handle the groupies. Or, rather, he handled them far too much, and Mum was really struggling with the quiet life in Cork. She wasn't cut out for standing at the school gates, not after being on the road for years, and she wanted to be back in the hub of things with the band *and*, as things turned out, with their manager.'

'Oh.'

'Yeah, she'd fallen in love with him apparently, which partly explained the move to Cork. It was an attempt to save their marriage, but when Dad helped himself to one groupie too many, she left him – and me. Dad had to leave the band, when they were at their absolute peak, and retire to the country to look after me, when he was only thirty-one.'

'Couldn't he have got child-minders?'

'Yeah, but there was also the problem of his wife sleeping with the manager, which made his position fairly untenable. So Mum stayed with the band and he left it. The band replaced him and she replaced me, with two bonny wee girls, who toured the world.'

Daniel exhaled. 'Tough shit.'

'It had its moments.'

'You must be pretty bitter?'

'I was very jealous at times. I mean, I sat on quite a few interesting laps as a child, and although Dad still has good friends in the business, it was really hard in my late teens when my ugly half-sisters were getting to every concert, every event, and appearing all glam in magazines. But I've grown out of that, thank heavens, and I've a much better relationship with my mother now. She looks like an Irish version of Bianca Jagger, you know? All dark and pouty. She was a real rock babe, I gather.'

'Your father never remarried?'

'Nope.'

'How did he survive? Financially, I mean.'

'Royalties. But it was horrible for him, seeing the band go on without him, playing his songs. Actually, they ran out of songs a few years later, so they came begging for more and he's still writing for them now. He does sessions, too, with other people, but he's lost interest in performing in public.'

'And your mother?'

'She lives in London. The manager didn't last.'

'Are you sure I wouldn't have heard of this band? I mean, if he's still writing for them, they're still out there.'

'Yeah, but they're old cronies now, doing a few gigs around the place. Old rockers no one can remember who don't have the wit to retire.'

'Jeez, you had an interesting childhood. While all that was going on, I was busy singing hymns at Sunday school.'

'I wish you'd tell me whatever it is you're supposed to be thinking about on this trip.'

'Tell me about the Croat first.'

Milenko had been right. Our relationship was a big problem. He could not travel during the high season, so I returned to Korčula at the end of June. He worked incredibly long hours, but it was enough to be near him, and he took comfort, during the busiest days, in knowing that I was there somewhere, round a corner. We never knew when we might run into each other. Any time he appeared unexpectedly, coming down to the waterfront to see passengers off or scurrying up the steps while I ambled down them, my insides twisted in delight.

The island had its own effect. Some mornings I took the water-taxi to Korčula for breakfast, and every time we came round the headland and the old town came into view, it made me smile. Even Milenko never tired of seeing the gathering of red roofs pressed together, the belt of green round its waist, and the spires – masts and churches – shooting into the clear sky. I loved walking its cool alleyways, looking up at the washing hanging between the houses – football shirts, vests, jeans – or I'd snoop round the yachts tied up at the marina, eavesdropping on the yachties. In the plaza, I'd buy cheese and fruit from the circular stone platform where there was a daily market and nibble them back at the hotel, while lying on the plinth and watching happy holidaymakers.

At some point, a hand would stroke my back and my day

would properly begin: Milenko was off duty. We'd take out the boat or drive along the Račišće road and swim off one of the hand-made piers along the waterfront there, talking and talking until Milenko had to return for a late shift. Those evenings he worked were hard. I ate alone, or sometimes with his parents, or I'd sit reading on my balcony, with the house-martins squeaking and flitting about, and the cypresses almost black against the white sky, like tall Christmas trees looming over me. Some nights, after his shift, we'd walk along the creek and find our spot on a wall, and Milenko would produce wine, bread and cheese, and we'd sit under the skies, my head on his lap, his low voice purring down on me.

I learnt about the hospitality industry: our time was not our own; time together would always be snatched between shifts. Generally, after a long day, Milenko was fit only for sleep, and that was not something we could do together until he returned to Ireland the following September. The first morning I woke beside him, in my flat, felt like the beginning of the rest of my life. With the freedom to do so, we spent a lot of time in bed. Milenko's restraint had vanished. He admitted to having been apprehensive about beginning an affair with me; it was easy, he said, with the holiday girls, to find a bush in the dark or to huddle in a boat by the pier, then wave her off a few days later, never to see her again. He had great stories about what he and his mates had got up to during hot summer nights, but by the time he met me, he had outgrown all that and, aside from the pressure inflicted by his parents, was longing for something lasting. It was likely that he would have to go beyond Korčula for a life-mate – he knew almost every woman on the island – but he fancied he might meet a nice girl in Zagreb or Split. What he was not looking for was someone like me: a guest, passing through. He'd already done that and didn't want to do it again, which was why I had presented a conundrum from the outset. There had been a Dutch tourist once, whom he had loved, but she had returned to her life and left him to his. He had feared a similar outcome with me; hence his reticence about embarking on something from which there would be no way back.

And there was certainly no way back when we lay curled against each other in my flat, able to relax in an embrace for the first time, skin on skin, legs on legs, hands everywhere. I loved to watch him sleep, wake, dream, stare vacantly out of my bedroom window in a post-coital slump, while we drank tea and fiddled with one another's feet, discussing things of no importance. Milenko was a tender lover, and determined. He sometimes approached me with an insistance that was irresistible. As when I took him that first time to Kilcrohane, on a grey afternoon, and we settled on a grass shelf overlooking the sea. His hands came inside my clothes, his mouth following close behind. I thought that was as much as we could manage, perched on an Atlantic ledge, until he moved down and I saw in his eyes that he meant to go on. I protested about being *al fresco*, exposed to the elements and to prying eyes. Milenko smiled, looked at the wilderness around us, said the birds wouldn't mind, and pulled at my jeans. I don't know if the birds minded, but I certainly didn't.

We were still cautious, as we tasted each other's lives and tried them for size. Weeks after our Irish break, Dad came with me to Korčula, when it was extremely quiet, and he and Milenko's father were like two old mates who hadn't seen each other since the sixties. They played backgammon, drank the local wines and went fishing. Dad was also attentive to Cecilia and sat with her on her terrace talking about the day and the time of year, and the simple things she liked to discuss. Watching our parents gel also brought us closer, and even more committed to the problematical future we never mentioned.

When Dad took Cecilia to Mass one Sunday, I couldn't

resist ribbing him. 'Don't mock,' he said. 'I wanted to give Milenko a break and a bit of a rest on a Sunday morning.'

I pursed my lips. Milenko had hugely enjoyed the break, but not a rest, in my bed. And also in my shower.

But Dad was in serious mode. 'Don't ever underestimate,' he went on, 'or undervalue Milenko's devotion to his parents.'

'I don't,' I said, then went on to prove that I did by adding, 'but it is frustrating that he rarely does anything without considering them first.'

'That should, above all, be a relief,' said Dad. 'It is to me.'

'Why?'

'Milenko knows how to care, Kadie.'

He made other observations. 'You've both grown up with largely ineffectual mothers, and fathers domesticated by circumstance. Men brought up in more conventional ways have often been a challenge to you, but Milenko is able to look after himself, as well as those around him.'

He was right, on every count, and so we continued, Milenko and I, with our long-distance love, until we found ourselves the following spring in Kilcrohane, and knew decisions had to be made.

We had taken a cottage there for a week. Living together agreed with us. We had bacon and white bread for breakfast, slurping at our teacups and mesmerized by the view beyond our window, of the peninsula on the other side of the bay and the sea in between, sometimes blue, sometimes grey, rarely still. We walked the empty roads and climbed the rocky shores, and sat in the evening on our gravel porch, marvelling at the way the sea glowed along the coastline. A golden halo, Milenko called it, as if Ireland really was a blessed isle. Sometimes we joked about whose isle was more blessed. Later, we'd bathe in the bedroom (there was a bath in the room), then stretch across the bed, still wet, and Milenko would press into me, as if trying to reach some better place, though there was no better place than where we were, that week.

He was very quiet, the man I chose. Restrained, and thoughtful. He spoke only when necessary, incisively and intuitively. Small-talk beguiled him, but he didn't need to say much because he wore his thoughts on his face, in those ever-changing expressions – the almost imperceptible bite of his lower lip, his deep eyes shifting sharply. The way he blinked, and when, also spoke volumes. He could be moody, petulant, and when we argued he infuriated me by contributing very little, refusing to respond to my taunts. It was like arguing with a statue. Impossible to win. But he was always quick to make up, and good at it, often taking the blame for the sake of restoring good humour, even when the fault was mine. But his silence was his most attractive attribute. In silence, I felt his love most deeply.

It could not go on. I feared that if he tunnelled any deeper into my love, into what I was and what I could be, he would come out the other side and be lost to me. We had to harness this, to catch it and keep it, and the unspoken finally broke through one day, when we were sitting on the steps at the coal harbour below the house. Milenko was subdued, moody. 'Only two days left,' he said.

'I could move to Croatia.'

'But what would you do? All winter. All year?'

'I can't get a job until Croatia joins the EU, but I could work unofficially. Helping you at the hotel and . . . you know that house on the other side of the creek? Dad's thinking about buying it – he needs to spread his capital – and I could do it up and rent it out. Maybe turn it into a couple of flats.'

'It's very quiet in winter.'

'This is quiet,' I said, gesturing towards the deep, cold water lapping below us and the perpendicular rocks that made this tiny corner a natural harbour. 'Where Dad lives is quiet. I can handle quiet. What I can't handle is another winter without you.'

He looked across at the peninsula opposite, moving his mouth around. 'It would be very difficult for me to leave Korčula. My mother . . .'

'I will never ask you to do that.'

'But how would you be if I took you away from your beautiful island?'

'Marginally better, I think, than if I took you from yours.'

Milenko wiped his hands on his jeans. 'I think,' he said, grimacing against the light, 'I think . . . it's no good.'

That was not what I had expected to hear.

He turned to me. 'One of us has to end this.'

There was no air in my chest. I thought we'd been moving inwards, but he was moving out. 'End it?'

'One of us has to move,' he said.

I breathed again. 'I told you. I'll do it.'

He looked around, then back at me. 'It's very hard to leave,' he said, and before I could protest, he put his hand on my lips and added, 'but it is even harder to take someone away.'

On our last afternoon we went to our favourite spot, a rock shaped like a great undulating wave, and watched the cormorants slither in and out of the water. It was a warm day. The blow-holes behind us were chuckling, not roaring.

I sat between Milenko's knees. It came as no surprise when he said, 'So you think you can leave them, your cormorants?'

I watched the silly birds I had loved since childhood. This was my own particular batch, my own brood, but I said, 'Course I can.'

Nor did it surprise me when he asked at last the dreadful question that had hung over us for months: 'But could you really leave Rollo?'

A lump gathered in my throat. 'Yes' was a word too far, so I nodded.

Then he said, 'Could you marry me, do you think?'

That surprised me.

13

Istanbul was as giddy as I was. I had never been so far east, and the moment I put my nose outside the carriage, an intimidating new world engulfed me: noise, colour, crowds.

Bewildered, I followed Daniel's rucksack through the station, holding one of its straps like a child. He made his way to an ATM so we could get local currency. More money, more notes, a change of set. I had hardly had time to blink in Budapest and had not yet recovered from seeing Milenko in Bucharest, but this was my wake-up call. I had to keep my wits about me and shake off the daze I had been wandering in. Breaking away from home had freed me. This had become a whole different trip, and with every day, every city, I felt closer to Steph. I was beginning to understand escape: not being where you should be was oddly gratifying.

I trailed Daniel on to the streets and was taken aback by the light, the high blue sky and the glimpse of waterways, busy with business. 'My God – from the Baltic to the Bosphorus in four days.'

'Come on.'

'Where are we going?'

'A hostel a mate told me about.'

'I'm not slumming it, you know.'

'Yeah, I get that.' He took out his travel guide to consult maps. 'It's a bit of a walk.'

A bit of a walk. And how. Daniel marched on, dipping through the dense crowds. We were travelling on his terms now.

'Can't we take a taxi?'

He sighed, forged on.

'Be careful not to lose me,' I called, hurrying along behind him. My holdall was pulling on my arm, as I changed it from one hand to the other, and my feet were hot and sweaty in my low-heeled boots. My coat, so cosy in Bucharest, was like carrying a dead body round my shoulders.

If Bucharest had been in black and white, Istanbul was Technicolor. 'When do you have to leave?' I asked Daniel's back, knowing I would never handle this place on my own and determined to book myself out ahead of him. The city roared in our ears.

'Tomorrow. Home Friday,' he added, as if it were a death sentence.

Brasov had been my first and only experience of a hostel, and whatever about the restrictions of his budget, Daniel was clearly enjoying bringing me down to earth, as he perceived it. When offered the choice of the ladies' dorm or sharing with him, I couldn't help but play up to it. 'Can't I have my own room?'

'It's a hostel, Kadie. You bunk in with whoever happens to be here.'

'I'm not sleeping with strangers.'

'Then you'll have to share with me.'

'Again? Is there an *en suite* this time?'

'You need to live a little,' he said ruefully, as we went upstairs.

'I figure I've lived quite enough in the last week to be entitled to a four-star hotel.'

The room was pleasant. The furniture was cheap – a desk, chair, double bed and a single – but the bedclothes were bright and colourful; I took the double bed, and was about to check in with home, when I changed my mind. In a few hours, I could come out of my foxhole, the crowded, vibrant warren of Istanbul, but for now I would remain unaccounted for.

From the roof of our building, we could see the Blue Mosque, its minarets spiking the sky and its main dome lying between them like a slumbering mammal or some extraterrestrial being sent to mind the bustling city. It was truly magnificent.

'Worth it?' Daniel asked.

'Oh, worth it, I don't know. It's so hard to grasp. I'm on the border of Europe and about to fall over the edge into Asia.'

'We'll go to Asia tomorrow. Then you can say you've been there.'

'Have you been here before?'

'No.'

'Seems like it.'

'You really are dim for a travel agent, you know.'

'Look, there's a world of difference between a travel agent and a seasoned backpacker.'

'You said it.'

'I really wish I could be as laid-back as you are, arriving in a place like this.'

'You get the hang of it. And if this goes on much longer – even *you*'ll get the hang of it.'

I blinked several times, convinced that the extraordinary skyline would dissolve and I would find myself somewhere else, dark and grim. 'It's strange,' I said, 'this jumping about like a flea. Someone dying on you is like a sort of slow strangulation, you know? But in city after city, hotel after hotel, it gets easier to breathe.'

'Maybe that's just because the weather's improving. So we'll do Topkapi and the Aya Sofya museum, and, obviously, the Blue Mosque.'

'Obviously.'

He stuck his nose into his guide.

'Three pages,' I said, 'three days per city. See the world with the *Lonely Planet*.'

'Better than not seeing the world at all. Let's go.' He disappeared into the building.

'"Let's go!" "Come on!" "Hurry up!" It's like being on an old-age pensioners' bus tour. Where are we going?'

'Aya Sofya.'

Along the way, we passed the Four Seasons Hotel – an enticing yellow building, like a castle, trying to lure me in. 'God, that's gorgeous.'

'It used to be a prison. The one in *Midnight Express*, no less.'

'A quick cup of coffee, perhaps?'

'Have you any idea what that would cost in there? . . . Oh, yeah. Forgot. Of course you do.'

The further south we travelled, the more I was acquiring the 'tourist' tag. That was all they saw, the crowds in the streets, when we ducked and dived along the busy pavements. They didn't see the friend, or lover, or daughter: they saw the Western tourist. It had been a gradual process from Stockholm down. But as my identity became more homogenized, so my surroundings became more diverse. The faces were darker, the men's glare more intense, their moustaches more uniform. The women were veiled, or shrouded, or heavily made-up and designer-clothed. As the weather diluted – it was warmer, softer – the flavours got stronger. It was like sliding down a tube, into a deeper, richer mix of life.

I wanted to remain unimpressed wherever Daniel took me, to prove that this was not the way to see the world, but when we walked under the magnificent dome of Aya Sofya – former church, mosque and present-day museum – I could not stifle a gasp. It was like being in an enormous golden bubble.

'Fifteen hundred years old,' Daniel said, staring up.

It was ludicrous, being me that day. A tourist in mourning, standing in a shaft of light on the great marble mosaics, thinking about God and heaven and Killian taken from us. It was not a question of missing him, there in that unfamiliar place. He would be missed more acutely at home, on the streets, on my sofa, in their cottage. It wasn't the missing of him that still made me shudder, it was the losing of him, his violent and unreasonable removal from my life. And yet, it was still possible to be awestruck. I wandered round the nave, looking up, comforted by its jaded beauty.

Daniel had his finger in a hole in a column in one of the side aisles. 'They say it weeps,' he said. 'If you make a wish and your finger comes out wet, your wish'll come true.' He took his finger out. We peered at it. Dry. 'Oh, well.'

'What did you wish?'

'Something that isn't going to happen apparently,' he said. 'Go on, your turn.'

'And what am I supposed to wish? Where would I start?'

'You could ask for the last two weeks to have been a very bad dream.'

'But if that comes true, I'll vanish on the spot and then what'll you do?'

My finger came out of the hole as dry as Daniel's.

When we emerged into the bright winter sunlight, he announced that we were going straight over to the Topkapi Palace. 'It's through a gate round the back.'

'First,' I said, taking out my phone, 'it's time I came out with my hands up.'

'You're *where*?' Dad roared.

'Istanbul. In Turkey.' I sat on a step, watching Daniel wandering around with his camera.

'I know where bloody Istanbul is. Get down, you wretched mutt!'

'What are the dogs doing inside the house?'

'What are *you* doing in Istanbul? And how the hell did you get there?'

'By train.'

'But why, for fuck's sake? I thought you were going to sit it out in Bucharest until Milenko went home?'

'I am sitting it out, just not in Bucharest and not alone.'

'You're still with that Daniel character? Milenko didn't like the look of him, I don't mind telling you.'

'Dad, you're a rock guitarist. Stop sounding like a bank manager.'

'But what the hell are you doing?'

'Enough with the inquisition, Rollo. This is your fault. You've shown more loyalty to Milenko than to me. Is he still there?'

After a moment he said, 'Yes.'

'Please ask him to leave. I want to come home.'

'Kadie, listen, there's been a development. Steph's in Vietnam.'

I exhaled. 'I knew it!' No. Milenko had known it.

'She faxed their solicitor, instructing him to have the body released from the mortuary for immediate cremation.'

My mouth fell open.

'His ashes are to be thrown around the Baltic or something.'

I stood up. 'No! No, this is all wrong! It isn't what he wanted.'

'Steph said his family can go ahead with whatever memorial service they want.'

'He isn't even to go home?'

'Apparently not. Marjorie is beside herself. She wants all of them back – Killian, Steph and her unborn grandchild.'

'But Killian didn't want to be cremated, Dad. I know it. We talked about it. And I told Steph. I told her!' Tourists turned to look at me.

'Nonetheless,' he said quietly, 'those are her instructions.'

'But can't someone speak to her? You could. You talk to her.'

'I have spoken to her. She phoned me about the dogs,' he said drily.

'And?'

'So I told her the dogs are pining. Actually, they're beginning to improve, but I'll tell her anything if it'll bring her home.'

'What did she say about Kill?'

'That was it. When I tried to change the subject, she hung up. Listen, Kadie, I'm not sure how much longer Marjorie can bear up. The solicitor isn't exactly keen to carry out these instructions when the family is so against it, and nor is the undertaker. She knows there's dissent and would rather it was cleared up to everyone's satisfaction before they do anything drastic. Let's face it, there's no way back from cremation.'

I winced.

'The trouble is, it's a bit hard to resolve when the relevant parties are all in different countries. James, their solicitor, feels Steph won't budge. He says she's convinced this is the best for all concerned.'

'Except Killian!'

'Take it easy, love. James is talking about going to Sweden to see if he can get the body released and brought home, without committing to cremation.'

'Good. Can he stop it happening?'

'Well, if nothing else, it would give you time to change her mind.'

'How am I supposed to do that?'

He hesitated. 'Actually . . . Istanbul is perfect. You're a third of the way there. Daniel must be some kind of lucky charm. Would you go the extra hump?'

A noise came out of me – some kind of humourless laugh.

'Kadie –'

'No way! Can't his mother overrule his wife?'

'Of course not.'

222

'But if her mind is made up, nothing I can say will change it. I've already tried.'

'Kadie, she's alone, only days after losing her husband in a ghastly car smash. This is hardly rational behaviour. Not only is she delaying the inevitable for herself, she's depriving everyone else of an opportunity to mourn. It's as if she wants to punish the rest of us for what happened to him.'

'Tell me something I *don't* know. Look – Steph has friends in Vietnam. Get in touch with them. They can sort her out on their verandas.'

'Most of the friends she had there have left, but we're working on it. Meanwhile, it would mean so much to Marjorie and Steph's parents if you went on.'

I wasn't laughing any more, with or without humour. There was a horrible inevitability to all this. 'Dad, this is mad. I'm in frigging Turkey, for God's sake, and I don't even know how I got here.'

'I know, love, but I've promised them that you would.'

'*What?*'

'This is getting out of hand. We have to do everything we can to –'

'Yes, but I'm the one who is having to do "everything". You can't go making promises to people. I'm totally knackered.'

'So you're happy for Killian to be cremated?'

He knew me too well. 'No, of course not, but why does it have to be me? Let the solicitor talk her out of it.'

'His job is to follow instructions. Besides, it's a hard thing to do from the other side of the globe. You could make eye-contact. Help her understand. She shouldn't be alone, Kadie. She really shouldn't. I know it's a lot to ask, but I'm looking further down the line than you are. If something happened to Steph, you'd never forgive yourself. You're tired and disoriented, but if things don't go right, you'll torment yourself for not doing everything you could do at the time.

And that time is now. You think I don't want you home? In the state you're in? I want this whole miserable odyssey to be over, but if you don't go to Vietnam, I will, because someone has to speak to Stephanie. We can't have Killian dumped in the Baltic with only his sister there to farewell him.'

'Don't say that. Steph wouldn't do that to him. She *wouldn't*.'

'They have it in writing. I thought you'd want to go and, let's face it, we can afford it rather more easily than anyone else.'

'But I don't have a visa or flights.'

'We've been working on that.'

I boiled on the spot. 'I see. I thought I was escaping by coming here, and all this time you people have been organizing my life for me.'

He talked over me. 'What's the story with visas for Vietnam?'

'Em . . .' I tried to make my mind work. 'Our clients get them from the London embassy. Ask Clara. She does most of the long-haul stuff.'

'I'll get her on to it and get back to you.'

'But I've no clean clothes!'

Daniel was tapping his watch. 'We don't have all week,' he said, coming back to me.

'Excuse me, but are you my husband or some yoke I picked up along the way?'

'Who's been rattling your cage?'

'Everyone. I'm going to Vietnam apparently!'

His eyes widened. 'I know you want to avoid Milenko, but isn't that taking things a bit far?' He took a slug of water. 'He's shacking up with your dad, is he? Not budging?'

'Worse than that.' I brought him up to speed. 'They've been planning to send me to Vietnam without even telling me. Because they think I'd "want to".'

224

Daniel nodded mildly. 'You do.'

That deflated me. I sat down again. 'It's Killian. He's still in that mortuary . . . and it's as if no one cares about that. But who am I to change her mind? It's between the two of them. It has nothing to do with me.'

Daniel leant back on the steps, closing his eyes against the winter sun. 'Nice place, Vietnam.'

'You've been there.'

'Twice, yeah. Love it.'

'Well, that's all very well, but sending me round the world isn't going to change anything,' I said, flapping my arms. 'It just isn't. I'm not doing it.'

'Tell me something,' said Daniel, his eyes still closed, 'has this got anything to do with the flight? If you weren't afraid of flying, would you . . . wouldn't you be on your way to the airport right now?'

'I don't know. I'm beyond making my way anywhere.'

'Here's a plan then. Come with me as far as Singapore. That way, you won't be alone on the long-haul. Ho Chi Minh City is only a hop from there.'

I shook my head. 'Please don't make it easy for me, Daniel. I really don't want to go. Anyway, I'd still need a visa.' I took his guidebook and looked up embassies. 'And there ain't no Vietnamese embassy in Turkey, so that'd mean going back to London and . . . oh, fuck, even longer flights from there.'

'Let's keep moving.'

We walked along the Court of the Janissaries to the ticket office. Topkapi was an enormous complex. 'We can't do the whole place,' I said. 'My feet are swelling. I need runners.'

'We'll get some in the bazaar later.'

Daniel was as irritating in tourist mode as he was endearing. In my ridiculously inappropriate boots, jeans sticking to my thighs, I walked uncomfortably across a huge courtyard.

'See?' he said. 'No queues. This is the time of year to travel.'

We joined a guided tour through the rooms of the harem. I was biting my inner cheek; my heart palpitated erratically. Hours and hours encased in a plane . . . and then what? Getting to Vietnam, tackling South East Asia, tackling Steph. The very interference, the presumption, would infuriate her. She had put herself out of reach for a reason – she didn't *want* to be reached. My loyalty was to her, not to our hyperactive families. But what of my loyalty to Killian?

'Whose mission am I on?' I asked out loud. 'I mustn't do this to pacify them at home. I can only do what is right for me and for Steph.'

'And what's that?' said Daniel.

'I've no idea.'

He was gazing up at the exquisite tiling work in the Sultan's privy chamber.

I followed in his footsteps. 'It's just . . . It's the way Killian's disappeared,' I said. 'I mean, he was around. He kept turning up, as if he wanted me to go to Budapest and Bucharest. He was guiding me until I swerved off course, which would suggest he's happy now with wherever she is and doesn't need me to go on.'

Daniel was looking at me.

'You think I'm insane, because I talk about him like that.'

'I don't know,' he said. 'I don't know about the dead.' We wandered on again. 'This is awesome, isn't it?'

I sighed wearily. 'Just another monument to another man's ego.'

'Ego is responsible for most of the world's great buildings. Anyway, this is way more beautiful, and the proportions are better, than Ceauşescu's place.'

'Three hundred rooms for one family?'

'If a man is going to have a hundred and fourteen children, and concubines and eunuchs, he needs space.'

My phone rang.

'Here's the story,' said Dad. 'The nearest Vietnamese consulate is in Ankara – no bloody use at all – so Clara suggests you stop off in Singapore and get the visa from the Vietnamese embassy there, which would be pretty handy because you'll probably have to change flights there anyway, yeah? . . . Kadie?'

I cursed myself for coming to Turkey. It made it so easy for them.

Dad went on. 'About flights –'

'Yeah, about flights,' I interrupted, 'tell Clara there's a Singapore Airlines flight out of here tomorrow. Get me a seat on that.'

Daniel cocked his head at me.

'Actually, we can get you on Air India tonight to Delhi, then transfer to Singapore.'

'It's Singapore Airlines tomorrow or nothing. Daniel's on that flight.'

'Really? Wow, that's a little weird, isn't it?'

'How so?'

'It's like he's . . . I don't know.'

I looked at Daniel's back. No wings. 'That flight is over twelve hours long, Daniel says, and I've some chance of keeping my marbles if I'm not on my own.'

'All right. I'll see what's doing.'

A voice inside my head kept telling me to stop this. To say no. But was it Steph's voice, or mine, or Killian's? Who was I supposed to be listening to?

'Do you want a word with Milenko?' Dad asked.

'Oh, do me a favour, Dad, book *him* a flight home!' I hung up.

Daniel came over to me.

'Can't have him cremated,' I said. 'Can't.'

★

227

We had to backtrack to get to the Blue Mosque. I was grumpy, tired, and confused. Daniel was chirpy, energetic, enchanted; every now and then I felt I had to remind him I was there. But the mosque, as we approached, was an uplifting sight, almost silver in the winter light, with its needle-thin minarets pointing at the sky and its multiple domes, like a stairway to the heavens, making it the most mesmerizing building I had ever set eyes on. I loved the way it laid claim to Istanbul, owned it. We removed our boots and went inside. It was like being in a vast jewel casket, and although I was not as moved as I had been in Aya Sofya, I suffered sensory overload. The chandeliers and hanging lights, the arches, columns, mosaics and marble, the stained-glass windows – two hundred and sixty of them, Daniel said – and the blue Iznik tiling and gold Koranic script almost overwhelmed me, but it was my feet that finally capitulated. I could stand no longer. My ankles were as thick as an elephant's, so I left Daniel gaping and went back outside. I struggled to get my boots on, then found a wall near the entrance to the courtyard and sat, content to enjoy the hue of the place. My eyes kept returning to those minarets. 'Up,' they seemed to be saying. 'Up, up!'

Then I saw him. Like any person, like one of the faithful, walking past the steps to the entrance. He glanced over; I shook my head. He raised his shoulders, then dropped them as he sauntered along. He wanted me to go on. I craned my neck to look up at the minarets and said, 'Thanks, God.'

When Daniel appeared, I said, 'Runners!'

We went to the bazaar. It was exotic, yet mundane, with locals shopping among the ambling tourists, but it was also a warren and we couldn't immediately find runners. There was everything else – jewellery, hardware, clothes, foodstuffs and spices, and men with shiny eyes trying to lure us down passages. 'From London? America? Australia?'

'Ireland.'

'Ah! Holland!'

Daniel allowed himself to be drawn into carpet shops and even into haggling, though he couldn't afford their smallest mat, and, of course, he had to try a hubble-bubble pipe, which he sucked at, his eyes wide. It would have been interesting, I thought, to have had his eyes for just one day, but the charms of the Grand Bazaar quite passed me by, especially with my phone going off every five minutes and my feet bursting.

Clara got me on to Daniel's flight – in business class. Bloody useless. What was the point of taking his flight if we were at opposite ends of the plane? The flight arrived in Singapore early in the morning, so Clara reckoned I could get the visa within hours and return to the airport for the evening flight to Ho Chi Minh City. She had booked me on to that, too, but if I missed it, I could pick up another the next morning.

I eventually found some runners.

That night, it was cheap food by the waterfront. This tourism business was non-stop, but a long shower had revived my feet, and my winter coat was welcome now against the chill night air. We ate off the stalls – grilled fish stuffed into bread. Tasty. I muttered that we'd probably get salmonella, but I was growing a new skin. Or perhaps I was shedding an old one. A slow death was spreading through my bones; it would complete its course. Losing Milenko would kill off whole parts of me. There would be no house on the hillside, no children raised on a beautiful island, but there could, perhaps, be something else, and this was a glimpse of it.

Feet. Feet into the fire. Sliding into the flames. Rugby boots and red and white striped socks, slipping, slipping, into the fire. Going, going . . .

I woke with a yelp. The room was dark. Daniel was breathing, deep and easy. I lay back, gasping. The call to prayer started up just then, haunting and pervasive, and released me from the nightmare. For all my professional patter about Istanbul's attractions, it was clear to me now that you could never really know anything about any place until you had heard it, and smelt it, and looked into the eyes of its inhabitants. As the muezzin called out across this heaving, waking city, I could feel the East pulling at me, pulling me on.

The anxiety began, as always, with a dry mouth. Daniel, insistent on having breakfast on another continent, had roused me early and dragged me down to the waterfront where we boarded a ferry to the other side. We wandered through a market in Kadiköy, then sat in a café, looking across the Bosphorus Strait, listening to the rumbling din of the city across the water. The satisfaction of doing the right thing washed through me. I was filled with a strong urge to go on. Dad was right: no matter how tired or depressed, I could not scurry home. It just wasn't in me to turn from Steph, and I couldn't bear to think of her being alone, so very far away.

As for the flight, I was in limbo. To go forward, or back, I needed an aircraft, unless I intended to travel alone overland from Turkey, which I didn't.

'Here,' said Daniel, on the way to the airport, holding out chewing-gum.

'I don't like gum.'

'*Chew*. It'll help.'

I chewed. Doing what Daniel told me to do usually worked to my advantage. The dry mouth was not so dry, and my anxiety became focused on chewing that piece of gum to death, with a fast and furious bite. But no amount of mastication could stop my mind going where it fancied and where it fancied was this: twelve and a half hours. Up there for nearly twelve and a half hours. How was it to be endured? And what about the terrorist threat?

There was a long, slow-moving queue at the check-in desks. 'This way,' I said, moving past the queue towards another desk.

Seeing where I was headed, Daniel turned to go back to the economy queue.

'Don't be silly, you can check in here too. Take advantage.' He loped towards me, uncertain. 'I don't suppose you'd consider upgrading?' I mumbled, while the woman behind the counter looked for my ticket.

'Can't afford to.'

'You know what I mean.'

He shook his head. 'Thanks, Daddy, but no thanks. Like I said, I'm not a charity case.'

'No. Just pig-headed and proud.'

Neither of us checked in our bags. Daniel's haversack was small enough for the overhead lockers and I wanted to keep my few belongings with me on the flight. Shopping was high on my list of priorities on arrival in Vietnam. Forget Steph, funerals and cremation: I'd be hitting the shops when this journey was over.

'They didn't search our bags,' I hissed, after we came through the security checks.

'They X-rayed them.'

'X-rays miss things. I could be carrying explosive putty.'

Daniel rolled his eyes. 'How *did* Milenko sign up for life?'

At the gate, he stretched out across five seats. He was game, I'd give him that. He'd waded into this whole story by accident, but he'd stayed there by choice. I walked up and down in front of him, looking at the boots, the worn jeans and his blue jacket bunched up under his head. A flicker of sadness ran through me. He had grown on me, and in twelve hours' time, presuming we survived the flight, I would have to leave him behind in the airport, like a security blanket.

I sat behind his head and flicked his bleached hair with my finger. 'It doesn't make sense, does it?' I said. 'A chance meeting, a crisis, travelling and more travelling, and then, just like that, goodbye.'

He looked up. 'It happens when you travel. You meet people in different places, form some kind of bond, then keep up the emails for as long as possible.'

'So we'll email?'

'For a while. Then it'll sort of drift off.'

'I'll bet you're lousy at keeping in touch.'

'Yeah, I am, but in this case I'll want to know what happens. You'll have to tell me.'

'I will. Of course I will. And the next time you're in Ireland . . .'

'Hey, if you start now, this is going to be the longest goodbye in history.'

When the flight was called, I thought I was going to be sick. I hurried into the queue and noted the business-class passengers arriving from their business-class lounge. Daniel sat up blearily.

'You're eager,' he said, coming to join me.

Half a day at thirty-four thousand feet. All that time for something to go wrong. Hours and hours in which the aircraft could develop a fault. Cars break down frequently. Machines are flawed. They don't always do what they're meant to. I hopped from one foot to the other, then hurried on to the 747, where I was directed into business class. Daniel went in the opposite direction. 'I'll come down in a minute,' I called over my shoulder.

The cabin hummed with its comforts. My seat was big enough for both of us. It seemed, as I stood over it, outsized, inappropriate. It would ease the long hours ahead, but it would be lonely too. A flight attendant was hovering, wanting to take my bag, install me, pamper me with a drink. 'I'll be back in a minute.'

Economy hummed with discomfort. It was crowded. People pressed into the aisles, pushing their belongings into overhead compartments, taking their seats and resisting my attempts to get past. I couldn't see Daniel. A flight attendant tried to redirect me to business class, but just then I saw Daniel's head in the middle aisle. He was reading and listening to his Discman. So damn cool. A pretty Asian woman was sitting beside him and the flight attendant urged me again to return to my seat. 'I want to change it. Would this woman mind swapping with me?'

'Are you sure?'

'Yes.' Daniel still hadn't noticed. I stood behind the attendant while she spoke to the young woman. She was ecstatic, got to her feet, disbelieving, and thanked me warmly. I smiled, as she gathered her things and was led off to business class.

I knocked on Daniel's head. 'Pride,' I said, pulling an earplug from his ear. 'Foolish pride. It's lovely up there.' I sat down. 'And you should see the menu!'

'If we're gonna die,' he said, 'as you seem to think, it doesn't matter what the hell class we're in.'

'We'd die more comfortably, that's all.'

'We?'

'I've downgraded.' He gave me a funny look, a smile, slightly bewildered, but also touched. 'And why do we have to be in the middle aisle? It's so squashed.'

'It's good,' he said. 'No windows to look out and see how high up we are.'

I stared along the row of four seats. It was very tight. On long-haul, when you needed more space, you had less space than ever. You couldn't even stretch out, with every single seat taken. 'Like chickens in a coop,' I said.

'Claustrophobic as well? Man, do I have my work cut out!'

The slight angels of Singapore Airlines, tiny women in exquisite uniforms, passed serenely among us. How could they be so calm? Who would choose this for a career?

'Seriously,' said Daniel, 'you're not going to blow, are you?'

'Shush. I'm concentrating.'

'On what? Oh, on your safe place, is it? A Croatian beach at sunset?'

'I'm thinking about all the things that could go wrong.'

'How does that help?'

'It means I've got everything covered. That there's no room for surprises. It gives me control – knowing what's going to go wrong.'

'You mean, terrorist attacks . . .'

'Yes.' I scanned Economy for shifty individuals.

'A fire on board?'

'I hadn't thought of that! Where are the fire hydrants?'

We were handed steaming-hot facecloths. I rubbed mine on my forehead, my sweaty palms. The doors banged shut. 'Oh, God! That's it. No going back. Christ. This isn't fair. The funeral could be over and we'd all be getting on with our lives, instead of being locked up in this great aluminium tube.'

'And what would you be getting on with exactly?'

God, he was irritating. So in-my-damn-face. 'I don't know, but I wouldn't be *here*, that's for sure!'

When the aircraft began rolling backwards, my anxiety rolled forwards. I could feel the weight of the thing in my bones. This lumbering mammoth could surely never get off the ground, what with the weight and baggage of four hundred people aboard. My head began to twinge. I put my hand to my temple. Oh, no . . .

'Oh, no,' said Daniel.

'If it *is* a migraine, there is absolutely nothing either of us can do about it.'

'Take something. Just in case.'

'I take enough pills without –'

'TAKE something!'

'All right, all right, don't shout.' I rooted in my handbag. 'I'll do you a double favour. There's no point taking a painkiller because I'm not in pain, but I'll take a tranquillizer, which will stop me having you for breakfast.'

'Doesn't sound like such a bad proposition,' he muttered, summoning the flight attendant for water. 'Man, they're beautiful. Singapore is a whole island of beautiful women.'

'You've been there before too?'

'A few times, yeah. Passing through. You'll like it.'

'I suppose I should have a Singapore Sling while I'm at it.'

'Aw, yeah. Can't miss that.'

'Daniel?'

'Yeah?'

'Em . . . what exactly *is* a Singapore Sling?'

He laughed. 'It's a cocktail: lemon juice, gin and cherry brandy. Expensive too.'

A video came on showing safety procedures. I watched avidly; made sure I knew where the exits were and felt under my seat for the lifejacket. Would I remember in a disaster how to tie it? And would my whistle work?

Daniel frowned. 'Christ, it's exhausting sitting next to you. Are you sure you don't want to go back to business class?'

He was very close, tucked up right beside me in those tight seats. The plane jolted over a few bumps. I grabbed his wrist. 'Oh, *shit*. All that fuel. We're a flying bomb. We'll explode on the runway. How could this thing possibly get off the ground?'

'The way it works is, the air sucks us up, see? We can't drop out of the sky because the air is actually holding us up. Planes fly because of physics, not in spite of physics.'

I opened one eye. 'That's supposed to mean something to me?'

'Birds don't fall out of the sky, do they?'

'They're made of feathers!' My fingers squeezed his arm. 'Oh, God, oh, help.' The engines roared into gear, my grip tightened, and my eyes were clenched shut so that every shiver of movement, every slight jolt was magnified inside my head. The aircraft revved up, began its acceleration. Faster and faster, bumps and lumps, groaning, straining and speed. All that fuel, tonnes of it, inside *the wings* of all places. Bomb. Time bomb. About to go off . . .

We were up. Sucked up. The roaring receded into a quieter moan.

I came to. I became aware of my surroundings, the work-aday sounds, the ping of call buttons and seatbelt lights, the announcements. I opened my eyes. There was a small screen on the headrest in front of me. Then I realized that Daniel had taken the hand that had been digging into his arm and was holding it, while he read the in-flight magazine. I squeezed his fingers in gratitude, but didn't take my hand away. Through all these days of stress, when there would normally have been hugs aplenty to get everyone through the ordeal, this was the first physical contact I'd had. I had gone a long way with only my father's voice at the end of the phone and Milenko's hesitant fingertips on my knee for sustenance. Daniel's hand was the first bit of comfort I had had in a week and I wasn't letting go. Instead, I took a chance. There could be no harm in being affectionate when we had only hours left together, so I rested my head on his shoulder.

'Aw, great,' he said. '*Pirates of the Caribbean* is on the movie channel!'

I had not looked at my watch for a long time. We had had a meal, we had watched a movie, it had grown dark outside and we had even endured another take-off and landing (and a hot, sticky hour on the ground) in Dubai. We had to be nearly there. To cheer myself up, I located the channel on which we could view our progress.

'What? Only seven hours! We've been up here longer than seven hours! Much, much longer! How could we still have five hours to go?'

'If the computer's wrong,' said Daniel, 'we're in big trouble, so you'd better hope that's accurate.'

'But another five hours!'

'Relax. It'll pass. Before you know it, you'll be in Vietnam with Steph.'

'Yeah, right. I find it hard to believe I'll *ever* see her again. She's like a puff of smoke.'

Daniel was contemplating the movie list again. 'What'll I watch now?'

'Maybe, ooh, I don't know – *Pirates of the Caribbean* for the third time, perhaps?'

'You should watch it. It'll distract you.'

So I did and it did, and it was true, what Clara said: Johnny Depp was to die for – only I didn't want to die for him there and then, at thirty-four thousand feet. And still the flight didn't end, though the movie did, and there were hours yet to go. Scrunched into our seats, I became more aware of Daniel, his physicality, how close he was.

Safe in the knowledge that we were, finally, about to go our separate ways, we had become quite cosy. When the lights went down and most passengers slept, we talked quietly in the dark. The lack of space, the powerlessness, and the seat up against my knees ceased to be irritants. They became like a nest. I relished its constraints, knowing that within hours I would be on the ground in a new continent, like a fledgling dropped into a very strange place.

We talked about his childhood.

'I can't believe your mother has no idea who your father is. I mean, you must look like someone, and how many men can she have slept with in one month?'

'Enough to confuse her.'

'Busy lady.'

'Too right. There were a couple of flatmates, a guy at a party, and she thinks another guy she can't remember.'

'You never went searching?'

'No point. It's a big hole. All I can do is make sure history doesn't repeat itself. I can't wait to have kids, and there'll be no mistaking their dad when I do.'

I smiled.

He looked bashful. 'You want kids?'

'We wanted a family, yeah. We weren't planning to wait too long either. We're neither of us spring chickens, but . . . well, some day, maybe.'

'It'd be great, wouldn't it?'

He said it as if it would never happen. 'Why so wistful?' I asked. 'You've got plenty of time, and you don't have a body clock to worry about.'

The veil came down again. End of conversation.

We drank champagne in the glow of his reading light, and as the hours drew on, we retreated into a slight, shared melancholy. We closed our eyes eventually, but neither of us slept.

When I went for one of my anti-bloodclotting walks, I looked out of the window in the rear door and saw that we were slipping towards day – a white line of light sat on the edge of the darkness. It was as if we were coming back to earth from space, from deep blue to bright light. A new, long day in a new world lay ahead, but all apprehension had gone. The tranquillizer had taken effect. I didn't care about finding my way around Singapore and going on to Vietnam. Singapore was visitor-friendly and highly efficient. It was simply a question of taking a taxi to the embassy, sitting around for the visa, and taking a taxi back to the airport. Not a fun day, but I kept my mind, like a pinprick, on that moment when I would arrive at the hotel where Steph was holed up. My only regret was that my adventure with Daniel Blewitt was over.

He had moved to the outside seat. When I went back, he put his hands on my hips and helped me past.

'It's getting bright,' I said. 'What'll happen when we land?'

'You'll go to Arrivals and I'll go to the transit lounge.'

'Funny place to say goodbye, in an airport corridor.'

'Let's see where we are.' He reached for the remote.

'Let's not,' I said, making him put it down.

Light filtered into the cabin as a few passengers opened their window screens.

Breakfast was served. We ate, hardly speaking. Our trays were taken.

Tired out, Daniel had become pensive. We sat quietly, aware of each other, as we felt in our ears the first drop of altitude, the start of the glide to earth. I had just about made it. The twelve hours were almost up. Only forty minutes to go.

Someone pulled up their screen at the end of our row and I turned towards the sunlight that beamed on to the passenger's lap.

'Kadie?'

I turned back. Beneath my blanket, Daniel's hand was on my knee. I glanced at the blanket, and at him. This was not cosying up. This was a hand on my knee. His face was very close, against the edge of his headrest.

'Yeah?'

'What would you say,' he said slowly, his eyes hard on mine, 'what would you say . . . to a Singapore Fling?'

His mouth, only inches away, looked suddenly, intensely, inviting.

'A . . . what?'

People began to stretch and stand up. Flight attendants patrolled the aisles.

'A stop-over. You know. Just a blast for one night. No strings. No complications.'

Hot facecloths were dangled before us. Neither of us took one: we were too intent on staying nose to nose. I was thrown, not only by this insane proposition but by a longing for him to come that extra inch. His hand moved minimally along my thigh, his eyes kept dropping to my chin, my mouth.

'You're mad,' I said.

'Are you?'

'I . . . What kind of a . . .'

'We could pick up our flights tomorrow.'

'But if we miss our flights today, they won't let us transfer just like that.' Extraordinary. I was considering it. Why else would I allow this conversation to continue?

'A severe migraine should cover any technicalities,' he said.

I gaped. 'How long have you been working this out?'

'It's coming to me as I go along.'

'I'm in love with someone else. Hopelessly. Irredeemably.'

Daniel sighed heavily, looked away momentarily and said, 'So am I, as it happens.'

'What? You're involved with someone?'

'In a manner of speaking.'

'Why haven't you mentioned it?'

'Didn't want to. Any more than you want to talk about Milenko.'

'But, then, it wouldn't be right.'

'You're currently single, aren't you?'

'*You're* not.'

'We have an . . . arrangement.'

'An arrangement.'

'We are currently enjoying something called an "open"

relationship – which sucks, by the way. So what about it?'

'I can't, Daniel.'

'Why not?'

'Because . . .'

'Because nothing. Let's do it. One day. One day out of life. What have you got to lose?'

'Any grasp on who I've been all these years!'

'You left her behind in Bucharest.'

He smiled, which didn't help the urge I had to kiss him. It was like a bad thirst.

'What kind of a girl do you think I am?' I said, with mock-indignation, and I was done for then, because I'd made light of it, and the time for serious protestations was lost.

'I think,' said Daniel, inhaling sharply, and then exhaling as he spoke, 'you're the kind of girl who should give herself a break.'

'It's a horrible suggestion. Low. Crass.'

'Come on, Kadie. Throw it away. Take a chance on the ridiculous.'

'What about Steph? Killian?'

'One more day won't make much difference.'

'You don't have a visa.'

'I can get one at the airport, same as EU.'

It made no sense. Why was I contemplating this?

The scrappy hair, the hollowed cheeks, the stubble, the nerve. That's why.

Milenko? Milenko was over, gone. *I will never go to your fucking country again.* The wound, raw. Daniel's green eyes, waiting, challenging. Mischief. A drop. Singapore. Passing through. Stopping off. All my life. Sensible. Sparing Dad further humiliation. Not being a rock star's daughter. All my life, *not* being a rock star's daughter. Never drunk in public. Never wild; arrested disorderly. Never seen with unsuitable wild cards. Like this one. Never, ever.

He held my eye, would not let up.

'Daniel.'

'Yeah?'

His lips, so close. Nice lips. 'I think I feel a migraine coming on.'

He smiled, but came no closer.

14

Somehow or other, Daniel pulled it off. I spent a lot of time lying across seats in the pristine, and very quiet, airport, with my arm placed strategically over my eyes, while Daniel did a lot of explaining, telling officials and airline reps that I had come down with a violent migraine and he had to get me to a hotel urgently. It was easy enough to change my scheduled one-hour hop across the South China Sea, but his long-haul, condition-heavy fare had to be carefully negotiated if he was to avoid paying for another flight – and availability was a problem. The Christmas rush to Australia was building up and the best they could offer him in lieu of his flight that day was one to Brisbane three days later. For the sake of one night with me, he would have to spend three days in Singapore. I told him he was losing his mind; he told me he was in no hurry to get home.

He kept moving me from one set of seats to another, but eventually he negotiated our way right out of the terminal and on to a hotel transfer bus. The humid warmth startled me. 'How many more weather systems am I going to go through by the end of this?'

We were the only people on the mini-bus. The air-conditioning was so bracing I had to pull my coat round me. I had almost convinced myself that I did have a migraine and was so genuinely exhausted that it was a relief not to have to rush to the embassy and then back to the airport to face another flight, another airport, another country. Nine days of fraught travelling had earned me this break. It was a necessity, not an indulgence.

'Where are we staying? Another hostel?'

'Nope.'

Phew. 'So why can't we get a taxi?'

Daniel looked down at me. Good chin, with enough stubble to make him appear rough and ready. 'Because I can't afford one, and this is *my* date.'

'We're staying at Raffles Hotel, right?'

'No, we're staying in a bland city-centre high-rise. Sorry.'

'I'll shout you Raffles.'

'They wouldn't let me past the door.'

Huge palm trees shaped like fans graced the streets. I was in South East Asia for the worthiest of reasons, and in Singapore for close to the worst.

The hotel was plusher than I expected, and I would hardly have called it bland either, when there was a large ginger-bread house covered with cotton wool standing in the light-festooned lobby.

'Christmas! I'd forgotten.'

'Three weeks to go.'

Daniel checked in. I tried to make myself behave, to end this ludicrous caper before it went too far. It was preposterous – checking into a hotel in Singapore for . . . what, exactly?

Daniel betrayed nothing, as if we'd been together for months and checking into a room together was perfectly normal, which, in some ways, it had become.

When the lift deposited us on the sixth floor, the first twinges of apprehension kicked in. Daniel marched along the corridor. The more blasé he was, the more attractive he became. He opened the door to our room. We went in. Two double beds; television; fridge; snacks and drinks. 'Are you sure you can afford this place?'

'My boss is a director of the chain. I get a discount. We're in Australasia now. My end of the world.' We went to the window and looked out at a city of skyscrapers. 'You wanted

Raffles?' He pointed at a low complex of old white buildings, just below us, nestling among the skyscrapers. 'There's your Raffles.'

'Wow. The real Raffles – *à la* Somerset Maugham?'

'Yeah, it's been refurbished recently.'

'Can we go and have a Singapore Sling there?'

'You and your expensive tastes.' His fingers were in his hip pockets, his shoulder against the window, his eyes on the streets below. It was the obvious moment to . . . begin, but his mind was where mine was not. 'We should get some kip and then go for your visa.'

Was he having second thoughts?

I turned on my phone, as I had been doing, with increasing reluctance. As soon as I was linked up with a Singaporean network, a text came in from Dad. 'New development. Ring when you land.'

'Damn, what's she done now? What time is it back there?'

'God knows. Irish? Romanian? Turkish? Let's just say that for them it's still yesterday.'

'I can't phone – I'd have to lie barefaced.' I thought about it. 'I'll lie by text instead. "Hi, Daddy,"' I said, as I tapped away. '"Am stopping overnight in Singapore. Migraine. Will be okay. Going Vietnam tomorrow. Had to rest. What development?"'

I was in the bathroom when his reply came. 'What does it say?' I called to Daniel.

He came to the door, reading, '"Cremation off. Steph talked out of it by her mother."'

Tears flushed my eyes. I sat on the bath.

Daniel continued, '"Now waiting for instructions for repatriation to go ahead, which she's faxing through. Suggest you carry on to Vietnam and see if you can get her home. But get better first."'

I covered my mouth, reached for loo paper.

'It was a close call,' Daniel said kindly. 'Have to say, I'm a bit emotional myself.'

'It's just . . . I've been having these nightmares about him burning and it being my fault.'

'Well, that's not going to happen now . . . I'll leave you to it.'

It was sorted. All sorted, through none of my doing. And the weird thing was – I was getting away with this little outrage, and *way* too easily. Perhaps it was part of a bigger plan. The post-Milenko plan.

Daniel was stretched across one of the beds when I came out. Was this the moment to sit beside him? 'Should I try to contact her, do you think?'

'Better leave it. Surprise her tomorrow.'

'I hope it'll be a good surprise.'

'Don't know about you but I'm buggered. Best thing is to sleep for a couple of hours, then get up and carry on. I'll set my watch to wake us at, say, twelve local time?' He fiddled with his watch, then buried his head in the pillow and fell asleep.

I stood by the window, wondering.

The beeping alarm dragged us from deep oblivion. My head was so muggy I thought I would never again be truly awake, but Daniel wouldn't let me be.

'Get up,' he said, looming over me. 'You can't give in. You'll feel okay in a bit.'

'Leave me alone.'

'Kadie, I've done this a thousand times. If you get up now, you'll sleep well tonight and there'll be no jetlag.'

'Maybe I didn't make myself clear. Fuck off!'

He pulled me into a sitting position. 'Breakfast.'

I fell back on the pillow. 'That was the nicest sleep I've had in my entire life and you ruined it.'

'I need food.'

Food. Had I misunderstood? When he'd said 'fling' had he meant something more innocent than I had assumed? Did he mean, perhaps, a celibate city-break? A detour between friends? Was he losing his nerve? Did I care? No. I had escaped. It was like getting on to that train to Istanbul. Going off-road. I had my own agenda: an unscheduled Singapore Fling, which . . . wasn't adding up to a whole lot.

Daniel took me across the road to a bakery called Ah Teng's that was part of the Raffles complex. It was lovely – banks of sandwich rolls and cakes, teacups and teapots, wooden chairs and marble tables, and chilling air-conditioning. Daniel insisted on going back to the hotel to get me a sweater, while I sat with a chocolate twist and a pot of decent tea. At a nearby table, a Western tourist sat alone, reading. At another, a Singaporean couple were talking animatedly. Young professionals. Everything was so smart and orderly and neat compared to Bucharest and Istanbul. So very moneyed. The tea gave a great kick. It was the best I'd had in weeks. Everything was better than anything in weeks. Steph had relented on cremation, with no help from me (I had travelled round the world, it seemed, to hear two words: cremation off), Killian would soon be on his way home, and I was far, far, far away from Milenko and the miserable mistake I had made.

Relief is warm. It flows through the veins like syrup. My task had been made unaccountably easier. All I had to do now was go to Steph and escort her home. With a tickle of guilt, I felt almost happy. My insides were in upheaval still, but with anticipation, and the anticipation cheered me.

My unlikely companion came back with my sweater, and when we'd eaten, we caught a cab to the Vietnamese embassy. I filled out the forms, paid an extra fee to have the application handled immediately, and more again to have my passport couriered back to the hotel when it was ready. I didn't want bureaucracy to get in the way of whatever it was Daniel had planned. When we came back on to the street, I said, 'I need clothes, Daniel. Singapore is one big shopping emporium, isn't it? Can we please, please, go shopping?'

'What happened to the jetlag?'

'My credit card will cure it. I need light, cool things. Sandals.'

'There's a big mall near our hotel. Sun City.'

'Lead the way.'

We asked the taxi to drop us back at Raffles. It was raining when we climbed out. 'Monsoon,' said Daniel. I thought he meant the shop, but he meant the weather. The Raffles arcade sheltered us as we went past its elegant boutiques – Rolex, Louis Vuitton, Kenzo.

'Aw,' said Daniel, stopping outside Gucci. 'This is probably what you want right here.'

'Give me a break.'

When we came to the end of the arcade, we had to make a dash for the lights, but roadworks on the other side forced us to cross back and go round a different way. At another junction, a pedestrian light turned red. We stood like a couple of soaked children, waiting to cross.

'Isn't this the place where you can get thrown into jail for jay-walking and chewing gum?' I asked.

'And where you're unlikely to get mugged or raped.'

There was a huge puddle at my feet, which would require a considerable leap to . . . No need. A car came past and flung the whole lot right over me. I was sodden from the waist down.

'Let's abort,' said Daniel. 'We can try later.' As we tracked back, the rain turned into a heavy downpour. And they call Ireland wet. We ran, barely able to see where we were going, until we ducked into a doorway for cover. It turned out to be the entrance to another shopping mall. We threw ourselves inside. Shops and shops and more shops.

I shivered. 'The air-conditioning is attacking my jeans.'

Daniel looked outside. 'One more dash will get us to the hotel,' he said, but I was off.

Skirts, shirts, tops, pyjamas, toiletries, underwear, more underwear; makeup, sandals, a bag, umbrellas. I couldn't stop. The prices, the stuff, the sheer wantonness. Daniel adopted long-suffering boyfriend mode, nodding or grimacing while I bolted in and out of changing rooms. The over-attentive assistants were so polite and gorgeous that I tried on whatever they brought and was a sucker for every special deal they offered. At one check-out Daniel said, 'If your dad's former band is doing two-bit gigs these days, how so much money?'

'Look, I earn too, okay? And I'll have you know that I have a very healthy relationship with my father's money. I pay my bills. He pays for my shoes.'

'Shoes?'

'I like shoes.'

In another shop, I was finally released from the clothes I'd been wearing for two weeks. I changed into a short black skirt and a neat white top. The clothes were designed for the Singapore winter, but they were far cooler than the woolly pyjamas, socks and jumpers I had carried to Stockholm. I felt so light. I had arrived in the other hemisphere.

Daniel, I presumed, had to do some purchasing himself – in a pharmacy, perhaps – and I wondered if he would remove himself at some point to do so. He did. When he came back, he said, 'Haven't you forgotten something?'

'What?'

'Suitcase?'

'Ooh, and I know just the place!'

In Louis Vuitton's, I selected a neat little case on wheels.

As I handed over my credit card, Daniel said, 'Has there ever been anything you haven't been able to have?'

'You know there has. Money didn't bring my mother back and it didn't stop everything falling apart with Milenko.'

We headed back to the hotel, passing a bright blue synthetic Christmas tree on the corner. It started raining again, but instead of opening a brolly, I spun round, my shopping bags flying out like the blades of a helicopter. 'Thank you for this, Mr Blewitt. Warm air, fresh clothes – and the rain washing everything away! It's fantastic!'

Back in our room, in the shower, I reconsidered our assignation. The point of Daniel's stop-over had not been shopping, or sleep, or food, but sex, pure and simple, and I was no longer sure I could go through with it. I stood, water pelting over me, thinking. Daniel would understand if I backed out; Milenko would never understand if I went through with it. Not that he would ever know, but that wasn't the point. It would be a hurt inflicted, if never felt. Although I was single, a free agent, this would still be cheating. Cheating on myself, if on no one else.

I came out of the bathroom, wearing the towelling robe provided by the hotel. Daniel zipped in behind me, cold in his damp clothes. I stood by the window. What now? What the heck happens now? Get dressed, I thought, that's the first move. Then, when he came out, I'd be sitting on the bed, fully clothed, and he'd know.

When Daniel emerged from the shower, a towel wrapped round his waist, I was still standing by the window in the robe, drying my hair with a towel and looking down at some children playing in the swimming-pool in the rain. A little girl jumped into the water. I wondered why she bothered. Daniel was suddenly behind me, kissing the back of my neck.

I leapt away. 'Stop!'

'Whoa.' He raised his hands. 'Sorry.'

'Don't come at me from behind! I hate that. Don't do that.'

'Okay.' He stood, uncertain. 'You've changed your mind?'

I glanced at the towel round his waist and at my robe. 'Do I look like I've changed my mind?'

He reached out and pulled me towards him.

It was strange to be held by someone else after more than two years, but not unmanageable. Relaxing into him, I absorbed the contact, the warmth of another person. With one move, this affectionate hug would become something else, but kissing would be slightly weird, almost too personal for us. In the mirror, I watched Daniel's tanned back and tattooed shoulder-blade as he made that one move – his hands coming inside my robe – and saw myself extending my neck the better for him to get at it. I looked out. Skyscrapers; yellow taxis; roadworks on the street below. Korčula came round a bend in my mind, its rocky girth floating on the shimmering Adriatic. I welcomed its uninvited intrusion, even as I welcomed Daniel against me. There was nothing bad, nothing sinful, in this. I was simply moving on, albeit with incredibly indecent haste. Thumbs found nipples and mouths found mouths. I yanked off his towel, he pushed away my robe, and we stood by the window, coiling round each other in an unlikely twist.

He was subdued afterwards, whereas I was giddy again. 'So. What's next for the Date?'

'Dinner. Chinatown.'

'Excellent.'

'There's a lot to do in Singapore. Pity we only have one day.'

My hand ran along his thigh, but my eyes went all the way to his ankles. He had lovely feet. 'Maybe I should stay for another day.'

He drew back. 'What about Steph?'

'Well, everything's okay now, isn't it? Panic's over.'

'Except for the funeral.'

'Yeah, but even if she agrees to come, it's still days off.'

His eyes moved around a lot before he said, 'A two-day fling might not be such a good idea.'

'Why not?'

'We wouldn't want to get caught up. *I* wouldn't want to, anyway.' He sat up. 'Having said that, I'm going to change your flight right now.'

Having done so, he hung up, saying, 'Spot the travel agent.'

My mobile rang. 'Damn. I told Dad I needed sleep.' I reached for it. 'Steph!'

'What the hell are you doing in Singapore?' she said.

'What the hell are *you* doing in Vietnam?'

'Why didn't you go home like I told you to? Rollo says you've had migraines. He said you've had to stop over because you're ill.'

I looked at the ceiling. 'I'm fine.'

'But what on earth are you doing?' she asked.

'We want you home, that's all. For the funeral. The family won't go ahead without you. They're afraid of the consequences if they do.'

'There won't be any consequences,' she said bitterly. 'They can do it their way and let me do it mine. I've conceded on every point. I wanted a cremation, they've got their burial. Now they want me at the funeral. I won't – *I won't* – see him put into the ground. That would be like punishing me, Kadie.'

'I know, but, Steph, listen. I'm tired. We're all tired, and you are too, and Killian's mum isn't well, and it can't go on. Have you sent that fax?'

'What fax?'

'So they can release the body to Deirdre.'

It was too blunt. I hadn't been ready, primed for this call, and it upset her, which brought tears on both sides. I apologized, I tried to comfort her, bouncing off satellites, and failed on all counts, while we cried into each other's ears.

'I haven't sent it,' she said. 'I don't know what to say, how to word it, and I hate being bullied like this.'

'You shouldn't be alone, Steph. It isn't good. I can't bear for you to be alone.'

Daniel got me a tissue and lay down behind me.

Steph sniffled and said the last thing I expected to hear. 'You might be right.'

'What?'

After a moment, she said, 'Kadie?'

'Yeah?' I grabbed Daniel's hand because I didn't know what she was going to say, and I wished he was Milenko.

'Come and get me, will you? I've reached the end of the line.'

'Oh, Steph, of course I will! I'm almost there.'

'Yes, but I'm not in Saigon. I came over to Phu Quoc.'

'The island?'

'Yeah.'

'So how do I get there?'

'You'll have to fly from Ho Chi Minh to Duong Dong, and when you get there, take a taxi to the Huangs' place in Bai Truong.'

'Hang on, I need a pen.' Daniel obliged. We went through the directions again.

'And if you have to stay overnight in Ho Chi Minh, go to the Alpha One hotel. They know me there. It's nice.'

'Okay, and we'll do the fax together when I come. Will you be all right till then?'

There was a pause. 'Yeah, I just . . . I don't know, maybe it was a mistake. I mean, it was good at first, to be here, but it's too strong, you know . . . I mean, he isn't here, is he? He isn't anywhere and . . . I just wish I could catch up with him.'

Her escape had not worked. I was stunned. Steph always

knew what she was doing, yet it had failed her, this great trek across the world. 'Well,' I said, 'I'm about to catch up with you. Small consolation, I know.'

'No, it'll be good. It's . . . I thought I wanted to be alone, but I don't. Not completely.'

I could not believe it. I had delayed by another day – just when she reached out to me. It was Stockholm all over again. 'Problem is, my flight isn't until the day after tomorrow,' I admitted, 'but I'll try and change it.'

'No, Sunday's fine. Once I know you're coming. Take a day out to get better.'

Daniel nuzzled my back between my shoulder-blades. His hand came over my breast, which made me take a sharp breath.

'You poor thing,' said Steph. 'Are you in a lot of pain?'

'A bit.'

'I'm turning off my mobile now, or they'll be on to me again. See you Sunday.'

'Okay. Steph?'

'Yeah?'

'Are you okay for money?'

'I'm throwing about my credit card, for once.'

'Well, if there's one thing I've taught you, it's how to treat a credit card with disrespect!'

'You know, you don't sound like you have a migraine.'

I bit my lip. 'I don't. It was more of a brainstorm.'

'How do you mean?'

'I, er, wanted a romp with this young stud I met.'

Steph laughed. It was a beautiful sound. 'Yeah, pull the other one. Oh, guess what – do you remember Shannon?'

'Your Aussie pal from Saigon, the one you lost track of?'

'Yeah, well, I've just found her. Or, rather, she found me. Some good things do come out of bad, it seems.'

'How'd that happen?'

'I don't know. Word got out about Killian and sort of filtered down the line, and she worked her way through the contacts until someone at home gave her my mobile number. She's been so sweet. She wants me to spend Christmas with her.'

'Oh, that'd be lovely! Maybe you could come back out after the funeral?'

'I haven't made any promises about the funeral, Kadie.'

'Steph –'

'We'll talk when you get here.'

A yawn escaped. 'Hmm, okay.'

'I've worn you out.'

'You haven't worn me out.'

'Must be all that shagging of the young stud, then.' She was sounding more like herself.

'Look here, you, don't move *one inch* until I get there.'

Daniel got up and started dressing.

'You're a sad case,' said Steph, 'coming all this way.'

'Killian told me to look out for you whenever he was away and he's away now.'

'Listen,' Daniel said, 'I'm delighted you two are catching up and all, but I'm hungry.'

'Who's that?' said Steph.

'The young stud.'

There was a very long pause. *'Kadie?'*

'Yep?'

'You've really got a man there?'

I sighed. 'Yeah, and he's hungry.'

'But you can't be . . . What about –'

'Don't even think about saying that word. I am currently unattached, remember?'

'I find that hard to believe, let alone remember! Are you completely off your head?'

'We are neither of us behaving rationally at the moment.'

'It isn't some seedy escort, is it?'

'He's very clean.'

'Jesus, I'm the one who should be coming to you,' said Steph. 'You've lost the plot!'

'There's a plot?'

'Kadie, be careful. You've never, ever been impetuous or irresponsible. You don't know how it's done!'

'No, but I'm learning.' She sighed indulgently. 'Oh, Steph, I can't wait to see you. I was beginning to think I was chasing a shadow.'

'You aren't, but I suppose I might be.'

We dined in a Chinese restaurant somewhere off a main street packed with shops and decked with Christmas lights. Things were on the up. Steph was okay, Killian would soon be on his way to Ireland, I'd get home for Christmas, and Daniel was . . . delightful. By making that daft decision on the plane, I had halted the downward spiral. By refusing to drag on, victimized and demoralized, I had turned the tide. I had voted for desire, a positive, forward force, and while I had been in the throes of pleasure, Steph had been coming ever closer. There had to be a lesson in there somewhere.

There were lessons all about us. As we ate, the heart was torn out of me by a middle-aged Chinese woman at another table who, half-way through her meal, started crying. She was with two young men, sons or colleagues, perhaps, who made no attempt to console her. The more she tried to stop the tears, the harder they flowed. Trying to hide behind her fringe, she wiped her eyes and dabbed her face, but the anguish in her expression made me want to go over and hold her. It was very hard, whatever she was going through, but the men just let her weep. Perhaps there was no consolation to be had.

'It gets passed on, doesn't it?' I said to Daniel. 'Things may be better for me this evening, but the unhappiness has simply moved on to someone else.'

'Jetlag's setting in,' said Daniel. 'Let's go.'

On the street, he held my hand; I took it away. We were lovers, not a couple. We had been intimate, but we weren't close enough to stroll hand in hand through Chinatown.

'What would your partner have to say about this?' I asked him.

'She'd be delighted,' he said bitterly.

'How so?'

'I was told to get off her case. I'm only following instructions.'

'Isn't that open to interpretation?'

'In this case: no.'

'But you haven't split up?'

He sighed. 'Nope. 'S not that easy.'

'Jesus, you aren't married, are you?'

'I wish.'

'Daniel . . .' There were so many things to ask him, but he stood looking at me with one eyebrow slightly raised, so I kissed him instead. It was better than it had been in the bedroom – less grasping; more personal and curious. Inevitably, we became heated, so we hurried to the hotel, where we fell into the room, pulling at one another's clothes, but had to stop for a loo break. In the bathroom, I slithered into a slinky nightdress. Daniel grunted in appreciation when I dipped past him, before stepping into the bathroom himself. Being desired was doing wonders for my general sense of well-being, but not as much as having fresh clothes. I slipped into the starched linen of one of the beds, leaving a corner of the blanket turned back. My conscience was certainly going to catch up with me about this, but it wasn't there yet.

Daniel was disappointed when he came out to see me stretched out, all shoulders and cleavage, the bedspread turned back in invitation. But the disappointment, he told me the next day, of finding me out for the count soon passed. He turned out the light, got into the other bed and joined me in deep sleep.

The combined noise of the air-conditioning and the drone of the early-morning rush-hour was soothing when I woke. The air-conditioning had made me think, during the night, that I was still on the plane. I had jumped several times when I felt myself sliding sideways, then remembered I was no longer on the jumbo, but safe in a bed on the ground – albeit six storeys up. I stretched, waiting for remorse to lay siege. It still didn't come, which was increasingly perplexing. I stared at Daniel's back. His hand came over his shoulder and fell limp behind his neck. There was no regret. Barely an ounce of guilt. It made no sense. I wasn't even sorry I'd done it. On the contrary, I was determined to do it again.

With one fluid movement I stepped across the divide between the two beds and slid in behind him. He didn't wake immediately, so I waited, my arm round his waist. When he began to stir, his hand came on to my arm and he stretched with something like a purr – a deep, contented gurgle. We lay quietly, waking, stroking. His stomach muscles rippled with pleasure at my touch. He turned, suddenly, and kissed me. It hit me in all the wrong places. I felt it in my chest, and stomach, even in my head. This was not the way it was meant to be with us, and yet we made love like that, side by side and kissing as if it was the only way to breathe.

'So what do you fancy doing?' Daniel asked, in the noisy restaurant, tucking in to white sausages, hash browns and baked beans. Breakfast in bed would have been my choice, but he had wanted to escape the room, I suspected, and reminders of the intensity of that waking session.

'What do you suggest?'

'We could go see the pink dolphins. There are fewer than two hundred and fifty pairs of them left in the world, but they breed them on Santosa Island.'

'Are they really pink?'

'They're born grey and turn pink as they get older, and they're really stubby, you know, with a long thin nose. They look a bit like slugs, but they're incredibly fast. It's a privilege to see them before they die out.'

'Not sold, really.'

'We could do the Bird Park or –'

'Or here's a novel concept: forget the sights – you've seen them all and I don't need to. Tell me instead – where is a nice place to *be*?'

The Botanic Gardens were lush, deep green and dripping. Like a sanctuary, they enveloped us. We were rained on, of course, and our umbrellas couldn't cope with the deluge, but the wet added to the feel of the place, and to my mood. The sticky air was liberating; it was lovely to be in light clothes, to get wet and not care. We followed paths past elaborate displays, ornamental trees and vast sloping lawns, through a suburbia of pretty blooms, exotica and floral peculiarities. We wandered through jungle, where dark strips of vegetation hung over us like raffia and ancient trees grew from a tangle of roots above ground, like strange creatures with a plethora of limbs. It was like being in the Garden of Eden. 'I hope Killian has gone to a place like this.'

'Hope it isn't raining as much,' said Daniel.

Thunder and lightning forced us into a restaurant at one end of the park, where we took a table on a terrace, surrounded by brown tarpaulin screens that had been pulled down to keep us dry. Through a gap, I could see the fronds of a palm tree dripping on to more greenery; the rain pounded the roof with tropical exuberance. I was in Somerset Maugham country. All that was missing were the planters and their wives, and their wives' lovers, smoking long thin cigarettes while sipping sundowners.

I came back from my reverie and noticed that Daniel was also elsewhere, but not in the Malaya of the pre-war years. That sadness had come again, so easily unveiled, really, whenever he stopped moving.

'Tell me about this girl,' I said, after we'd ordered Singapore *laksa*. 'You know everything about me, after all.'

'Not why you broke off your engagement.'

'Milenko doesn't know why either, so it wouldn't be fair to blab about it to everyone else. So, come on, you distract *me* for a change.'

The waitress brought chopsticks.

'Have you come away to sort out where the relationship is going?' I asked.

'Aw, I know where it's going,' he said. 'In fact, you could probably say it's already got there.' He fiddled with the chopsticks, turning them round in circles. The restaurant was empty except for two men in khakis and boots. They were speaking Dutch. Dutch planters!

Daniel made an attempt to change the subject, or so I thought when he said wistfully, 'I used to have the best job in the world.' Then I realized that he had, finally, begun talking to me. 'When I left school, I wanted to get away from the minister, so Ma sent me to Ireland to meet the rellies. I did Europe with a cousin before heading back, but instead of going home, I went to Australia and worked my way up the coast, doing whatever job I could find. A real bum's life, but no one was watching, no one cared, and that was sweet. After a year or so I landed in Airlie Beach, up the northern coast of Queensland. Sailing excursions go out from there, headed for the Reef or around the Whitsundays, so there are lots of boats needing crews. It was easy enough to get work – especially as I'd sailed since I was a kid – and I was taken on by one of the companies, as a dogsbody at first, but I worked hard and climbed up the ropes. It was a great life, taking tourists round the islands for snorkelling and diving. But I had my eye on the same ship everyone else did – the *Solway Lass*. She's a schooner, a tall ship, you know, a real beauty. She has quite a history too, but now she takes people on de-luxe trips round the islands. I'd no experience on tall ships, but after a lot of grovelling, I got on as crew. I worked on her for two and a half years.

'Anyway, that's where I met Libby. She came aboard as a passenger with some friends. It was love at first sight, both ways. Getting involved with passengers isn't allowed, but we couldn't help it.' Daniel shook his head. 'She's great, you know. Gorgeous, smart, really gutsy. I was gone. Out to lunch. I loved my life in Airlie, but Lib's from Sydney, so we carried on long-distance, me going down to see her every possible opportunity, until I decided, to hell with it. Libby couldn't move, she was still in uni, so I moved to Sydney about a year ago.'

'You gave up the *Lass* for a lady.'

'Yup. I shacked up with Libby in Tamarama.'

'Quite a compromise.'

'No, it's fine. Sydney's all right, and it gave me the chance to do some courses, get more qualifications.'

'And a good job.'

'Eventually. At first I crewed with a company that sails tourists round the harbour, but now I'm with this lady who has a magnificent boat, forty foot, eight berth, and I keep her in shape and take the boss and her cronies out whenever she wants to impress them.'

'Sounds nice.'

'Yeah, it's a cushy number. Well paid, dead boring.'

'What does Libby do?'

'She's a climbing instructor. We both love outdoor stuff, bush-walking, white-water rafting, surfing – you name it, we do it. We're going to set up our own outdoor activities centre up the New South Wales coast in a few years' time, after we've travelled some more.'

'Travelled alone, like this, like you're doing?' A loud crash of thunder made me jump.

Daniel fiddled, looked trapped. 'No, that wasn't really . . . what we had in mind.' He grimaced at the rumbling thunder, then forced himself on. 'A few months ago, we had, you know, a pregnancy scare. Lib got into a total panic. So did I, at first. She was just getting her career under way and earning for the first time, and she couldn't believe it could happen just then. I mean, she was so stressed, she wouldn't even do a pregnancy test. She didn't want to know.'

'I can relate to that.'

'Oh? You've had a scare?'

'Look, we've all had scares. Nothing serious, in my case, but you do want to put your head under the pillow and hope it'll go away.'

'She wasn't under the pillow,' said Daniel, 'she was under the floor. But the thing was . . .'

'What?'

'. . . I got to like the idea,' he said quietly.

'Of having a child?'

He nodded bashfully, as if admitting to some shaming misdemeanour. 'That's when we started,' his hands flapped out in opposite directions, 'diverging. With every day that passed, I got more excited. I thought, My own kid – how cool is that? I couldn't help it, I really wanted it to happen. But it was a total nightmare for Lib. Her career doesn't exactly lend itself to pregnancy and it wasn't part of the plan. Not for a long time. A *very* long time, I discovered.'

'Oh.'

'Yeah,' he said, jerking his head to the side. '*Oh.*'

I put my hand on his forearm.

'She ranted on about the things she wanted to do, like climbing all the world's highest peaks, and I told her it'd be fine, that we could do all that *and* have kids. I mean, it was understood that we were in for the long-haul together. But when she heard me talking like that, about having the baby if there was one, she went off the deep end. *No bloody way*, she said. She told me she'd be having an abortion, and that it was non-negotiable. I . . . It was . . . I'd never thought about it. Abort my kid? Without my consent?' He looked round for a waitress, though we didn't need anything. 'She had no problem with that.' There wasn't much air left in him when he added, 'No problem at all.'

Our curries were served. Three porcelain bowls on wooden trays. 'She said all the usual stuff – *her* body, *her* life . . . Yeah, maybe, but *my* kid. I've always been pro-choice, pro-abortion – anything to be on the other side of the fence to the minister – but when it's personal, when it's your own kid in there, it isn't so simple.' He looked at me suddenly. 'I tell you, it was a real shock to me too, realizing I wanted a kid, but I figured we'd manage. It would have put Libby's career back, sure, but only by a year and I'd have taken up the slack then. I'd have raised the critter and worked round it. It could have been done, is all I'm saying. And it's not like she's nineteen – she's twenty-five. We still didn't even know if she was expecting, but the whole thing kind of grew out of nowhere. It was like this great big plate had been put down between us and we didn't know what to do with it. When she finally did a test, it was negative, but we weren't convinced. She went on being late. Every day was like a year. We dreaded the next test, because instead of hanging over the thing together, we knew we'd be at opposite ends of the room. I was freaked out.

I knew if it was positive, we'd be in for some serious shit. It's almost impossible for a bloke to legally prevent a woman having an abortion – some guys have tried it, but–'

'You would have gone that far?'

He looked into the food. 'I don't know. I was pretty desperate. It isn't about inflicting motherhood on someone, it's about . . . taking care of what's yours. I love Libby, she's the best thing I've ever had, but if I had a three-year-old kid who ran into the street, I'd be expected to run in front of a truck to grab it, right? But with abortion, we're supposed to drive our girlfriends up to the clinic and make them tea afterwards. I didn't want to fight it out, I didn't want that between us, but I didn't see that I'd have much choice.' He caught my eye. 'This must sound like I'm total scum.'

'Why? Is it only scum who want to have kids?'

'It's just – it's one thing going through life not knowing who your father is, but going through the rest of your life not knowing who your child was, I couldn't have handled that.'

The sadness was beginning to make sense. I dreaded the next bit. 'And was she pregnant?' I asked quietly.

He sighed heavily. 'We don't know. I came home one day and found her curled up, cramping so much I nearly took her to hospital. She was almost haemorrhaging. We wondered if it was some kind of miss. And I still wonder, because there was something about her those weeks. Something about me too, and I can't get away from this feeling that I've lost something recently.'

'Maybe you have,' I said. 'Women often say they know they're expecting even before they're late. Why should men not have similar instincts?'

He shook his head. 'I'm sure it was nothing.'

A nasty thought crossed my mind – that his girlfriend had had an abortion without telling him. 'But you and Libby, you weathered it?'

'Yeah, we got through.'

The rain became heavier again.

'Good, eh?' Daniel said, pointing at my curry.

'So why the open relationship?'

He groaned – he figured he'd done enough work for one meal – but I couldn't let him off now. 'We had this trip planned since way back, but when things went a bit sour, Libby decided not to come. She said I'd freaked her out with all the talk of kids, that I'd gone middle-aged overnight, and she had a point. Anyway, that's when she started talking about being non-exclusive. She said putting air between us would give us a fresh perspective, a chance to spread our wings. All the usual arguments.'

'You could have refused.'

'I can't stop *her* being non-exclusive.'

'No, I suppose not.'

'I never thought I'd do it. Nor did she, I reckon. I think she feels pretty safe about that.'

'But that's the trouble about open relationships. They *aren't* safe. It allows the possibility of one party becoming involved elsewhere.'

'You said it.'

'And, anyway, if she wants to mess around, why doesn't she just leave you?'

He looked up. 'Because she loves me.'

'Oh, Daniel, what kind of love is that?'

'Any kind of love is worth hanging on for. It isn't that easy to move on – for some of us,' he said pointedly. 'And maybe being non-exclusive is the way to get past this low patch.'

'Yeah, and maybe you should just break up.'

He held a piece of meat between the chopsticks and gazed at it. 'See? That's what I don't get about you. Why rush into breaking up? Why have you taken off without even talking to Milenko? So he stuffed up, but what happened to forgiveness?

Everyone deserves a fair go.' His stepfather's rantings had taken root.

'That's as may be, but I don't buy this we-can-sleep-around-and-still-love-each-other thing. The love bit doesn't fit.'

'But you love Milenko, and can still sleep with me.'

'. . . Yes. I don't understand it.'

'People do it all the time. Relationships go through all sorts of permutations. And I've too much going with Libby to give up on it just because we hit a bump in the road.'

More like a pothole, I thought.

We made faces about the deafening noise of torrents on corrugated iron.

As we were leaving, the waitress offered us plastic capes. We pulled them on and wandered through the orchid gardens, holding hands and looking like two garbage bags.

Raffles Hotel entranced me. We could see the whole revamped complex from our room. It took up a whole block and, apart from the boutiques and bakery, there were open-air bars, gardens and fountains, although the sight of palm trees dripping with fairy-lights took some getting used to. I loved the white porticoes and red tiles, the lush greenery and shuttered bedroom windows because they left me in no doubt that I had, somehow, made it to the tropics.

I took Daniel to High Tea in the Tiffin Rooms. From the front, the hotel looked like a Christmas cake, white icing and a big red sash. A doorman with a splendid moustache stood sentry in frock coat and feathered hat, ready to turn back people like Daniel, who favoured shorts and flip-flops. He was refused access because no shorts could pass through the lobby. I was in a micro-mini, but Daniel had to go back to our hotel to change.

I went on in to take our table, draped in linen and set with Raffles cups and saucers, and ordered tea. When Daniel returned, appropriately clad, we made our way to the buffet at one end of the room. It was hard to know where to start: omelettes, curries, finger sandwiches, cakes, buns, scones, fruit, weird-coloured jelly things, tiny sponges, desserts and gooey chocolate cakes were laid out before us. Breakfast, lunch, dinner and tea all on the same table. I began with a selection of salmon, cucumber and egg sandwiches and returned to my seat. The waiter hovered. Every time we twitched, our cups were refilled. When we cleared our plates, they were swept away and replaced with clean ones.

'It must be okay then,' Daniel said, 'to go back for more?'

My chair was pulled from behind me as I stood up. This time I chose scones and cream, and slivers of three cakes – chocolate, sponge and lime. Back at our table, our napkins had been placed across the armrests, just so, and fresh cutlery had appeared. 'Exquisite,' I said, sitting down. 'Thank you.' The waiter appeared with more tea. 'Absolutely exquisite.'

'Later we should have a Singapore Sling in the Long Bar upstairs. It's the longest bar in South East Asia,' said Daniel.

We worked our way through our second helpings. 'About Libby,' I said, 'this – us – isn't about getting back at her, is it?'

Daniel looked up. 'Aren't you getting at Milenko, slightly?'

'I have no reason to get at him.' My cup was topped up. 'If you and I had met some other place –'

'We've met in loads of places!'

I laughed. '– or some other time, I'd have liked to carry on. There. God, it's easy to say things when you know you won't be seeing each other again.'

'I can't say I'm looking forward to tomorrow.'

'Me neither, but you have to get home. Libby's playing a blinder, Daniel. This open clause has taken your eye right off the ball.'

'The ball being . . . ?'

'Children.'

He shrugged that off.

'Do you know what struck me most about you when we met? You seemed lonely, and no one in a healthy relationship should be lonely. Maybe you're hankering after the child that wasn't, or the chance, the possibility missed, or maybe there *was* a child and deep down you know it, and you're in mourning, just like me.' He looked at me, then down at his buns. 'Either way, don't underestimate the children thing, because it's insurmountable if you don't agree about it. You've recently realized that you want kids with the woman you love. That's wonderful. But she doesn't, and that's shite, so maybe you should go find someone who does.'

'You don't beat around the bush.'

'Why would I beat around the bush? Think of Steph. Think of me. Libby doesn't know her luck.'

Around the room, the head waiter was taking photos. Everyone wanted to have their photo taken having tea in Raffles Hotel, but they weren't all tourists. Some businessmen were having an evening meal, four young Muslim women had come in for a celebratory afternoon tea, and a Western woman was sitting alone, writing on a notepad.

My cup was refilled. 'Do you think it'd be really disgusting if we went up a third time?'

'Who's counting?' said Daniel.

My chair was whipped away. 'What to eat this time? Omelette, maybe, for breakfast?'

The Muslim women were giggling behind their hands at some private joke, their eyes flickering. 'Maybe that's what I'll do for my next birthday,' I said, when napkins had once again been flapped across our laps. 'Bring all my girlfriends here to tea.'

Daniel frowned. 'Are you sure I've never heard of your dad's band? I mean, you do seem to be seriously loaded.'

'Royalties can be good. Even if you have just one hit.'

'And that one hit was?'

'Well, there was more than just one.'

'Give me a name! Hell, I'm not going to run to the papers saying I shagged so-and-so's daughter in Singapore, you know.'

Our friendship was well established. It was safe to proceed. 'Black Daffodil.'

The inevitable double-take. The penny dropping. At times like this, I often felt inclined to take an emery board from my bag and file my nails, but I didn't have an emery board.

'You're kidding?'

Besides, my nails didn't need filing.

'Your dad was with Black Daffodil?'

'Wrote most of their songs. Still does, actually.'

'But they're awesome!'

I let it run.

'I won't say I have most of their CDs, because I don't – I'm more into U2, if that's allowed?'

'Of course.'

'But I saw them live once. At an open-air gig in Auckland.'

'They're still on the road.'

'So your dad is . . . Ah, shit. Rollo King! Founding member who left.'

'Ssh!'

The woman who had been making notes looked over.

'But he's an awesome lyricist. *Man*. And I've spoken to him!'

'Keep your voice down.'

'That's unreal. Totally unreal!'

'So let's drop it and enjoy the fruits of his success. What *is* that jelly stuff?'

He kept chuckling after that, as we worked our way through even more food. 'We need a walk to work all this off,' he said, his belly visibly distended.

'There are other ways of burning calories.'

He winked. 'You're on.'

This time, there was no falling asleep. When I stepped into the shower, Daniel joined me. *'Don't* stand behind me!' So he turned me round and soaped me all over until I was covered in a creamy gel, and we slid against each other, and into each other, and it seemed a pity that our impromptu fling had to end.

On the bus the next morning, there was a knot in my stomach, but it wasn't the airport knot, it was the goodbye knot. Daniel was not in good form. We had not really succeeded in making the fling uncomplicated. 'I suppose we get on too well,' I said.

'Yeah, we didn't factor in the Eastern Europe effect.' He turned, his face as close to mine as it had been on that long flight when he had said, 'Fancy a Singapore Fling?' – words that still made me flush with desire – and said, 'Regrets?'

'None. Libby is taking a big chance. She's going to blow it.'

'You're blowing it too. With Milenko. You should go back to him.'

We drew up at the airport. 'That would be a big mistake.'

As we got up, Daniel grabbed my shirt and kissed me across the top of a seat. 'You're *my* big mistake.'

'That's one of the nicest things anyone's ever said to me.'

I had checked in over the phone, which meant I could go straight through to the departure gates, but we dallied over a watery cup of coffee.

'What time is your flight tomorrow?' I asked him.

'Nine p.m.'

'God, what are you going to do to kill time?'

'Hell knows.'

'You could go see your pink dolphins.'

'Or I could go to Vietnam. I feel personally responsible for getting you and Steph together, especially since I delayed you. And I know the place.'

It was so tempting – let him handle everything – but I said, 'Enough of the avoidance therapy, Mr Blewitt. Go home and sort things out with Libby.'

'What will you do all day? Sit it out at the airport?'

'God, no. I'm going to go to a little hotel Steph knows, the Alpha One, and take a room and get a shower. Chill a bit. I couldn't face six hours in any airport, and I've no mind for sightseeing.' I tried to catch my breath.

He reached for my hand. 'You make yourself worse with all the puffing.'

'I can't help it.'

'You don't exactly inspire confidence. You're gonna get yourself lost over there.'

I glanced around. 'I should go through.'

At the departure gate, passengers were queuing, holding their bags and boarding passes at the security barriers. I checked again – pass, passport, ticket. Daniel watched me, smiling. 'I wish I could go with you. Keep you calm.'

'Me too.'

'Really?'

'Of course,' I said, hugging him. 'You make everything so easy. Even outrageous behaviour. But I can't go on taking advantage of you.'

'I hope you get that funeral you've been looking for,' he said, into my ear. 'And maybe I'll come see you in Ireland. one day.'

'Do – but leave it until Singapore is well and truly behind us or you'll cause havoc.'

We kissed long and thoroughly, and tenderly. 'If it doesn't work out with Libby,' I said, 'go back to that boat, would you? I think you miss her.'

'Yeah, and you drop me an email when you get home.'

'If ever.'

'You're nearly there.'

I stepped away. 'See you.'

'Hope so.'

'I'd still be lost in Transylvania if it weren't for you, Daniel.'

'Ditto.'

'You say the nicest things.'

'I do, don't I?'

As I inched away, he stood watching, carrying the awkward body language of the person left behind on a station platform, looking up and down the concourse, and then at me, a single grin, the mouthing of indecipherable words. I behaved like the person on the train, looking back. He was still standing there, watching, when I put my bags through the X-ray machine, and I thought about his Dylan CD and how we'd danced to 'Standing In The Doorway' the night before, by the window of our room, with the Discman tucked into Daniel's jeans and each of us holding one end of the headphones, and Daniel's arm tight round my waist, his pelvis pressed into mine, rhythmic, and Bob's coarse-voiced despair about dancing with strangers and the mercy of God searing through me, while Raffles Hotel twinkled below us, all dressed up for Christmas, and Singapore, lit and busy and making me wish I could stay much longer, dancing with Daniel to Dylan.

15

Ho Chi Minh City was everything Daniel had warned me about: heavy, sweaty, manic. Singapore had been Western enough to be familiar, its wealth and order both comfortable and comforting, but Vietnam was very different and by the time I'd collected my new suitcase, I was already thrown off kilter. I had a passing longing for Daniel to ease my way, and then thought, No. This journey was changing me, and would possibly change my life. So much was being packed into the same event – Killian's death – that I would surely be unrecognizable to myself at the end of it, wherever that might be. I pointed my trolley towards the exit and stopped to gather my wits. It would be frenetic; there would be a scurry for taxis, hunger for dollars, but I would do it with Daniel's kind of confidence. I was a travel consultant; I had crossed the world; I should be able to cross Vietnam without getting lost. Swallowing hard, I threw myself into the congested crowds around Arrivals.

The hand came from nowhere and grabbed my wrist. The white cuff, pristine, turned back. There were people between us, but he had a hold of me, he had me, like a handcuff. I couldn't take my eyes from the fingers gripping me, the bone of his wrist, and I wished to be gripped like that for ever.

Delight, sorrow and fury harried me like taxi touts, until he managed to come alongside. There was such a crush, we had to work to free ourselves and the trolley from the bustle, as if we were driving a dodgem car together. Somehow we found an empty spot of airport big enough for the three of us.

Milenko looked down at me with a cautious smile. My relationship with Dad would never recover.

'At last you're here.' He touched my shoulder lightly.

I couldn't speak.

'Are you better? I thought I would have to go to Singapore.'

'Singapore?' I spat. 'You said in Bucharest you'd never set foot in Ireland again! What are you doing *here*?'

Almost visibly tongue-in-cheek, he could not resist saying, 'This is not Ireland.'

'Don't be smart.'

'I was angry in Bucharest. You should know I would not give up so easily.'

'But how . . . *when* did you get here?'

'Last night.'

He seemed so cool, so integrated into the backdrop. Sunglasses, cream cotton trousers and a white linen shirt, half open. He was set up, sartorially, for the tropics, as if he'd been living in Vietnam for years and had merely come to meet me at the airport.

'I'm at the hotel where Steph goes,' he told me, 'but she isn't there.'

'I know. She's on Phu Quoc. I'm flying to Duong Dong this evening.'

We got a taxi. I slid across the back seat. Milenko got in beside me. His large hands were restless and uncertain on his knees. Brave, impetuous, adorable man.

'I can't believe Rollo did this after Bucharest,' I said.

'Why not? You can't believe he worries for you? Anyway, it has nothing to do with Rollo.'

'Oh, right. How else did you know what bloody flight I was on?'

He ran his palms along his thighs. 'When you agreed to come to Vietnam, I made arrangements. Rollo couldn't stop me.'

'Did he try to?'

He shrugged. 'We knew you'd be mad. We are prepared to take the consequences.'

I suffered a momentary zap of pity for Dad. It was hard to be angry when he was so far away, when I was cut off from him. He so much wanted us to be happy that he had risked inflaming my wrath by encouraging Milenko's impulsiveness. But when, finally, he heard why I had left Korčula, he would feel very badly about doing this to us.

'How did you get here?' I asked.

'I went to London to get a visa and Clara booked me on to a flight.'

'Why do you insist on making this so difficult?'

'You cannot shut me away in a box, Kadie.'

Kay-dee. 'I'm not trying to, but I resent the assumption that I can't manage. I don't need your help.'

'I am not here to help. You and Steph, you can do what you like,' he said.

'So why . . . ?'

'In Ireland, people kept asking questions, questions. Why were we not getting married? What happened? Even teasing me about you. Of course, I had no answers for them, and I will not go back to Croatia like this. With no answers. I will not go home until I know why my life has been cut into pieces.' His chest heaved and his eyes, intense and watery, reached out. No wonder I had run. This was what I was fleeing – the visible manifestation of what I had done. The thinner face and sweaty hands; the physical desperation.

I looked out, seeking distraction. It was like being in the middle of a tornado – everything flying around us – bikes, motorbikes, hats, faces. Nothing like the languid and lush place Steph had described: a country like a huge, slow river. Ho Chi Minh City was more of a gushing stream.

At the hotel, Milenko headed straight for the lift. I stopped

275

at Reception. He threw out his hands in exasperation. 'I have a room already.'

'I'll get my own. I want to shower and change.'

'For Christ's sake.'

I checked in and was given a key. We went to the lift and stepped in. Together, in a tiny space. Those eyes, that narrow mouth, the indentations in his face where his wisdom teeth had been.

'The migraine must have been bad. Three days you were ill?'

'I couldn't get a flight yesterday.'

'Clara said there were plenty of seats between Singapore and here.'

'I needed to rest, all right?'

The doors opened. Milenko followed me along the corridor to my room. 'I'll call you after I've had a shower,' I said, holding the door.

'Kadie, stop this!'

'What?'

'We were to be married soon, but I can't come into your room now?'

'I've been travelling. I want a shower. What's wrong with that?'

'Listen,' he grabbed my elbow and pushed me gently into the room, 'it's not going to be like this.'

'Like what?' We sat on the end of the bed.

'I will not allow our future to be decided in such circumstances.'

'These were not the circumstances in which it was decided.'

He glared at me, shaking his head. 'You left me standing there like a fucking idiot, with no explanation, nothing, taking off like—'

I interrupted, saying quietly and slowly, 'Milenko, I know all this, but what has it got to do with me having a shower?'

He did a double-take. I smiled. He smiled too, then covered his eyes. '*Isuse!* You give me so much work!'

I put my hand up to touch him, then withdrew it.

He turned sharply, looking at me over his arm. 'Don't shut me off, Kadie, not here, not now.'

I stood up, snapped open the clasps on my suitcase.

'I should be allowed to know why my marriage is over before it began.'

It had seemed so simple the day I had left him – break it off, leave the country and never endure having to see him or be with him again. How very straightforward it had been. 'I have to phone Steph. Tell her I'm here.'

I couldn't get through. My text didn't deliver either. *Pending.* 'Shit. She's still off. I'll try the hotel.' I rang Reception and a few minutes later they called back with a connection to Bai Truong.

'Mrs Enright is not here,' a cheerful voice informed me.

My heart jumped. 'What do you mean?'

'She is on the beach.'

'Oh. Okay. I'll call back. Thanks.' I hung up. 'I'm going for that shower now.'

Milenko was not for moving. I didn't want him there. I was afraid he might see Daniel's fingerprints all over me, so I went into the tiny bathroom and undressed there.

After my shower, when I came out to get clothes, Milenko was lying on the bed, hands behind his head. 'I will come to the island with you,' he said. 'Steph won't mind.'

She'd be delighted. Nothing would make her happier than seeing us together, I was sure. '*I* mind.'

'Then stay here tonight.'

'I can't. She's waiting for me.'

He swung his feet to the floor, leant on his knees and looked at me. 'We had a promise between us, Kadie. You can break that, but if you don't tell me why, here in this city, I will follow you to that island and all the way back to Cork until you do.' He meant it. He had more than demonstrated his determination. This was the strength of his love: his intense sincerity. Had he broken it off with me and flown, I would have done the same, would have gone in pursuit. Nowhere would have been too far. Ours had not been a relationship that could easily be left behind.

'I didn't fly across the world to have lunch with you,' he said, with contempt.

'You *can't* come to Phu Quoc.'

He stood. 'Then I am going downstairs to change your flight until tomorrow. Steph will understand.'

I didn't stop him. Didn't want to. I got dressed, relieved – and not a little impressed – that I had managed not to throw myself naked on top of him, because there was no more appealing prospect. Daniel had made no dent, no dent at all, in my attraction to, and longing for, my former fiancé. Daniel was a will-o'-the-wisp; Milenko, when stern or cross, had the presence of a hurricane, and was all the more alluring for it. Relaxed, or a little drunk, he could be slightly boyish, but subdued and serious, when he seemed to retreat behind the walls of his body and became like a great corporeal thought, he was irresistible. Still, I *would* resist.

We went in search of lunch. The flurry of the city made the view outside my head much the same as the one inside: a maelstrom. Confusion. A chaos of unfamiliarity. And something hot, too; sticky and sultry and . . . sexy. Pleased that he was getting to see my new gear, I had dressed for Milenko, in a grey silk dress and high white sandals.

'Were you all right in Singapore?' he asked.

'Yes, fine, but after the headache passed, I needed time out from phone calls and instructions. And there was no urgency, once I'd spoken to Steph and the cremation was off.'

'How long have you had contact with her?'

'Since I got to Singapore. I spoke to her the other day, but then she switched off her phone. She's as fed up with being hounded as I am.'

He took my arm to cross a street. Motorbikes – hundreds of them – came at us like a battalion. We stood, waiting for a break, but they just kept coming. Other pedestrians, we noted, stepped right out and crossed without stopping or hesitating while the bikes swerved deftly round them. We followed their example, and survived. The humidity was defiant, not cosy like Singapore, but challenging. Sweat dripped off me. The air was hazy with fumes.

'Where are we going?'

'I don't know,' he said. 'This place is crazy.'

It was a sharp reminder that I was no longer with Daniel, who always knew where he was; Milenko, like me, was in an alien world. We wandered through heaving streets, looking into restaurants and cafés, until we found one to our liking. We stepped in. Air-conditioning.

We ordered what we recognized. I was glad Milenko was there, that we were sharing this madness at last. I had missed him so much, had wanted so badly his companionship and steady wisdom. I had gone to Istanbul to keep distance between us, but now he had thrown himself into my path and I had to decide how much I could take. For how long, in these conditions, could I keep myself from him? Was that his plan? He knew me; he knew, probably, that he could break me down by simply staying near me for long enough. And how long would that be? Days? Weeks? *Hours?*

'You must ring your father.' He looked at his watch, made some calculations. 'In a few hours he'll be getting up. You can ring then.'

'I'll ring him when I feel like it. He shouldn't have told you where I was.'

He held my eye. 'He could not have stopped me finding out.'

A breath of air came out of me, as if from crushed bellows.

'Please let me come to this Dong Dong place.'

'Duong Dong.'

'We'll talk to Steph and take her home to the funeral and . . .' he smiled, ever so slightly '. . . maybe by then I'll have changed your crazy mind.'

'Don't even think it.' *Don't even think it, my love.*

He ran his hand across his mouth.

'How are things at home?' I asked.

'Crazy. Everything is crazy. And when Steph said Killian was to be cremated . . . oh, the crying and the weeping and the worry that he should not have a proper service! Already, he had not . . .' He made the sign of a blessing.

'The Last Rites?'

'His mother finds that hard. Like mine did, with Dario.'

'Poor Marjorie.'

'She is ill and even Rollo –'

'What?'

'It's hard for him. He is trying to help Marjorie, and you, and then people were coming for the funeral to stay with him, and had to be sent away again. And those dogs! Everything is breaking. Their tails, they keep going whoosh-whoosh, knocking things off tables.'

'They're getting into the house?'

'A bit. He tries, you know, but . . .'

Homesickness came into the place like a soundwave, bringing a yearning for my father and the smell of Ireland. 'Mum?'

'She's . . . the way she is.'

'Has she gone back to London?'

'No, she is staying with Rollo until the funeral.'

'And that'll be any day now.'

He hesitated. 'The undertaker has still not received instructions from Steph, and even when she does . . . nobody wants the funeral to go ahead without her. You have a heavy burden. If I go to this island, I might be able to help persuade her.'

'I'm not going to bully her. And I won't let anyone else do it either.'

We meandered back to the hotel. When we had to cross another busy street, Milenko put his hand to my elbow and then, as we crossed, took my hand. I was so alarmed by the bikes skirting my arse that I let him, but when we got to the other side, I withdrew it.

In my room, I tried Steph's hotel again, but it was engaged. It made me uneasy. I was already a day late because of Daniel and now I was unable to tell her that Milenko had delayed me again. I should have rushed straight to her, instead of shagging a Kiwi for no good reason. There was every good reason, however, for losing a day to Milenko.

He took the receiver from my hand and left it off the hook, upturned on the table. 'No more with Steph. Tell me what I did.'

He threw himself on to the bed, never taking his eyes from my face. It was getting harder, much too soon. The longer we were together, in this small room in this strange world, the more difficult it became to remain aloof, to keep up the performance. The hardest part was trying to stop him feeling my love. He wasn't actively attempting to break me down. He was simply waiting to hear my explanation and probably hoping that whatever it was could be rectified, reconsidered, here, far from our families and wedding arrangements. But I had not lightly flown Korčula.

I lay down beside him. We watched one another until our lids were heavy. We slept. Milenko was jetlagged and we were drained from the strain of being together but apart. The air-conditioner and the cacophony of horns from the streets hummed us into oblivion.

Two hours later we woke, none the better for it. Milenko dragged himself to the bathroom. I dozed. He collapsed again beside me. For another hour, we tossed and turned and stretched. He waited; I struggled. He deserved to have answers; there was no doubt in my mind about that, but was it right to inflict them on him?

We had not been naïve about marriage. We knew it would be tough at times, but we had good raw materials, not least this ease between us and the compatibility of our temperaments, and it irked me to see these go to waste. But I had learnt that a marriage is made up of many other elements, which I had foolishly overlooked.

The two of us, laid out like that together in light clothes, made me think of Mauritius. Specifically, of our honeymoon in Mauritius.

'What are you thinking about?' Milenko asked.

'Mauritius. You?'

He rolled on to his side. 'I was thinking how nice it is to be near you, even though you won't touch me or care about me.'

'I care. This is not about loving or not loving you.' Before I could stop myself, I had touched his face.

'What is it about, then?'

Where was God when I needed Him? Or even Killian. Where had Killian gone? This was huge, metaphysical. Who would tell me what was the right thing to do? Milenko's misery was powered by curiosity and bewilderment; but the reasons he sought would throw him into a far deeper crisis.

'Tell me.'

'I can't.'

He grabbed my arm, then lightened his grip and stroked the back of my hand with his thumb. 'I know you love me,' he said quietly. 'It doesn't go away, like that, in a night. And I know you loved me that day I was coming from Zagreb, because I heard it in your voice. It came from here,' he lightly touched my stomach, 'not . . .' his hand moved to my hip '. . . anywhere else. What happened, Kadie? Something happened.'

Time stretched out, expanding like an image in a hall of crazy mirrors. Several moments passed before I was able to move my head in some sort of acknowledgement.

His hand still on my hip, Milenko said again, 'Tell me.'

Hanging over me, just there.

It had taken only hours, a handful of hours, until we found ourselves thus, alone and slipping towards each other, with little resistance to call upon and too little space between us.

I turned my face from him, but couldn't draw away.

With one finger to my chin, he made me face him. Time took another slow stretch.

He didn't kiss me; I didn't kiss him. We kissed each other, falling into it, dropping towards it until it had begun almost without our doing. His lips and tongue were on me again, with me again. This was the kiss before the first and after the last. Nothing would ever be like it.

We broke off, gasping. Milenko ran his chin along the backs of my fingers, questions alighting in his eyes, disappearing like fireflies; then he held me tight, pressing the air from my lungs. Tears slipped from the sides of my eyes. We should have stopped there, but we were too ravaged to be wise. We threw ourselves in once more, as if hoping to salvage those lost weeks.

I was going backwards, but he thought we were going forwards. When would I tell him?

Not yet.

I pulled his perfect tropical shirt from his appropriate cotton trousers and over his head, kissing his chest, his nipples, his belly, in a great hurry down to his belt. He pulled me back up and painstakingly opened every button on my dress before pushing it off my shoulders with near reverence. He reached down to my foot and squeezed it – a familiar, affectionate gesture. He loved my feet; I loved that he loved my feet. He moved his hand to my calf, my thigh. I opened his belt, bit into his shoulder. We shoved off his remaining clothes and my own, and gripped one another with arms and legs, and someone knocked on the door.

'Shit!' I pulled a sheet over me. 'You go.'

'I can't go like this! I need a minute.'

'Feck.' I jumped towards the bathroom, grabbed a towel, calling, 'Who is it?'

There was another rap, a gentle one.

I pulled the towel round me and opened the door a fraction. *'Jesus!'*

Daniel smirked. 'Picked up some other poor bugger already, have you?'

I stepped out, pulling the door behind me. 'What the fuck are you doing?'

He stepped back, stung. 'Making another big mistake, it seems.'

'But . . . how did you get here?'

'Grabbed myself a visa from the embassy and got the next flight.'

Milenko opened the door behind me, his trousers pulled on. Their faces almost fell off their heads.

I stood between them in a towel. 'Excellent.'

'What's he doing here?' Milenko asked, calm and cool.

'I . . . I don't know.'

'Don't mind me,' said Daniel, backing off along the corridor. 'I just wanted to make sure you were okay, but I'll be on my way. No sweat.'

I called after him: 'But how did you . . . Where are you going to go?'

He had no answer ready for that, because he had not been ready for this. 'I'll . . . I'll, ahm . . .'

'We'll all go to dinner,' Milenko said, turning back into the room.

'Yes! Wait, Daniel. We'll meet you in the lobby in five minutes.'

He walked backwards, looking mischievous. 'Might take you a bit longer than that to explain,' he whispered loudly.

I cursed.

Back in the room, Milenko stood with his hands on his hips. 'Why is he following you?'

'Why are *you*?'

'How does he know you are here?'

'Look, sit down and stop being so macho about it.' He did so. 'We travelled to Istanbul together. Did Dad tell you?'

He had not. Probably wise.

'Daniel was going there anyway and I went along because . . . because . . . Wait a minute. I don't have to explain anything to you. We've broken up.'

'So there *is* something to explain? Like maybe why you were so long in Singapore? Would he be the migraine by any chance?'

'Milenko.'

'Would he?'

'All right, he *was* in Singapore and you know what? It really helped. I was cracking up and exhausted, so we took time out, and it set me up for the next leg. I knew where Steph was and she knew where I was, and it was great to get a break from all the flying and hassle and family shit. We were tourists, that's all.'

Milenko looked as if he wanted to stand up but couldn't. 'You don't waste time,' he said quietly.

'That's not fair. Have you any idea what it's been like since I left Korčula?'

'Of course I do. It's been worse for me.'

'Not worse. You can take my word for that.'

'But you're the one who ended it! Why is it so hard for you? It's what you *want*.'

'It *isn't* what I want! I need you, and I want our life together.'

'So have it,' he shouted, standing up. 'Have it. I'm here, take it.'

'I can't!'

'Why not?'

It came suddenly – the dark, the night, the breathing and nausea. I put my hand over my eyes and sank on to the chair.

Milenko leant into my face. 'Why not?' But he saw that I was trembling, and thought it was because he'd shouted, and he knelt on the floor, kissing my neck. 'I'm sorry. Christ, I'm sorry, Kadie. I didn't come to fight.' I held his head against me. He nuzzled my breasts, kissing them and me.

I pulled back. 'We can't. Not now that you've arranged dinner with Daniel. Why did you do that?'

He sat back on his haunches. 'We can't leave him alone. He was good to you in Romania.' He shook me lightly. 'But it should have been me.'

'I wish it had been.'

'Why has he come, Kadie?'

'I don't know. Honestly. He's supposed to be going to Australia.'

'Not any more.'

'He's lost his way, that's all. I'll set him right. He's . . . Please be nice to him. We may have our problems, but he has his.'

Milenko shook me gently again. 'What is going on with you?'

'I'm no good without you, that's what. Being without you is terrifying.'

He reached for his shirt.

'Don't,' I said, taking it from him. 'Don't.'

Dinner was interesting. Daniel was as efficient as ever. He flagged down a tuk-tuk, in essence a motorbike with extensions – a roof and seats. We squashed into the back and he directed the driver to a restaurant he knew. The putter of motorbikes was like the purr of a giant cat sitting on top of the city.

'The Saigon river,' I said to Milenko. 'It's perverse.'

At dinner, neither of us ate much. I had no appetite, caught as I was not only between two men but between two such recent lovers. I could not look at Daniel, for fear he would see the lingering glow of sex in my eyes. My cheeks were flushed, my legs like jelly, and even the delights of Vietnamese cuisine could not distract me from one moment in the bedroom, which kept replaying inside my head. When Milenko had put his hands under my knees and pulled my hips to the edge of the chair, I had said, 'I've stopped taking the pill,' but he came into me anyway, his eyes hard on mine, and I let him.

Daniel didn't prevaricate. 'So, you're back together. That didn't take long.'

Milenko said, 'It took much too long. I should not have left Bucharest.'

'So you'll both go over to Steph?'

Neither of us knew the answer to that, but Milenko nodded mildly. I said, 'What are *you* going to do?'

'I'll head back to Singapore, then Sydney.'

'That's quite a few flights you've missed.'

'Yeah, and I'm sorry for stuffing my nose in where it isn't wanted, but I . . .' He glanced awkwardly at Milenko. 'With me knowing Vietnam, I thought it might be helpful.'

'So many knights in bloody armour,' I said. 'You're as bad as each other. Unreconstructed males.'

Milenko turned to me. 'You're terrified of flying and you get migraine.'

'You've no sense of direction,' Daniel added, 'you hate every single form of transport, and you don't understand even when people speak English. Then there's the claustrophobia, the emotional baggage . . .'

'Yes, I'm such a disaster,' I said, 'and yet you two can't seem to manage without me.'

'I just meant to help,' Daniel muttered.

'Your help won't be necessary now,' said Milenko.

'Yeah, I get that.'

'I'm sorry, Daniel. It was good of you to change your plans, but you're just avoiding going home,' I said, coming on all maternal.

When Milenko left us to go to the bathroom, Daniel chuckled. 'You have to see the funny side – I mean, what a dork.'

I bristled. 'Milenko?'

'No, me – running after a woman who already had another guy running after her.'

'What possessed you?'

'I thought maybe there was something . . . that it might have been worth it. But if I'd known it wasn't over with him, I would never –'

'It *is* over.'

'You think? It feels pretty hot from where I'm sitting.'

I sucked in my lips.

'I hope you know what you're doing,' he said.

'You should know by now that I have absolutely no idea what I'm doing, or what I'll do next.'

What I did next, later that night, was to tell Milenko why I had left him. After saying goodnight to Daniel, who took Milenko's room, we lay on the bed cuddling, enjoying the comforting contacts that had been so badly missed. Eventually we made love again, without the pent-up frustration of earlier, but slowly and surely, and when we climaxed, it came from such depths that a surge of weeping shook me. Milenko held me, but said into my ear, 'Do you know what it's like when you lose someone and you don't know why?'

'Haven't we just lost Killian like that? Though, I know, I shouldn't compare.'

'Why not? Losing you was not so different. You were there, and then you were not.'

'But Killian's gone for ever. You can replace me.'

He pulled out of me. 'How can I replace you,' he asked, 'when I don't know why I lost you?'

'If you think I hurt you by leaving you, it will hurt even more to know why I left.'

His eyes barely flickered. 'You left me standing on that quayside on a beautiful morning and there were cars and people and I didn't understand.' He rolled off me. 'It was like the day Gabriella drove away, saying, "Over, over!" I couldn't work, couldn't see my parents. I drove up and down the island, twice, but I couldn't go to my friends because it was embarrassing – to lose two beautiful fiancées. I knew you meant it. There was something in your eyes. Something I didn't understand. As if you were disgusted with me, or even . . . afraid of me.'

I *had* been afraid. Afraid of what he might find out.

'Very late, I went home. My parents had not gone to bed. They had heard you had left Korčula. I told them: "It's over, finished. Failure, again. No woman wants to marry me." They stared at me. And then the questions. Questions, questions! Why? What about the wedding? All the family going to Ireland? What were we to do? My mother got excited and my father, he sat at the table and he was shaking. His hands were shaking, Kadie, and he looked like he would cry, but I comforted him and said I'd be okay, even though I thought I would kill myself.'

'Don't say that.'

'But I felt it. I couldn't see what it would be like to get up another day and another week and another month without you. I didn't know how to get up even the next morning, so I didn't. I lay there all day and all night with my phone and a bottle, sending SMS and phoning, but you weren't answering. My father listened to me going on and on: "Is there something in me? Something bad I can't see?" It was like being sick, you know – dying, but not dying.

'We had to tell the family *again*. So humiliating. Milenko is not getting married after all. I wanted to leave. Dad suggested our relatives in Zagreb, but I was too sick to go anywhere. I went to Gabriella's house and woke her and her family in the middle of the night and I tried to force her to tell me why she had left me, so that I could understand why you did, and she looked sad – no, shocked, as if she pitied me – and I thought maybe she would tell me, but she made raspberry tea and stroked my face and told me not to be upset. She held me against her and her breasts were going up and down like there was something in there she couldn't get out, but she said she had left me because she was not in love. She gave it away. You are lying, both of you. How could I have picked two such different women who break their engagements? It's not possible. Gabriella is going to marry her boyfriend, but she doesn't love him. I could feel it in the way she held me. And when I left – she made me leave – she was crying too.

'Everyone was crying. My mother had not stopped, but she didn't know why. She'd ask about plans for the wedding, or say, "Where is Kadie?" We were in a nightmare. Aunts, uncles, everyone calling over to talk about it. Pretending to be helping, but they were thinking, Poor Milenko. Can't get a woman. Must have some disease. They probably think I beat my women. My aunts, the looks they gave me. Disgusted. Not sympathetic at all. I went for a swim. It was bloody cold but I swam out and a boat nearly knocked my head off. It felt good to take a risk and not care. I only swam back because of my mother.

'And then Killian died, and saved my life.'

I held him to me, and his tears – or mine – wet my ear. 'I would never have done this to you if . . .'

'If what?'

'If there was some way not to.'

'You don't like Korčula, is that it? You're not happy there?'

'I *love* Korčula.'

'My mother, then? She's too much, I know, but I can deal with that. I'll do anything to make it easier for you.'

'It isn't your mother.'

'Is it Rollo? You can't leave him?'

'No.'

We lay some time more.

'Kadie?'

'What?'

'Marry me. For Christ's sake.'

I was weary with his unhappiness, and with carrying it. I wanted to let it go, to drop it, but how could I pass the burden on to this gentle man and abandon him to its weight? The temptation to do so was overwhelming, here, so far from home, so much in love, in this exotic, clammy world, which seemed to invite confession.

'I feel I will never eat again,' he said, his mouth against my face, 'because the food would pass through me since there is nothing left of me. And I will never sleep again, because inside my head, I will never stop thinking, wondering. I'll never dream again, because I'll be afraid to see you there. That's what I feel like. Empty clothes on the floor. There's just air where I used to be.'

I turned to face him and, for a few moments, cherished the love in his eyes that would soon be gone.

'Why has the person who makes me taken me apart?'

'I made a terrible mistake,' I whispered. 'Please don't hold it against me . . .'

16

A loud rapping on the door woke me. Through the slits of swollen eyes, I saw that it was nearly midday.

'Kadie?' Daniel called.

I opened my mouth, but my throat had closed up. Slowly I dragged myself from bed and opened the door, barely covered by a sheet.

'Christ.' He closed the door behind him and pulled the sheet properly round me. 'What have you done to each other?'

'You've seen Milenko?'

'He was checking out. He looked . . . badly shattered.'

I bit on the sheet.

'What happened?'

'I told him why I can't marry him.' I retreated to the bed, where I curled up with my back to him.

'Kadie, you have to get moving. You can't miss another flight.'

'I'm not going anywhere. Ever.'

He sat down behind me on the bed. 'Should I get you tea or something?'

'I hope I'm pregnant.'

He could do nothing with me. 'Look, I have to go soon too.'

'Good.'

'We can go to the airport together.'

'We're not going anywhere *together*, Daniel.'

'But you need to shift it if you're going to get to Duong Dong.'

'You know,' I said, my words slightly slurred, 'you were wrong about me being your big mistake.' I looked over my shoulder. 'You were *my* big mistake.'

'Thanks.'

'You're very welcome. Now, why don't you just run along, like a good boy?'

His eyes narrowed. 'If you have regrets about Singapore, don't take it out on me now.'

'I don't have regrets. If we hadn't stopped in Singapore, I'd have no clothes.'

He caught his breath.

I twisted round, coming out of the sheet, aware that my nipples were inches from his wrist. 'And even if I did have regrets about you, they would come to nothing against all the other regrets that are swamping me right now.'

'You're very sweet this morning.'

'Go home, Daniel.'

'You're the one who needs to go home.'

'Just clear off, will you? I don't need your bloody fussing and organizing.' I leant on my elbow and kicked off the sheet. He took it all in, his expression dour. 'At least you've still got Libby. Go and fix it.'

'Don't patronize me,' he said. 'Poor you, you can't have Milenko back, even though he was here last night and you were eating and breathing and sleeping together, but you've sent him off, like a kicked dog. It's destroying both of you, and you have the nerve to tell me all *I* have to do is "fix it".'

'Yeah, because you *can*, and because you and Libby are being bloody careless. Playing stupid games.'

'And you haven't been careless?'

My befuddled brain didn't know what he meant.

'You're the one who's done the cheating, aren't you?' he said. 'Back in beautiful Croatia.'

'Piss off.'

294

He stood up. 'If I didn't know better, I'd say you were drunk.'

'If I was drunk, I wouldn't ask you so politely to get the fuck out of here! I'm sick of the sight of you.'

The door didn't close quietly behind him because he didn't bother to close it. He left it open, forcing me to hobble over with a sheet dangling round my feet to shut it. Then I went back to bed.

It was easy, letting Daniel go. It could not be otherwise, not after I had watched Milenko zip closed his bag and look at me, not wanting to leave in silence but unable to speak any more. We had talked for most of the night. It had been like throwing someone precious and vital to my being into a deep mine. He had sat on the edge of the bed, caving in. I had expected something else. Fury, perhaps. Aggression, even. I thought he might fling me across the room after hearing about this betrayal of who he was and what he'd been and done, of everything that held substance for him.

He had been, for a while, like a panther, slick, black, pacing. Then he had been sick. I held his brow over the lavatory bowl, crying and consoling, but there was nothing in it for him. And there was nothing at all he could do, for himself, for me. He had been coherent at times, and in turn persuasive, bloody-minded, argumentative and, finally, bereft. There was no way round it. He simply caved, as I had done, and there was no way of reconstructing him.

In the early hours, he had been mute. He lay, curled on the bed, foetal, ashamed and humiliated, and I had wanted to get into him, to get inside that curved chest, those rigid limbs, but I lay behind him, unable to reach. For an hour, we scarcely moved. Then he had packed. I wasn't sure where he would go, but suspected the airport, where he would board whatever flight would have him. He was so wretched. His clothes seemed to be in tatters, though they weren't. He looked quite tidy on the outside, but in my eyes, and in Daniel's too apparently, he was torn and wrecked. His struggle for words was not entirely lost. 'I'm sorry,' he had said finally, his hand on the side of my neck. He shook his head at the inadequacy of the gesture, of the word, but it was all he had.

For twenty-four hours, I lay mourning him. Nobody knew where I was; least of all me.

The taxi was sticky. It was a miracle that I'd got into it at all. Had it not been for Steph, I would have stayed in that room until someone came to scrape my remains off the sheets. But I had somehow managed to overcome paralysis. I had, eventually, lifted myself into an upright position; anguish proved even heavier on the vertical, balanced precariously like a concrete building on my shoulders, drilling me into the ground. It wanted me down, and it gave me a headache, but I managed to book another flight and to go through the motions until I found myself on the way to the airport. Steph would understand the delays, but I dreaded switching on my phone. The pellets that it would fire might knock me over.

I was sickening by the minute, but I would get to Duong Dong. One last leg. A short leg. I would make it.

Phu Quoc Island, from the map in the hotel, was like a figure of Christ pointing to the right, hanging in the Gulf of Thailand. On this pearl drop of beaches and jungles, Vietnam had spread into Steph's blood when she had frolicked there as a teenager. I was impatient to see it all: the sea, Bai Truong, or Long Beach, and, most of all, Steph.

The fretful street scenes on the way to the airport reminded me of all the travel documentaries I had watched, snug in my living room with tea and biscuits, enjoying the spectacle without the discomfort. It seemed I had roused myself from stupor only to find myself in a Michael Palin programme.

Trolleys stacked high with green bananas; three people on a pushbike – Mum, Dad and baby wedged in between; hens in baskets; kids with dinner-plate eyes and silky hair I wanted to stroke; and women – with loves and hurts and intrigue like mine, but lives so different, neat and exotic in their straw hats and pyjama-like suits, carrying their loads of fruit and veg and every other thing on a balance over their shoulders. I blanked out, went somewhere else and came back again.

It could not be put off. I switched on my phone. My inbox was full, but my eyes were jumping. I held the phone at arm's length to focus. Two messages from Steph saying, 'Where are you?' Several from Rollo – apologies, from what I could make out with dodgy vision, and pleas to phone home. I had left him in no doubt that seeing Milenko would be detrimental to us both, and it had been, but he had allowed his fondness for Milenko to overrule me. Now he would not be hearing from him again and I could not leave him in the dark with his worries, especially when he was being hounded in turn by Killian's family for every scrap of news. So I rang my mother's mobile, waking her. The line kept breaking up, but I told her I was on my way to Duong Dong and asked her to pass this information on to any interested parties, then I whined about Dad and Milenko.

'Kadie, listen to me,' she said. 'Can you hear me?'

'Just.'

'Stop being so pig-headed about Rollo. He only did what any father would do.'

'Any father would put his daughter's feelings ahead of her ex-fiancé's! From the outset he . . . Mum? Damn. I'm losing you, hello?'

Gone.

Reading texts in the back of a taxi had been a very bad idea: I felt much worse.

There was a bloke in the front seat beside the driver. Killian.

He turned and winked. I hoped he would come with me all the way to Steph, that she might see him too.

But where was Milenko? Was he sitting in an airport? Singapore, perhaps? I could imagine his face, could see his features working to figure it out. My stomach twisted into worms of misgiving. I should not have told him.

A woman in a pink jacket and conical hat was cycling alongside us. Suddenly there were two of her. I covered my eyes. *Christ.* Double vision! I clenched my eyes, then opened them again. No focus. None at all. Double vision. Triple. Full-blown. I'd never had it before. I tried to blink it away. It wouldn't go and my system erupted. Shouting at the driver to stop, I opened the door and threw up over the back of a motorbike. 'Take me back, please. Hotel. The hotel!'

The chambermaid was finishing my room. I stumbled in, feeling my way, closed the shutter and lay down. Double vision was a regular feature for some sufferers, but it was new to me, and terrifying. I held my phone at arm's length and wrote to Steph: 'Delayed. Will come.' I may not have hit the right keys, but it was the best I could do. As the message was sent, my battery went down. I threw aside my phone, rolled over and surrendered myself to the worst migraine I had ever experienced.

The pain, initially, was almost comforting. It behaved in a recognizable manner. It was what it was. But then it transcended even itself and became so severe that I wished my head would simply explode and be done with it. Instead it imploded. There was no way to contain it. Away from my own hard bed, the agony was several extremes beyond intolerable. This migraine shredded me mercilessly. I cried out more than once, in my dim, brown room.

The hours of reeling, screaming inwardly, tossing and writhing went on. I was closed in, trapped behind a pane of glass.

Sleep wouldn't come, or oblivion, so the battle raged into the night. I could barely see the room, the fluttering, flittering, hazy world around me. At times I believed myself at home, at others I thought Daniel was there. Always Daniel. I longed for Radio 4 and the gentle hum of its voices; sometimes that worked – normal voices in the normal world distracting me into sleep.

There was a black-out of some kind; when I came round, my eyesight was steadier. Only one room and it wasn't jumping. The streets were quiet, but their silence was more alienating than those purring engines. I had never been so stranded, and never, ever, so lonely. 'And I thought Budapest was bad,' I said out loud. 'I should have gone home then. Should have gone home.' There was no Rollo to bring me a glass of water, to soothe my forehead with a damp cloth. There would be no Rollo to bring that miraculous cup of tea when recovery set in. The bumpy soft mattress made everything worse, because I could not put my neck where I needed to. Nor, as coherency improved, could I rest easy with myself. What would Steph be making of my no-show? I was racked with remorse at letting her down, at my infidelity with Daniel, my destruction of Milenko. But I railed against Killian – how could he, now unworldly and celestially informed, have dumped me here? Could he not at least have got me to Bai Truong before this happened?

I called home. 'Kadie! How are things?' Dad said cheerfully. 'Swimming in the South China Sea, are you?'

They hadn't even missed me. Was Steph in contact with no one?

'I'm still in Saigon. Couldn't go. Migraine.'

'Oh, Lord. So soon after Singapore?'

'Prevailing conditions are contra-indicated.'

'You poor love.'

'I need water, Dad. It's early hours here and I don't know

if there's anyone downstairs. Could you ring Reception and see if someone could bring me some, but tell them to leave it outside the door. I haven't the energy to explain.'

'But where's Milenko?'

'Gone.'

A pause. 'Oh. I see.'

'I warned you.'

'Kadie, listen, I'm sorry about him going out there, but your mother crumbled under the pressure and I don't blame her. The guy is distraught and –'

'I thought *you* told him.'

'I wouldn't dare, but –'

'Dad. Water. Please.' I held on to my head until, a good twenty minutes later, I heard rattling outside the door. When I felt able, I retrieved the cool bottled water. I drank half of it, and finally slept.

A clearing. A knock on the door, then it opened and a small, busty woman came in, softly, softly, carrying a tray, and put it on the bedside table. A pot of tea. She smiled. 'Better?'

'A little. Thank you.'

'Your daddy he phoned and ask me bring you tea,' she chirped.

'What time is it?'

'Four o'clock.'

A whole night, a whole day.

Time to face the music. I plugged in my phone. Two missed calls from Steph and two voicemails. The first was predictable: she was seriously pissed off. 'Kadie, what do you mean "delayed"? Are you off on a spree with yer man? I mean . . . are you still planning on turning up, because if you are, could you please let me know? I really want to get out of here now and there are seats on tomorrow's flight back to Ho Chi Minh.

300

I can't hack it much longer. It's so cut off, and Shannon's mad to see me, so if you're not coming, I'll go and stay with her. Please ring as soon as you switch on.'

The second voicemail had been recorded that morning. It was less predictable. 'Okay, still no word, so I'm off. You're clearly not coming and Shannon won't let up, and we won't get another chance like this after the baby comes. I hope you're enjoying your brainstorm. Maybe, when you have a minute, you might tell them at home that they can do what they want and I'll come home when I want. I'm sorry you came this far, but this isn't really about me, is it?'

So I would not have to go to Duong Dong after all. I felt only relief. I could hardly begrudge Steph. She must not feel 'cut off'. That was exactly why I was pursuing her – so that she wouldn't be lonely. But now I had to find Shannon. What a palaver. Years before she had moved to Hanoi, which was when Steph lost track of her, but she might have moved back to Ho Chi Minh City since then. Call in the rescue service.

'Thanks for the tea, Dad.'

'How is it?'

'It was the worst ever. I had double vision and everything.'

He sighed heavily, and for the first time sounded like an old man on the end of the line. My old dad.

'But it's getting better,' I said. 'I'm upright, and I won't be going to Duong Dong.'

'Why not?'

'Steph has given up on me.'

'Oh, shit.'

'No, it's okay, I know where she is. You know her friend Shannon, the Aussie who lives here? Apparently someone at home put them back in touch.'

'Yeah, when the word got out about Killian, it filtered through the grapevine to Shannon and she got linked back to us. So they've made contact, have they?'

'Yeah, do you have her number?'

'I can get it. Why?'

'Because that's where Steph is. I thought I'd go there tomorrow.'

There was a very long pause, over beyond.

'Dad?'

'Are you sure that's where she's gone?'

'Yeah, she said so, and it stands to reason. Seeing as I didn't show up.'

'But, Kadie, Shannon's in Australia.'

'Huh?'

'She moved back some years ago.'

'What? No! She can't have. Steph wouldn't go to *Australia*.'

Dad said quietly, 'Poor thing. She must be completely disoriented.'

'No, I don't believe it. I'll phone her. 'Bye.' But Steph's phone was off again. I sent a text: 'I'm here. I've been sick. Don't leave!'

Silence.

I rang the airport. Yes, there was a Sydney flight, and it was just about to leave. Then I rang the Australian consulate. Yes, they issued visas to EU passports over the counter.

She'd gone.

While I had been writhing in my bed, she had been within a few miles of me, getting her tickets, visas, and going away.

There was no point getting excited. I couldn't afford to. I ordered more tea and bread and stayed calm. Her old pal was offering mothering and comfort in sunny Australia, while I had gone off the radar. She had not even known I was in Vietnam. On the other hand, I'd said I was coming and I came. She told me she had reached the end of the line; clearly, she had not. Maybe she never would. On a radio down at street level, I could hear 'Sail On' by Lionel Ritchie. Sail on, indeed.

Dad called back. 'I've just heard that the undertaker in

Sweden has finally got that fax from Steph, giving instructions for the repatriation to go ahead. She took her time about it.'

'Is that what they've been waiting for? Is it enough?'

'Written instructions – sure. The undertaker is happy to proceed on that basis.'

'So Killian will be brought home?'

'Without delay.'

'That's something, I suppose.'

'You see? You haven't wasted your time.'

'But none of this is my doing. It wasn't even me who talked her out of cremating Killian. And what am I to do about Steph?'

'Leave her be. She's in good hands, by all accounts. You've done what you can.'

'Will they hold the funeral for me?'

'I'll make sure they do. Get some rest, Kadie, then head for home.'

'I'm not sure I have the energy.'

'Don't be silly. We'll have you back before you know it. I should never have asked you to go that far.'

'No, you shouldn't. It served no purpose.'

'When do you think you'll be fit to travel?'

'I've never been fit to travel.'

'I'll make sure Clara books the shortest possible flight.'

'Just one more thing, Dad. You and Mum need to know that Milenko could have been spared. We needed to be kept apart. I told you that. Now that we've spoken, he'll never be the same again and his life will never be the same, and I could have spared him if you'd heeded what I'd said. On his behalf, I'll never forgive you.'

That night, and for much of the next day, I sat on my balcony, looking down at the street below. What a way to see a place – from a balcony. But being alone was the best thing. With

Daniel, I had allowed myself to be needy. Now it was just me and the roar of the city, and the dense Vietnamese days, and the giggling children taunting me from balconies across the street. In all this commotion, I could at last be still, and stillness restored me.

At some point, when I was sitting there, it came to me that it had been right and fair to make love with Milenko, to have told him what happened and to have seen him go. An end for us both. The story had been told, the man I loved devastated enough to leave me for ever. He would no longer pursue me. I would probably never set eyes on him again.

Something else came to me, in my groggy, post-migraine state: there was only one way left for me to go.

The long flight passed in a daze. I watched the movies and ate the food. Every emotion had been drained out of me. Even the fear was gone. *Birds rarely drop out of the sky*. Didn't care either way. Let it drop. Explode. Nothing to lose.

That I really had nothing left to lose was emphasized by a song on the Easy Listening channel, a song that had the means to tear the heart out of me but, like a person cutting herself, I listened to it anyway. There had been a party in Korčula that summer, an engagement party, thrown by Milenko's parents and held on the terrace of a nearby restaurant, where we ate under a rattan roof, a brick stove smoking our fish in the corner, and all Milenko's friends, and many of mine, gathered with our families for a long celebratory meal. After dark, the tables had been pushed back to make room for dancing. Someone put on the Grace Jones version of 'La Vie En Rose'. Other couples dispersed, leaving the floor to Milenko and me, and a rope of friends gathered round us. I was in my element. Happy out. Everything was, as the song said, *lovely*. My parents beamed at their charmed daughter; Marin sat with Cecilia, nodding to the music; Ger and Clara flirted in the corner with

Croatian cousins. We danced, the two of us, teasing with our hips, seducing with our shoulders. Milenko was at my fingertips, a glass of wine in his hand, another on my waist, loving me with every move. It was, I suppose, our wedding. Our union. Or as close as we would ever get to it.

17

Early morning Sydney. South of our north; summer of our winter; day of our night. I was upside-down, inside-out, and discombobulated. Clara, who had groaned when I had asked her to reroute me to Sydney instead of Cork, had also booked me into a city-centre hotel, but it was too early, when I arrived, to check into my room, so I was directed to the mezzanine that overlooked Reception. Self-service breakfast, again. Were there no hotels left, I wondered, where you didn't have to make your own toast? Breakfast had globally become a do-it-yourself job, from dangling teabags to pre-boiled eggs, and moving racks dumping toast on to trays. So I did-it-myself, sat down and scrambled around for my bearings.

Australia. I had sold it so often. I knew its attractions, but had never been inclined to go. Way too far. Now I had arrived by default. Maybe I was getting into the swing of this travelling lark, though this could hardly be termed travel. More like being on a pogo-stick, bouncing up and down, never quite sure where exactly I would land and having little time to see it anyway, before being projected into the air again. But if nothing else, my perspective had changed. The earth was not shrinking, as we travel agents liked to think. The earth was a behemoth and we were sitting on the rim in hordes and bunches. Nor was Australia, as I frequently told my clients, a mere 'hop, skip and a jump' from Asia. If Australia was on Asia's doorstep, it was a very tall step, as I had discovered on that long flight. When, finally, the jagged edge of the Northern Territory had come into view, I had been captivated. The red continent. It took us nearly four hours to cross two states.

Rollo had been adamant. No bloody way, he said. Absolutely not. I was coming back to Ireland, not going on a bloody wild-goose chase to Australia! But it was quite simple to me. I could not turn back without Steph. I had almost snatched her; I had heard her and giggled with her, cried with her; to retreat would be like reaching the gravitational pull of Mars and blasting away from it. There were things to be said and a promise to be kept. Besides, I had built up such momentum that I was unable to stop myself. Only seeing Steph would do that.

Her friend Shannon lived quite far south on the New South Wales coast. I was not prepared to risk alerting them to my arrival, lest it prompted Steph to bolt. Far better to rent a car and drive down, in the hope of surprising her *in situ*. The prospect of driving alone through such an unknown continent filled me with apprehension, but apprehension had become my constant companion and we had learnt to tolerate one another. All the same, I needed to get my bearings before I leapt into a car and headed south.

Or so I told myself. There was another mitigating factor: Daniel. Daniel, whom I could not think about without wincing. We were once again in the same city, crazy as that seemed, and I would not rest until I had apologized to him. Perhaps I should have agonized over whether it was fair to contact him in this place where he lived with his girlfriend, but I had no stomach left for agonizing. There had been enough of that and, anyway, I could not resist the opportunity to do to him what he had done to me and Milenko.

Voices rose from the lobby. A row was building between the receptionist and some departing guests. I moved closer to the railing. The guests were complaining about being overcharged. In their view, the receptionist's attitude left much to be desired.

I made more toast and returned to my ringside seat, feigning distraction from what was actually preoccupying me – how to approach Daniel. He had given me his mobile number, which, now that he was back in Sydney, would be in use. But it was a Saturday, and he could be at home, curled up in bed with Libby. After much deliberation and with one eye on the rumpus downstairs, I chose to hide behind the veil of cyberspace and sent a text: 'Morning, Daniel.' Inspired, actually.

It took some time for the message to go all the way back to Ireland to pick up my network and come back again, but there was certainly a pause in there as well, on his part. He replied, 'Good to hear from you' – a little cool, certainly – and 'Are you home at last?'

'Nope.'

'Still in Vietnam?'

'Nope.'

That gave him pause, but he was warming up. 'So where's she led you now?'

'Fancy a coffee?'

It took him so long to reply that I sent another one: 'Or shall I come knocking on your door à la Daniel?'

It was painful to imagine him staring at his phone, wishing he had never befriended me, slept with me and, above all, given me his number. The holiday fling had caught up with him on his own turf.

Finally, 'Where the hell are you?'

'Sydney.'

Oh dear, the silence. Another *Christ-what-have-I-done?* silence. But then he asked, 'How'd you get here? Did you swim?'

We agreed to meet an hour later in the Victoria Centre,

which was apparently near my hotel. Downstairs, a manager had joined in the fray: he sided with his receptionist and sent the guests packing. The anarchist in me, who had so often wanted to do the same to difficult clients, rejoiced.

A walk down to the quays drew me up short. Summer it may have been, but it was breezy, and positively cold compared to Vietnam. The skies were high and bright, the financial district of Sydney businesslike, the waters choppy. I wandered past waterside cafés, busy with people having coffee with friends, and wished I was not so very far from my own friends. I stopped by a railing to look over at the deep blue Pacific. Another sea, another ocean.

Meeting Daniel was unnerving. Determined not to compromise his situation with Libby, I planned to keep it short. But my belly did a back-flip when I arrived at the Victoria Centre and saw him waiting at the entrance. He nodded at me. Definitely chilly.

'This gets more ridiculous,' he said simply, leading me inside, where once again the jolly Yuletide atmosphere threw me. A girls' choir was singing carols beneath the staircase in white gowns. It made me shiver. I could cope with just about everything, but this proximity to Christmas – only ten days away – was one test too many.

We took seats at a café on the busy concourse. People pressed past us with parcels, tourists gazed into windows at didgeridoos and boomerangs.

Daniel plopped two cappuccinos on to the table.

'I'm sorry for springing up like this,' I said quickly. 'You must think I'm a piece of gum, stuck to your shoe, but after my behaviour in Saigon –'

'That isn't why you came over, is it?' he asked, alarmed.

'No. No, I'm still trying to catch up with Steph. She's staying with a friend of hers further south.'

'She came to Australia?' He stirred the frothy coffee. 'Why doesn't that surprise me?'

'Daniel, I'm so sorry,' I blurted. 'I was foul. Filthy to you.'

He looked up without moving his head, the green eyes sharp.

'My behaviour was appalling. I don't understand what came over me, but I'm sorry you were on the receiving end. That's all I want to say. I'm leaving Sydney tomorrow, but I had to apologize first.'

Still nothing. What did he want? More grovelling? All right. 'It's just . . . it had been a hard night. That's no excuse, I know. There *is* no excuse. I was rude, unfriendly . . .' still nothing '. . . unappreciative –'

'You were cruel is what you were.'

Nowhere to look.

'No one's ever done that to me before,' he said. 'Used my attraction to her as a weapon.' He was angrier now than he had been at the time, in that far-off room in Saigon. It had been preying on him. 'Stripping off and cursing me at the same time . . . I mean, stuffing it in my face like that, that was . . .'

'Cruel, yes. But like you said, it was as if I was drunk. That's what it felt like. I didn't mean any of it.'

'Yeah, but you *enjoyed* it.'

And I could still feel it too, the sense of power in lying naked in front of him, knowing it was tempting and tormenting him, yet getting some kind of nasty kick out of it. 'Why would I get any pleasure out of that?'

He looked at the feet of Christmas shoppers hurrying past. 'To spread the pain, I suppose,' he said, relenting.

'Please don't remember me that way.'

He raised one eyebrow. 'Aw, I dunno. You looked pretty good.'

I smiled. 'Thanks. That's very big of you.'

We sat for a while, the sound of happy consumerism buzzing around us.

'How the hell did Steph end up in Australia?'

'She got tired waiting for me and went elsewhere for comfort.'

'Where is she?'

'A place called Moruya – is that how it's pronounced? Have you any idea where it is?'

'South of Bateman's Bay, I think, but how do you know she's still there?'

'I don't.'

'Does she know you're coming?'

I raised my eyebrows. 'You don't think I'd give her another chance to abscond, do you? I plan to turn up unannounced.'

'What about the funeral?'

'It's under way, thank God, but it's taking a few days to organize, and they're still hoping that in this tiny window of time, I'll help Steph change her mind so that we can make a final dash for the line.'

'You people don't take a hint, do you?'

I ate foam off the teaspoon, shaking my head. 'I'm not the advance party any more. I've given up on that. But she thinks I've been shagging you in Singapore instead of going to her when she needed me, when the truth is that I got the mother-and-father of a migraine after you left. I let her down, sure, but not quite as mindlessly as she believes, and I have to set her straight on that.'

One side of his mouth smiled. 'And that's it?'

'Oh, all right, so maybe I *would* like to get her home in time. I can't help it. There's this picture in my mind of the two of us standing in the front pew and Steph saying to me, "I'm glad I'm here," or "Thank you." Something, you know?'

'That's –'

'Wishful, I know, but going through a death without a

funeral is like being stuck in the middle of a sentence, and I'm afraid of leaving her there, stranded, wishing she'd done things differently. It's going to be hard enough as it is. I've seen it – in Milenko's family, how they tiptoe round his brother's death, pretending they're fine, while in fact, every day is less beautiful, less fulfilled, less worthwhile than it would have been. It's one of the things I most admire about Milenko – the way he bridges the gap between his life with Dario and his life without him. He manages to continue, and helps his parents continue, without letting go, but without giving up, and it's like they're stuck on a traffic island. Steph has it all before her, and I don't want it made any worse by regrets.'

'But how much longer are you going to go on?'

'I'll be home for Christmas. That's it. If Steph doesn't come, so be it.'

'Great, but flights are hard to get this time of year.'

A cold sweat broke out. Flights! Christmas! The travel agent's nightmare – those two words in the same sentence. 'But I can't get stranded here!'

Daniel shrugged.

'Oh, God, sometimes it seems like I'll never get home. That I went away for a weekend and couldn't get back.'

'You will.'

'When, though? *When?*'

'In a couple of weeks this'll all seem like a very strange dream.'

'I hope so.' He shifted uneasily. 'What about you? Are you going to Auckland for Christmas?'

He licked white foam from his lip. 'I should but . . . gotta better offer.'

A better offer from Libby, I surmised. I didn't particularly wish to acknowledge her existence. The conversation hit a dead end. A glass rooftop allowed the summer light to filter in on the deep red decorations and dark wood panelling of the

Victoria Centre. I was becoming accustomed to the incongruity of Christmas inside and summer out.

'Still seem odd to you?' Daniel asked, following my gaze.

'Yes, but I welcome the contrast, seeing as I was due to have a Yuletide wedding.'

'When exactly was it to be?'

'A few days away now.'

'All cancelled?'

'As far as I know.'

'This is weird,' said Daniel, fiddling. 'I feel like there must be some train or plane that needs catching or a hotel room to book into.'

'There is! I *do* have to check in.'

'Ah, that's better. Let's go.'

My room was like a small apartment – the sleeping area had a gigantic double bed and was separated from the bright sitting room by a glass partition. There was a kitchenette and the large bathroom offered the source of all happiness: a washing-machine.

'You could live in this place,' Daniel said.

While I was loading the machine, he boiled the kettle, then we sat at either end of the grey couch, dunking teabags.

'Would you have preferred if I hadn't got in touch?'

He jiggled his teabag over the cup. 'I'd have killed you.'

'Not if you didn't know I was here.'

He threw his head sideways.

'How are things?'

'Good, yeah.'

'How's Libby? Did absence make the heart et cetera?'

'We're fine,' he said, nodding. 'You could meet her, if you like.'

I almost spat out my tea. 'You're joking? Does she know about me?'

'Yeah.'

'Everything?'

He looked at me sideways: not bloody likely.

'Maybe you *should* have told her about me and then she'd realize what an idiot she is.'

This new Daniel, the one I didn't know so well, retorted, 'Libby may be a bit confused about stuff right now, but she's no idiot.'

'Sorry. I didn't mean . . . It's just . . . you seem a bit low.'

He tucked his foot under his thigh, the tanned knee inviting me to place my hand on it. 'Ah, you know. Back to a job I don't much like. No holiday is ever long enough. Except for you. You're in such a hurry to get home.'

'I'm not on holiday.'

He put his cup on the table. 'I'm with Steph on this. Why is everyone so intent on getting her home, when it'll be such a horrible place for her?'

'Because the longer she leaves it, the harder it will be. Or maybe you know better? Has your trip resolved things for you?'

He pressed two index fingers into his brow. 'It gave Lib what she needed – space. It put a heck of a lot of space between us, more than she bargained for but, no, I can't say it fixed things. Not in my head anyway.'

'Maybe time together over Christmas will help?'

'I'm heading to Queensland for Christmas. To see some mates.'

'But what about Libby?'

'She's spending it with her folks.'

'You're not invited?'

'Yeah, but . . . I want to see the guys.'

I felt for him. The relationship was as kaput as mine, but neither of them seemed able to face it. ' "What are you meant to do," ' I quoted, ' "with all the love that lingers, After things go wrong?" '

314

'Black Daffodil?'

'Rollo King. Very well interpreted by the Daffs.'

'He has a point,' said the unfamiliar downcast Daniel. 'It's stopping the love bit that's hard. How do you do that?'

'You're asking me?'

He stood up. 'I've got to go check on the boat. You should get some rest, but don't –'

'I know, I know. No more than two hours. I'm an old hand now.'

'I'll pick you up at three and show you around.'

'Won't Libby mind?'

'Why would she?'

That put me in my place good and proper.

Through four or five cities now, Daniel had tried, but failed, to make of me a Lonely Planeteer and he wasn't giving up. I *did* want to see the opera house (and find out if it was smaller than I expected, like everyone said), but first he drove me to Bondi and on to a couple of pretty coves south of it. There seemed to be a city beach round every bend. My eyes were always drawn to the surfers, huddles on the glittering horizons, being lifted over the swell of the waves they had rejected, twisting round to watch the sea behind them, until the one wave deemed fit to tackle was spotted, far out, and they lay down and, at the given moment, paddled like crazy. It was mesmerizing.

We'd become adept at seeing the world's great cities in a matter of hours. The opera house (not smaller than expected) was easily done, later that evening. We took all the relevant photos of me, and him, and us, with the great shells rising behind us, the dark window panels like the teeth of a grinning whale.

'That's where you'll get the best view of Sydney,' he said, gesturing behind me. 'Up there. See the people climbing?'

There were tiny figures in groups on the arc of the bridge.

'It's the new must-do experience – climbing the Sydney Harbour Bridge. We could do it if you had more time.'

'Thank God I don't.'

Daniel had arranged to meet Libby. I couldn't escape it without appearing to have placed more importance on our fling than he did, so I had to play eager. She joined us when we were having a drink at a bar on a terrace beside the opera house. When I saw her (lovelier than expected) striding towards us in a sleeveless white T-shirt, a tan skirt to match her skin and sunglasses nestling in her short blonde hair, I understood Daniel's predicament. She was trim, sporty; radiant, in fact. She greeted me with a dazzling smile and gave Daniel a warm smooch. He sat between us – his passionate, single-minded girlfriend and the basket case he'd picked up on holidays – without a trace of awkwardness. Ho Chi Minh City in reverse. But introducing his long-standing partner to his lover of one week earlier (for whom he had flown to Vietnam, no less) was a cinch for him, I realized, because he was very secure in our friendship. It made me warm to him even more, and it made me protective, because he was not a happy person in Sydney. He and Libby needed to restore whatever it was that had been so good or, failing that, get out of it.

We had dinner under the bridge, in a courtyard behind an Italian restaurant. Libby was keen to impart the history of this, the Rocks area of Sydney. She was proud of Australia and kept telling me that I must do this, and this. I kept repeating that I had no time. When her enthusiasm bubbled over, I was inclined to say, 'My friend is in a zinc-lined coffin in the hold of an aeroplane and my wedding cake is being eaten by toothless residents of an old people's home. I couldn't give a fig for convict history.'

They drove me back to the hotel. They seemed easy

together, and she was positively glowing. I wondered who it was she had slept with while Daniel was away.

The next morning he led me out to the highway. On the pavement outside the hotel he said, 'Give me a call when you come back. I really have to meet the elusive Steph. If she doesn't want to make the funeral, maybe you could allow a couple of days here?'

'I'm pretty keen to get home.'

'I know, but it's a long way and you'll never come back, not with your record.'

'When are you heading north?'

'About three days before Christmas, so you'd better get back before then.'

'If I had my way I'd have a quick cup of tea while Steph packed her bags and be back by this evening for the next plane out.' I shook my head. 'What are the chances?'

He smiled, but I couldn't see his eyes through his dark glasses. 'Right,' he said, 'so keep on my tail – it'll be for a while, and when I turn off to the left, off the highway, you carry on and it should take three to four hours to get there. Stop for a break in a place called Berry.' He jumped into his car.

I leant over his open door. 'It's possible I won't see you again.'

'I'm trying,' he said, grinning, 'I'm really trying, but somehow it just doesn't seem likely. You know what a bugger it is to get gum off your shoe.'

'Sod off!'

I would never have found my way without him. I followed the bumper of his car for an hour until he waved and veered off. I continued alone, gripping the steering-wheel as if I'd take off if I let go. The highway was busy: lorries as big as villages shook me as they overtook, leaving me too nervous to do more than throw a glimpse at the scenery. I thought I sighted a white pagoda rising out of some trees at one point, but maybe I had blinked with my South East Asian eyes. My brain had perhaps not yet caught up with me and was all confusion in this Antipodean landscape.

Berry was quaint – old buildings with overhanging roofs shading the sidewalks – but it enjoyed none of Sydney's refreshing breeze, so my introduction to the real heat of the Australian summer was sudden. It was dry; still; suffocating. I stepped into an art gallery to cool down and found myself among moody paintings of the bush, of oceans and gum trees, and one of an open road slicing through red earth, which I bought and had shipped to Dad. In a café, I had French toast and tea, but was too jittery to eat much. This was truly the last leg. Steph was within my grasp. All I had to do was get there.

I hit the road again, passing a hitchhiker who looked like Killian. Was Killian, in fact.

The highway narrowed and emptied, allowing me to relax enough to look around and realize that this was, truly, the bush. Gum trees, black-barked and white-barked, burnt and alive, flashed past. The earth really was red. Orange. Toasted by the sun. The blue sky, the dusty grey-green gum leaves reaching towards it, and the pencil mark of road running in a dead straight line were just like the painting I had bought. It was huge, magnificent, and it made me feel pathetic, steering my little car through this prehistoric continent as if we meant something, which we didn't. The car and I were ridiculous, a ladybird scrambling across Australia's vast hand.

The next compass point was Bateman's Bay, but it wouldn't come. The hills went up and down and I, like a surfer on a board, went up and down over them but, like the perfect wave that never came, Bateman's Bay remained beyond the brow of the next hill and then the next mountain. I had to creep down to the coast round hairpin bends, and finally reached Bateman's Bay after three. My heart was racing. Not far to Moruya. Not far to Steph. It seemed unreal. Steph was not there, Steph wasn't anywhere at all. Steph was gone, like Killian, into the ether and she'd taken their baby with them. This close to where she was meant to be, I was filled with the conviction that I would never see her again.

The road became even emptier, the warning signs for kangaroos and koalas increased, and when I finally drove into Moruya, it looked to me like the Promised Land. I had an address for Shannon, unearthed by the ever-snooping families, and went into a newsagent's to ask for directions: out to the roundabout, turn left, follow the road a long way until I came to . . . I had been too hyper to concentrate on the rest, so I reached a point when I didn't know where to go next. Summer homes peeked out from behind tall trees and shrubs. The place had the beachy, sandy feel of a seaside community. I pulled up beside two women who were walking languidly along the road, carrying cartons of milk. It was holiday time. I asked if they knew the Culazzos.

'Sure do. Everyone knows everyone round here.'

'Ah. Like Ireland, then.'

'Carry on, follow the road round the bend, and take the third left. It's the last house down the lane.'

'Thanks.' I skidded out of the sandy roadside. It was nearly four o'clock. 'Please God, Killian, *whoever* – make her be there!'

White house, on right. Had to be it. My arms and legs were shaking. Steph might have been watching from a window, might have seen this strange red car drawing up and be waiting to see who got out. I felt watched as I locked the car, thinking, *Enough, enough, enough.*

A porch ran along the side of the house. I stepped up to the front door, pulled out the screen and knocked. The door opened, but there was no one there. I glanced into a bright, open-plan living area. A little face appeared round the door. About three years old. Blonde. Curls. 'Hello. Is your mum home?'

At which point the cute pixie hollered at such decibels that I leapt back, 'MUM!'

A woman hurried out from the right and offered a tentative hello.

'Shannon?'

'Yes.'

'Hi. I'm Kadie Kingston.'

Her hand went to her open mouth. 'Kadie? As in –'

'Yes.' We took in the faces we knew from photographs. Her hair had changed colour to a deep red, and she had wide blue eyes. 'I don't believe it,' she said. 'You came all this way?'

'She is still here, isn't she?'

'Not right now, I'm afraid.'

I felt faint. 'Why not? Where's she gone?'

'Goodness me, come in, come in! She's told me all about you!'

'I can just imagine.'

'She'll be so surprised! She thinks you're –'

'What?'

'With someone in Singapore, I think she said. But you're not. You're here. It's wonderful. Let me get some tea.'

In their vast kitchen-cum-living room, everything was blue and pale yellow, and tidy. I was in a style magazine. A kitchen. A *home*.

'No, really, I –'

'A hot chocolate, then.'

'I just want to see Steph! She hasn't left, has she?'

Unfazed by my tone, Shannon picked up her smart aluminium kettle. 'She's on the beach, but she'll be back soon.'

'Which way?'

'I beg your pardon?'

'The beach – is it far?'

'Nah, it's right out there.' She led me on to the back porch. 'See that path? It'll lead you over the dunes and on to the beach.'

'Thanks. If you don't mind I'll . . .'

'Nah, off you go!'

'But if I miss her – if we don't cross paths, please, please, don't give her any hint that I'm here.'

I climbed a steep sandy hill, through twigs and bushes, and, following the path to the left, ended up in someone's backyard. I backtracked, worried that I'd get lost in the bush and die the careless tourist's death. A noise behind me made me jump, though not as efficiently as the wallaby that leapt off into the bushes. I followed another track, came into a clearing and walked down the side of the dune, then across a flat to another mound. I could hear the ocean. There was an opening in the dunes, beyond which the beach stretched in either direction, a hazy expanse of untamed wilderness.

Now what?

There were a couple of flags over to the left and people swimming near them. In the other direction, a lone surfer was sitting on his board beyond the breakers. There were a few odd blobs along the curve of beach. Walkers. Steph was probably one of them, but if I went in pursuit and she was actually down at the other end of the beach near the flags, I'd miss her, while if I perched myself right there, she would have to pass me to get to the house.

I wandered on to the beach. Green water, sharp waves, sand that sings when you walk on it. The sun was beating down, and it was windy. Dried seeds, rounded like a dandelion's but much bigger, were running down the strand and hopping, kamikaze-style, to their demise in the water, where they went soggy and limp. One or two scraped the backs of my legs as they passed.

I shaded my eyes and looked to the left, past the flags. At that end, which was much closer, there was a sizeable gathering of rocks. I looked again in the other direction – the beach tapering into infinity – and back towards the dunes. Steph was there somewhere. I could not let her slip through my fingers again. Having no idea how she would receive me, I did not want our reunion to take place in front of Shannon. There was a knot in my throat. I twisted in both directions. The wind was hot.

There was a figure on the rocks at the end of the bay. I screwed up my eyes, but it was just that: a figure sitting on top of a huge rock. I was drawn towards it, so I took off my sandals, scampered across the burning sand to the water, then headed towards the flags. More and more convinced that the figure was Steph – it would be just like her, staring out to sea for hours on end – I hurried along the water's edge, past a few children running in and out of the waves and past the muscle-bound lifesaver in his red Speedos and wraparound 'sunnies'. My feet sank deep into the sand and energetic waves rushed round my legs, trying to throw me off balance, but the closer I got, the stronger became the thumping in my chest. It was a woman . . . in a loose, floaty dress. My blood pounded. It *was* her: facing the horizon, long hair trailing out to the side. I struggled on, slow when I wanted to rush. The beach impeded me. Beyond the waterline, the sand was too hot to walk on, but in the shallows it slid away, making me overbalance in my attempt to hurry. I fell on to one knee and cursed.

'Why don't you just get in?' a voice called behind me.

The figure was clambering down the side of the rocks – had she seen me? I took another heavy step towards her.

But that was no Australian accent . . . and that question had been directed at me. I swung round.

Steph was lying in the foam of the waves, her elbows in the sand, her bump protruding. I had walked right past her.

I plonked down, into the water.

18

'You daft idiot,' she said. 'Now you're all wet.'

'You told me to get in.'

The sea gushed round my legs. It wanted me in. It kept pulling, like someone sucking out a sting, but I held firm, planting my fists in the sand. A strolling couple glanced at me. I must have looked pretty silly, sitting there in the foam in my little white skirt and yellow top. 'I couldn't take another step,' I said to their backs, as they went past. 'Not another step.'

A wave carried Steph closer to me.

I sagged into myself, leaning over my knees.

Steph pushed herself backwards until she was alongside me.

'*Christ,*' I said.

'What?'

'I need to get my legs waxed.'

She snorted, and so did I, and then we couldn't stop. The laughter kept coming, receding slightly, then bursting out again, as we sat, shaking, in the shallow surf. It was one of the most satisfying moments of my life.

When the hysteria subsided, Steph said, 'I suppose we should do all the huggy-wuggy stuff.'

But the sea was doing all the huggy-wuggy stuff for us, pushing us together in its playful waves.

'Aren't you mad?' I asked.

'Why would I be mad?'

'Well, my no-show, for a start.'

'This is hardly what I'd call a no-show. In fact,' she put her mouth against her shoulder, 'this is the nicest thing anyone has ever done for me.'

I put my hand on her ankle, an ankle very dear to me.

'But all the same,' she added, 'what in God's name are you doing here?'

'I'm not sure, now you ask.'

'Where have you come from?'

'Oh,' I said emphatically, 'from many different places!' We laughed again.

'But why? What possessed you?'

'Killian possessed me. The last time I saw him, he said, "Take care of Steph," and that's what I'm trying to do. You're not making it easy, I might add.'

Steph frowned. 'I wonder what he meant.'

'He said stuff like that all the time.'

'But just then, before he went away. Maybe he had some sort of premonition.'

'Hardly. It was a pretty obvious thing to say, with you pregnant and sick, but as it turned out, it gave me onerous responsibilities.'

'I told you to go home.'

'You also asked me to come and get you.'

She looked sheepish.

'Mixed messages, wouldn't you say?'

'A bit,' she conceded. 'Sorry.'

'I *was* on my way to Phu Quoc, Steph – literally, going to the airport – when I got this monster migraine and had to turn back. I was in Saigon when you came through.'

'You went to Vietnam?' She sat up. 'But I thought you were in Singapore! That the stud delayed you.'

'Milenko delayed me.'

She gaped. 'He was in Singapore too?'

'He was in Saigon when I arrived.'

'Jayzus.'

'Yeah.'

'*And?*'

'And nothing.'

'He went all that way and –'

'We finalized our separation.'

'Oh, Kadie! I thought it was just a blip.'

'So did everybody. Anyway, seeing him took a real whack out of me, and then I got that headache and the days dribbled away. I'm really sorry for leaving you in the lurch, but I could barely look at my phone, let alone use it.'

'I'm the one who should be apologizing.'

'Steph, what are you doing? How can you be here?'

'Because I can't bear to be at home.'

'But there are others to consider. Do you so dislike Marjorie that you can make her wait and wait to bury her son? And Deirdre was away from her children for nearly two weeks. And what about Killian? While we're sitting on a hot sunny beach, he's nowhere. In a coffin. Waiting for you.'

She looked at her feet. 'I told them to go ahead.'

'Marjorie won't allow it. She wants you to be there. She's afraid – we're all afraid – you'll regret it if you aren't.'

'So you're Marjorie's emissary, are you?'

'Don't be ridiculous. I had to see with my own eyes that you're okay, because running around the way you've been doing doesn't exactly inspire confidence.'

'I know. I'm sorry for taking off like that.'

I sighed. 'Oh, don't be. I was useless in Stockholm. A complete prat. Said all the wrong things. I didn't know what to do.'

'Me neither, but . . .' she smirked '. . . how the hell did we end up in Australia?' We dissolved into another fit of giggles, making jokes about the how and the where and the when of it all. It was so great to see her, alive and fleshy, slightly sun-tanned and freckly, no longer the wan ghost of those short Stockholm days, when she had disappeared from sight.

'I should have waited for you in Phu Quoc,' she said. 'I thought it'd be good for me there, like going home, but after a few days I got panicky. There were happy couples everywhere, honeymooners, and it didn't feel right at all, and when you didn't show, I started losing the run of myself, and Shannon was at the end of the line, saying, "Come, come, you'll be all right." I had to hang on to her voice. So calm and certain. Coming here seemed such an easy option.'

In Shannon's place, I would have done the same thing, would have wanted to nurture Steph, draw her to me. Our instincts had been the same.

'Anything was better than going back,' Steph went on. 'I mean, I've managed to antagonize everyone. Even Mum and Dad are cross. I thought you were too.'

'I've had my moments.'

'I'm glad you didn't give up.'

'Are you? I wasn't sure . . .'

'Look, I didn't mean to come this far either, you know,' she said ruefully, then took another deep breath, as if inhaling the landscape. 'But I'm so glad I did. I love it here. It's so different from home. So wild. This beach has great soul.'

'All the same, we have to go home, Steph. We can have whatever kind of service you think he'd like, but you have to go through the process or –'

'My God,' she said, 'you've come all the way from Sweden and you *still* haven't changed the record.'

'You have to grieve! Running around the world won't change that. It's something that has to be done, just like Killian has to be buried.'

'It *is* done,' she said quietly. 'I am grieving. I've done little else.'

I looked down the strand, the way I had come. A hazy

figure stood in the sea-spray, watching us. He was wearing a grey jacket. He waved. After a moment, I raised my arm and waved back. He turned then, and walked away, into the haze. My breath caught in my throat, like a sob.

'What is it?' Steph asked.

He was gone already. 'Nothing.' I moved out of the cold water.

'Who were you waving at?'

'Did I wave?'

I could hear the rattle of every railway mile, the beep of every text, the acceleration of each aircraft . . . Every single mile revisited me in a flux of tears and I looked over her shoulder to where Killian had been and knew I had seen the very last of him.

Shannon greeted us on the back porch. Two of her three daughters were jumping on the trampoline, their pigtails staying down when they went up and going up when they went down.

'You found each other.'

'Eventually,' said Steph.

'Now I really *will* make tea.'

There were freshly baked muffins and biscuits on the table. Joy of joys: comfort food. It was just what I needed to bring me back to earth. While Shannon and Steph talked about the children, I scoffed the muffins and had several cups of tea, too mystified to contribute. 'I'd better get myself into a guesthouse,' I said, when the afternoon began to fade.

'No way,' said Shannon, 'you must stay here – if you don't mind that.' She pointed towards a tent on the sandy lawn.

'That's my room,' said Steph. 'You're welcome to share it.'

'Can I handcuff myself to you?'

'Excellent,' said Shannon. 'I'll get on with dinner.'

'A nice kind of a refuge,' I said, glancing round the garden. 'And the first home I've been in in three weeks.'

'They've been so good to me. They've told me to stay as long as I like.'

'Oh? And how long would you like to stay?'

Steph picked up her mug, held it in front of her face. 'I'm not ready to go home, Kadie. You'd better get your head round that.'

I sighed. 'And when, exactly, might you be ready?'

She peeked round the mug. 'Don't know.'

'Right.' I stood up. 'That's it, then. I'll tell them to go ahead with the funeral. Marjorie can't hold out any longer. And nor can anyone else. If you insist, Killian will be buried without you, which I don't happen to think is fair.'

'It isn't a question of being fair. It's about what I'm able to do.'

'His wife should be there.'

'His wife is there.' She put her hand over her heart.

I stood with my hands on my hips. 'You're with the fairies, d'you know that?'

'And I always have been and that's why he loved me.'

'Loves you,' I said. 'Always loves you.'

She put her fingers over her lips and looked across the garden. My presence was inevitably bringing much to the surface and would continue to do so, because I would not leave off. I would not allow this peculiar location of bush and sand to throw a veil over where we really were – this unspeakable time in our lives.

I took her wrist. 'Steph, I'm going to call Dad and tell him to go ahead. Please, please, tell me you will never regret this.'

Her eyes filled. She watched the children going up and down, their pigtails going down and up.

'Because if you regret it, ever, even once, I will blame

myself for not bringing you round to the right decision in this very moment in this very place, and I wish you would spare me that.'

'Go on,' she said. 'Do it.'

Dad was tired. It was five a.m., but we talked for an hour, as I walked round, past Shannon's basil and tomato plants. Beyond her fence, a spiky thing, like a big porcupine, emerged snuffling and sneezing and poking its long snout nose into the dirt while I told Dad that I had failed. Steph would not be coming home. But he had good news: Deirdre had not failed – she had brought her brother back to the oul' sod. He was resting in the funeral parlour. Dad said he would go round to Marjorie's first thing to instigate arrangements.

'I hope it won't be the day after tomorrow,' I said.

'I'll push for tomorrow. I know you didn't want to miss it, but this is for the best.'

'Yeah . . . and all things considered, it's best for Steph too. She's eating again, and there's a bit of flesh on her. If I dragged her away, she might get back into that state again.'

'That will make sense to them.'

'How are you, Dad?' I hadn't asked in quite some time.

'I'm fine. Just not getting much sleep. There was commotion about an hour ago and when I went down the little one had helped herself to a box of Swiss chocolates in the living room. Scoffed the lot! It's like having kids all over again.'

'What was she doing in the living room?'

'Oh, I don't know. She must have pushed the door.'

'You mean the three doors between the utility and the living room? You're going soft, I swear.'

'You'll be pleased to know,' I told Steph, 'that your beloved mutts are fine. Dad's spoiling them. He's even letting them sleep by the fire, I think.'

330

'They must be so confused,' she said. 'I'm glad he's being good to them.'

'Indulging them, more like. One of them helped herself to a large box of Swiss chocolates an hour ago. He barely even complained.'

'Sorry?'

'She upended the box and munched away.'

'But that's toxic! Chocolate is poisonous for dogs, especially good stuff. Ring him back quickly.'

'Huh?'

'Quick. Call him. She could die!'

'From chocolate?' I dialled the number. 'Don't be daft.'

'I'm serious. Too much could kill a young dog like that.'

'But she's the size of a pony . . . Dad? Wake up.'

'Humph?'

'You might have murdered the dog.'

'Tell him she has to throw up,' Steph urged. 'He has to make her vomit!'

I told him.

'Aw, what?'

'Tell him to make her drink water and Persil.'

'*Persil?*'

'Yes, he's to make her eat Persil automatic. The powder,' Steph said.

I told him.

'Would that be bio or non-bio?'

'Dad.'

'Okay,' he said. 'I'll do it. First thing in the morning.'

'I don't get the impression you have that much time,' I said. 'You have to do it now.'

We listened while he went downstairs. I was right. The dogs were clearly asleep in front of the fire, *my* fire, in *our* living room. 'Come on, sweetheart,' I heard him say, 'we have to go and get sick.'

We listened across those thousands of miles and several satellites as my father explained to the Irish wolfhound that she was a very bad dog, should not have eaten the chockies and had to have her stomach pumped. He asked us, 'So would that be Persil on the rocks or just –'

Steph took the phone to coach him through the procedure. The puppy didn't much like the frothy mix; Dad had to force it down her neck in a bottle. He wouldn't let Steph hang up until 'this wretched mutt gets sick, do you hear?'

I stood in the evening sun, watching her standing on that wooden porch, admonishing my father, and I thanked God or Killian or whoever it was who had put me right there in that place at that time. I lifted my face. And I'd even get a tan.

Shannon was baking at her expansive blue counter when I went inside. 'All sorted?' she asked. 'The funeral?'

'Yes.'

'For the best, I'm sure.'

'I hope so. I've had my fill of fraught phone calls. Now everyone can get off Steph's case and let her be.'

'When is it happening?'

'Tomorrow, probably.' I looked out to the porch. 'Is it the right thing, do you think, to let it go ahead without her?'

'I'd say so. I guess this is just her way.' She poured a buttery liquid into a tin. 'I wish I'd met Killian. He sounds lovely.'

'He was great,' I said. 'No more, no less.'

'You know, Kadie, you'd be very welcome to stay for Christmas.'

'Oh, no, we couldn't. I mean, thank you, but we have to get back.'

She looked up as she scraped the last of her mix into the tin. 'Steph has, ahm –'

'Already said she'd stay?' I asked, aghast. 'But she can't!

We can't. It's impossible. I have to get back, and she has to come with me. Otherwise she'll end up doing that journey alone – and that'd be madness, don't you think? Thirty hours' travelling, pregnant and bereaved?'

'That's why I was suggesting you should join us too.'

'I'm sorry, but I can't. Dad's been dealing with a lot, and we don't have much in the way of extended family – there's just the two of us. With everything that's happened, it would be too miserable for him if I wasn't there for Christmas.'

'Two of you? My word, I'm having fourteen people for Christmas lunch!'

Steph appeared in the doorway. 'Fancy a walk, Kadie?'

Absolutely.

We walked towards the rocks at the end of the beach.

'Shannon seems to think you're staying for Christmas.'

Steph put her nose up in the air, to breath in the sea-spray. 'I am. I couldn't face it, alone at home.'

'You wouldn't be alone. You don't even have to be in the house.'

'Of course I'll be alone.'

One of those spindly dried balls hit my ankle. 'Ow.'

'I'm going to be a single parent soon, Kadie. This is my last chance to do what I want. I'm eating better, and sleeping, and I just want to enjoy this place a bit longer.'

'But how *much* longer?'

Huge waves were hitting the rocks, spraying foam sky-high, then leaping over the incoming wave as they retreated, creating more aerial waterworks. It was spectacular.

Steph had to shout above the roar. 'I can't face the grey skies and family fuss and everyone pitying me. Can I please get past Christmas?'

I dug my fists into my pockets. Some way out, a surfer took a dramatic tumble, a wave tossing him over, like a person flicking a speck from his shoulder. 'All right. But I'm not hanging about. Can't. I've nothing left.'

'But it's such a long flight,' she said, dismayed. 'You'd have to do the whole thing alone and . . .' she patted her tummy '. . . I probably shouldn't travel alone either, in my condition.'

I eyeballed her. 'Your point?'

'I was hoping we could go together. It's not like I'd be delaying you indefinitely, because they won't let me travel beyond the thirty-fourth or thirty-fifth week, or something like that, so we'd have to go before then.'

'And when's that?'

'Around the end of January.'

'The end of January.'

'Well . . . maybe not that long.'

Suddenly that beach seemed like the loneliest place in the world. There were figures in the distance, walking, and surfers tackling big waves, but it was desolate. 'I feel so cut off, Steph. From everyone. I'm losing track of what's really going on.'

'I know.'

'But if I leave without you, what guarantee do I have that you'll follow before you're banned from flying?'

She kicked her toes into the sand. 'None. I could happily stay for ever.'

'That's blackmail.'

'So it's in your best interests to stay. If you don't, you might miss the birth of your godchild.'

'Please don't joke. I need you at home.'

'Then wait for me. A few weeks, that's all I ask.'

There was news when we returned to the house. The funeral was set for the next day. Everything was moving forward apace. Over the course of a long phone call with the Enrights, agreement was reached about readings and music. It would be a light and loose ceremony. Deirdre and her mother were exceedingly malleable: anything to get this service under way. Steph was also malleable: Killian would be buried with his father. She had no intention of ever visiting his grave.

She showed no signs of regret. If anything, she seemed relieved. It was slightly surreal. Shannon's husband, Ricardo, an engineer of Italian extraction, jollied conversation along during dinner, sparring off Steph as if they'd known one another for years. I couldn't rise to it. With the funeral fiasco coming to an end, I was done in.

Later, we lay in the tent, the ocean grumbling beyond the dunes. 'I fall asleep to it every night,' said Steph, 'and wake to it every morning. That, and the kookaburras.'

'No wonder you don't want to leave.'

'I wish *you* wouldn't. Shannon's happy for us both to stay.'

'I know, but you're like part of the family. Maybe I should push off?'

'No way. You can't be alone on what would have been your wedding day.'

'I'd like to see a bit more of Sydney.'

'Sydney or the stud?'

'Both.'

Steph sighed. 'Kadie, why – *how* – could you let yourself be with someone else so soon?'

'Easy. Missing Milenko. Missing Killian. Missing you.'

'What's his name?'

'Daniel, and he isn't a stud.'

'But where did you pick him up?'

'*He* picked *me* up, literally. Off the floor of a train when I'd collapsed from a migraine.'

'I still don't get how you could be unfaithful to Milenko.'

'Me neither. All I know is that the sex stopped me exploding like a pressure-cooker.'

'But you liked him? It wasn't just the sex?'

'Of course I liked him, and we'd already been together for

over a week – all the way back as far as Transylvania, so we were hardly strangers, which made it a bit weird in a way.'

'And now?'

'Now he's like something I borrowed, then handed back.'

'To whom?'

'He's involved with someone else.'

Gasps in the dark. 'And that didn't bother you either?'

'Not enough to stop me. They're *in extremis*.'

'They always say that.'

'I'm the one saying it, not him. He can't see he's flogging a dead duck where his relationship is concerned.'

I could feel Steph looking at me. 'Seems to me you'd be mad to see him again.'

'Trouble with that is, I already have.'

'Kadie!'

'Don't worry. It isn't about to flare up, not with his girlfriend around, and anyway, we're both embarrassed about it, especially after Vietnam.'

'What's Vietnam got to do with it?'

'Seems . . . I was unfaithful to Daniel.'

Steph sprang into a sitting position. 'You slept with Milenko?'

'You could say we consummated our break-up.'

'Bloody hell. Do I know you at all?'

'And then Daniel turned up.'

'In Saigon?'

'Yeah, in Saigon. Keep up. And, well, it was all quite jolly, really.'

She screeched, then sniggered, and we became hysterical again when I told her about Daniel's passion-killing timing and the fraught dinner that had followed. We weren't sure what all this laughing was about, after so much crying; all we knew was that it was very, very good, and it took nothing to set us off.

'Isn't it weird,' said Steph, lying back after we'd calmed down, 'the way one story bleeds into another? You left Milenko, and Killian was killed, and here we are in a tent in the backyard of someone I haven't seen for years.'

'Someone who can't stop baking.'

'I know I shouldn't ask you to stay. It isn't fair, on top of everything else.'

'No, it's fine, it's just . . . me. Unlike you, I need the comfort of the familiar right now. But I'm not sure I have it in me to go back without you.'

'Yeah – that long flight – all on your own.'

'That wasn't what I meant.'

'If you stayed, it'd keep the pressure off me. From the families, I mean.'

I sighed, defeated. 'I suppose I could do worse than experience Christmas Down Under.'

'I won't keep you long,' she said quietly. 'Promise.'

'Please don't.'

We slept. Six hours later, I woke to the sound of the kooka-burras and the ocean. The removal of Killian's casket to the church would have been taking place around then. There would be no ceremonial closing of the coffin in the funeral parlour: it had been too long for that. But his sister and mother would be standing close as it was placed in the hearse, and they, along with the gathered crowd, would walk behind it to the church, where another crowd would be waiting. This funeral had, no doubt, become notorious. Busy-minded women, who knew little of Steph, would scoff behind their prayers at the widow who did not show. Lying on my back in a stuffy tent, I could hear the shuffle of feet along the street, could feel myself a part of the slow-moving cortège. Could imagine myself in it, with them. A stab of pain: Milenko, collar up round his neck, cold and sombre beside me, suffering again his brother's loss. Dad, harrowed to find himself walking in the dark night behind the boy who had been such a presence in our family, such a pest, such an imp; Deirdre, supporting her mother for the second time in two years; and Killian, up ahead, the Pied Piper, with most of the town on his heels, on his way to a sleep-over in the church on the eve of Christmas week.

Steph slept through it. A magpie gurgled. They didn't sound like ours, these southern magpies. When Steph woke, she looked at her watch. 'He'll be there now, in the church.'

'Yeah.'

'Alone all night. God. I wish they wouldn't do it to him. Cremation must be so much easier on the soul.'

'On the soul that wants it.'

We had breakfast on the porch; I graciously but unenthusiastically accepted an invitation to spend Christmas. Christmas on the beach. Cold turkey. Yay. Dad and I had spent every Christmas together since Mum left. When I was little, Dad was in demand, invited to every imaginable gathering all over the world, but he had not once deposited me at the airport for the flight to London. Instead, we had established our own routine, a fairly traditional one of open fires and friends and mulled wine, and my marriage would have changed little, because Milenko had agreed that since we would be living in Croatia, we would spend every Christmas in Cork. Now, for the first time, the tradition would be broken.

Dad didn't mind too much. He was in bed when I phoned. It had been a trying day. The removal had gone smoothly. The church had been overflowing. 'We went to Marjorie's for drinks afterwards, but we came away early. Tomorrow's going to be a long day.'

'Tomorrow's already here,' I said.

'And I hope to get some sleep before we catch up with it,'

338

he purred down the phone, his voice low and . . . very mellow in spite of everything. Getting the funeral under way had clearly taken a load off him. 'Killian may not have been ready to die,' he said, 'but he sure as hell is ready to be buried.'

'Dad!'

'Sorry.'

'Have you been smoking dope? You sound weird.'

'It's late, sweetness. Remember, you're down there and I'm up here.'

'Up is right.'

'Well, I am a bit high, comparatively speaking.'

'Look, you won't be lonely over Christmas, will you?'

'It'll be fine. I'll miss you, of course I will, but you're the one who needs to relax, so don't be worrying about your old dad. We'll all be together soon. You and me and the dogs.'

'You're sure you don't mind?'

'Kadie, everyone's going to be so relieved when they hear you're hanging on to travel back with Steph. Her parents are thrilled you've caught up with her. You're doing the right thing, and I've had enough company recently to do me a lifetime.'

'But I ordered the biggest turkey in Christendom, because of all the people left over from the wedding. There's spiced beef and hams and . . . thousands of mince pies, all on order.'

'We'll get through it.'

'You won't! There's enough to feed legions. Cancel the orders.'

'Right, right.'

'He won't do it,' I said to Steph. 'I'll go home to find rancid meat in the fridge.'

'Poor Rollo.'

Suddenly, there was commotion all round us. We were going to the beach – a different beach. I would have liked to stay quietly at the house and have time with Steph, but she was jumping around with the kids, all excited about going surfing. She wanted to be carried in the flow of family life, where her unhappiness could be drowned out by the demands of three loud under-sevens.

It was a short drive to Shelley Beach. The three girls bounced around in the back of my car, the antithesis of my heavy mood. The dull longing to be in Ireland was aggravated by the prospect of several long weeks, maybe, before we could set off.

My phone beeped when we were spreading towels on the sand. Daniel. He made me laugh. Another wholly improper proposition: Christmas in Queensland. Steph looked at me quizzically.

'He's going up to see some mates,' I explained, 'and now that I'm staying on, he thinks I should join him.'

'Girlfriend?'

'Going to her parents.'

'Handy.'

'Hmm. I'm not sure what he's up to, but it's a non-starter, so . . .'

My shoulders were tight, burnt, from the day before, and my shins too, and the sun was nipping at those overdone bits. I watched Steph and Shannon run into the surf with the children, while I covered myself with sunscreen. This was a manageable beach, the waves tamed further out by a reef and coming to shore abashed, unlike the hyperactive sea round the outcrop to the right. A stroll to the end of it revealed another shorter curve of bay beyond. I paddled there, then watched as Steph put one of the girls on the boogie board and pushed her off into a wave. Killian was due to be buried; Steph was on holiday.

A baby, wearing a yellow bodysuit and a pink hat, was

crawling around near me, delighted by the feel of the sand. She pressed handfuls between her fingertips and chortled as it slid away. Had everything gone to plan, I would have had someone just like her before very long. Watching her gurgle, I felt trapped, locked into a childless future, from which, at that moment, I could see no escape.

Steph was trying to kneel on a surfboard, her bump making surfing something of an odd choice of acquired new skills. Sometimes she slid off the front, sometimes the back, but once or twice she actually got to her feet. Shannon and her girls applauded every effort. It was so repetitive, so all-consuming, every small gain needing encouragement, that Steph was absorbed. Though I had questioned every move she had made since Killian's death, I was acquiring a new set of eyes. Even from this distance, Steph looked lonely; a person with another person inside, both of whom were missing someone else. They were alone now, left only to each other, and for all her frolicking, I could see the nakedness, the exposure. How brave she was, to keep on her feet after the violence she had suffered. She had been assaulted, mangled. Many would say her duty and restitution lay in Ireland, that she should stand by the grave and see her love delivered into it, that she should weep and throw a rose and receive the mourners. Instead she was gambolling in surf, living and nurturing, and it comforted me that she would not be witness to those dreary funereal scenes, would not be pushed about by the grief of others. Enough that she had lost him, that her baby would never know its father. Enough.

This, I thought, is where she should be – swimming in life-enhancing waves under a hot sun. Because seawater heals. The earth heals.

Finally, Steph grabbed a towel and joined me in my stroll, through pools and foamy shallows, and we spent the day of Killian's funeral talking and basking like seals.

I kept looking around, hoping to see that figure, that shrug, but he was truly gone.

In the evening Steph grew quieter and went for a long walk. It was still early in Ireland; nothing had started yet. I also sought solitude and lay on the trampoline, staring at the fading blue of the day. Every now and then I gave a little kick, and bounced gently. Shannon could be heard yelling at her angels. It was almost dark when Steph came down the path. We had a subdued meal on the porch. Shannon and Ricardo kept the conversation bland. The children were parked in front of the television and we sat on chatting until, around nine, Steph suggested we go to the beach.

'In the dark?' I looked at Shannon.

'You'll be all right if you don't go too far,' she said. 'It's a good idea. You don't want to be here with the kids rushing around. You'll want a bit of quiet. We have torches and you should take some blankets, and a flask, if you like.'

We set off with all this – and muffins. If we were to commune with Ireland, I wasn't quite sure where the muffins would come into it. We hiked over one low dune, and then another, until we could see the white line that cut into the black night where the waves were breaking on to the shore. We sat, trying to imagine the scene at the church – the coffin by the altar, the gathered mourners who had come and gone and come back again, and I could not escape the stark image of an empty space in the front pew.

'Who do you think will carry it?' Steph asked.

'The coffin? Who would you have asked?'

'Ferdia and Paul, Bill. Dad. Your dad.'

'Dad? Really?'

'And Milenko, if he'd been there. Do you think he's there?'

'He would have been. He wanted to be. But not now.'

'Thank God we're not having any of those hymns Marjorie was planning.'

'You can thank me for that, not God. There'll be some rock and soul and good readings.'

'I wish I'd decreed that no one wear black.'

'And no black ties,' I said. 'I hate the way men always wear black ties.'

'I'd have insisted on Christmas ties, with Santa and reindeers on them.'

'And balloons outside the church.'

We giggled. 'A stripper at the do afterwards!'

Killian's funeral, as we would have had it, became more outrageous, and we were right to laugh when, far away, a sombre ceremony was taking place for a man who had rarely stopped laughing.

'What time is it beyond?'

I shone the torch on my watch. 'Half eleven. Dad'll be doing his thing around now.'

'My favourite?'

'*My* favourite. "The Ones That Got Away".'

'God, I'm glad I'm not there! That would crack me up totally.'

'I'm glad *I*'m not there. Dad'll probably blubber and make a show of himself.'

Twelve thousand miles away, those men she had mentioned, or others, would soon be carrying Killian's coffin from the church. I could not imagine it. It would be taken into the graveyard nearby, the cortège following, while we sat on a sand dune, the sky heavy with mysteries. It was a different sky, a southern sky, nothing like the one my father would see when he emerged from the church into winter light, with Killian on his shoulder.

The ocean seemed subdued, cutting into the quiet with subtlety and consideration.

Steph wept and raged. He should not have been taken. He should *not* have been taken, should not have been hurt. Where was she to go, what were they to do? Why had she married him? This was the moment I had dreaded – the point at which regret would hurtle out of nowhere like a monster and take her apart, but the sound of the surf soothed her and the rage subsided. In time, she said quietly, 'This is so much better. No crowds, no handshakes, no useless consolations. Killian isn't in Cork – he's out there, in the sky and the sea.'

'And right here.'

Like a screeching woman bursting in on her lover's tryst, my phone rang.

'Hello?'

'It's all done.' Rollo's voice was low. 'Can you hear me?'

'Yes.'

'Where are you?'

'On a beach.'

'Well, it was a lovely service. Good readings, good music. And Killian's buried now, God rest him.'

I couldn't speak. Nor could he.

'Where are you?' I asked eventually.

'Walking back from the cemetery for the after-do with your mother.'

'How are Marjorie and Deirdre?'

'Better, I think. Steph?'

'Better too.'

'We're very proud of you, Kadie.'

My throat tugged. 'Did you carry him?'

'Yes.'

'Thanks. I love you.'

'We love you too. Both of you.'

Feeling the first chill of night, we pulled the rug round our shoulders and cried. Then, dried out, we toasted Killian with warm tea and muffins.

Steph suddenly jumped to her feet. 'Jesus Christ! I hope there aren't any deadly snakes sliding around here!'

We were too wound up to sleep when we got home, so we made hot chocolate and had just parked ourselves on the porch, when Steph repeated the performance – lifting off her seat. 'Fuck, that's the biggest spider I have ever seen!'

There was a huge brute, the size of our hands, looking at us from the roof of the porch. 'Sit down,' I said. 'I'll keep my eye on him.'

She sat, eyes lifted to the roof. I sipped at my cocoa. Then Steph looked at me. 'So,' she said. 'Go on.'

'Huh?'

'You were telling me about Milenko when we were rudely interrupted by the gardaí.'

'Oh, God, haven't we had enough emotion for one night?'

'Time's up, Kadie. Spill. We don't want to talk about it on your wedding day, do we?'

'Nor should we talk about it on the day of Killian's funeral.'

'You said it was tough. Rough stuff, you said.'

I stared at the stars glimmering over the shadows of the trees beyond the garden. I longed to share it, to speak of it, and was desperate to find some comfort for my ordeal, but there was no question of dumping it on Steph. She had enough to be getting on with, and she needed to believe that whatever I had been through, I would be all right. Besides, however compassionate she felt, it would surely seem rather tame compared to her trials. She might even, with some justification, be tempted to say, 'But at least he's alive.'

I would have to find my own cure, somewhere, and soon. With every day that passed, I was more and more in need of it.

She nudged me. 'What happened, Kade?'

It was so brave of her to ask, so generous, but I said, 'Not tonight. Tonight is Killian's.'

19

In the southern hemisphere, my would-have-been wedding day dawned ten hours earlier than it should have. Neither the kookaburras nor the magpies chortling registered with me when I woke up, nor the slightly damp tent, nor the early sunshine brightening the cream canvas. An overwhelming urge to text Milenko lay on me like a board. There was only one thing I wanted to say.

Once again, I began the day by projecting myself to the other side of the globe. At that time, at home, had things gone ahead, we would all have gathered on the eve of the big day. Old friends, family, cousins. My dress would be hanging in my room at home; my half-sisters would be applying their fake tan; people would be calling in, bunking down, getting tipsy. Milenko and his slightly bewildered parents would be holed up in some nearby hotel, along with his Croatian groomsmen, suits hanging, shoes polished. Black Daffodil, all of whom had accepted the invitation, would be creating a stir in town. Photographers' fingers would be twitching.

I rolled over on the thin mattress. Steph was sound asleep. Tears fell across my nose and dropped on to the sheet. I fiddled with Steph's hair. At least I had done something right recently.

I shuffled out of the tent. Shannon was sitting on the porch, reading in her dressing-gown. 'You're up early,' she said.

'What time is it?'

'Nearly eight.'

Ten p.m. at home.

Shannon poured me tea. 'You okay? You look a bit . . .'

'Puffy, yeah. Hard night.'

She was such an embracing person: a glow came off her, a glow of friendship, and those big watery eyes always shone with amazement and delight. She reminded me of that spa in Budapest, bubbling with a warmth that spread into your bones. She'd be worth a few thousand miles of flying, I could see that.

'I broke off an engagement once,' she said. 'He was a real bastard. We have to do drastic things sometimes.'

'Milenko isn't a bastard.'

'Oh. I see.'

The morning was fresh, but it would be hot later. There was no trace of the night before. I had gone to bed in a black hole and woken up on summer holidays.

'Was it going to be a big wedding?'

'Big enough,' I said. 'But after Stockholm I would have pulled everything back. There would have been no heart for it.'

'I guess.'

'In fact, it would have been the saddest wedding I've ever been to.'

The zip in the tent went up; Steph crawled out backwards in a T-shirt. Not an exceptionally pretty sight at that early hour. I raised an eyebrow at Shannon. 'Not quite bridesmaid material.'

Steph came towards us, eyes half-closed. 'Is that a pot, I see? A cup?'

Shannon poured.

'Nectar.' Steph patted my arm. 'Well, this is the way all wedding days begin: the girls having a cup of tea and looking like shite after the night before. When are we due at the hairdresser's?'

Perfect: a friend with no sense of pathos. 'In about twelve hours. I hope Dad remembered to cancel that appointment . . .'

'Shit,' said Steph. 'How many was it for?'

'Eight women. We were taking over the place.'

'But first our plans for the day here in the southern hemi-sphere,' said Shannon.

'We have plans?'

'Absolutely. Annihilation.'

'Of what? All bastards?'

'Of all matters bridal. Ricardo'll mind the kids. We'll have breakfast in town, then I'll take you south to a very special place: Mumballa Falls in Biamanga National Park. Dinner on the way back.'

I was touched. 'Thanks,' I said. 'I hope Milenko has someone like you to help him forget.'

Two things happened before we left: Steph spoke to Killian's mother for the first time in three weeks. Her silence, her break from the world, was unravelling. Marjorie was meek, and more caring towards Steph than she had ever been, urging her not to travel until she felt up to it. Steph, in turn, was appreciative, but not apologetic.

Then, when we were packing a picnic, the house phone rang again. Shannon handed it to me. It was Daniel, and his voice swiftly and incomprehensibly reduced me to the quivering state of infatuated adolescence. 'Howzit going?'

'Okay.'

'Today's the day?'

'The day that isn't, yeah. Is that why you rang?'

'Er, mostly to find out about Queensland.'

'You were serious about that?'

'Yeah. Me and some of the guys from the *Solway* are having a bit of a get-together. You'd love it, and you'd see a bit of the country too.'

'It's sounds great, but . . .' Where were the buts? Was Libby not a major but? Clearly not. If she didn't want her seat on the bus – I did. It sounded fun, and I really wanted to see him. 'I can't leave Steph,' I said.

'That's a real shame.'

We had breakfast on the veranda of the Air Raid Tavern on Vulcan Street. It was the first chance I'd had to take in my surroundings without being in a rigid state of uncertainty. Moruya didn't stretch very far – a broad main street, cars parked on either side – and the bar-cum-café, where we had coffee and French toast, was open and bright, the antithesis of a cosy Irish pub, where my friends would have been gathered . . .

'Stay in the here and now,' said Steph. 'It's much less painful.'

She had a point. On the flip side of my own world, few comparisons could be made with Cork. In Moruya, New South Wales, on that twenty-first of December, people whom I had never seen before and would never see again were going about their business. They gave me scarcely a passing glance. I was spared from running into people who would otherwise have been at the wedding and were pretending they had forgotten all about it. I was not examining the skies and thinking, Yes, it would have been a perfect winter wedding, or even, Bollocks, we should have got married in June. I didn't have to wake in a quiet house or witness Dad failing to hide how much he was feeling my hurt; I didn't have to drive past the church and other pertinent locations, or fill my day in some strained way that would numb the senses. Australia did all that work for me. Thanks to Steph, I found myself in the unpronounceable town of Moruya, where nobody knew that I wasn't supposed to be there at all.

And yet, Australia notwithstanding, I wanted only to curl up on the ground and shut out everything around me. But Steph was making such an effort, suppressing her own despair to shield me from mine, so I smiled and gossiped and pretended they were distracting me.

We travelled south. In the back of the car, I cradled thoughts of Milenko, hoping that he would be asleep, not lying awake, and that he might even forget what day it was. But what chance of that? Unlike me, he had no escape. He was surrounded by family and friends, all of whom had probably lost money in cancelled flights, and every way he turned would be reminders of the life we'd had and the one we'd planned.

Steph and Shannon were chatting as if no years had passed. Like all good friends, they didn't need to catch up; they simply moved along. I looked at the back of their heads and thought: They'll always have this. No matter that they might not meet for another twenty years, they'll always have this special time binding them. It had been Shannon, not me, who had caught Steph when her husband died, and neither would ever forget it.

We drove through undulating pastures. The living trees standing around in huddles were spectacular enough, but it was the dead eucalypts, burnt and white-barked, that looked singularly Australian. They were like bolts of lightning staked in the ground.

Self-pity slouched over me. Killian's funeral and Steph's restitution had resolved almost everything, but peeling back those problems had re-exposed my own. I was staring once again at my original wound and wondering what to do with it. I envied Steph her Shannon and this plateau of stillness, where she could steady herself and find the means to go on, but this stasis, so recuperative to her, was like a rack to me. Flickers of fretfulness were returning to my stomach. Events in Korčula remained like slime on my mind. They had gone nowhere, had merely stood behind a screen while I travelled. I had to outpace them, outrace them. If I got moving again, surely they would eventually fall behind.

I was no longer in pursuit, perhaps, but I was still in flight.

Impulsively, I sent a text to Daniel. 'About Queensland. Can I reconsider?'

He phoned immediately. 'Please come,' he said. 'You'll need to shell out a few hundred dollars for accommodation, but that's not a problem, right?'

'Right.'

'It's a very special place we're going, and a change of scenery will make time go faster,' he went on, 'and, heck, why not go all out and tick off another destination? Like I said, a travel agent should see the world. Even an unemployed one.'

I was up for it. Anything would be better than smiling through someone else's family Christmas, with fourteen relatives and several over-excited screaming kids, and even – though it was hard to admit it – Steph's loneliness. I would be dealing with that, long-term, when we got home; Shannon could handle it in the meantime. The big family gathering filled me with dread: working our butts off to get the food ready, working our butts off to tidy up afterwards – like at weddings and funerals – and in between, a party on the scorched beach where Killian had left me.

The two heads in the front seat were gabbling on. Happy out, as we'd say in Cork – happy enough. In the tropical north, with Daniel and his mates, I, too, would be happy out, because I, too, needed a friend.

'You've gone quiet on me,' said Daniel. 'Come on, Kadie, give it a go. This is a once-in-a-lifetime opportunity. Take my word for it.'

'I'd love it, Daniel, I would.'

'But it'll be a long drive, very long, so you'd have to get back to Sydney tomorrow.'

'I'll talk to Steph. Stand by.' We hung up.

'I wasn't so far off the mark,' Steph was saying. 'Killian was a rat when he was single, wasn't he, Kadie? Anything in a skirt.'

'Listen, lads, em . . .' I leant forward. 'How would you feel if I took a rain-check on Christmas?'

They both turned, Shannon only briefly, then glanced knowingly at each other.

'Queensland, is it?' said Shannon.

'What about the girlfriend?' Steph asked.

'Not going, like I said.'

'That's hardly the point, though, is it?' said Steph. 'I mean, it's one thing throwing yourself at a stranger, but getting embroiled in someone else's terminal relationship . . .'

'I have no intention of resuming the affair.'

'I'll bet *he* does.'

'I think you should go,' said Shannon. 'I'm all for Daniel.'

'You are?' I said.

'But you don't know Milenko,' Steph said to her. 'I feel for the guy. God knows what he's going through today, and here's Kadie – replacing him.'

'I'll never replace him. Any more than you'll replace Killian.'

'So why Daniel, or anyone, at this stage?'

'Anaesthesia,' said Shannon.

'Rebound, you mean,' said Steph.

'Rebound is good,' said Shannon.

I leant forward with my phone, showing a photo of Daniel that I'd taken in Singapore.

Shannon repeated, 'Rebound is good, especially when it's *that* hot and in no position to make demands.'

'Excuse me, but Daniel is neither Rebound nor Anaesthesia. Daniel is Friend, right? We've known each other for a few weeks, during two days of which we had a little waver towards the bedroom. He's simply offering to show me some of this amazing country. So, can I get something straight,' I said to

Steph, 'you've no objections to my going away for Christmas – you're just concerned about who I'd be going with?'

'It's messy,' said Steph. 'You might get hurt.'

'I'm so saturated with hurt, there isn't room for any more.'

'And Milenko?'

'Milenko's over. When are you going to catch up?'

A couple of hours later, we arrived in a national park and drove along dirt tracks through forbidding woodlands, dense and high and hissing with the unseen, until we came to a picnic area in the shade. We carried the *eskie* – cold box – down to the tables and were setting up the picnic when Steph's eyes widened. 'What the hell is that?'

An oversized lizard, about two metres long, was coming out of the bush.

'Oh, er, that's a goanna,' said Shannon, sitting on the table and lifting her feet. The goanna lumbered towards us. 'They're harmless, really,' she added, standing up on the table.

We jumped up beside her. 'If they're harmless,' I ventured, 'why are we standing on the table?'

'Well, if they bite – and they sometimes do – it can be nasty.'

'How nasty?'

'Ahm, the bite tends to reappear on its anniversary.'

'On the goanna's anniversary?'

'No, on the anniversary of the bite – for the rest of your life.'

'You're kidding?' said Steph.

'This country is *weird*.'

'He doesn't belong here,' said Steph.

'No, no, he does. He's native.'

'I mean he doesn't belong in this century. That thing is prehistoric. Look at the way he walks – he's obviously exhausted. He's been wandering around since the Mesozoic era and can barely put one foot in front of the other.'

'You call that a foot?' I said.

'Oh, God, here's another one.'

'Are we going to be able to eat?' I asked. 'You know, my wedding breakfast and so forth?'

'Ahm . . .' Shannon glanced at the picnic box a few metres from the table. 'Maybe not immediately.'

'So we just stand here till . . . they become extinct?' asked Steph.

'This is great.' I laughed. 'Instead of standing at the altar saying, "I do", I'm standing on a table being stalked by two prehistoric lizards whose bites never forget their anniversaries.'

'Don't make me laugh,' said Steph. 'I need to pee.'

'Not again.'

'The eco-loo's over there,' said Shannon, pointing towards a hut between the trees.

'But . . .'

'They're fine,' said Shannon. 'They can't keep up, just jump and run.'

With several hops and a few silly skips, Steph made it to the loo, leaving us creased up on the table. The goannas wandered slowly to and fro, but wouldn't decamp. When Steph came back, she grabbed the picnic box *en passant* and lifted it to the table. We ate with our legs crossed, drank white wine, waved the infuriatingly persistent flies away, and didn't notice when the goannas left.

Shannon began packing up. 'Now, let's swim.'

We followed her along a descending path to the falls. A series of pools snaked its way down the stream, in high and low steps, with one deep watering-hole near the clearing where we emerged. There was no one else there.

'It's a sacred aboriginal site,' said Shannon, 'but people have been swimming here for over a hundred years.'

We hopped across the rocks. The water slithered down crevasses and slipped over the brim of pools.

'Beautiful.'

We made ourselves comfortable on a flat rock by the largest pool. It was too glorious, too *other*, to go on thinking about The Day. All I wanted was to lie in the sun, my hand trailing in cool water and think about . . . *Daniel?*

I sat up. 'That can't be good.'

'What?' said Shannon.

'Daniel. He keeps coming into my head, which isn't right, really, not on my wedding day.'

'Better than moping.'

I looked over my shoulder. 'Do you think I'm a real slag for getting off with him?'

'Yes,' they said together.

'And then I slept with Milenko. Oh dear.'

'That was unfinished business,' said Shannon.

'No,' said Steph, 'that was love.'

'But how is it possible to like someone so much when I'm in love with someone else?'

'Chemistry,' said the women together.

'It knows no rules,' Shannon added, with a sigh. 'Thank heavens.' She clambered up the side of the mini-cliff-face to the ridge above our pool.

'You should go,' Steph said.

'Up there? No way.'

'Queensland. Just listening to Shannon makes me realize . . .'

'What?'

'Well, she's all for it, and you know what? She's right. You should go. You've earned it. Go and have a blast with the young stud. It might save your head. I shouldn't have been so stuffy about it.'

'You're concerned about Milenko. That's fair enough.'

'Yes, but if you're determined not to go back to him there's nothing anyone can do about Milenko, God love him, and

Daniel won't make a blind bit of difference to what he has to deal with.'

'But I've come all this way to be with you, and now I'm asking to skive off.'

'You don't have to hold my hand. I asked for time, but that doesn't mean you have to watch over me. As long as we fly back together, I don't mind about Christmas.'

'Are you sure?'

'Look, it's going to be hard with or without you. Truth be told, it might be that bit easier if you aren't around to remind me of home and all that stuff we always did at Christmas.' She stretched her neck, her face lapping up the sun. 'I'm so glad we're not there. You've no idea. I'm sorry about the wedding, but this is the best day I've had since the cops came knocking. I don't feel so . . . panicked.' She shaded her eyes to look at me. 'There's just one thing, though.'

'What?'

'Don't let this Daniel character fall in love with you. That would be unfair, and careless.'

'It would also be impossible – in view of our respective situations.'

'Your respective situations make you both extremely vulnerable.'

Shannon was looking over the rim, about twenty feet above us.

'You're not going to jump?' I called.

She was, and she did, dropping into the dark pool, splashing water all over us.

'Thanks for the cold shower,' I said, when she spouted to the surface.

'How deep is that pool?' Steph asked. 'It's so black.'

'Fifteen, twenty feet. Don't know, really.' She climbed out and clambered up the ridge again. This time she hurtled down a natural slide in the rocks that twisted her sideways as it flung her into the water. She emerged again and swam over.

'You're pregnant and bereaved, so I don't expect you to join in,' she said to Steph, 'but *you*'re just depressed because you don't have a wedding to go to, so come on, Kadie, get in, or are you Irish afraid of a bit of cold water?'

'You don't know the meaning of cold water. No, it's the twenty-foot drop that bothers me.'

'Look, when you're old and grey and your eighteen grand-children gather round and ask what you did on your wedding day, are you going to say, "I lay in the sun like a great white blob," or are you going to say, "I jumped into the ancient, sacred waters of Mumballa Falls"?'

'I hope I'm going to say, "I married your grandfather"!'

She was not to be dissuaded. We climbed up the slippery ledge to the next level. Beyond the rock-face that dropped into the pool, there was a series of smaller pools, the rocks smooth and reclining, like armchairs submerged in warm water. It was quiet up there, but for the tinkle of the stream. We were in the heart of the bush. The trees crowding round the waterhole were majestic, yet hostile. Cranky flies fussed in my face. This place was certainly sacred, and haunted by its own memories, but I lay in a warm Kadie-sized pool, my head resting against the curved granite, and concentrated on the present. Shannon talked down to Steph, their chatty voices incongruous in the sizzling air.

'Time to jump,' Shannon called.

'Must I?' I got up, moved towards the edge and peered into the deep pool. 'There could be a monster down there, waiting for me in the depths.'

'Remember those grandchildren by the fire.'

I took three steps back. 'On the opposite side of my wedding day, I . . .' I ran out into air '. . . jumped into the unknown,' and dropped into the water with such a screech that the Aboriginal ancestors were surely startled.

Silence engulfed me as I went down. It was dark. Not transparent like the sea. Dark and very cold, and powerful as it sucked me in. It was the place I had wanted to be all morning – a black and silent hole, a surrender to nothingness. As my feet got colder, I feared something would grab my ankle and pull me further down, so I gave a kick, a flip of my feet, and headed up to the light.

We were well ready for tea and lemon cakes when we reached the heritage town of Tilba late that afternoon and settled on the veranda of the Tilba Teapot.

'What would you say,' Shannon asked me, 'if Milenko walked by right now?'

'I'd say, "Where's the nearest church?"'

'Ah, so I haven't succeeded.'

'Oh, you have,' I said. 'Today makes absolutely no sense at all, and I'll be for ever grateful to you for that.'

We set off again and wound our way along the Princes Highway. In a matter of hours at the salon back home, my hairdresser would be tapping her foot and wondering where on earth her bridal party had got to. New South Wales probably wouldn't occur to her.

We stopped in Narooma for dinner. Parking on a verge overlooking an inlet, Shannon said, 'Go grab a table while I order.' Nonplussed, Steph and I sat at one of the picnic tables. The sun was dipping, the gulls were scavenging, and the tide was out. Shannon came back with fish and chips.

'I thought we were going to some posh place?' Steph protested.

'Nah. Kadie wants a dinner she'll remember.'

I smiled. 'And I'll certainly remember this.'

At the next table, two couples were also eating fish and chips, while their children – two girls and two small boys – were playing with eels and blue crabs on the sand. We sat on one side of our table, watching the sun set behind trees across the sound.

Nodding towards the next table, I muttered, 'They're Irish.'

'Nah,' said Shannon. 'Aussies.'

'They're Irish, I'm telling you. You can't get away from us.'

'Aussies.'

Steph said, 'It isn't complicated, girls. One family is Australian, the other is Irish.'

Wherever they were from, I was drawn to the two women, sitting opposite each other chatting, their knees crossed under the table, their sandals drifting off their heels, and I recognized the comfort of a long-standing bond. Had things turned out differently, Steph and I could have been like them one day – Milenko and Killian discussing particular boats resting in the sand, our children playing together . . . As if reading my mind, the mothers stopped talking, entranced for a moment by the sight of their four children, some way across the strand, making their way back, all in a row, tinted pink by the light. The women smiled at one another, in that intimate way, then ate more chips.

Much later, back at South Head, I stood under the polka-dot sky. The children were asleep, Ricardo waxing his surfboard, and Shannon and Steph's voices were drifting out from the kitchen. The Australian accent, slow but higher, and the Irish, low but faster. The spider was on the roof again. It was late morning in Croatia. I punched 'I love you' into my phone and sent it.

We waited, the spider and I. I walked the length of the porch. Beyond the garden fence, marsupials were shuffling around for their nightly feeds. Minutes later, my phone beeped. With shaking fingers I opened the text and read, '*Volim te.*' I love you.

20

Another huntsman spider – Ricardo had identified them for me – was inside the canvas when I woke the next morning, spread out to its full and considerable width, just above Steph's head.

Dilemma.

The spider itself wasn't strictly the problem – they give a fair nip and I didn't relish the prospect of handling it. No, the real problem was Steph. If she woke to see him thirty centimetres from her face, she would lift off the ground, hit the canvas and the spider would drop. A terrible prospect. There would be bloodcurdling screams, limbs everywhere, trampling and rushing and not finding the exit, while the panicked spider would also be all limbs and crazed disorientation – and I'd be stuck in between.

I considered my options: there was no receptacle with which to catch it, but any such attempt would wake Steph and the same scene would unfold. She would rip the canvas with bare hands to get out. I looked up at the huntsman; it looked down on me. Ugly devil. Legs as long as my fingers. Tough call, to be born a spider. I was terrified – of what would happen if Steph woke. There was only one thing to do. Since I could not get rid of the spider, I would have to get rid of her. Pulling on my heels, I eased myself towards the opening of the tent in my sleeping-bag and slowly pulled up the zip which . . . was properly closed. How had he got in? How long had he been there? Had Steph been sleeping with him for days now?

The huntsman moved a leg – oh, Christ – but then stopped

to see what I'd do next. I put out my feet, my knees, my legs, until I was fully outside the tent. Then, kneeling back into it, I found Steph's feet in her sleeping-bag. She didn't stir. I grabbed her ankles and pulled.

They were heavy, the two of them, but I slid her out on to the lawn. She groaned. I stepped over her and pulled down the zip.

'What?' She covered her eyes. 'What the hell?'

'You'll thank me.'

'Why?'

'Monster fucking spider in –'

She levitated, all right. Lifted skywards, swung round in mid-air and landed on her knees facing the tent. 'Where is he?'

'Inside. But we're outside, as you can see. And, judging by the size of it, it was probably a she. They're always bigger, aren't they?'

'Was it near me?' she gasped.

'Look, you've got to get over this phobia or you'll pass it on to your child. It's so silly. You must learn to control it. I was in fear of my life in there.'

'I know. Some of them are deadly! You can die in minutes.'

'I wasn't afraid of being bitten, I was afraid of you!'

She looked up at a still dull sky. 'What time is it?'

'Six thirty.'

'Oh. What do we do now?'

'We could get back in and sleep more?' That didn't appeal. 'On second thoughts, I'll make tea. I need to hit the road soon anyway.'

On the porch, sitting in our sleeping-bags, Steph said, 'Will you tell me now why you called off the wedding?'

Desperate to unload, to get her take on it, I opened my mouth to begin, but a sideways glance forestalled me. Steph looked so peaceful and rested, her hand instinctively stroking her belly, that I couldn't bring myself to shatter the moment. 'Let's not,' I said.

She sat still for a moment, then said, 'Yes, let's not. I thought I wanted to know, the other night, I thought I could handle it. Now I'm not so sure. There's so much in my head, so much going on, I just don't think I'd have anything for you, whatever happened. I'd be no good to you, Kadie.'

'That's absolutely fair.'

'But you're okay? I mean, you're handling it?'

'I'm okay.'

She tried to read my face, then flicked her head to indicate she'd failed. 'Well, it's all very peculiar, is all I can say. Such a lovely man. Do you mind if I have him?'

'You could do a lot worse. Steph, are you sure you're okay about me going away?'

'Of course. I'll be fine. This place is doing me so much good I can barely quantify it.'

'I can see that, but we can't stay away much longer. You're becoming very pregnant. Let's meet in Sydney before New Year?'

'Don't press me, Kadie.'

'All right, but please don't make me wait until the end of January. I couldn't hack it. Let's go as soon as Christmas is over. Please?'

Steph shivered. 'How big, exactly, was the Mrs Spider?'

On arrival in Sydney early that afternoon, I checked into my hotel, handed the car back, and met Daniel. He looked good, but I didn't notice. Friends don't notice such things.

'You need a bit of exercise and fresh air before we hit the road tomorrow,' he said, 'and I know just the place to get it.'

Manly Beach? Bondi? He wouldn't say. We ended up in the Rocks area again. 'What's this about?'

He pointed up. The Sydney Harbour Bridge loomed over us.

'No way.'

'But I've shelled out a packet for cancellations. You can't miss it.'

'Oh, I think I can.'

'The view is spectacular.'

'Don't care. I'm not good with heights. I'm not a disaster, but I'm not good.'

'It only takes three hours.'

'*Three hours?*'

'Yeah, with the training and all.'

'Training? For what? How to fall feet first?'

He set off along the pavement. 'You want to see Sydney, don't you?'

'I *can* see it. Lovely opera house,' I said, pointing at the cream shells. 'Lovely harbour.' I looked up. 'Average bridge.'

'Think of all the things you've done in the last few weeks that you've never done before.'

'Right, and I'm thinking about the mistakes I've made too. Like *Singapore*, for instance!'

He smiled and opened the door to the building.

'I must be losing my mind.'

Daniel really did look horribly well, better than he had in wintry Bucharest or sultry Singapore. He was also more cheerful than he had been the previous week, but that was his disposition. He was predisposed to the good mood, and in spite of his troubles with Libby and boredom at work, he was affable, even endearing company. I wished I had not met Libby and had no conscience about her, but I had and I did, so I appreciated Daniel from one remove. But only one – and a very narrow one at that.

'We have to take off our clothes?' I hissed, during the

introductory talk. Not only did we have to wear cotton jumpsuits, we also had to leave behind watches, cameras, handbags and earrings. 'One of these items dropping on a car on the highway below could cause a substantial accident,' explained the facilitator. Sweat moisturized my lower back. We were breathalysed, asked to sign a form of consent and handed our deeply unflattering jumpsuits. Once dressed, we were herded past the communal bucket of sunscreen. 'This is disgusting,' I grumbled. 'I feel like a . . . a . . .'

'A what?'

'. . . a *tourist*.'

Handkerchiefs on rubber-bands, neck-bands for our sunglasses, and headphones completed our get-up. Everything was attached to us and we were attached to the bridge. 'Don't worry,' said Daniel, 'I'll be right behind you.'

'Oh, goodie. So if I fall, you'll come down right after me?'

I was placed behind the leader because I was a nervous candidate. Once clipped on to the safety line, there was no going back. I couldn't say, 'Erm . . . actually, I don't think so. I'll just pop back the way we came.' I was hooked on and would have to go all the way to the end. The only reasonable explanation for finding myself attached to a two-hour, 440-foot climb had to be that I was trying to impress Daniel, he of the gifted, climbing, outdoorsy girlfriend. In contrast to Libby, I had thus far presented as a hypertense, high-maintenance, over-emotional *piece of work*. There couldn't be much to this bridge lark.

The commentary, delivered by our guide, Jinny, began with a vivid description of how bubonic plague kills – it hit the Rocks area of Sydney in 1900 – so we stood on a mesh walkway, that shook with traffic and wind, high up in the underbelly of the bridge, and heard all about suppurating sores and madness and mucus. I thought I might actually throw up only five minutes into the climb. We then trundled along this see-through catwalk, below which we could see – oh, way too much – until Jinny announced that we had come to the hard part. We had to climb five ladders, one person at a time, and I was the first to go. It was tight, steep, and lonely. Forget vomiting – this time it occurred to me that I might actually lose the head. But there was nothing for it, as had become the pattern in the last month, but to go onwards and upwards. Oh, God, for ever upwards.

The ladders brought me up and over one of the highways. 'Wave at the cars,' Jinny had said below.

Wave? Take my hands off the handrails and wave?

'But be careful how you go about it. One climber accidentally hailed a taxi.'

A taxi . . . bliss!

There was a guy waiting at the top. 'Hi! How's your day going?' he gushed, helping me on to a platform.

'You really don't want to know.'

'Aw, are you Irish? It's snowing in Ireland.'

'Sorry?'

'Guy came past earlier. Irish guy. Said he got a text this morning saying it was snowing over there.'

I mopped my brow and wished I was home.

They would insist on telling me how high we were: the drop from there to the sea was so many hundred feet, and from the top of the arch was so many more hundreds of feet . . . But climbing the curve of the bridge was more pleasant, except for the 'light breeze'. 'We climb in winds up to a hundred kilometres per hour, but it makes it a bit hard to hear the commentary,' said Jinny. 'In fact, you can see the scratchmarks from fingernails on the iron here from those windy climbs,' she joked. She wouldn't let up about rivets – all the burning hot rivets that had to be thrown from worker to worker when the bridge was being built, with no such thing as a safety harness. Of the six million rivets in the bridge, only ten thousand were dropped. That 'dropped' word again.

The view was spectacular, no doubt. I didn't look. I wanted only to forge ahead and get off the thing, but we kept stopping. With Sydney Harbour spread out behind us, the opera house far, far, below, and the huge Australian sky not so very far overhead, Jinny had to take photos of the group, and of the groups within the group, and we also had to stand about while the group ahead of us, and all in it, had their photos taken. Progress was slow, but no one minded because it allowed ample opportunity to appreciate the view – or the drop, down, down to the highway far below, and down again to the sea below that.

At the very top, we had to cross a rickety walkway to the other side of the bridge. Halfway across, a large red light, affectionately known as Blinky Bill, straddles this mini-bridge. 'If you kiss under Blinky Bill,' Jinny explained, 'tradition has it that all your dreams will come true.'

'Stop again?' I snarled at Daniel. 'To kiss? Up here? Is she kidding?' I stepped out to follow Jinny across. It was terrifying – a mere grille like you'd put a couple of chops on separated me from oblivion. I gripped the rails, not sure where to look, and was about to hurry under Blinky Bill when Jinny called, 'Stop there!'

Move out of my way. 'I'll skip this photo, thanks.'

'I'll take you and your partner.'

'No, really. I'm not stopping and he isn't my partner.' I stepped out, but my foot never touched the grille. Instead, it whirled round. Daniel had taken my elbow and spun me round to kiss me. The group clapped.

I pulled away. 'What d'you think you're doing?'

'Making all my dreams come true,' he said.

'Well, *don't* do it again!'

But he did, and I did, hands firmly gripping the rail, and it was very, very nice.

'That'll make a good photo!' Jinny called.

Daniel grimaced. 'I hope Lib doesn't see it.'

I didn't care what Libby saw because, bliss of bliss, we were on our way down. Down, down, wonderfully down low, easy steps, along the gentle curve of the bridge, with the suburbs laid out to our right, the harbour snaking round them, and ferries tootling along right beneath us. But then we had to negotiate those ladders in reverse. Jinny said, 'Sometimes the train drivers like to tease climbers by blowing the horn, so be prepared.' Inevitably a train came along when I was half-way down. The whole structure shook, the train driver hooted, and I clung on for dear life.

'In eight years of construction, only six men died,' Jinny prattled on, 'and only one of those fell. An Irishman fell and survived. He knew he had to fall feet first, so he turned himself around and hit the water so hard that his boots were shoved right through his feet and he was torn all the way to the groin. But it was during the Depression, so he was back at work four weeks later.'

When we reached the ground, I said to Daniel, 'I want the T-shirt.'

'I'll get you the T-shirt.'

'The one with "I climbed the Sydney Harbour Bridge" on the front, "and I'm a fucking eejit" on the back?'

We went straight to my hotel, straight to my room. Daniel pressed me against the back of the door; I tried to push him off, but his mouth kept getting in the way of my protests. He reached down to my thigh, lifting my skirt. 'Stop,' I said.

'Can't.'

'But you're with someone, *remember*?'

'Not very.'

'Look, if you'd had the good sense to break it off with her, I might be persuaded, but . . .' He was persuasive. I responded, then resisted. He persisted; my lips slid down his neck and across his shoulder. We were sweaty from the climb. Restraint struggled to engage. 'This isn't Singapore,' I said, 'this is *her* town.'

'Geography doesn't come into it,' he said, his fingers probing, finding.

It was too good. I made it easier for him. Steph's words were competing with what he was doing: *careless, unfair, vulnerable*. Daniel's mouth was trying to swallow mine. Something kicked in. I manoeuvred him into the bathroom and backed him into the shower cubicle. 'Shower,' I gasped, and turned on the cold tap.

'Agh! Bugger you!'

I leant back against the tiles, panting. 'Cool us down.'

Daniel screwed up his face to let the water splash over it. 'Is this working for you?' he asked. 'Because it isn't for me.'

'It wouldn't be fair.'

'Why not? She hasn't changed the rules. We're still open.'

I stepped out, pulled off my wet skirt and took a towel, handing another to Daniel.

'I take it that's a "no"?' he said.

'You shouldn't have introduced us. I can put a face to her now, and I've seen how much you care about each other.'

'Things change. Things are changing all the time.'

'What's that supposed to mean?'

'I've had a revelation.'

'Oh?'

'Yeah.'

'And?'

'There's no such thing as a No-ties Fling.'

I squeezed my hair into the towel. 'Don't start talking like that. We're too much in love – with other people.'

'I know something else too.'

'Dazzle me.'

'The bloody cold shower didn't work, so don't stand there in a towel telling me we aren't going to do it, because we bloody are.'

Drops of water slithered down his chest, his shorts dripped on to the floor. 'I like a man who's decisive,' I said. 'But not here and not now.'

He stared at me, catching his breath. 'So let's hit the road.'

We spent three days on the Pacific Highway. The drive from Sydney to Airlie Beach didn't look like much on the map, until I remembered that most of Western Europe would fit into Australia. We were driving, effectively, from southern Italy to Ireland. Daniel warned me to expect hot, sticky and very, very long stretches. I told him not to worry. His car was air-conditioned, the music was good, the scenery was likely to be quite interesting, and we were in motion again. And motion brought stillness: the fretfulness in my stomach was already receding.

As the miles disappeared under the grey bonnet, accumulated tensions dropped off me and got left somewhere on the road behind. Steph was found, Killian mourned, and my non-marriage had been consigned to history. There was nowhere else I should have been.

'Maybe this should become my gap year,' I said, 'seven years too late. Maybe I'll stay in Queensland and cut sugar cane or pick pineapples and hang out with students.'

'There'll be plenty of cane where I'm taking you.'

'Where *are* you taking me? It had better have hot running water, mosquito nets and a swimming-pool.'

'And if it doesn't?'

'God, we're not going troppo, are we?'

He shook his head ruefully. 'What *was* that Croat thinking, signing up for life?'

'Does Libby know I'm with you?'

He nodded. 'She's relieved I've got someone to share the driving.'

This pair! What were they like? 'She might not be so relieved if she knew about Singapore.'

He made no comment.

'Remind me – why *are* you two still together?'

He glanced over, his eyes shaded by sunglasses.

'It won't be any easier just because you do it slowly,' I said. 'This way you keep stabbing at each other, trying to kill it off – a long break, infidelity, rows, reconciliations – but it isn't working. Why don't you just *do* it?'

'Because I turned everything upside-down for her. Left the *Solway*. Moved to the city. Took a job I didn't want. Went on *our* trip to Europe *alone*. Are you telling me all that was for nothing?'

'Not for nothing. For the good times. But good times end.'

The journey was long, sometimes dull, and it left a trail of impressions in its wake: making sandwiches at Wallabi Point, where puffy clouds sat motionless in the sky and the ocean glowed gold; the neatly rounded hills of northern New South Wales looking slightly posh and middle-class; cooling dips on beaches that stretched into infinity and, later, the refreshing call of the Pacific extracting its price – layers of dried salt and sand scraping my skin. In one little cove, I asked Daniel about sharks and was told, 'I'll let you know if anything rubs up against me.' Neil Young, I decided, was born to be listened to on the road.

Whenever we stopped, the bush sizzled loudly like natural static, and when we picked up free wake-up coffee at a café-cum-museum full of old motorbikes, telephones and lists of the war dead, I found photocopies of a poem called 'Miss Me, but Let Me Go'.

Sometimes I slept, and woke in darkness, the white lines of

the road flashing under us in the headlights. Daniel wouldn't let me drive at night.

'Why not?'

''Roos. They're dangerous after dusk. They come out of nowhere.'

'Will we stop then, so you can rest?'

'It isn't rest that's on my mind.'

'Give over.'

We crashed out in roadside motels. When Daniel lay on his back, in the small hours of that first morning, with one arm across his chest, I was unable to resist touching his fingers. He opened his eyes, then closed them. Croatia was impossibly distant; Daniel deliciously close.

Early-morning DJs dragged us from stupor each day with traffic reports and weather forecasts, while neat postmen in orange and blue uniforms went about their rounds on motorbikes. When we ran into a ferocious storm with bloated, purple skies, the radio reported that the biggest hailstones to be seen in thirty years were smashing windscreens in Gladstone. I caught myself stashing it all away to tell Milenko when I got home. I couldn't help it. The habit of his love was engraved in my thinking. It would take more than this detour to fill in the grooves, and it was comforting to keep him near me, in heart and mind, even though I never *would* get to tell him about the burnt plains, or the blue-blooded eucalypt forests, or my first sighting of kangaroos – a clan relaxing in the gloaming, their ears twitching and claws scratching their bellies as they lay back, Nero-like, watching us watching them.

A cute little church on the brow of a hill, white with a green steeple, reminded me of Sunday mornings in the Lalić household, when Milenko took his mother to Mass while his father minded the shop. Cecilia would be ready at eight for Mass at ten. Arriving from the hotel, I would find her at the breakfast table, holding her handbag, saying we mustn't be late. Tousled and grumpy, Milenko usually appeared with ten minutes to spare, but after a shot of coffee, he would rush up to change and return all smart and shaved, only to find that Cecilia had wandered off, or changed out of her good clothes, or started making soup. We'd scurry around, trying to find her, reorganize her, get her into the car. At such times Milenko was at his most tender, and most mischievous. He wasn't above telling bare-faced lies just to get her there, and had a tendency, when exasperated, to lapse into English. 'Please, Majko, don't be a miserable old bag!'

After the service they went, every week, to the graveyard. I watched from the car, aching with love, as he shepherded his mother to Dario's grave, his tie flapping over his shoulder, and handed her fresh flowers and blessed himself to pray with her, holding in his own emotions like unruly children in a playpen. He once told me that when he missed his brother most acutely, he went to the graveyard alone at night to sit by the grave and talk to him.

I jerked awake, and was battered with disappointment to find myself on the Pacific Highway.

'You fell asleep,' said Daniel, stroking my knee.

That evening, while eating fish and chips in the car somewhere near Noosa, watching lightning flashing high over the dark sea and rain pounding the bonnet, I decided I'd had enough. But at just that moment, Daniel set aside his chips, licked his fingers, said, 'That was one sticky day. Let's have a shower,' and stepped out into the sheeting rain. Looking through the windscreen at him, I said, 'No, this time a shower won't do it,' and got out. He was standing with his arms extended, wet through, and smiling. I took the smile from him, swallowed it. He tasted of grease and salt and rain, and he groaned like a lion having a thorn pulled out of its paw. The rain splashing into our eyes, he felt for the handle, pulled open the door and shuffled me on to the back seat. Singapore, it seemed, was already too long ago.

It was good, being back with him. It was good resting my hand on his thigh while he snoozed and I drove, the following afternoon, through a landscape that scarcely altered for six hours and in which even I struggled to find points of interest.

Sometimes we stopped in petrol stations for sandwiches that looked like they'd been made in the 1960s and were shaken from the torpor of travel by cheerful demands of 'And how's *your* day been so far?'

'Welcome to Queensland,' Daniel said, the first time we heard it.

Queensland. Gin Gin Station, Raspberry Creek, Old Emu Road, Little Pig Creek, Disaster Bay, Bli Bli and Kin Kin and the Shire of Woocoo . . .

The weights that held me down were loosening their grip, certainly, but not without resistance. It was impossible not to think about what Milenko was doing while I was living easy, when I knew too well the pain he was in, the effort it must have been taking him to get through every single hour. He would have loved to be wherever I was, and where I was, on Christmas Eve, was cane country.

21

Daniel grew wistful as we neared Airlie Beach. This was his first return trip since he had left a year earlier to be with Libby.

'Aw, I love it up here. Really love it,' he said, looking across fields of green cane and billboards advertising holiday camps. We had returned to the tropics. 'They were the best two years of my life.'

He was excited about seeing the mates with whom we were to spend Christmas. Sailors all. What would I have to say to a bunch of sailors?

'Don't worry about it.' He smiled.

We had quickly become tender, affectionate. Our encounters, in motels and on dusky beaches, had become more intense, and the comfort we sought from one another was reaching deeper. It was risky, but we considered ourselves immune to serious attachment when we each had one eye on someone else. Whatever happened, I knew that I would be able to let him go. Within weeks, I would be gone from him, and I would no doubt remember him thereafter with fondness and occasional yearning, but reaching the end of this unlikely fling in unlikely places would be but a speck to the catastrophe of losing Milenko.

We drove through the outskirts of Airlie Beach in the early afternoon, past shopping malls and holiday parks. 'Phew,' said Daniel, cruising down the main street. 'Three hours to spare. I honestly didn't think we'd make it.'

'Now he tells me.'

Airlie Beach was like the capital of the gap year – youngsters everywhere and Australian accents hard to find. Daniel took me straight to the lagoon, a vast curving swimming-pool behind the shops, surrounded by palm trees and parkland. Hot and bothered, I threw myself into the water. 'Ugh, it's warm!' I slithered my limbs around Daniel and we bobbed about, unwinding. 'Is it far to this place we're staying?'

'Nah, but the guys won't be there till after four, so we have time for a bit of shopping, if you like.'

'I like.'

He encouraged me to buy lots of beach stuff – not that I needed a great deal of encouragement: bikinis, hats, sunglasses, flip-flops . . . Daniel shook his head in bewilderment. 'What it must be like to be rich.'

'We're not rich. We're very well off.'

'What it must be like to be very well off.' We went to the checkout. 'Do you think he'd like me, your old man?'

'Does it matter?'

'Wouldn't mind impressing a former rock star.'

'You'd impress him.'

He fiddled with some earrings on a stand. 'Maybe I'll call by some time . . . in that life where Libby and I travel the world with our kids in the camper-van.' He looked out towards the sunny pavement.

'That'd be great.'

He turned back to me. 'It isn't going to happen.'

He was starting to let go. His travels around Europe had not done it. An affair with a stranger had not done it either, and neither had coming home to Libby, but here, back in his other life, the fog was beginning to lift. He was drifting out of Libby's reach.

He drove us out of town to a vantage-point from which we had a panoramic view of the harbour. We got out. Daniel scanned the sea, shading his eyes. It held him riveted, until he said, 'There she is.'

'Who?'

Among the catamarans and yachts sailing to and fro, a tall ship was coming towards the marina under full sail. 'Oh!'

He shook his head wistfully.

'Oh, Daniel. She's beautiful.'

'For over two years,' he said, 'that was home, for most of the time.'

Her cream sails were being taken up, one after the other. 'Ten of them,' said Daniel. I could see little figures on the cross-bars, high up the mast, pulling in the huge sails. 'Come on. We've got stuff to do.'

Near the marina, he took me into an office where he was greeted like the prodigal son by two women who hugged him and asked after Libby. He introduced me. 'A mate of mine from Ireland.'

'Oh, yes, you booked her in,' said one of them. 'Welcome to Airlie.' She considered me, head to foot. 'You'd be a medium, I reckon.' She disappeared out the back.

'A medium what?' I asked Daniel.

'For the stinger suit – wetsuit.'

'I don't need a wetsuit.'

'Yeah, you do, if you want to go in the water. There are some nasty beasties – stingers, you know, box jellies – around these parts this time of year and, believe me, you don't want to get stung.'

'No, I don't suppose I do.'

'They don't usually come down this far, but you can't risk it. Some are no bigger than your fingertip, and transparent too, so you don't see 'em coming. I knew a guy once, got stung. Said he'd rather die than go through that pain again.'

When the woman came out with my wetsuit, I grabbed it and tried it on. Horrendous. Worn by at least two hundred people before me, it sagged between the legs, and was about as flattering as a rubber Baby-gro.

'Perfect,' said Daniel.

At half six, he led me along the quays to the ship to meet his friends. He was greeted on deck by an ecstatic crew; there was much back-slapping and bawdiness before he remembered that I was still standing on the pontoon. He helped me aboard. It was getting dark. The boat was smaller than its majestic entry to the harbour had suggested, and the four crew members who greeted us were barefoot on the timber deck and wearing black shirts with the *Solway Lass* insignia inscribed in white. They handed one to Daniel. 'Get into gear, Volley.'

There were no bags or backpacks on deck, no evidence that these men were about to go anywhere.

It was only me, of course, who was about to go somewhere.

The bo'sun, Billy, said to Daniel, 'Gotta get on, Danny. Kadie's in eleven.'

They dispersed. 'Danny' cocked his head at me. 'Welcome to the *Solway Lass*. Hot and cold running water, great food, swimming-pool, even.'

So many different words tried to form in my mouth that none succeeded. I'd been comprehensively had.

'It's a three-day cruise,' he hurried on, 'around the Whitsunday Islands. But it's a boat and you hate boats and wouldn't have come if I'd told you, so I didn't tell you.'

'You . . . What about Christmas?'

'We do Christmas real well,' he said, looking up.

I followed his eyes to the rigging, to the ropes and sails rucked up like curtains, and saw a Christmas tree perched at the top of the mainmast. 'I thought we were going to relax by the beach?'

'Oh, you *will* relax. And there will be a beach.'

The boat creaked. 'How old is this thing?'

'She's over a hundred years old,' he said proudly.

'Oh, God. We'll sink.'

'Nope.'

'I'll get seasick.'

'I doubt it.'

'I'm not a group person, Daniel.'

'You don't have to be.' He took my hands. 'You don't have to be anything. Or do anything, for anyone. Not even me. See, I've signed up as a volley. We always have a volunteer, someone who's prepared to muck in, do the washing-up and stuff for the privilege of a trip, so I'll be on duty and out of your hair. The time is *yours*.'

'Are you telling me I sat in a car for three days in order to spend Christmas in a tub?'

He looked at me oddly.

'What?'

'I thought you'd throw a fit,' he said. 'Head for the nearest four-star hotel.'

I turned my head to the side, my eyes still on him. 'Whatever made you think that, Mr Blewitt?'

My cabin was cramped and dark – there was no porthole. Daniel threw my bags on to the single berth that lay over a double, saying, 'You won't be seasick. You'll be on deck most of the time.' Then he inhaled. 'Ah, the smell of the timbers.' There was commotion over our heads, voices calling out and the patter of feet on deck. 'Here come the passengers.'

He brought me back along the dark corridor and showed me the women's bathroom at the foot of the broad staircase that led up to the deckhouse. It had only two loos, which doubled as shower cubicles.

'But don't flush during the night,' Daniel explained, 'because there won't be any water.'

'I beg your pardon?'

'It'll be flushed first thing in the morning, when the generator comes back on.'

'Oh, God. And I have to shower on the loo?'

'More or less.'

'I'll never cope.'

'Yeah, you will.'

People were coming down the stairs with their luggage. Daniel went to work.

Within a very short time, we were puttering out of the harbour. The skipper, Matt, gave a welcome talk on deck to the thirty or so strangers with whom I would be spending Christmas. There were student backpackers, older couples and a family with young children. I wasn't sure how I'd cope with loos that didn't flush in the night, a bunch of strangers and no porthole in my cabin, but at least I had a decent double bed and a decent bloke to share it with. Daniel was introduced as the volunteer, and as a former crew member who had abandoned ship, he was also the lowest life-form in the food chain. Everyone laughed.

As a sailor, he was well cast. He looked the part. The black shirt and bare feet suited him. This was the piece of Daniel that had been missing: his natural habitat. He stood behind the captain, with his hands behind his back, while the cook prattled on about housekeeping. The friendly lights of Airlie Beach were drifting into the distance. Other lights could be seen far off, on the edge of islands, but after Airlie Beach disappeared behind a headland, it was very dark indeed. This was going to be one strange Christmas . . . I would remain for ever grateful to Daniel for that.

After sending a general text to everyone who had contacted me on Deirdre's phone, wishing them Happy Christmas and telling them I was running away with pirates, I buried my phone in my bag. Daniel had warned that if he saw me using it even once, he'd throw it overboard, so I metaphorically threw it overboard myself.

He was serving hot sausage rolls and pies on the maindeck. When he came to me with the tray, I swiped as many as I could, because there would be no more food before breakfast, and ate them sitting on the bench that ran along the rim of the boat, enjoying the soft night breeze and listening to the water lap round the hull. This, surely, would stop me thinking about Korčula.

When I went down to have a shower, a forlorn-looking Dutch girl was coming out of the bathroom, her pyjamas soaked. 'I knocked the shower handle when I was on the toilet,' she said.

In contrast, I had the best shower I'd had in days, then went to my cabin to dress for a nice Christmas Eve drink with my volley. The next thing I knew, I was stretched diagonally across the bunk and Daniel was shoving me aside. 'Happy Christmas,' he whispered, lying down.

'What time is it?'

'One.' He ran his lips along my arm. Delicious. Such gentle wakening. Sleepy and friendly, I cuddled up to him.

'Listen,' he whispered, 'I have to bunk in the crew's quarters.'

'What?'

'Shush!'

'You mean I have to sleep down here alone?'

''Fraid so.'

'But we're supposed to be spending Christmas together!'

'We are together.'

'And I've paid for a double berth!'

'So you'll have loads of space to yourself.' He kissed me.

I held my arms tight round his neck. 'What if I won't let you go?'

'Oh, and there's one other thing.'

'What's that?' I purred, grinding my hips against him.

'Shagging passengers is against the rules.'

'*Excuse me?*'

'Shush up, will you? You'll get me thrown off.'

'Are you *serious?*' I hissed. 'Are you telling me you've brought me out here for three days' *celibacy?*'

'You're not going to make this difficult, are you?' he asked, breathing very heavily for someone who was on the point of not having sex.

'I never make anything difficult,' I said, running my hand down that lovely firm stomach. He grabbed my wrist and held it away. 'For God's sake,' I grumbled, 'you're not even a proper crew member.'

'Yes, I am. Sort of.'

The man in the next cabin, just behind the partition, was snoring. He was so close, he might have been in bed with us.

'But who's going to find out if we bend the rules a little?'

Releasing his grip on my wrist, Daniel kissed me and did a bit of hip-grinding of his own. We were in business. Again, I reached down to touch him. Again, he took my wrist, saying into my neck, 'So I'm going to go off to my bunk now and you're going to go to sleep. We've got a long day tomorrow.' He got up.

'You rotten tease!'

'Now you know how I felt in Sydney.'

'Bastard.'

'Happy Christmas,' he whispered, letting himself quietly out of the cabin.

'Bastard.'

I woke, not to the sound of kookaburras and cicadas but to the lap of waves against the hull right behind my head. I was lying close to water level with the Coral Sea just behind me, and it was Christmas Day. I thought about home and then thought, No, sod it. Not another day lived on Irish time. I'd be there soon enough. I would never be here again. This Christmas Day would be lived for itself. And for *myself*, as Daniel had said.

Apart from the sound of children in the distance, the ship was quiet. It was seven thirty. I pulled on shorts and a bikini top, and almost tripped over a parcel when I stepped out of the cabin. Santa had come. There was a present outside every closed door. I opened my gift like a child – a box of chocolates. As the only present I would get, it gave me inordinate pleasure, and made me think of hot-air balloons. Specifically, of the hot-air-balloon trip over Mauritius that was to have been my Christmas present to my husband.

We had moored in the lee of an island, wild and wooded. The sea was a strange light green. No, blue. No, turquoise. All of the above. It was already hot. But this 360° vista of natural beauty had competition: breakfast laid out on a table by the galley – bread for toasting, jam, Vegemite, cereals, fruit, tea, coffee. I helped myself and sat on the timber bench, balancing a plate on my lap and wondering how we'd manage Christmas dinner without tables.

Billy was helping one of the kids feed bread to a school of flat grey fish.

'Are they edible?' the boy asked.

'Fusiliers, yeah, you can eat them.'

'What do they taste like?'

Billy looked down at the nibbling fish. 'Soggy bread.'

Suddenly Daniel appeared, hanging off a rope above me, with a piece of toast in his other hand. 'Happy Christmas.'

It sounded absurd. 'Same to you.'

'Sorry I don't have a present.' He glanced at the island. 'Not one you can unwrap anyway.'

'I don't have anything for you either.'

'You're here.'

I squinted up at him. 'We'd want to be careful, Daniel Blewitt.'

'Why's that?'

'This could be going somewhere it was never meant to go. And I don't mean geographically.'

He bit into his toast. 'That's what I was thinking. And the geography of it isn't so great either.'

'Maybe you should drop me ashore before it gets complicated?'

'You'd be dead in a day.' He jumped down. 'Eat up. You're going bush-walking later.'

Bush-walking? On the Coral Sea?

A huddle gathered round an excited young couple, who had become engaged the night before in their cabin. Everyone fussed around, congratulating them. I looked out at the island, sickened.

Dad had been the first to know when we had come back that day, smug and silly, from Kilcrohane, with the blessing of the cormorants. He'd opened a bottle of Krug and we'd called Milenko's parents. Then we blew the news wide open and everyone rolled round for an impromptu party. No one was as surprised as me, except Milenko, perhaps, who could not believe I had accepted him.

I turned back to the couple. What timing. What a location. What a memory to pack away, already, in their marriage box, along with the fortuitous bottle of Champagne that had, by pure fluke, been put outside *their* door, because Santa had run out of presents.

'It's the kind of thing that happens on the *Solway*,' said Billy.

After breakfast, we motored over to see one of the Whitsunday Islands' most spectacular views. I knew about Whitehaven Bay. I had seen it in brochures and travel magazines, but had never expected to get there. We were ferried over to Tongue

Point and dropped on a beach, then Billy led us up a steep track to the top of the hill. The students, recovering from their hangovers, groaned about the sticky heat, others gasped with effort, and someone up ahead was talking about Yasser Arafat, but when we reached the top of the promontory and found ourselves perched over paradise, we were silenced.

There was a cove to our right and a shallow river, more sand than water, snaking its way out of the hilly island. Crescent-shaped sandbanks altered the hue of the multi-shaded channels, creating boomerangs of colour, and across the inlet, beyond a hook of rainforest, Whitehaven Beach was an incandescent white line, a perfect curve, separating the light green sea from the wooded shore. Below us the water was crystal clear, further out transparent green, azure over there . . . Swathes and arcs of cream and blue stretched to the horizon, which was potted with islands. Sacred, it was. Divine.

A hot wind scorched our overheated bodies. Cameras began clicking and whirring. People found their voices, caught their breath.

'There's a stingray, Dad!'

At the foot of the hill, dead wood, like well-placed sculptures, had been pushed on to a tiny beach, and a stingray wafted in the shallows.

Daniel appeared, stepping on to the platform. I smiled over my shoulder. 'And I didn't even have to unwrap it, just like you said.'

'We're going over there next. We'll stop by the beach for lunch.'

We had to be dragged away, but there was compensation on the *Solway*: hot mince pies and morning tea. We sat on the benches munching and chatting, as we motored round to Whitehaven Bay, where the anchor chain rattled. Guests began to struggle into their wetsuits and the great brass bell rang out.

'What's happening?'

'Pool's open,' said Daniel, as people started jumping overboard. 'Told you there'd be a pool.'

I squelched into my suit, clambered down the ladder and settled waist-high into the deep water, where I bobbed about like a buoy. Some of the guests were swinging off the Tarzan rope and plopping into the thick soupy sea near me. 'It's the second saltiest sea in the world,' Daniel called down to me, leaning on the wooden rail.

'Aren't you impressed with me?' I called back. 'Floating around with my hands and feet exposed to translucent jellies the size of a fingernail with a sting so painful even morphine won't touch it? I wouldn't have done this a month ago, you know.'

'Glad to see I'm finally having some effect.'

'It has nothing to do with you, silly.'

'I know,' he said, half smiling. 'I know.'

A look passed between us, intimate and slightly startling, as we shared a thought for Killian, who never got to swim in the Coral Sea or take his chances with the jellies.

After lunch, Billy ferried us over to the beach, where we stepped barefoot on to the finest silica sand in the world. No shoes allowed on Whitehaven Beach. The heat was overpowering. I sat in a long cotton dress, sheltering under my broad-brimmed hat, and watched the captain play ball in the surf with the children. Straight ahead, our schooner was lined up against the horizon, as if carefully poised for a portrait, all ropes and rig and masts, her green hull low in the water. Daniel had stayed on board doing chores. I sought him out, trying to work out which of the figures on deck might be him. He had become compelling. My eyes were always looking for him; at every given minute, I wanted to know where he was and what he was doing, and that was good for neither of us.

But I had found my cure. The *Solway Lass* was healing me. I felt rested, still. Already I could think about Milenko without the walls of my gut folding over. I should have been married by then, but on a ship made to ply the seas of heaven, the Korčula option had lost some of its glow. This pristine, protected beach, with its scrunchy white sand, didn't seem, at that moment, so bad a trade-off.

The sails were hoisted that afternoon. Daniel sailed. As a former crew member, he could enjoy the real tasks as well as polishing the brass. He climbed the rigging with one of the others, his nimble form scurrying up the mast and out across ropes that he held between his toes. Concern that he might fall was mitigated by the fact that he would fall into the water, so with sheer delight I watched the great canvas sails drop at his bidding. The wind curled into them. He was a natural: the sun-bleached hair, the firm build, even the tattoos had come into their own. This is where he should be, I thought, not working on a rich woman's gin palace in Sydney Harbour.

There was more motion under sail, so I sat in the narrow passageway outside the deckhouse, looking at the horizon as prescribed, and having tea and biscuits with a soft-spoken Scottish woman called Jill, who was queasy.

'We got married a year ago,' she said, 'but put off the honeymoon until now.'

'Lovely.'

She followed my gaze as Daniel helped Billy secure ropes. 'How about you?'

'I *should* be on my honeymoon. In fact, I hope my ex remembered to cancel.'

'Oh, I'm so sorry.'

On cue, Daniel stepped over our knees, saying to me, 'Mind if I use your cabin for a bit of a kip?'

'Is that allowed?'

He looked up at the sails, said, 'Yeah, I'm only the volley,' and flicked his head towards the deckhouse.

'Feeling better?' I asked Jill.

'Yes, thanks, the biscuits helped.'

'Okay, well . . . I might just . . .'

'Go for a bit of a kip?' she asked.

Daniel was stretched out on his belly on my berth. 'Off duty?' I asked, lying down.

'Yeah, knock-off time. I'm buggered.'

'So what exactly are the penalties for sleeping with a guest?'

'Disembowelled and tossed into the sea.'

'It must happen a lot. Billy is seriously dishy. I wouldn't mind a slice.'

'And the guests who do it are pelted with rotten eggs.'

I ran my hand along his sweaty back. 'Did you ever succumb to the charms of a pretty guest?'

'Libby.'

'Before Libby.'

'I thought about it once or twice. Or maybe three times. But it wasn't worth losing the job.' He glanced over his shoulder. 'Have you any idea how seriously amazing you look from fifty feet up?'

'If that's a line, you'd better follow up on it or get out of here right now.'

He chortled, put his head down again and didn't shift. Good. Pelted eggs would be worth it. He was hot from the sun and he smelt of the sea. I straddled him (with difficulty, in view of the upper berth) and pressed the heels of my hands into the small of his back. He groaned in appreciation, so I worked his shoulders, his back, then turned round and massaged his thighs and calves, confident that it was having the desired effect. With cramping hands and a crick in my neck, I lay down. Daniel sighed deeply. It had worked, all right. He was asleep.

★

On deck, hearing the skipper call, 'Strike sail,' I slipped down to the cabin to wake Daniel. 'Does that mean something you need to know?'

'Yeah, we're bringing in the sails,' he said, scurrying to the task.

When the job was done, he took the wheel, and I took a gin and tonic on to the roof of the wheelhouse. Green islands wandered by.

'I keep imagining myself stranded on one of them,' I said to Daniel. 'How long would I survive, do you think?'

'Not long.'

'The sea looks like someone's put food colouring into it. And it's all gloopy.'

'Gloopy?'

'It moves differently – slowly. Is that the high salt content?'

'Reckon so.'

I lay back, listening to the rhythmic clunk of the wheel and the voices on the radio inside the wheelhouse. When Billy joined Daniel, I eavesdropped while they caught up on news – the trip round Europe, the gossip from Airlie.

Then Billy dropped his voice. 'So what's the deal here? What about Libby?'

Behind my sunglasses, I opened my eyes. The wheel spun gently between Daniel's fingers as he glanced in my direction. 'It's complicated.'

'I figured as much,' said Billy, 'being Einstein and all.'

The Christmas lights came on at dusk. The crew donned their loudest Hawaiian shirts and the guests were asked to dress in our Sunday best. The only vaguely dressy piece I had was a cream silk dress with a low back and slits up the side. Two long timber tables were put in place on the maindeck. Drinks flowed; conversation and laughter too. On the sultry Coral Sea, the Christmas atmosphere was every bit as potent as by my fire at home, especially over a dinner of roasties, turkey, veg and booze. Some of the students who had seemed home-sick that morning had forgotten about their families. We were no longer strangers; not after having been to heaven together.

Feeling slightly contrite, I retrieved my phone and gave Dad a call from the bow, the only place with a signal. He sounded lonely. He would have lots of company later on: the food I had ordered in for those left over from the wedding would now be enjoyed by people left over from the funeral – Killian's extended family were joining him for dinner. None-theless, Dad was having breakfast alone in the kitchen and we had never before been apart on Christmas morning. I felt the gulf. He pretended not to.

'How can I be lonely with four hounds tripping me up at every step?' he said. 'Gerroff! That's my brekky.'

'Don't tell me they're in the kitchen now?'

'Here, have a rasher, then. What was that, Kadie?'

Back on the foredeck, cruise hell was unfolding: the Party Piece. It wasn't so bad – some tricks, some bending of bodies round a broomstick – until an eager young couple got up with their guitars to sing. They were hopeless but, in the spirit of the evening, were enthusiastically received, which encouraged them to sing again. Their second offering was a ballad by Black Daffodil. Daniel, who had only then managed to slide in beside me with his dessert, said quietly, 'Is it really weird when this happens?'

'You get used to it.' They warbled on. 'Sort of.'

'Agh, that's dreadful. I hope it isn't one of your father's.'

'It is.'

'Are you all right?' asked Jill. 'You look like something painful's going through you.'

'There is.' Dad, it seemed, had written the world's most dreary dirge. 'I can't bear it,' I said to Daniel.

We shuffled off the bench and discreetly wandered to the front of the ship, where Daniel climbed over the bow into the rope netting that was suspended like a large triangular hammock and stretched out to the tip of the bowsprit. It sagged but he walked on it as if it was flat carpet. 'Come on.'

It was quite a job, getting me over. I wobbled and overbalanced and my feet slipped through the holes, so lying down was the only solution. The Christmas tree twinkled above us. I put my hands inside Daniel's Hawaiian shirt, but pleasure quickly turned to frustration. 'This is hopeless! You can't seriously expect us to fumble around like teenagers in these conditions, what with the sun and the sea and you climbing those ropes half-naked . . .'

'Just wait till we get back to Airlie.'

'What happens in Airlie?'

'Shag our brains out.'

'I'll bet you the full set of Daffodil CDs and DVDs that we won't make it to Airlie.'

'You're on.'

'You're really prepared to settle for three days of harmless necking?'

'Are you suggesting I'm only in this for the sex?'

'You're *supposed* to be in it for the sex. This is meant to be a purely physical relationship.'

'Except it isn't, is it?' he asked.

'I don't know what it is, Daniel. I only know I'll never make it to Airlie.'

'I feel so used.'

Seduction can be difficult in a net, but I did my best, helped by a backless dress that slipped effortlessly off my shoulders (when I manoeuvred my shoulders out of its way) and eventually succeeded in focusing his attention. There was only so much taunting one man could take. We wobbled and writhed like trapped fish. I waited for him to say, 'Meet me downstairs,' because he had to. He simply had to. There could be no retreat from this.

There was indeed no retreat, not even to the cabin. There was so little between us, hardly anything between us, that it was done before we could speak. We could so easily have been caught, chanced upon, and our situation was so ludicrous that I giggled when I came and couldn't stop.

'You!' I said. 'All that talk of monkhood and a condom in your pocket all the time, you chancer.'

'With you around, I'd be mad not to.'

He readjusted his clothes and scampered on to the ship. Allowing for a respectable gap, I pulled myself into a sitting position with a view to standing, but the netting wobbled and my legs went astray. It was like trying to find footing on the sea itself. Grabbing hold of the bowsprit, I pulled myself up, but my feet kept slipping through the holes. The sound of whistling wafted from the foredeck; they'd stopped murdering Dad's song. I struggled to the bow and, with graceless effort, managed to heave myself on to the rim. But then I was stuck. My shoulders were over the rim, my hips on it, my legs were hanging out to the side, and my dress didn't know where it was going. The slightest movement and I would slip off into the sea and nobody would notice. With a great pull, I spun myself round and fell on to the deck, the dress askew. I pulled it up, and down. It had otherwise survived the rough netting.

'Right,' I said. 'Won't be doing that again.'

There was commotion on the maindeck. So much for not being a group person – if something was happening, I wanted to be right there in the middle of it, so I hurried back to find all thirty-two guests leaning over one side of the boat. Suddenly they hurried past me and leant over the other side. 'What's happening?'

'Dolphins!'

'Where?' One very large dolphin, a mother, and her not very small baby were swimming around in the glow of the *Solway*'s lights. They kept going under the boat, so we hurried from one side to the other trying to catch every glimpse of fin, every flurry of silver, every splash of tail, until the *Solway* must have been rocking. Often they swam out into the black sea and we waited patiently until they were sighted again. Finally, people settled back to their drinks, but I kept watch, looking for the silvery blue dash, zipping around in the deep. It was a gift from Killian, I was sure. A benediction.

We stayed up that night, with the younger lads and crew, sitting on deck, drinking and talking. There was dancing too. We played REM, Chili Peppers, U2 and Black Daffodil. Coldplay's 'Green Eyes' seemed to have been written for Daniel, or so I fancied when we danced, holding hands and grinning stupidly at one another like a couple of, well, lovebirds. The next track ruined all that, with its maudlin lyrics going on and on about missing someone. I went to the bow to escape it. The dolphins were gone. There would be no escape; there was no place in the world, no time in my life, when Killian would not come, would not remind me that I missed him, *missed him*, and would always do so, and that every high, every good thing, would be punctured by the loss of him.

Later, I fell asleep on Daniel's lap and when I woke, I was covered with a blanket and my head was on a towel. I had slept on deck. Whatever next? There were other bodies strewn around me. I went in search of Daniel and found him on the roof of the wheelhouse, sitting against the mast.

I cuddled up to him for warmth. 'What time is it?'

He looked at the sky. 'Probably around four.'

'I slept for a while then.'

'Yep.'

I ran my toes over the bridge of his lovely foot.

He inhaled deeply and said, 'Tell me. It's about time you told me.'

A sudden shiver made me jump. A breath of light showed itself on the horizon. 'Just when I'm trying to leave it behind, you ask me to go back.'

'I'd like to know, before you go.'

'And I'd like to tell you,' I said. I went to the deck to collect the blanket, brought it back and pulled it round us.

'That last day,' I began, 'less than a month ago, Cecilia was in great form. She lit up when she saw me, just like she did whenever Milenko appeared, which was lovely. She was apprehensive about the trip to Ireland, but she had a stunning Italian outfit lined up and I told her she'd outshine the bride on the day. It all pleased her so much – her beloved son finally marrying and soon after having babies. What really thrilled her was that we weren't moving away. She was always thanking me for not taking Milenko off to Ireland.

'Anyway, he was at a tourism conference in Zagreb and it had been good for me, having to handle things alone those few days. I'd spent the first day at our house supervising work, and taking it all in – an unbelievable view, granted, but also this whole new life, and I started getting homesick. With the final move getting so close, apprehension kicked in. I fretted about having committed myself to too much – marriage to someone from a completely different background, to his family, their history, and to life on an island hours from the nearest city.

'Milenko's dad, Marin, sensed that I was struggling and did his best to distract me. He stopped me going out to the empty house and insisted I work in the office until Milenko got back. I spent that last day there, in the office, doing computer work and going over stuff with Marin. We worked hard. He showed me figures – government projections, their own projections, the plans for an extension, et cetera, and when I had to go out to the house that evening, he drove me there and spoke to the builders for me. But looking at the kitchen – still without units – gave me another jolt. It was so empty without Milenko, and it wouldn't be the only time he'd be away, and I thought, This is it: home. Bye-bye, Cork, Steph, Clara, Rollo, Lough Ine and Kilcrohane. When Marin realized how low I was, he reiterated how much it meant to all of their family, but to him personally, that I had agreed to make the move. They had already lost one son, he said, and didn't want to lose another. He promised they would do everything possible to make me feel at home, and he gave me his hanky to wipe my face, and even made me laugh.

'He insisted on taking me out to dinner to cheer me up. He was chuffed about my enthusiasm for the family business and all the ideas I was bringing to it, and he was excited that so many of their relatives were making the trip over for the wedding. It was a nice evening, he kept everything upbeat, and I did feel a lot better, so I kissed his cheek, like I would Dad, and said thanks for cheering me up. On our way back to the hotel, Milenko called me to say he was hitting the road and should be back at about two.

'"Two?" I said. "But how will you get across?"

'"Goran's coming with the boat. I'll leave the car in Orebić."

'He promised not to disturb me, but he was actually pleading to be allowed to do so because we hadn't seen each other for three days, and with this dose of pre-wedding nerves, I was as keen to see him as he was to see me. I turned away from his father and muttered, "No, do."

'Milenko said, "Hmm?"

'"*Do* disturb me."

'Unfortunately his father overheard me and he didn't say another word on the way home. He obviously disapproved. We always behaved so well in front of his parents, mostly to avoid unsettling his mother, but I thought Marin would be more understanding. I got that badly wrong. Asking his son to come to my room at two o'clock in the morning was clearly a big mistake. When he dropped me outside the hotel and I said thanks, he said, "Yes, yes," and drove off. It was mortifying.

'I rang Milenko straight away. "I've obviously shattered all his illusions about the pure Irish virgin."

'"He knows we sleep together."

'"Does he?"

'"Of course. He isn't ignorant."

'"But why would he react like that?"

'"It's embarrassing for him, hearing you talk like that, and he won't be pleased about me going to your room in the hotel. You should have been more careful."

'"I was just asking you to call in and say goodnight. For God's sake, we'll be married in a few weeks."

'"So you still want me to come, later?"

'"Yes. *Come*, later."

'"Stop it, Kadie." *Kay-dee.* "I'm driving."

'But I went on, telling him what I was planning to do to him and getting him all heated. He reciprocated by speaking Croatian, which always got me going, but he was driving winding roads, so I told him to hurry, because I wouldn't sleep until he got there.

'But I did fall asleep,' I told Daniel. 'I . . . At first I didn't think I had. It was only afterwards I worked out that I'd been completely out of it when I registered the sound of the door closing, and then I drifted off again, happy that Milenko was back, and I didn't come round properly until . . . When I woke again, he was lying behind me . . .

'He . . . he was pressed against my back. I was irritated that he'd started without me, without waking me properly, but he pushed back the blankets and . . . I, you know, responded.'

Tears had made an inconspicuous arrival. I wiped them

from my face. 'He . . . his hand . . . you know, my breast, and kissing my neck, and I was writhing . . . *enjoying* it,' I whispered, 'and I was pushing against him and . . . and,' Daniel squeezed my wet fingers, 'and we . . . he . . .' The words had become inseparable from the sobbing.

'What?'

'I put my arm over my shoulder, to pull him closer and it was then . . .'

'What? Tell me what that bastard did to you.'

'It wasn't Milenko,' I whispered. 'It was his father.'

Daniel stood up.

'I leapt from the bed, my nightdress half off me, but the room was dark, I didn't know where he was . . . He said my name – he sounded surprised – and I heard him shuffle around and thought he was coming at me, so I screamed at him to get out, go away, get out. That frightened him, and he rushed to the door, but he couldn't get it open; he was cursing, pulling and yanking at it and saying over and over, "Don't tell. Don't tell." He'd totally panicked and finally the door opened and he disappeared.'

I wiped my face, but it was very wet and I kept wiping and wiping and my hands just got wetter.

Daniel stared down at me.

'I felt so sick,' I said. 'I locked the door and had a shower, and then about an hour later, Milenko came. He tried the door very quietly, and there was a pause – he was confused that I'd locked him out, but he rattled it gently a few times and then went away, because he's a darling adorable man who only ever wanted the best for me, and I'd flirted with him and aroused him and promised to be waiting, and he came home to a locked door. He didn't even try to wake me or whisper my name, he just tiptoed away.'

Daniel put one hand against the mast, looked over his shoulder; I could hear him breathing. Had there been space, he would have paced. Then I felt his eyes on me again. 'What did you do?'

'I didn't know what to do. I had to think, but my mind was in a fuzz, and all I knew was that it was my fault, that I'd been too friendly – that kiss in the restaurant, he must have misunderstood, and all my gushing gratitude – and I knew that getting out of there, leaving, was the only thing I *could* do, so I started packing, madly, and it wasn't until later that I realized the marriage was off. Off. Off. *Off.*'

'No,' said Daniel, hunkering down beside me. 'That can't be right.'

'But how could I go through with it? To protect Milenko and his mother I would have to protect that bastard, which was just what he wanted – that I say nothing, that I live with them and say nothing – for what, twenty, thirty years? Have that between me and Milenko? Or maybe he even thought we'd carry on – have little trysts whenever his son was away. And Milenko *would* be away quite often and I'd be stuck on an island with that man!'

'*Christ.*' He turned to me. 'You didn't tell Milenko anything?'

'No. I mean, I considered it – all night. Tell him. Don't tell him. Run to him for protection. But Milenko adores his father, reveres him. They work together. Their livelihoods depend on each other. If I'd come between them, if there'd been a rift, how would his mother have coped? My only option would have been to pretend it never happened, but in that dark, dark, endless night in that room, I was convinced it wouldn't be a once-off. That he'd done it once and he'd do it again. And . . . if we had a daughter, who's to say . . .'

'Shit, no.'

'What do I know? The guy tries to hump his own son's fiancée . . . I mean – where does it end? How could I ever be sure? Can you *imagine* what my life would have been? Family occasions, children being born, and all the time being afraid of him and hiding it from my love, my partner in life. Wanting to vomit every time he came close. Oh, Daniel, it was the longest night of my life! I was terrified he'd come back – terrified of everything. Even of Milenko. What made it so ghastly was that I'd responded to him, I went with it. I was *turned on*, for God's sake.'

'You thought it was Milenko!'

'I know, but he could use it against me! He could have told Milenko I'd seduced *him*, and then who would he have believed? His beloved father or his fiancée?'

'Maybe you could've –'

'What? What could I have done? Tell me.'

'Have you considered reporting him?'

'For what?'

'Molestation. Attempted rape.'

'But that would destroy the other two.'

Daniel shook his head. 'I don't know, Kadie. I mean, I thought Milenko had cheated on you or murdered someone in cold blood in the war – but he's blameless.'

'That's what I've been trying to tell everyone!'

'So maybe you should have taken time out, gone home and thought it through from a distance before doing anything drastic?'

'I didn't have that luxury – not with the wedding looming. I had to think fast – about his mother, their family, the business. Milenko has spent years educating himself and developing that hotel. It's his life. In Ireland, he'd end up working for some hotel chain, if he was lucky. And we could live with that, maybe, but he cannot leave his mother, not after what happened to Dario.'

'Do you think she knows what she's married to?'

'I'm sure of it. That's why he panders to her. How did I never see it? How did I miss what a sleaze-bag he was?'

Daniel stood up again and leant against the mast. 'What did you do,' he asked, 'afterwards?'

'I packed. I had so much stuff. But the real problem was getting off the island. In winter the car ferry still runs, but not frequently, and I had to get off quickly, before I saw his father again or had much contact with Milenko. I was terrified I'd tell him, that I'd blurt it out in anger, so I decided to go for the car ferry at eleven and packed just one bag so that I could walk there.

'Milenko came to my room around nine, with breakfast. He took one look round the room – the tornado that had gone through it, the empty cupboard – and the realization that something really, really shitty was about to happen spread across his face like pallor. I made it up as I went along, told him I couldn't go through with the wedding. I blurted stuff out, stuff you hear in the movies, rubbish, total bullshit. He argued, said it was wedding nerves, homesickness, on and on for . . . I don't know, an hour maybe, but he couldn't break me. He came after me, when I left the hotel, begging me to reconsider, and he grabbed me, holding my elbows so hard it hurt, and tried to make me see sense, but I broke down. I was completely beside myself, and it scared him. Alarmed by the state I was in, he put my bag in his car and drove me to the ferry. He offered to drive me to Dubrovnik, but I wouldn't let him, so I left him there, looking up at the boat . . . completely bewildered.

'Next thing, I found myself in Orebić, across the sound from Korčula, waiting to go to Dubrovnik. There was a bus later that evening, so I spent the day sitting in a café, looking across at Korčula. I'll never forget what it looked like that day.'

Daniel touched my head.

'Somehow I found my way home. I couldn't get a flight for two days, so I waited in a small hotel in Dubrovnik. I switched off my phone and never left my room. I was terrified they'd find me, that Milenko's father would come, trying to change my mind, or threaten me or God knows what. I didn't eat, or sleep. I just counted the hours to that flight. I told Dad I was coming home early – Milenko was already hounding him – but there were to be no questions. "Just pick me up at the airport," I said, and he did.'

Daniel was very still. After some time he said, 'This is . . . unreal. You've lost Killian and can't do a blind thing about it, but to lose your fiancé because of this pathetic excuse for a man . . . It isn't right.'

'I thought . . . I thought I could just leave and break Milenko's heart and never see any of them again, but I didn't count on him coming after me.'

Daniel cursed quietly. 'Vietnam. What did you say to him?'

'That his father had made a pass at me and that I could never trust him again and never wanted to be near him or in the same room or even the same country.'

'Christ.'

'You think I shouldn't have told him?' I looked up at him.

'God . . . I don't know. I suppose . . .'

'He was desperate, Daniel. So full of self-loathing – I couldn't bear to see it and be the cause of it. He deserved to know that he had done nothing wrong, that he's a good person and a good son.'

'How'd he take it?'

There were no words for it.

'Poor bastard.'

'It was like . . . having pulled out his heart, I went in there again and pulled out his liver and his spleen and every part of him,' I cried. 'He was raw meat when he walked out of that room and I did that to him.'

'His own father did it.' Daniel crouched down again

and stared into brightening darkness. 'Did he see any way round it?'

'We tried. We really tried, all that long night, looking at every conceivable solution, but . . . Cecilia is insurmountable.'

'It's sexual assault. You really should have him charged.'

'Milenko would never live it down and his mother would never recover.'

'So you pay the price, the two of you, and he gets off?'

'That's about the size of it.'

'Fuck.'

Dawn was spectacular – not because of any particular performance by the sun, which rose unobtrusively, but because of the way the islands gradually revealed themselves in the thin light, mostly green but with cheeky bays of cream sand nestled against them. They squawked and squeaked with wildlife. I lay cosy with Daniel, against the mast, and it made for an extraordinary start to the day.

'So that's it,' he said.

'What?'

'You. Not approaching from behind.'

'Hmm. As for waking up and finding a stranger in my room in Brasov . . .'

He tightened his arms around me. 'I'm behind you now.'

'And I'm so glad for it.'

He kissed my forehead. 'What will Milenko do?' he asked.

'Beat the shit out of him, I hope.'

'That would be too good for him. I'd fucking shoot him myself.'

'Milenko has seen enough of shooting and killing. You know, that night in Saigon, he talked about the war. About what a dirty, filthy war it was, neighbour against neighbour, and how degrading it was to be part of it. He said he had thought he could never feel so degraded again.'

The first tickle of heat came off the sun, which was well above the sea, though the islands still seemed to be dragging themselves out of a deep and mysterious fog. 'I wonder where the dolphins went to,' I said.

22

This Boxing Day was rather different from the slovenly affair it could be at home. After a few hours' sleep, I went up on deck. Daniel was polishing the brass, his most important job after cleaning out the holds. The deck was wet, recently washed; it smelt good. A mother was reading a Harry Potter book quietly to her children at one of the tables. Coffee was brewing. White clouds stood around the sky. A murmur of voices touched the early-morning calm, along with the slush of the sea against the hull and the gentle hum of the generator. It was my favourite time of day, I decided, and I realized as I stood there, taking it all in, that something had changed. Me. I felt different. Telling Milenko about his father had been an ordeal unlike anything I was ever likely to go through again. Rather than disperse the load, it made it more dense, because the pain had been made two-fold: Milenko's grief and humiliation, as well as mine.

In contrast, speaking to Daniel *had* helped, like an inhaler on a wheeze. I felt cleaner, fresher, and was already more resigned to what had taken place and to its consequences.

But Daniel was another matter. The way he was going at those brasses, as if trying to polish them out of existence, suggested he was struggling with what I had told him. It was so seedy, so very disgusting, I realized, that it could even prey on someone much removed. A good thing, then, I had not told Steph.

I felt even better after going snorkelling later that morning. My breathing was laboured in the snorkel, water got into my ill-fitting mask and fish kept swimming into my eyes, so it wasn't quite as elegant a performance as seen on travel programmes, but I could not be unmoved. Schools of colour fluttered by; others, individuals, flipped past, unbothered by the intrusion, and in a deep crevasse that cut its way through the seabed, the water was as dark a hue of blue as I had ever seen. Reefs grew out of it like mushroom clouds. My spirits lifted higher as the sea got darker. I sent a thought to Killian, *I hope it's as lovely as this where you are.*

Back on board, Daniel joined me for morning tea at one of the long tables. He was low, and had been since dawn.

'I guess the old guy can't help himself,' he said.

'Yeah, yeah. His wife is vacant and his first-born is dead, but other people bear heavier burdens without destroying anyone else's life.'

'Could you and Milenko live with his mother in Cork?'

'The damp would kill her, and she'd have to leave all her sisters and her own mother.' I shook my head. 'I suppose I should be glad he did it when I could still get out.'

'Could you live on the mainland?'

'Too close.'

'Maybe –'

'No,' I said. 'I've had plenty of time to think about it and I wouldn't change what I did. I'm not sure what else I could have done.' I watched Daniel, longing for affirmation.

None came.

'You don't really think I should have stayed, do you? Gone through with it?'

After a moment, he said, 'That assumes Milenko would have gone through with it.'

'How do you mean?'

'Maybe he would have, but . . .'

'What?'

Daniel wouldn't look at me. 'He might have found it hard

to . . . be with you – you know, physically – after his father had been all over you.'

'Oh . . . *God*.'

'No matter how much he loves you, it would have preyed on him. It would on me, anyway, if I had a father. Maybe I'm better off without.'

My stomach looped over. Had I become disgusting to Milenko? 'But we made love.'

He looked up. 'Before or after you told him?'

He read my face, then rubbed my arm.

'I've made it worse for him, haven't I? He's probably in a state of revulsion. I shouldn't have let him touch me, should I?'

'Stop beating up on yourself. You don't hold all the cards. You never did. This is about his mother and his father and even his brother . . . The way I see it, it was out of your hands.'

'Does that mean I did the right thing? Leaving, I mean?'

'You really want my opinion?'

'*Yes*. I want someone to tell me that I haven't thrown away the best chance I had and the best man I'll ever meet! I had to make that decision in unbelievable circumstances, alone and in a hurry. Don't you think I'll spend the rest of my life wondering if it was the right one?'

He held my eye for a moment. 'Kadie,' he said sadly, 'you hadn't a chance, the both of you. Not after that. That marriage could never have worked, even if you'd tried. Every time there'd be a quibble, a row, you'd bring up his father, and he'd make it your fault. Think of the culture, the small community, the tragedy they'd already had, and then his own father emasculating him. That's no ghost in the closet, that's a fucking corpse on the dining-room table. How could you have got past that, even with love?'

I held the back of his hand to my lips, crying again.

'Sorry,' he said.

'No. Thank you. I've had to wait so long to hear someone say that.'

He kissed my forehead. 'But I might be wrong. Maybe Milenko'll get in touch some time.'

'Yeah, and maybe the Coral Sea will turn pink.'

I loved to watch him sail. Seeing him climb the rigging was spell-binding, and vaguely arousing.

'Get your buttocks over the futtocks!' Matt called up to them.

'I beg your pardon?' I said to him.

'It means climbing over the cross-trees on the ratlines.'

Of course it does.

Daniel worked his way out to the end of the bar, sixty feet above us, a silhouette against the sky. The sails came down gracefully, billowing pillowcases, and ropes were pulled in and tied, as Billy and Daniel called out to one another. Jill and I craned our necks. The *Solway Lass* came into her own, the sails pregnant with wind, and pushed us across another idyllic day.

Silence stretched out between me and Daniel. We had allowed ourselves to be taken where we should not have gone and it was too late to do anything about it, so we found ourselves facing a separation that should not have mattered, but did, as we tumbled into another hopeless entanglement. It was a strange place to be, and stranger still on a boat with forty other people. Sharing my disaster had, inevitably, brought us closer: he felt badly for me, and for Milenko. He brought me a coffee that afternoon when I was resting in my cabin, and leant over to kiss my neck, collar-bone, breast. I tried not to be predatory, but I felt so close to him, so much in need of him. If I responded, he might be gone, disappeared upstairs in fear of his skipper, so I remained passive until he brought his legs on to the bunk. We snaked out of our clothes. The couple in the next cabin chatted to one another, right beside us. They could surely hear us breathing, hear the creak of the bunk as Daniel moved quietly against me, could maybe even feel the shudder when he came.

He made a quick retreat afterwards, but I followed him on deck and sat on the bench while he coiled and secured ropes.

'I don't get it,' I said. 'How can we go on like this, not even in love?'

He grunted. 'Aw, I think we are a bit.'

'A bit what?'

'In love.'

'Doesn't that make us rather fickle?'

'Not in my book. If good things didn't happen in the middle of bad times, we'd never survive.'

'And what are we supposed to do with it, this little bit of love?'

'Enjoy it.'

'And then leave it on the quayside, I suppose?'

He shook his head, still working with his ropes. 'Take it away with us, wherever we go.'

'No. I vote we drop it with the anchor. Drown it.'

'Geez, and I'd never have taken you for a romantic . . .'

'I'm a pragmatist.'

'It doesn't always fit into little boxes, you know,' he said. 'Isn't that why it goes wrong – because love or chemistry, or whatever you call it, suits itself and goes where it bloody well wants to?'

'But where does that leave us?'

He had no answer.

The cook summoned him to the kitchen. A radio in the wheelhouse called out conditions and messages to boats. Billy took over the coiling of the ropes and Matt shouted, 'The sun's over the yard!'

'What does *that* mean?'

Billy smiled. 'Time for a drink.'

'Why don't you people speak English?'

Nimble as Daniel, he hopped round the netting, tying ropes round the bowsprit. 'And this is how you make your living,' I said.

'Yeah, it's good.'

'But how do you manage a private life when you're away so much?'

'You don't. People always say, "Wow, what a great life," but it's hard if you have a family. If I had a girlfriend or kids, I couldn't do this.'

'Would you give it up?'

'Depends on the girl.'

'Daniel gave it up for a girl.'

Billy nodded. 'Can't say he looks that happy about it, but.'

'He misses this life, I think. This ship.'

'For sure. But it's a bad idea coming back. Makes you realize what you've left behind.'

'Now that I've seen him at it,' I said, 'I can't imagine him making a living away from the sea.'

'Me neither,' said Billy. 'Not for him, and not for me.' Then, without taking his eyes from the ropes, he said, 'You're Irish?'

'Yeah.'

'Great sailing nation, Ireland.'

Our island haven for the night had a rock formation on its upper ledges that looked like an angry face. The sea was as flat as a window. On deck, people read in the nearly gone light; the generator hummed. Plates rattled in the galley, and a smell of toast filtered out.

When I came across Daniel deep in conversation with Matt, he caught my eye and directed me away. I went back the way I'd come.

He found me later, reading on the deckhouse. 'Sorry about that.'

'That's okay. Were you and he talking about what you should be talking about?'

'What's that?'

'Getting your job back.'

Daniel sat back, his hands locked round his wrists. 'That's a non-starter. Libby won't come up here.'

'No, well, of course Libby doesn't do anything Libby doesn't want to do.' He fiddled with his leather bracelets. 'Does she have the slightest understanding of what you've given up for her?'

He neatly changed the subject. 'Would you mind going back to Sydney alone?'

'He *has* offered you a job!'

'No. They want me to volley on the next trip, that's all. Someone's dropped out. It'd mean you'd have to make your own way back. You could take the ferry to Hamilton Island and fly from there. Or you could charter a private jet in Airlie, of course.'

'Yeah, right.'

'Would you mind?'

'If it keeps you on this boat a day longer, I don't mind at all. What about your boss?'

'She's away for another two weeks. I'm sorry, Kadie. I had hoped we'd be able to take our time going back – go to Fraser's Island and . . .'

'Oh, no, Daniel. Enough! Even if you had the time, I need to get home. I have to get back to Steph and pack her up and put her on a plane. I can't hold out much longer. I want to see Killian's grave while it's still fresh. By the time we get there, there'll be weeds growing out of it and everyone else will have moved on.'

'But Steph might not be ready to go.'

'I *know*. I wish I hadn't promised her I'd wait.'

Daniel's eyes were on a junk about half a mile away. 'If I'm going to volley again, it means tomorrow . . .'

'Yeah. So much for the Great Shag in Airlie Beach.'

'That's not what I was thinking about.'

'Me neither.'

'But there's a slight chance you'll still be around when I get back to Sydney, right?'

'Daniel, what exactly would you be going back to Sydney *for*?'

He fiddled, looked about, scowled. 'I don't know,' he said finally. 'I don't know any more.'

'What did Matt say? Is there any chance of work here?'

'With the company, maybe, on one of the yachts, but with my tall-ship experience, I'd probably get back on soon enough.'

'Then you must stay.'

'You think?'

'Definitely. You need to live this out a bit longer. You're too young to settle for a flat in the city for the sake of someone else's career. That's what people do when they're *my* age.'

'Oh, your advanced years . . .'

'You know, you said to me once you'd go over a cliff for Libby, but the thing is – you already have. It's time you turned that fall into a dive, Daniel.'

I was in a boat, Korčula town behind me. We were coming round the headland. I was looking, looking, straining to see. When the hotel came into view, I could see sunbathers on the quays and children in the water, and the great bank of cypress trees hiding the grounds where Milenko would be. But then I saw that he was at the bar by the quayside, dishing out ice-creams, slopping great balls of pink and green into cones. Melting colours were dribbling down his wrists. We motored closer, my heart racing, bursting. Suddenly, Milenko whizzed past us in a speedboat, standing tall and proud and not even looking at me, and we were caught in its wake and my boat got smaller and we rocked and rocked until we lifted on our side and . . .

The sea slapped against the back of my head – the Coral Sea, not the Adriatic. Morning had come.

Arms came round me. I jumped. Daniel nuzzled my neck.

'Must you sneak up on me like that?'

'I didn't sneak up. You were a long way off.'

'I'm trying to extract myself from a dream.'

'Nice one?'

'Sort of. I dreamt I was going home, and home was Korčula. Home *is* Korčula. But now I have to go back to Cork, instead, and start all over again.'

Daniel rubbed his unshaven chin into my neck. 'You could stay here.'

'Tempting.'

'Seriously?'

I shook my head. 'It's too far, Daniel. It'd be like exile.'

'A change of scenery is always good.'

'I've been changing the scenery for a month now and it hasn't made a blind bit of difference to what has to be done. I have to go back to Ireland and consolidate. I need to shed all the Croatian stuff, get to where I was before Milenko, and somehow learn to live without Killian.'

'And will I feature in there at all?'

'Of course. For what it's worth, I'm dreading tonight. I love being with you.'

'But I'm a long way down the list, right?'

'Not as far as you should be.'

As we headed back towards Airlie Beach, the lazy sense of well-being I had enjoyed for three days began to curdle. I packed without reluctance. The cruise had been a balm – everything Daniel had promised – but any more would have been endurance. I wanted only to return to Moruya to collect Steph. Being with Daniel had been sweet, restorative, but it was becoming harder. That morning, with time running out, he made love to me like a man on a mission and at the height of it I told him I loved him, because he deserved to hear it and because, at that moment, I did.

23

Bags and backpacks were piled on deck. Last-minute photos were being taken, email addresses exchanged. We had been asked not to disembark until an official group photo had been taken and, as we pulled into our berth, a photographer hopped aboard. On the quayside boxes of provisions were lined up for loading and a guy was waiting to collect our wetsuits.

The photographer sorted us – the tall lads behind, the women sitting in front, the crew peppered over us. Billy threw himself across our laps, causing yelps and squeals. His elbow rested on my knees. We cracked jokes while we posed, and people looked on from the quay, smiling at our antics.

Just as the photographer clicked his camera, I saw him.

'*Jesus.*' I pushed Billy. 'Get off! Get off me!' He swivelled on my lap, slid off and landed heavily on the deck. I stepped over him and ran downstairs.

The cabin had been tidied. Fresh sheets and blankets were neatly folded at the end of the bunk. I pressed myself against the wall. *Oh, God, oh, God, oh, God.*

'Kadie?' Daniel rolled back the door. 'What the hell . . . ?'

'I'm not getting off. Don't make me get off!'

'You have to.'

'How *could* they?'

'Who? What?'

'Dad. Milenko. *Everyone.*'

He touched my shoulders. 'What's happening? You're shaking.'

'*He's here,*' I hissed.

'Milenko? Bloody heck, that guy doesn't give up.'

I tried to shake my head but it would barely move.

'Not Milenko? Who? Oh, Christ.' He stepped back. 'Not –'

'He's out there. Waiting for me. I'm not going. I'll take the next trip.'

'Are you serious?'

My head kept jerking about.

Daniel's voice dropped several notches. 'He has some bottle.'

'I won't see him. I'm not getting off!'

'Calm down. Wait.' He sat me down. 'You have to get off. Every berth is booked from here till February. And you can't hang about – they're getting ready for the next lot. We'll disembark and –'

'No!'

'Look, maybe you should hear what he has to say. He's come so bloody far. This might be your way back.'

'You said yourself there was no way back.'

He sighed, and stared at me. 'I might have been wrong.'

'I'm not going anywhere near him.'

'He can't touch you. I'll be there. Really, Kadie, you can't stay.'

'You won't leave me?'

'Not for a minute.'

'Seriously, Daniel. Not one minute?'

'I know what he did, remember? So, come on. Let's see what he has to say and send him on his way.'

He eased me into the alleyway and manoeuvred me up the stairs. The photo had been taken, emotional farewells were all but done. People were staggering away from the *Solway* on their sea legs.

'I'm sorry,' I said to Billy.

He checked his elbow. 'It'll mend.'

'She had good reason.' Daniel looked over my shoulder. 'The guy in the grey suit?'

'What's he doing?'

'Watching us.'

'You okay?' Billy asked me.

'See you later, mate,' said Daniel. 'Ready?'

'You go first.'

We stepped off the boat. Daniel was like a shield in front of me. He stopped a few feet from Marin Lalić.

'May I speak with you, Kadie?' he asked, craning round Daniel.

I couldn't look at him. 'Leave me alone, please.'

'I have come twenty thousand kilometres. Five minutes only.'

I didn't know what to do.

'How did you find her?' Daniel asked. Around us, caterers were lumping boxes of cornflakes, muesli and Vegemite on to the *Solway*. We kept getting in their way.

Lalić raised his shoulders, as if it was obvious. 'Kadie's father and her friend Stephanie have been helpful.'

'Fuck.'

Lalić held out his hand. 'You're Daniel, yes?'

'Do you have a car?'

'Yes.'

'Follow us into town.'

We hurried along the pontoons and through the car-park. I was so aware of him behind us, following, creeping . . . I jumped into the car and held my arms over my head. 'That voice!'

Daniel leant towards me, and I didn't care if Milenko heard about it. His father had personally thrown me into Daniel's arms. 'Can you hack it?'

'I don't know. What'll I do tonight when you're back on the boat? I can't be here alone with him. What am I going to do?'

'Stop panicking for a start. We'll get rid of him before I

leave, and if we don't, I'll think of something. Meanwhile, hear him out. It might turn out to your advantage.'

'Don't you leave me, not for one second,' I said. 'If you need to pee, tell me and I'll go too.'

He started the car. A hire car pulled up behind us and followed us up the winding road out of the marina. We turned towards the town centre.

'This is the last straw,' I said. 'I am *never* speaking to Dad again.'

Daniel braked suddenly, pulled in and stopped the car. Lalić almost hit us. 'Your father,' Daniel said, 'has no bloody clue what this guy did, so stop being such a bloody prima donna! He just wants you to be happy with the guy you chose to marry and if that means sending your almost father-in-law round the world to plead with you, then you can hardly blame him!'

'It is *exactly* because he doesn't know what happened that he should not have done this! This is one interference too far – and as for Steph! What was she thinking?'

'Don't make me mad, Kadie. These people are doing their best for you. I wish I had as many people lining up to help keep me and Lib together.'

'Maybe they're not lining up because they don't happen to think you *should* stay together!'

Milenko's father could certainly see us arguing.

'They should *not* have told him where I was!'

'You don't even know what he said to them. But you can be sure of one thing – this guy lied his way out here. Your dad's grasping at straws. He has no idea what an asshole Lalić is. After all, *you* didn't tell him. If you had done, do you think we'd be sitting here now with old Fuck-face right up our backside?'

'Jesus, Daniel,' I hissed. 'You choose *now* for our first fight!'

He let off the brake and swerved back on to the road.

417

'There's only one thing that matters here, Kadie,' he said quietly. 'Do you still want Milenko?'

'Yes.'

'So this is your chance.'

Refusing to leave his elbow, I went with Daniel to get the coffee in a café near the lagoon. Then we sat opposite Lalić, who was agitated and miserable. I watched the kids going by in trunks and sandals, and tried to hear what they were talking about. Such an odd place for this encounter, a tropical paradise, embraced by hills of virgin rainforest.

We waited while Lalić struggled to find the words he had gone to such ends to deliver. He removed his smart jacket. 'Kadie,' he began, his voice husky, 'I ask you, please, not to punish my son for my mistake.'

I didn't react.

'His heart is broken. He is broken. I did it, yes. I am a worthless person. But I ask your forgiveness for his sake.'

Daniel screwed up his eyes, and drank some coffee. It *was* excruciating.

Lalić's hands were shaking. I had no compassion. 'If you come back,' he went on, 'I will be invisible to you. This is my promise. I ask you to come back. Please do not make Milenko suffer more.'

The mention of his name undid me every time. 'I am not the one who is making him suffer.'

Lalić nodded to the side, conceding the point.

'Did he send you?' I asked.

He shook his head.

'Does he know you've come?'

'Yes. Cecilia very much wanted me to speak to you.'

'Cecilia knows?'

'Only that you have left. She hopes I will change your mind . . . Milenko told her it would never work. He doesn't speak to me. He has only spoken to me once since his return from Vietnam.' He looked at me with reproach.

'Milenko had a right to know about his father.'

He sighed heavily.

'Is he all right?' I asked. Beneath the table, my hand gripped Daniel's.

'He is very silent. You should come back.'

'You can't really believe that I could return and we'd all play happy families together? You have shamed him, and shamed me. There wouldn't be room in one marriage for that much humiliation.'

'I am his father. He will forgive me one day.'

'I doubt that,' said Daniel.

He didn't look at either of us. 'How can we make this better?'

'We can't.'

'But I am asking you not to make Milenko pay like this. His future. His life. I beg you. For Milenko and his mother. This is too hard a punishment for a whole family, and for your family also.'

'Leave my family out of it.'

'Do not hurt everyone for what I have done.'

'You haven't even apologized.'

'What do you mean? I have come all the way across the world, leaving Cecilia at Christmas, to apologize. I am very sorry for what has happened. I cannot explain very well. It can be lonely . . . Cecilia – '

'Oh, right. It's her fault, obviously.'

'Your own son,' said Daniel, as if the words slipped out involuntarily.

Lalić looked debased, and still I felt nothing. 'You've wrecked my life,' I said.

'No, no, you can have it again! Forget about me. You will see nothing of me.'

'You plan to leave?' Daniel asked.

He hunched his shoulders again. 'I cannot do that. Milenko's mother . . . she knows what I am, but she does not want me to go, she could not manage, but you will not see me. I will –'

'Just as I didn't see you coming that night.' Nausea rose in my throat. This was him. This crushed old man had pressed himself against me. I covered my eyes, turning away from the table. 'You've made a pimp of him. Gabriella stills loves him – do you know that?' I turned back. 'You did it to her too, didn't you?'

Drawing back, he said, 'No . . .' in that unfinished European way, almost casual, as if the suggestion was perfectly ludicrous. 'Gabriella . . . Not at all.'

'Maybe not, but she felt it. She knew you might, one day. She was smarter than me. She saw what you were.'

He had lost weight. His skin sagged under his eyes, his arms were wrinkled with loose flesh, making him appear much older than his sixty-six years. The dashing debonair man I had known was gone. And good riddance.

'Why are you so determined to sabotage Milenko's happiness?' I asked, feeling increasingly removed and disappointed. With every word, he was failing me. He had no magic potion, no quick fix to make all this . . . disappear. 'What is it? Jealousy? Is that it? You're jealous because he's a better man than you are?'

'Or do you want to hurt him for still being alive?' Daniel said.

That shocked me, and Lalić too. He didn't like having to contend with Daniel. 'I love my son,' he said to him, as if Daniel could not possibly understand what he was talking about, which was probably true.

'You have a mighty strange way of showing it,' Daniel replied, without a flicker.

'I am weak, yes. But Milenko is not.' He turned to me. 'He

is all we have left. I have already lost one son, and now I am losing another. That is why I have come so far. I will do anything, anything you want. Please will you consider returning?'

Daniel glanced at me. Here, he seemed to be saying, was my chance. All I had to do was take it. But what of Milenko? What would *he* have me do? Where did he stand, now?

'Can I tell him you will come?' Lalić urged.

I came back from where I'd gone to – Milenko's eyes, and face, and love – to the tropical garden. 'So you can save the day?' I said. 'Sorry. You've done it before. You might do it again. And I might not get away so easily next time.'

'But my wife and I, we will retire, on the other side of the island. I will never come to your home.'

'Never see your grandchildren?'

He flinched.

'And what would that be like for Milenko and Cecilia?' I shook my head. 'This is what you have done. You can't undo it – not even by flying half-way round the world. I only wish you could.'

Daniel leant towards me.

Lalić glanced at him and said to me, 'This is to hurt Milenko? He is not hurt enough?'

'How dare you presume to stand in judgement over me?'

'You cannot love him,' he said.

'I beg your pardon?'

'You cannot love Milenko if you find someone else so quickly.'

'You shabby little *shit*. I love Milenko more than you know how. I have left him because I love him, even though I will never, *ever* love anyone like that again!' Daniel's grip on my wrist loosened. I stood up. 'I hope Milenko can find the happiness he deserves with a woman you don't fancy!'

*

421

We drove out of town to a guesthouse perched on the brim of a hill. 'He won't find you up here,' Daniel said. 'Tomorrow take the ferry to Hamilton and get a flight out as soon as you can.'

We were led down steps to a dark, non-air-conditioned room, with a tiny balcony overlooking Shute Harbour. Green islands sank into the green sea and yachts lingered in their coves.

'I'll stick around if you like,' said Daniel. 'Matt'd understand.'

'No, he wouldn't. Anyway, Lalić can't do any more damage than he's already done. I'm not afraid of him now.'

'What a sad little man,' he said. 'He isn't even a class-one sleaze, he's almost too pathetic for that.'

'Maybe I should have listened to him.'

But Daniel once again endorsed everything I'd done, every decision I'd made. Meeting Lalić had made it even clearer to him: in a family like that, a tiny, tight little family, I would always feel at risk, he said, or at the very least uneasy. He agreed that the only conceivable solution would be for Milenko to take his mother and move to Ireland, which was beyond the mother and therefore beyond the son. We were trapped, all of us, in his father's horrible lapse.

Daniel pulled out his phone and switched it on. It beeped with incoming messages. He stepped out to the balcony to call Libby and closed the sliding window behind him. It was casual at first. Lots of 'Really? . . . no kidding? . . . yeah, it was awesome.' His voice dropped. Low, seductive. He was smiling. Not breaking it off then. It ended on a low note. He leant on the railing, then looked over his shoulder through the window at me.

My own phone was full of messages, all with the same information: Lalić is coming. I would have been warned, if I had turned on my phone. Steph wrote that he had come bearing a message from Milenko. Dad's version was similar – Milenko had pleaded with his father to find me and prevail upon me. As if. Milenko would never have subjected me to the man again, but Dad had no way of knowing that Lalić himself was the problem. In good faith, he would have seen a father prepared to travel the world for the sake of his son's happiness. He had given him Shannon's address, and Steph had sent him to Airlie Beach, believing he was the messenger and knowing the enormous respect in which I had always held Milenko's parents.

Daniel came in. 'So?' I said. 'Did you tell her you're staying on indefinitely?'

'No. I said I'm going back to Sydney after this run.'

Funny, I thought, how I had abandoned a relationship that was good for me, but he could not escape one that was bad for him. He'd tried everything – travelling, giving her space, going back in time, even me – but he was pinned down by his love for her.

I stared at the wall. 'He's made me feel so guilty about Milenko and Cecilia. Maybe I should go back for their sakes – whad'ya think?'

With a sudden jerk, Daniel flung his phone on to the bed. 'Stop asking me! I'm hardly a neutral party, am I? I mean, it wouldn't exactly be in my interests, would it, if you were to go back to Milenko now?'

'Daniel . . .'

He shrugged and sat down by my legs.

'You haven't ended it with Libby, though, have you?'

'Of course not.'

'Then how can you say –'

'I haven't ended it because I wouldn't do that over the phone.'

'You mean, it *is* over?'

He looked over his shoulder. 'I've had a revelation.'

423

'. . . Dazzle me.'

Our voices were quiet, almost fearful.

'When you said to Milenko's father that you'd never love anyone like that again, it was like a punch in the gut. I suppose I'd been hoping you would, one day.'

I put my arms round his neck. 'But there's no point to us, Daniel. There was never meant to be.'

'Yeah, and you can stick to that, because you're still so in love with your Croat, but I'm up the creek without a paddle.'

'You're on the rebound, that's all. Once you're back on the *Solway Lass*, surrounded by pretty girls in bikinis, you'll forget about me.'

He took my palm and kissed it, and looked at me, and I knew it wasn't rebound. Not for him, and maybe, even, not for me.

By six, we were back on the quayside, where the *Solway* waited at her berth for another lucky bunch of travellers. I didn't know or care where Lalić was.

Daniel hesitated. 'This sucks,' he said.

'Yeah. It's no wonder we didn't quite manage it all those other times . . . Still, I need to get back to Moruya and get that woman on to a plane, and *you* need to sail.'

'Oi, lover boy, get your ass into gear,' one of the lads called, which was just as well. Neither of us had the stomach for the slow goodbye.

'Come and see us, won't you?' I said. 'Get that autograph off Dad.'

'If I come, it won't be his autograph I'll be looking for.' There were whistles and cat calls from the crew when we kissed. We moved slightly away, to the end of the narrow pontoon.

'You'll cope, will you?' he said. 'Flying home? Twenty hours or more?'

'I'll think about my special place.'

'Your dad and the lake?'

'No, you on your *Solway Lass*, and I'll forget there's nothing between me and the ground except air.'

He pulled me against him. 'And nothing between you and me except air.'

'But so much of it,' I said, welling up. 'Way too much of it.'

Billy came along the planks, prattling to the group of guests bunched up behind him. Seeing our faces, he stopped. The group stared over his shoulder at us. 'Er, right,' said Billy. 'All aboard.'

We gave it another hug, before Daniel stepped on to the deck. 'The French never say, "I'll miss you,"' I told him. 'They say, "You will be missing from me." You will be missing from me, Daniel Blewitt.'

I could not take my eyes from the tall ship as she motored past all the other boats. I walked along the marina, trying to keep up. I could see Daniel in the dusk, moving around. If nothing else, I had returned him to his rightful environment. My phone beeped. Daniel waved. I waved back, then glanced at my phone. Steph.

It read: 'Let's go home.'

I let out a yelp. 'Yes!' I looked up. The *Solway* was making her way between the end of the piers. I was in the wrong place. I ran back along the marina, then down one of the piers, calling, 'Daniel! Daniel!' He would never hear me above the splutter of the engine, but I ran, willing him to sense it, to look for me. I couldn't see him on deck, but I ran after the ship, still calling his name, until I heard an 'Oi!' He was hanging off the bowsprit, waving. I jumped up and down. 'I'm going home!'

'Huh?'

I held up my arms and pointed at my phone. 'Going home!' I shouted. 'We're going home!' And I did a little tap-dance at the end of the pier.

The lights of the *Solway Lass* came on. Daniel, invisible now in the dark, let out a 'Woo-hoo,' as the tall ship made her way out to the Coral Sea.

The sad brown eyes of the smallest dog looked up at me from where it rested on its paws. The other three were stretched out in various stages of oblivion around the back lawn. It was a fine early-summer afternoon.

'Go on,' said Dad, from the deckchair next to mine. 'Admit it. They're quite sweet, really, aren't they?'

'They're walking, talking Brillo Pads! Honestly, Dad, enough is enough. Steph can manage. She's sorted now and it's time they went home.'

He was affronted. 'You can't mean that?'

'Why not?'

'Oh dear.' Rollo looked at the hounds. 'Time for the truth, dogs.'

'What truth?'

'I . . . The thing is, I don't want to give them back.'

I snorted. 'Yeah, right.'

'I'm serious.'

'God, you are, aren't you?'

''Fraid so.'

'Tough shit,' I said, 'Steph will have something to say about that.'

He patted the ears of Mirabel, the mother. 'I don't think so.'

'Dad!'

'Look, they've grown on me, all right? And, more to the point, they think this is home now and they're way too big for Steph's place. She can't manage all four of them.'

'But she wants to breed them.'

'Not since the baby came. So I offered to hang on to them and she's pretty happy with that. She's going to take Mirabel when she's able, but she wants to offload the pups.'

'You mean you two have already agreed to this?'

'Weeks ago.'

'Oh! She's been covering for you! All that stuff about waiting to get a shed built . . .'

He nodded sheepishly. 'I put her up to it. I knew you wouldn't have them otherwise.'

'You horrible, deceitful old man. I hate dogs. Honestly. I go away for five weeks and come back to a dog pound!'

He chuckled. I considered my new house-mates. In truth, they quite looked the part, lolling about all grey and wiry, like in an ad for a country-house hotel.

The sliver of lake that we could see from where we were sitting was glittering in the sunlight. I loved our home. At times like this, I was glad I had not had to leave it.

'Hello?' Dad said quietly.

'What?'

'When are you coming back to us, sweetness?'

'Hmm?'

'It's been five months, Kadie. Killian is gone. Steph is getting on. Your godson is a charmer. You've got an exciting new job. But you're always miles away – in Korčula, I suspect, or is it the Whitsunday Islands?'

'I'm thoughtful, not miles away. And I'm happy, all right? As much as I can be, so don't go asking for more.'

'I just wonder, sometimes, if you're ever coming back.'

'I am back,' I said, getting up. 'Isn't that the whole problem? I'll make tea.'

In the kitchen, I put the kettle on the Aga and looked out to where Dad was sitting. He was right, of course. I *had* been living in my head. Fantasizing about the future that could never be had helped to get me through the empty days in the

428

winter and spring. My dreams were variations on a theme: Milenko coming to find me. The fantasy never changed much. I would be wandering in the orchard, where the apple blossoms were sighing with floating petals, and I'd hear the gentle thud of the back door. I would not turn, as I listened to the footsteps soft across the grass. Then a hand, Milenko's hand, would come over my shoulder and pick a sprig of apple blossom, right by my face, and offer it to me as he gathered me against him.

I would say one word: 'Cecilia?'

And he would reply, 'She is with the one she loves, and she insists that I, also, should be with the one I love.'

How simple it seemed. But the fantasies were always distraction, never delusion. Milenko could not come. Not ever. And so, in more generous moments, I wished for something else, something almost possible: that Milenko and Gabriella would be reconciled, their joint understanding of his father clearing the way for them, and they would marry and have babies and make Cecilia happy. I prayed that Milenko, too, would be happy, that he would one day let me go, as I was, slowly, letting him go.

But I was still prone to daydreaming and one day, Clara had caught me at it when I was waiting to have lunch with her in town. She goaded me until I shared it with her – the apple-blossom version.

'And then what?' she asked. 'What happens next?'

'We'd get married, stupid, and honeymoon on the *Solway Lass*, where we'd watch Daniel hanging off the ropes with a bronzed beauty in a skimpy bikini draped round him.'

Clara frowned.

'On second thoughts,' I said, 'scrap the bronzed beauty. It would just be Milenko and me, relaxing on deck, while Daniel clambered up the masts . . . Actually, scrap the ship. It would be too full of memories of Daniel and me . . . you know.'

'Yes, inviting disembowelment. Does he really have to go on honeymoon with you?'

'No, it's just–'

'It's just you can't *quite* imagine a happy outcome without him, can you?'

'Of course I can.'

'Ok, so instead you'd . . . ?'

'Well, Milenko and me, we'd stay home, by Lough Ine, just the two of us, and we'd walk hand in hand through the gardens with the architect, discussing what alterations needed to be made to change the house into a first-rate country-house hotel. There.'

'And then you'd look at the architect's plans for the granny-cum-granddad flat you'd need for Cecilia and Rollo, right?'

'*Wrong*. We'd take the boat across the lake, and row out of sight, where I'd rip off Milenko's clothes and have it off in the bottom of the boat, just like we started.'

'And would Daniel still be flying off the ropes? Out of a tree, maybe?'

'Jesus, Clara, you're making him sound like Tarzan. What's your point? You loved Milenko.'

'I did. But when you talk about Milenko, you get all dark and broody. When you talk about Daniel, you cheer up again.'

'But that's inevitable. I didn't lose Daniel the way I lost Milenko.'

'Funny,' she said. 'I wasn't aware you'd lost Daniel at all.'

I put a packet of biscuits on the tray and waited for the kettle to boil. Of course it was harder to think of Milenko. An ugly cloud sat over my memories of Korčula; it had been tainted, its sweetness sucked away, while thoughts of Blinky Bill and huge hailstones and frisky sex in weird places were bound to make me smile.

Daniel was still in touch. He had returned to Sydney, as promised, only to be dumped unceremoniously by Libby, over the phone. The *Solway Lass* puffed out her sails, and had him back. He emailed whenever he had shore leave. He was, I could tell, as happy as a pig in muck, and he had only once 'or maybe twice' risked being disembowelled since Christmas. He still made me smile. I remembered with tenderness the ease he had brought me and the way he had brought it. He had been like a guardian angel, delivered to my side by Killian, when I most needed one. As for our affair, it was better to have been together with love, I believed, than to have been together for the sake of it. And there *had* been love. This much had become clear to me: we *can* love in two directions at once. I wished I had not been quite so intent on batting it away. In my more brutal, and lonely, moments, I accepted that that had been a mistake, that instead of throwing away another chance, I should have hung on to Daniel as Rebound, Anaesthesia and Friend.

Dad smiled when I brought out the tray. He was looking better. Killian's death had been hard enough, but the story that I had finally brought home to him – that I had been molested by a man he considered his friend – had knocked him around further. Paternal guilt savaged him. He should have seen it, should have protected me . . . And then anger had its fill: anger at himself, at Marin, even at Milenko for letting it happen – a useless, boiling anger that had no place to go and sapped his energies as he tried to comfort me. In the end, he had succumbed to a bad flu, from which he was only now recovering.

I chuckled as I poured.

'What is it?'

'Us. We're like residents in an old people's home. The war-wounded, with our tea and biccies on the lawn.'

We were still sitting there an hour later, reading the Saturday papers in the evening warmth, when the doorbell rang inside.

'I'll go,' said Dad, getting up. The four dogs, like his senti-
nels, woke simultaneously and went after him. All five of them
came back a few minutes later. Rollo stood in front of my
chair, looking down at me.

'What's wrong?'

'There's a young man here to see you. Some bloody
foreigner.'

I shaded my eyes to catch his.

'And he has *loads* of luggage.'

I couldn't speak.

'A lifetime's worth of luggage, I'd say.'

We stared at one another. 'Jesus, Dad. Which one? Which
one is it?'

He looked up at the house and back at me. 'Do you really
have to ask?'

I couldn't remember how to breathe.

'I'll send him out,' said Dad, turning on his heel.

There was no wandering into the orchard. I couldn't move.
I sat with my back to the house, rigid. Thoughtless. One of
the dogs nosed the packet of biscuits and found her way into
it. I couldn't stop her.

Then, suddenly, I laughed.

I didn't quite hear his footfall, but I sensed it. My eyes filled.
His shadow fell over me. I still couldn't move.

He hunkered down and reached out to ruffle the dog's ears.
I stared at the worn cuff, the khaki sleeve, the long bronzed
fingers that I loved.

'You shouldn't be eating those, should you, mate?' he said
to the dog, with a tentative glance at me.

A look passed between us, intimate and satisfying.

'What are you doing here?' I asked quietly.

He grinned. 'See, I've had a revelation.'

'. . . Dazzle me.'

There *is* such a thing as a no-ties fling.'

432

'Yeah?'

'Yeah. It's just that we're no bloody good at it.'

I smiled. You're not telling me you've left that ship again, are you? How stupid is that?

'Not stupid at all . . . unless there's someone else you'd rather have seen?'

I put my hand to his face, unshaven, rough. 'No, Daniel, there's no one else I'd rather see.'

He kissed my palm. 'Sweet as.'

Acknowledgements

My teenage daughters, Finola and Tamzin, are great proof-readers and harsh critics. I could not do without their honesty, advice and enthusiasm. With this book in particular, they travelled the road with me – literally and figuratively. It is entirely theirs.

I would also like to thank the following people: Marina Brajkovic, Mostar, for help with matters Croatian; Philippa Rennie, Auckland, for knocking ingrained Aussie-isms out of my head and replacing them with Kiwi-isms; Catherine Reilly and Allen Grimwood, Moruya; Peter Lindgren, and his parents, Nils Olof and Ingrid Lindgren, in Stockholm; Henrik Druid of the Karolinska Institutet, Stockholm, and Carina Söderquist-Meyer, of Söderquist Undertakers, Stockholm; Maria and George at the Rolling Stone Hostel in Brasov; Fiona Riordan of Getaway Travel, Ballincollig; Lynn Crowley, again, this time for Budapest and Black Daffodil; Sue Leonard and Iris Haldemann; Anne O'Brien and Henry Woods; and my long-suffering migraineurs, Ger Layton, Pernilla Lindgren-Vizard and William Merivale, for making me *think* I know what it feels like to get migraine.

I am most grateful to Eavan Boland for allowing me to quote from 'The Lost Land'.

Thanks once again to all at Penguin Ireland – Patricia Deevy, Michael McLoughlin, Cliona Lewis and Brian Walker; the London team at Penguin UK; and special thanks also to my excellent copy-editor, Hazel Orme.

I would especially like to thank Captain Mark Edwards of the *Solway Lass* for his invaluable help on tall ships and tall-ship vernacular; Al Grundy of Southern Cross Tours; and our crew on the *Solway*

Lass, particularly Dave; and skipper Marty. And here's a nod to the ship herself.

It goes without saying that any outstanding mistakes are mine.

Finally, the double act that keeps me going – my agent Jonathan Williams and husband William, without whom.

Woodstock
Cork
November 2005